CRIMSON GREEN

Withdrawn

CRIMSON GREEN

A QUINN PARKER
NOVEL OF SUSPENSE

BRUCE ZIMMERMAN

HarperCollins*Publishers*

This book is for
María-Pía Marta Paulsen Urdangarin
(and any other name she cares to tack on).

HarperCollins books may be purchased for educational, business, or sales pro-
motional use. For information, please write: Special Markets Department,
HarperCollins Publishers, Inc., 10 East 53rd Street, New York, NY 10022.

FIRST EDITION

Designed by R. Caitlin Daniels

Library of Congress Cataloging-in-Publication Data
Zimmerman, Bruce.
    Crimson green: a Quinn Parker novel of suspense/by Bruce Zimmerman.—
1st ed.
        p.   cm.
    ISBN 0-06-017069-7
    1. Parker, Quinn (Fictitious character)—Fiction.
    2. Psychotherapists—California—Fiction. I. Title
PS3576.I48C75   1994
813'.54—dc20   94-14751

94 95 96 97 98 ❖/HC 10 9 8 7 6 5 4 3 2 1

When a man wants to murder a tiger, he calls it sport: when the tiger wants to murder him, he calls it ferocity.

—George Bernard Shaw

— 1 —

When I opened Brad's locker a single sheet of paper fluttered loose from the top shelf and floated down to the floor like a dying butterfly. I watched it drift and settle and then stared at it awhile. The paper hadn't been there the last time I'd rummaged through the locker, less than an hour ago. After a few seconds I bent down and picked it up, quickly, almost guiltily, as though I were trying to palm somebody else's dropped wallet. The page was blank except for a single typewritten sentence at the top: "Brad—lose this ternament real big tomorow or both you and your family will be killed." I read the note again, then slowly folded the paper three times and tucked it in my back pocket.

A deserted room is, by definition, quiet. But suddenly the locker room at the Pebble Beach Golf Links seemed especially silent. The kind of silence that is only possible when someone else is consciously not making noise. I stood rock-still. Listened in that foolish way for the sound of the perpetrator's footsteps, sneaking away. But all I heard was water dripping from a distant faucet and voices emanating from beyond the room itself. Spectators heading out onto the course. Vendors selling souvenir programs. I took the note out of my back pocket and read it again. The words hadn't rearranged themselves. They were still misspelled. They still threatened Brad and his family with violent death.

"Hey!"

The voice jolted me. It was the ancient locker-room security guard. He was standing twenty feet away, hands on hips, mouth open, narrow head tilted at an angle. Normally he stayed perched on a little stool at the entrance to the locker area, but now his rheumy, bloodshot eyes were filled with a kind of flabbergasted incredulity at my very presence.

"You're Parker, right?" he said.

"Yes."

"Brad Helfan's caddy?"

"That's right."

"Then why in *holy hell* aren't you out there?" he shouted, jabbing a bony finger in the direction of the golf course. "Your man's about to tee it up, for Christ's sake!"

"He sent me for a candy bar," I said.

"A *what?*"

"A Snickers bar. He's hungry."

The guard rolled his eyes. Now he'd heard everything. "For the sweet love of—get whatever the hell you need to get and *move!* Jesus H. Christ! The television cameras're ready to roll!"

Despite the theatrics, the guard was right. I didn't have the luxury to stand around and be stunned by what had floated out of Brad's locker. Not now. Twenty thousand people were lined up along the first fairway. Another twenty million were tuned in at home. I reached back in the locker, grabbed Brad's Snickers bar, and hustled past the security guard. Instinctively, I tapped my back pants pocket and felt the folded death threat still there. It had grown in weight and bulk since I'd tucked it away. But no. That was impossible. It couldn't have gotten bigger. I was almost certain that was impossible.

I walked briskly past the practice putting green and pushed my way through the crowd, ducking under the ropes surrounding the first tee. Brad stood there, waiting. He shook his head as I approached.

"Thought we'd lost you there for a second, Quinn," he said with a curious smile. "What took so long?"

"Had to use the bathroom," I said.

Brad squinted at me. "Two minutes before tee time?"

I shrugged. "When you gotta go . . . "

I did my best to assume an I-haven't-just-seen-a-death-threat expression, but Brad wasn't buying it. He took the Snickers bar and peeled away the wrapper, looking at me suspiciously the whole time. "Something wrong?" he said.

"Like what?"

"I don't know like what. You look funny, is all."

"Nothing's wrong," I said. "I went to the bathroom, you've got your Snickers, all's well with the world. Quit worrying about me and get your mind on your golf game."

Brad took a bite from his candy bar, shook his head to let me know I wasn't fooling anybody, and took his driver out of the bag. Then he wandered over to the other end of the tee box to take his warm-up practice swings and chat with some fans.

I watched him. If you sat down and tried, you couldn't have hand-selected a more unlikely candidate for imminent superstardom than Brad Helfan. He was short and stumpy, with uncombed brown hair, tinted eyeglasses, and drab, ill-fitting clothes straight from the Wal-Mart discount rack. A basic, everyday, blue-collar guy who loved cold beer and greasy chili dogs and had a West Texas twang that cut across the nerve endings like tin foil on tooth fillings. Amazing. Last week he couldn't afford the two-dollar deposit on his motel television key. Three days ago he sat and fretted the extra fifty cents required to add cheese to his quarter-pounder. But now "my man" was teetering on the brink of fame, glory, and unimagined wealth. After two rounds of the most important tournament in professional golf, Brad Helfan—longest of improbable long shots—was at the top of the leader board. He was forty-eight hours and thirty-six holes away from winning the United States Open.

I forced myself to go through the motions of what a caddy needed to do. Checked to make sure we had plenty of balls.

Counted the clubs in the bag. Toweled the last speck of dirt from each of the irons. And while I worked, I made a firm and conscious decision to ignore the note in my back pocket. It was a hoax. A prank. Had to be. Some illiterate bozo who didn't know the limits of a joke thought it would be funny to stick a death threat in Brad's locker and see if the easygoing nobody from El Paso would rattle. That's all it was. And I'd be damned if I was going to show something like that to Brad moments before the most important round of golf in his life.

The official starter with the hand-held microphone shuffled some papers, nodded at a crewman working the television booth, and cleared his throat. Things were about to get under way. I took a deep breath. Gazed out at the sea of smiling faces crowding the tee area. Firm decision or not, I did a quick, cursory scan for potential killers anyway. But it was an exercise in foolishness. There wasn't a glaring psychopath as far as the eye could see. No green drool or sharp fangs or crazed Charlie Manson eyes. Just an innocuous sea of beaming faces staring in Brad's direction, all of them caught up in the excitement of rooting on this affable, unlikely underdog.

"Ladies and gentlemen . . . " The tournament starter clicked on his microphone. The din of talk around the first tee died down instantly. "We come to our final twosome of the day. First, playing out of Palm Springs, California, by way of El Paso, Texas . . . Mr. Brad Helfan."

Brad shyly smiled at the applause, tipped his visor, and continued to warm up at the other end of the tee box, swinging easily, stretching the muscles in his legs and arms. Then a hush descended and Brad ambled over to the left side of the tee box to get ready to hit.

I felt my resolve weaken. What if the death threat *wasn't* a hoax? Brad was my old high school golfing buddy, but the fact of the matter was, we hadn't seen each other for many, many years. I knew virtually nothing about his life in the interim. Maybe Brad had made some serious enemies out there. Both you and your family would be killed, the note said. Both you and your family. A small, cold knot formed in my stomach and then fanned out to the rest of my body. I didn't have the right to stay quiet. I didn't have the right not to tell Brad what had been waiting for him in his locker. It wasn't my call. I had to show him the note. That was that. As soon as we started walking down the first fairway, I was going to dig it out of my back pocket and show him.

Brad stood over the ball in the electric silence, shrugged the last bit of tension from his shoulders, and took his swing. The shot started high and to the right and stayed right. At the top of its arc the ball rattled into the high limbs of the trees guarding the right side of the fairway two hundred yards away and came straight down in thick forest. The crowd groaned, Brad winced, and a different thought suddenly shouldered its way into my overcrowded brain.

So far Brad had slipped into the role prescribed to some sacrificial unknown at every U.S. Open. It was almost mandatory that an obscure club pro from the boondocks would go unconscious, shoot the flat-out greatest round of his entire life, and jump into the first-round lead. It happened every year, as surely as the sun rose in the east. Names like Herb Drimmler, Jay Stutz, and Werner Grossenbacher would—for one shining afternoon—elbow aside the Nicklauses and Trevinos and Palmers to stand atop the golfing heap. But what rises in the east inevitably sinks in the west, and it was equally compulsory that this same club pro would then be offered up to the golfing gods by shooting an absolutely dreadful second round. He would fade quietly back into the anonymity that was prescribed to him from birth, never to be heard from again.

But Brad had put a slight wrinkle in tradition. After shooting an opening round sixty-eight on Thursday, he followed it up with a solid sixty-nine on Friday and found himself, incredibly, clinging to a share of the lead at the halfway point. Conventional wisdom still held that his collapse was inevitable. Preordained. Every column in the morning *San Francisco Chronicle* had said it. Every condescending sports announcer on TV had predicted it. The United States Open was simply too big; Brad Helfan, unfortunately, too small. Though the gallery would not admit it, this element of impending disaster comprised a significant part of their current morbid fascination with Brad. How hard would he fall? What would be the components of his prime-time belly flop?

Brad wandered over to my side, shaking his head at the errant tee shot, and the starter clicked on his microphone again. This time he introduced Raymond Floyd, Brad's playing partner and tournament co-leader. Brad and I watched as Floyd teed it up and scorched a perfect drive down the center of the fairway. Applause from the gallery, and our group trundled down the slope of the tee box.

The insidious thought that had crawled into my brain the moment Brad drilled his tee shot into the trees was plain and direct: Maybe I wouldn't have to say anything at all about the death threat. The note had told Brad to lose and lose big. As we walked I looked out at the thousands of fans lining the first fairway. Gazed up at the overhead ABC television cameras, trained on Brad's every move. The first two rounds hadn't been anything close to this. Brad had been teamed with two other mediocre unknowns, teeing off in the dewy chill of dawn, accompanied by a ragtag handful of moms and dads and bleary-faced girlfriends who constituted the entire gallery, finishing up about the time the marquee players were just getting under way. But this . . .

Yes. This problem might solve itself. The natural course of things might have Brad losing big without the pressure of locker-room death threats. As I walked down the fairway, bag slung over my shoulder, I found myself almost wishing for it to happen. I vaguely hated myself for harboring the thought, but there was nothing I could do about it.

The gallery to the right parted so we could go into the dense forest and find Brad's tee shot. The ball was almost dead stymied, up against the base of a eucalyptus tree. Brad exhaled loudly, shook his head, and let his shoulders slouch.

I stood off to the side and waited for him to decide what to do next. The cold knot in my stomach turned a little warmer.

*   *   *

Five hours later our twosome trudged up the eighteenth fairway toward the final green. It was almost dusk. With each step Brad took, the crescendo of applause widened, deepened, grew loud enough to drown out the sound of the crashing Pacific to our left. He'd put his third shot on the long par-five twenty feet from the cup. Now it was simple. If he made the putt, Brad Helfan would tie the Pebble Beach course record and open up a commanding three-shot lead on the rest of the disbelieving field going into the final day of play. My legs felt numb beneath my hips. It was only the memory of walking that kept me walking.

Brad's extraordinary round was to be defined by the very first hole. He punched a low, slicing three-iron away from the eucalyptus tree, running the ball to a point thirty yards in front of the green. Then, to the uproarious delight of the crowd, he spun a wedge right over the top of the flag where the ball bit, backspinned, and rolled directly into the cup. A certain bogey had somehow turned into a miraculous birdie, and he was off and running.

For the rest of the afternoon Brad Helfan could do nothing wrong. Every putt fell in. Every bunker shot nestled up inches from the pin. His drives were true, his irons crisp and accurate. As word of Brad's exploits spread, more and more people joined our group until the mob trooping down the eighteenth fairway was almost more than the USGA officials could handle. It was dream and nightmare combined.

We reached the green and I stood off to the side, focusing on the blue-green ocean rather than the tournament, the world fuzzy and unreal. I watched Brad calmly drain the twenty-footer to tie the course record and listened to the crowd go berserk. In the midst of the pandemonium I managed to hug Brad, slap him on the back, say all the congratulatory words a proud caddy is supposed to say to his conquering golfer. But my gestures were mechanical, preprogrammed. I had a wild, irrational urge to take the death threat out of my pocket right there and shove it into his hands, but before I could let the impulse take root a half-dozen marshals surrounded us, forming a protective circle so we could be escorted past the cheering, hand-waving crowd toward the press tent. Brad had a scorecard to sign. There was an astonished sporting world he had to tell his story to.

At the entrance to the press tent we winked our temporary good-byes and I went to the parking lot to put the clubs in the van and wait. The excitement hanging over the Pebble Beach Golf Links was almost palpable. It hummed like a tuning fork in every branch of every tree.

I put the clubs in the van, then leaned against the driver's door and waited. In my back pocket the sheet of folded paper began to throb and pulse like a living thing. Like the persistent beating of an obscene and malignant heart.

— 2 —

I was fifteen minutes into my wait when Hank appeared at the edge of the parking lot. He was snacking from a carton of something, and even from a hundred feet away I could see the huge grin on his face. He saw me and hurried his pace. I took a deep breath and braced myself.

"I told you!" he said. "Didn't I tell you? Tell me I didn't tell you!"

"You told me."

"Damn right I told you!"

Hank Wilkie, for better or for worse, is my best friend. He claims five foot nine on his driver's license, and for the sake of maintaining the peace I don't quibble with him the extra inch. He's slender, with straight, medium-length brown hair, gentle blue eyes, and a strong, stubborn chin. Hank is married to Carol Scardino, who happens to be my other best friend in the world, and between them they have two small boys who draw me crayon pictures and keep my refrigerator magnets occupied. Hank's job resumé reads like a minimum-wage checklist of a failed life, but he couldn't care less. Ask him what he does and he'll tell you that he's a stand-up comic, and as such doesn't get overly preoccupied with the more mundane aspects of life, such as generating a stable income. Besides, as he is often quick to point out, if we were living on Mercury where a year zips by in a more reasonable eighty-eight days, he would be generating a comfortable annual income from his comedy.

Hank is also a native New Yorker and, despite almost ten years on the West Coast, is never completely comfortable when out from under the cold shade of a city skyscraper. Three months ago he couldn't have told you the difference between a five-iron and a tire iron, but now he fancied himself an authority on the grand old game of golf.

"Where's Brad?" he said, approaching the van, munching on a ketchup-drenched french fry.

"In the press tent."

"What a round!" Hank said. "Did I or did I not tell you so?"

"We just went over this, Hank. Yes, you told me so."

Hank gave me a funny look, continued to pick at his french fries. "Is it my imagination, or are you demonstrating a strange lack of joy at what Brad just pulled off?"

I pulled the piece of paper out of my back pocket and handed it over. "Read this."

"What is it?" Hank said.

"Just read."

Hank licked the excess ketchup off his fingers and opened the page. He read but didn't react.

"I found it in his locker just before the start of the round," I said.

Hank handed the paper back to me, refocused on his french fries, and shrugged. "So some kook is trying to make him lose. Didn't work, did it?"

"What if it isn't a kook? What if it's real?"

Hank gave me a look. "Come on, Quinn. Famous people put up with this kind of shit all the time. It doesn't mean a thing. You toss it in the trash and get on with your life."

"You think so?"

"I *know* so."

There was sudden commotion at the edge of the parking lot. A handful of people came around the bend, all moving together in one tight little knot. I could make out Brad's tinted glasses and uncombed hair in the middle of the drifting pile.

He was smiling and signing autographs and trying in a polite way to break free of his admirers. Finally a man in a uniform came to Brad's rescue and asked the fans to let him go. Brad scribbled one last quick autograph, then hurried in our direction, smiling, letting his tongue hang out in a demonstration of mock exhaustion.

"You're not gonna believe this," he said. "That last woman there said she thought I was sexy! Gave me her damn business card in case I got lonely tonight! Guess that's all it takes. Drive it straight and sink a couple long putts."

Hank shook Brad's hand and reminded him that he was the one who had predicted third-round greatness and Brad said yep, that was right, and dug down in Hank's carton for a french fry.

"Let's go eat!" Brad said. "I'm starved. Whatever you two guys want is fine with me. Champagne wishes and caviar dreams! The sexy one here's gonna treat!"

The three of us climbed in the van, me driving, Hank up front with me, Brad in the backseat next to the propped-up set of clubs. I fired up the engine, shifted into first, and coasted toward the parking lot exit.

"What the hell's the matter with you, Quinn?" Brad said with a smile. "I go out and shoot sixty-four and you look like you just lost your last friend on earth."

Hank and I exchanged glances. The hell with it. I reached into my back pocket with my right hand, steering with my left, and held the death threat over my right shoulder.

"I found this in your locker this morning," I said.

Brad didn't take the paper right away. His face was frozen in a funny sort of half-grin, like I'd told a joke he thought he understood but maybe didn't. When I didn't grin back his smile faded and he took the folded note.

"This was in my locker?" he said.

"Yes."

"Who put it there?"

"Why don't you read it," I said. "Then we can talk."

Brad settled back in his seat, still looking at me, the eyes behind the tinted glasses now filled with a new seriousness. The man directing traffic out in front of the Del Monte Lodge waved us through, and I merged into the flow of traffic.

Nobody spoke for the next twenty minutes. Not a single word. Nothing. I inched my way through the stop-and-go congestion of Pebble Beach and got out on the Pacific Coast Highway, going north. Hank ate his french fries. Brad slouched in the backseat, pale and deathly quiet, the unfolded death threat resting on his lap. Finally Hank licked his fingers and held the soggy carton under my nose. "Want some?"

I took a peek. The few fries left had turned to ketchup-soaked mush. A thick red smear of room-temperature sludge, coagulating at the bottom, vaguely evocative of the floor of the Entebbe airport.

"I'll pass," I said.

"Sure?"

"Positive."

"Then we better find a place to dump it," Hank said. "Carton's starting to leak."

"Just put it on the floor."

"It'll make a mess on the floor."

"Trust me," I said. "This van has endured messes other vehicles only dream about."

"Some day that will be a colorful and interesting tidbit in your biography," Hank said. "But for now please just pull over. It'll take five seconds to dump this thing in a trash can. Save the environment."

"Since when have you ever been concerned about the environment?"

"Since I'm about to put ketchup stains on a pair of pants that Carol paid sixty bucks for last week, that's when."

I wasn't in the mood to argue. Not with Brad in the backseat, half-catatonic. So I took the Seaside exit, found a supermarket on the main drag through town, and swung the van around back where the Dumpsters were. Hank got out, carefully cradling the carton of fries in both hands. He took a half-step toward the Dumpsters, then froze, took a half-step back, leaned his head in the window.

"Uh-oh," he said.

"Now what?"

"Trouble."

I bent down and saw what Hank was looking at. A skinny, teenage stockboy was standing on a concrete loading dock thirty feet away, glaring at us. He clutched a broom, and silhouetted against the dying sun he looked as grim and determined as Gary Cooper in *High Noon*. The kid knew precisely what we were intending to do but this was his loading dock and we weren't going to do it. Hank smiled blandly and held the carton of fries aloft, demonstrating how insignificant it was compared to the vastness of the empty Dumpsters, but the kid was unbudgeable. This wasn't a public garbage site. During his watch, *nobody* was putting a carton of anything anywhere.

"Better keep the engine running," Hank said under his breath. "This could get ugly."

Hank took the fries and headed in the direction of the Dumpsters. I propped my elbow on the steering wheel and glanced in the rearview mirror at Brad's listless profile in the backseat.

"What do you think?" I said.

Brad shook his head, said nothing. I shifted sideways on my seat and looked back at him.

"Can I see it again?" I said.

Brad hesitated a second, then silently handed the paper over. His jaw muscles were working, and he wouldn't look at me. I read the single typewritten sentence for the tenth time. Brad was in the middle of an emotional nosedive. It was time to put an optimistic spin on things to try to bring him out of it.

"Notice how they spelled 'tournament' and 'tomorrow,'" I said, grinning.

Brad squinted. "What?"

"The spelling. It's horrible."

"So?"

"So we can automatically eliminate all past and present spelling bee champions."

Brad continued to squint. Then it clicked that I was trying to make light of the situation and he went back to ignoring me. Sat there next to his propped-up golf clubs, eyes vacant, running the tip of his left thumb slowly back and forth across his lower lip. The silence in the van deepened.

"Look," I said. "Hank thinks it's just somebody fooling around, trying to mess with your head, and I'm inclined to agree with him. Put it out of your mind. It's probably some crackpot, that's all. A prank. The world's full of screwballs, and screwballs like to hassle celebrities, and I realize it hasn't sunk in yet, but that's what you are now, Brad. A celebrity. Watch the ten o'clock news tonight if you don't believe me."

Brad cleared his throat and faced me directly for the first time since we left the Pebble Beach parking lot. "We've been outta touch a long time, Quinn."

"I realize that."

"Fifteen years at least. Longer."

"What's your point?"

"My point is that maybe you're my caddy and old high school buddy and all that, but there's a lot about me you don't know. Some stuff's gone on during those fifteen years I'm not too proud of."

"What sort of stuff?"

Brad didn't answer. He just kept his left thumb going back and forth over his lower lip.

"Stuff that makes you think this threat might be for real?" I said.

"Yes."

We fell silent again. There was no arguing that Brad and I had been seriously out of touch. Our friendship had never been a particularly deep one to begin with. We were just two guys who happened to go to the same high school in San Francisco and ended up playing together on the varsity golf team. After graduation Brad left California for his native Texas on a golf scholarship and that was the last I'd seen of him. Peggy Lewis, his high school sweetheart and eventual wife, sent Christmas cards the first couple of years, but that was it. The cards stopped, the phone never rang, and Brad and Peggy faded into the elephant's graveyard of most casual high school acquaintances.

Then one foggy San Francisco night a month ago the phone *did* ring. It was Brad on the other end, mumbling apologies and wondering how the heck I was doing, anyhow. I was so surprised I could hardly speak. Brad was sorry as hell that he'd more or less dropped out of sight, but things had been kind of tough. He and Peggy were divorced five years now. She was living in Sacramento with their daughter, Alison. He was back in California, too, based pretty much down south in Palm Springs, getting his golf game in shape. In fact, that was the main reason he was calling. Kind of a strange thing had happened. He'd upped and shot a couple of the best damn rounds of his life and qualified for the U.S. Open. And seeing how this year it was being played at Pebble Beach, in my neck of the woods, and seeing as how he didn't really have a caddy to speak of . . .

I refolded the death threat and handed it back to him. Brad put it in his shirt pocket without a word. It was time to abandon the false optimism and get to the bottom of things.

"Do you know who wrote this note?" I said.

"Yes."

"Who?"

"It's complicated."

I shrugged. "Go slowly enough, even I can handle complicated."

Brad stared at the back of the seat for a moment or two. "Let me think on it awhile. Haven't ever talked about any of this with anybody and I want to get it straight in my head before I start blabbing away."

"Take all the time you want."

I left Brad to his troubled thoughts, turned around straight in my seat, and focused instead on the escalating drama of the leaky french fry carton. Hank and the stockboy were not making a whole lot of progress. The kid had actually come down from the loading dock to physically position himself between Hank and the Dumpster, legs braced, broom at the ready. Hank wearily looked back at me, a can-you-believe-this-asshole look, and I pointed at my watch. It was getting late. We were hungry. Hank nodded, took a millisecond to weigh the long-term consequences, then casually ended the deliberations by sky-hooking the french fries high over the stockboy's head and into the empty trash bin. The stockboy was too stunned to react. He just stood there, openmouthed, aghast, trying to assimilate the immensity of the transgression while Hank turned and strolled back to the van.

"That's it," Hank said, climbing in next to me. "No going back now. You be Bonnie and I'll be Clyde."

"What's the problem?"

"Think plural, Quinn. Problems. We are in direct violation of a dozen city health codes, several county ordinances, and probably a commandment or two." Hank shook his head. "The little twit threatened to call the police on us! The *police!* Over a bag of french fries!"

"We need to think about dinner," I said. "There's a good Mexican restaurant in San Juan Bautista."

Hank frowned. "Where's that?"

"About thirty miles north of here. Thought we could use a change of scenery. Get away from the crowds. Avoid autograph hounds."

"Fine with me," Hank said. "But keep an eye out for roadblocks."

I got back out onto the Pacific Coast Highway going north, flicked on the radio, and fumbled with the dial till I picked up a live broadcast from Pebble Beach. The announcer was talking about Brad's exploits. The pressure handled. The course record tied. The shocking three-shot lead opened up on the rest of the field. The announcer said that if Brad were to hold on tomorrow and win, he would be the greatest long shot to capture a

U.S. Open championship since Jack Fleck beat Ben Hogan in 1955. And on it went.

I thought it might cheer us up, but the announcer's enthusiasm only made it more painfully obvious how little we were celebrating. So I turned the radio off and we drove the rest of the way in silence. The thin white tip of the carefully folded death threat peeked out the top of Brad's shirt pocket, and it took a surprising amount of concentration not to glance at it from time to time in the rearview mirror.

3

It was dark by the time we reached San Juan Bautista, and the restaurant I had in mind was packed. I don't know why that surprised me. It was U.S. Open week in Monterey and it made perfect sense that a sizable chunk of the two hundred thousand fans swarming the Peninsula would think to drive out to a lovely nearby mission town on a Saturday night to eat. But I was surprised anyway. The normally placid streets were mobbed. Every gift shop full to bursting. Parking nonexistent. I inched my van through the narrow cobblestone streets and shook my head. There might be autograph hounds to dodge yet.

We got the last table in the joint, outside on the second-floor patio area next to a raucous wedding reception. On the drive up Brad had roused himself somewhat from his stupor. The color was back in his face. A pretty Hispanic woman with lush dark hair took our margarita orders, and when they came we all clinked glasses and made predictable toasts. Hank and I piled high the accolades, placing our Lamborghini orders for when Brad was rolling in his inevitable millions. Brad drank his margarita, said two Lamborghinis wouldn't be a problem, and actually managed a sheepish smile. The death threat—at least for the moment—seemed to be forgotten.

We downed our drinks, ordered another round, downed

those, went through the motions of weighing the need for a third round, and by a vote of three to zero decided what the hell. When the third round came, Hank scooted back from the table and announced that he had to use the little boys' room and nobody was to touch his drink in the meantime. I invoked the broom-wielding diligence of the supermarket stockboy as an example of how ferociously I would guard his margarita, and Hank wandered off, satisfied.

"I like your buddy," Brad said.

"One of the best," I said. "Infuriating at times, but one of the best."

"You said he's a comic?"

"Aspiring. He makes some money at it, but not enough to pay the rent. Right now he's on a roll, though. Remember the bubble gum when you were a kid that came wrapped in a little paper that had a cartoon on it?"

"Sure."

"Some company back in Wisconsin has decided to cash in on the nostalgia craze and they're resurrecting it. Calling it Tripple-Flipple gum. They hired Hank to write the jokes."

"Really?"

"Scout's honor. Hundred bucks per joke. This bubble-gum contract is worth more than he's ever made doing stand-up."

"Stand-up comedy . . . " Brad slowly shook his head. "Man, that's gotta be a tough racket."

"Not as tough as leading the U.S. Open."

Brad ignored that. He took a deep breath, linked his hands behind his head, and looked out over the cobblestone street below. "Pretty little town."

I nodded. In truth, I preferred the old San Juan Bautista of dusty sidewalks and winos in the park and dark bars of ill repute where nary a word of English was spoken. But a number of years back the local chamber of commerce woke up to the sound of heavy tourist traffic rumbling right past their town toward the Monterey Peninsula and decided to siphon off a bit of that vacation money for themselves. The result was a major sprucing up, and now the town oozed the tame, fit-for-consumption brand of "authenticity" that your average tourist is able to safely digest. But Brad had made his first positive statement in a very long time and I was going to champion it home. He was working up his courage in a roundabout way to talk about the death threat.

"Did you ever see *Vertigo?*" I said.

"What's that?"

"The Hitchcock movie with Jimmy Stewart and Kim Novak. He's the cop who's afraid of heights."

Brad bit his lower lip and thought. "That the one where at the end she runs up to the top of a building and jumps out?"

"It was a bell tower, and she fell instead of jumped, but yeah. You've got it."

"Saw it a long, long time ago."

"That bell tower scene was filmed right here," I said. "About three blocks from where we're sitting."

"No kidding?"

"After dinner I'll show you."

"Sounds good."

We drifted into an awkward silence. I let it go on for almost an entire minute, then I leaned forward and put my elbows on the table. "So how about it, Brad? You had the whole drive up and three strong margaritas. What's going on with this death threat?"

Brad kept his eyes on the street. "Tell me something, Quinn," he said at last. "Did you ever wake up one day and realize there was something bad inside you?"

"Bad?"

"Yeah. Something dark and scary that you never knew you had before?"

"Not sure I'm following you."

"No?" Brad forced a smile, but still wouldn't look up at me. "Thought you were a phobia therapist."

"I am."

"Then you must run up against all kinds of dark scary things."

I nodded. "Sometimes."

"Because I've got one of those dark scary things," Brad said. "True fact. It sat there inside me not doing anything for thirty years. What do they call it when volcanoes aren't doing nothing, but aren't dead either?"

"Dormant."

"That's it. Dormant. Then one weekend I went up to Las Vegas from El Paso to play in a pro-am, and my dark scary thing wasn't dormant anymore. It came wide-open alive." Brad paused, turned to finally look me in the eye. "Found out I liked to gamble, Quinn."

"Lots of people like to gamble."

"Unh-unh. I found out I liked to gamble more than any-thing else in the world. Remember how I used to smoke, even back in high school? Two packs a day?"

"I remember."

"Shoot, I quit that, no problem. Tossed the cigarettes in the trash one day and forgot about it. But gambling . . . gambling was a whole 'nother animal. Inside a year I pissed away every-thing I had. Wife and family. All our savings. Lost my job at the club. After Peggy kicked me out I went ahead and moved up to Vegas and really bottomed out."

"I can't picture it, Brad. Not you."

"Well, start picturing. I never was a big drinker, but in Vegas I hit the bottle heavy. Never had a dime except whatever I picked up hustling golf that day, which usually wasn't much. Things got so bad I'd go to the casinos and hang around the nickel slots just so I could drink for free."

"Do what?"

Brad smiled. "Next time you're in a casino, take a look. Every thirty minutes or so the house sends around a cocktail waitress to give people at the slots a free drink. Course, it's not really free. What it makes people do is stand there feeding more money into the machines waiting for their freebie. Fifty cents worth of watered-down booze ends up costing them a roll of quarters, but they don't put it together like that. Gam-blers are the dumbest shits in the world, Quinn, and I'm includ-ing me in that. I'm putting me at the front of the line. Anyway,

I'd hang around the halls with my hands in my pockets till I saw the waitress coming and then I'd go quick and jam a nickel in the slot like I'd been playing all night and order my drink. Take it around the corner and guzzle it. Half-hour later she'd come around again and I'd hurry back to the slots with another nickel. Used to get royally buzzed every night for about thirty cents."

There was a roar of laughter from the revelers to our right and Brad drifted off from his narrative, seemed to lose his concentration. Things were getting touchy-feely over there. Someone had produced a garter belt and the bridesmaids were lifting their gowns to mid-thigh, offering to model it. Tuxedoed young men clustered around. The bride leaned over and gave the groom a particularly lascivious kiss and everybody whooped and hollered.

Brad stared at the newlyweds. "What about it, Quinn? Think they're gonna live happily ever after?"

"Sure," I said. "Why not?"

Brad picked up his margarita and took a healthy slug. The tequila was kicking in. I wondered what was taking Hank so long. Maybe he was twiddling his thumbs in the men's bathroom, carefully reading the fine print on the state sanitation codes, giving Brad and me a block of time to talk in private. Hank Wilkie *does* have his rare moments of sensitivity to a situation.

"Anyhow," Brad said, refocusing, "make a long story short, Peggy divorced my worthless ass, packed up Alison and her bags, and moved back with her folks in Sacramento till she could get on her feet."

"She's been in Sacramento all this time?"

"Yeah."

"I'm surprised she never called me."

Brad lowered his eyes. "Things've been kinda tough for her. Point is, getting back to what I was talking about, after a while even I figured out Vegas was killing me. I got myself in some serious money troubles so I went off to the desert."

"The desert?"

"Palm Springs. Indio, actually. Bought me a used Airstream, twenty-eight-footer, parked it out on an old empty lot, and set up shop on the cheap."

"Doing what?"

"Mainly trying to get myself back on track. Quit drinking. Even quit gambling except for poker once in a while. Hustled a living on the golf course, but this time did it right. There was this guy, Leonard, who set up the games, put up the stakes. I kept twenty percent of whatever I won and he covered me if I lost. As long as I didn't lose too much, it was a good steady income. Because of my looks I had all the action I could handle."

"What did your looks have to do with it?"

Brad leaned back from the table, slapped his beer gut, held out his arms. They were the burly, muscled arms of a pneumatic drill operator. "Come on, Quinn! Do I look like a guy who's going to finesse home a downhill left-to-right eight-footer?"

"Not really."

"Damn right not really! I got no illusions. I look like something that oughta be pullin' a cart and shittin' in the street, but that's where I got my advantage. Most hustlers in the desert are your typical California types. Big and tall. Perfect tans, perfect teeth, perfect everything. These guys look like they were born and raised on the first tee with a three-wood in their hands. Scares the pigeon off. But me . . . "

"And you did well?"

Brad shrugged. "Didn't have to hang around the nickel slots no more. I mean, look at Michael Jordan. Remember a couple years back? Gambling at golf he lost what? Hundred and fifty grand? And that's just what the government knows about. You can bet your ass it was at *least* twice that much. Lawrence Taylor the same thing. What I found out in the desert is that some of the very best golfers in this country never go on tour."

"Why not?"

"Money's too damn good hustling!" Brad said. "No travel.

No entry fees. The pigeons come right to you. I remember one time I completely cleaned a guy out, guy from San Diego, he was walking up the last fairway with tears streaming down his cheeks. Bawling his eyes out, like a little boy! He sidled up close and begged me to accidentally on purpose screw up so he wouldn't lose his house. The guy'd put his *house* on the line! Said he'd give me thirty grand on the side and nobody'd know nothin'. I would've done it that time just because I felt so sorry for the dumb shit, except losing on purpose with Leonard was a good way to get your skull aired out, so I didn't."

"You beat him?"

Brad nodded. "Canned a twenty-footer for birdie on eighteen, just like I did today, and took every single last cent off the guy. Somebody told me later he tried to kill himself. Took about a hundred pills and they had to pump his stomach."

"The note in your locker," I said. "You think it's from Leonard, don't you?"

"I *know* it's from Leonard."

"What makes you so sure?"

Brad lowered his eyes. "I owe him some money."

"How much?"

"Forty thousand and change."

There was another drunken roar from the wedding party to our right. I waited till the noise subsided, then slowly shook my head. "Doesn't make sense, Brad."

"What doesn't?"

"Leonard. The note told you to lose, right?"

"Right."

"But if you win this tournament you get a Sunday afternoon check for two hundred fifty thousand dollars. Endorsements'll bring you in another million, minimum. I don't know which way Leonard's head is screwed on, but if you owed *me* forty thousand dollars I'd be your number-one cheerleader out there tomorrow. I sure as hell wouldn't be telling you to *lose*."

"Leonard must have some bigger bet down, then," Brad said. "Some other kind of bet where he wins megabucks if I lose big. I just don't know. All I know is it's him."

I slumped back in my chair. "And you're sure it's for real?"

"Positive."

"Not a doubt in your mind?"

"None."

"Then our next move is simple, Brad."

"What?"

"We go to the police."

I wasn't prepared for Brad's reaction. It was as though a switch had been thrown and ten thousand volts surged through his body. He was immediately alert, erect, eyes bright and alive behind the tinted glasses. "No way, Quinn! Forget the police!"

"All I'm saying—"

He hit the table hard with his fist and the silverware rattled. Hank's margarita sloshed and spilled. "No goddamn police!"

A group at the next table glanced over at us. I leaned forward and lowered my voice.

"Would you please calm down and listen to me a second. If this threat is for real—"

"No, Quinn." Brad clamped one meaty hand on my forearm and gripped very, very hard. *"You* listen to *me*. I know who I'm dealing with here. You don't. These people, they'll come after Peggy and Alison if the police start sniffing around. It won't just be me. It'll be my family. They even said so in the damn death threat."

"Brad . . . "

"No 'Brad' anything!" he shouted. "Swear to me right here and now! No matter what, no police!"

"Okay," I said defensively. "Whatever you say. No police. Just keep your voice down, for Christ's sake!"

"Swear it!"

"I just did. No police."

Brad released my forearm, leaned back in his seat, and instantly reverted to his earlier sullen form. We were through talking.

Hank eventually wandered back from the bathroom and we ordered our meals. When the food arrived the three of us ate in an edgy silence, Hank glancing at me curiously, me giving him a we'll-talk-about-it-later look. To our right the wedding party continued to provide a wild and giddy soundtrack, great hopes fueled by alcohol and youthful optimism. I was thankful for the diversion.

After dinner we strolled to San Juan Bautista's main square and stood for a moment in the warm, breezy evening, looking up at the bell tower where decades ago Kim Novak had fallen to her cinematic death. Brad was distant, preoccupied, troubled.

"So that's where she bought it?" Hank said.

"The very spot."

Hank sighed. "I remember the first time I ever saw Kim Novak. Some old movie on T.V. I was just a kid. She was wearing this tight, clingy sweater and right there I suddenly understood that being an adult was going to be a lot more fun than being a kid."

"*The Birds* was filmed near here, too," I said to Brad, trying to draw him into the conversation. "Up the coast in Bodega Bay. And the Joseph Cotten movie was shot in Santa Rosa. I forget the name of it . . . "

"*Shadow of a Doubt*," Hank said.

"Right," I said. "*Shadow of a Doubt.*"

Brad didn't say anything. He wasn't interested in Hitchcock trivia. We were silent for a long half-minute, then Hank said, "What do you suppose it was about this area that got old Alfred's morbid imagination going?"

"Hadn't thought about it."

"Must've been something," Hank mused. "Hitchcock picked up on something."

Brad wasn't thinking about it, either. He just kept his eyes on the high bell tower where Kim Novak, filled with fear and regret, had hurtled to her death on the tiles below. Then we turned as if on cue and wandered back to the van.

It was almost ten o'clock by the time Brad and I got back to Chick Bratton's house in Pacific Grove. Chick was an old friend of mine, a registered nurse and single mother, who'd loaned us her funky little house while she was down at a Club Med in Mexico somewhere seeing if she could rectify the "single" aspect of her dossier.

We'd dropped Hank off fifteen minutes earlier at his hotel in Monterey and I reminded him to take a taxi out to the course early the next morning to pick up his fourth-round ticket at the main desk of the Del Monte Lodge.

Chick's house was silent and dimly lit. I opened the door first and scuffed around in the darkness near the entrance, thinking there might be another note. There was. I reached down as if fumbling for a dropped key, palmed the single sheet of folded paper, and tucked it into my pocket before Brad could see what I was doing.

I threw some logs in the fireplace and for an hour we sat around the warm glow, the two of us, talking strategy for the final round. We went over likely pin placements and how playing conditions would be different if the wind kicked up. We discussed club selection and how Brad was going to cope with the icy disposition of John Ratcliffe, his fourth-round playing partner and closest competitor. We did not talk about Leonard.

A few minutes before midnight Brad stood and stretched and said it was time for him to hit the hay.

"Can I ask something without you flying off the handle?" I said.

"Fire away."

"Are you going to try to win this thing tomorrow?"

Brad finished another yawning stretch and looked down at me. "Say what?"

I repeated my question.

"You mean, am I going to lose the tournament on purpose?" he said. "Go into the tank?"

"That's what I'm asking."

"You read the note, Quinn."

"Forget the note."

Brad nodded an exaggerated nod, like I'd just come up with an obvious solution that had somehow escaped him. "Oh!" he said. "Okay! Sure. No sweat. All I'll do is forget the note."

I sighed, gave it a few moments so his sarcasm could dissipate in the evening air. "All I'm saying is this, Brad. It sounds like you've made some mistakes in the past. Mistakes with your career, with Peggy, with the family. But you have the chance tomorrow to fix a lot of it. I'd hate like hell to see somebody scare you away from it."

A reluctant smile tugged at the edges of Brad's mouth.

"Know where I live, Quinn?"

"Where you live?"

"Yeah."

I shrugged. "All I know is what you tell me. You live in Palm Springs."

"Not exactly," Brad said. "Point of fact, I live in a dinky little camper out in Indio, thirty miles east of Palm Springs. Got it parked on a little patch of desert north of town they were gonna call El Dorado Estates, except the Estates never got built."

"Maybe the developer should've called it something different," I said. "El Dorado Estates is a lot to live up to."

"How come?"

"El Dorado was the legendary lost city of gold," I said. "People've been looking for five centuries and haven't found it."

"No kidding?" Brad said. "Lost city of gold. Well . . . could be yet. If I shoot another sixty-four tomorrow it might turn out to be El Dorado after all. There's a sign out there next to the camper, pointing the way. That old sign might turn out to be right anyhow. Wouldn't that be a royal kick in the ass?"

We fell silent. The fireplace popped and hissed and lit the room with agitated shadows.

I cleared my throat, sat up straighter. "Getting back to what I was saying—"

"About me blowing the tournament on purpose?" Brad said.

"That's right."

Brad shook his head.

"Put it out of your mind. Fact is, El Dorado or not, I'm too broke to kiss this off. Peggy and Alison need the money bad. I messed up their lives but good back in Texas and this is a chance to . . . I don't know. Make it up to them a little. Maybe even patch things up. Who knows? Me and Peggy've been kicking it around. So don't worry. If I lose tomorrow, it'll be because I choked. Plain and simple."

"And Leonard?"

"I can settle up with Leonard later."

Brad gave me a wink and we went into our respective bedrooms. Once my door was closed I sat on the edge of the bed, turned on the end table lamp, and unfolded the note I'd picked up off the floor. It was an exact replica of the note Brad had found in his locker, misspelling and all, just in case he bypassed the clubhouse locker room and missed the first one. I refolded the note and put it in my wallet.

I got into bed but couldn't sleep. I was thinking of what Brad had told me at the restaurant in San Juan Bautista. Leonard. The nickel slots. The high-stakes hustling and the guy who'd gotten his stomach pumped. Strange the way he always referred to Palm Springs as "the desert." An image came to mind of Brad swaddled in a turban, skin blackened by the relentless sun, lips blistered, eyes bleached to colorlessness. Lawrence of Arabia with a putter and a six-iron. But of course "the desert" in Brad's case had nothing to do with sand or heat or geographical terrain. To Brad Helfan "the desert" meant something else entirely.

At last I drifted into a fitful sleep. A strong wind was blowing off the Pacific, and the windows creaked under the strain. In the middle of the night I woke with a start. A light was still on in the living room. I checked the digital clock by the side of the bed. Two twenty-three A.M. Then I heard a sound. A strange, soft, plunking sound, at regular intervals, like the slow drip of a leaky faucet.

I quietly got out of bed and cracked open the bedroom door. It was Brad, standing in the middle of the living room in his T-shirt and boxer shorts, barefoot, faintly illuminated by the glow of the dying embers. He had his putter out, and was methodically stroking golf balls across the carpet toward an inverted water glass that had been set on its side at the foot of the couch. Sitting on the coffee table was the locker-room death threat. It was unfolded and propped against the lamp, face up, where it could be read and reread with ease.

I softly closed my door and went back to bed.

—— 4 ——

We got out to the course the next morning a little after ten. Brad signed autographs in the parking lot and slowly made his way to the locker room. He seemed in pretty good shape, considering. Had eaten a decent breakfast back at the house. Wasn't especially nervous. On the drive in from Pacific Grove there'd been no mention of typewritten death threats or debts owed or ghosts from "the desert" come to visit. I was almost beginning to feel hopeful about the day ahead. Almost.

There were no further messages waiting for us in the locker, so while Brad changed his shoes I struck up a conversation with the same locker-room security guard who'd howled at me the day before. He was about seventy years old and sat on a stool at the entrance, legs wide apart, bent forward from the waist, bony elbows on bony knees. The guy was pipe-cleaner skinny, with watery eyes and arthritic fingers stained yellow from nicotine and a nose that looked like it had had about a quart of bourbon strained through it every morning since early childhood.

"Don't envy your job today," I said, flashing my most casual of smiles.

"What?"

"Your job. It must be tough with everybody and his uncle trying to get in here."

The guard harrumphed. I'd seen the word "harrumph" in books, but I'd never really heard one until now. "They can try all they want," he said. "Tryin's not doin'."

The guard looked off down the hall. He wasn't in the mood to chitchat with a lowly caddy. He kept his elbows on his spread-apart knees, torso bent way, way forward, like a three A.M. drunk down on the sidewalk, doing his woozy best not to vomit in the gutter.

"Come on," I said. "All these people. Total confusion. Somebody must slip through the cracks."

"You see any cracks around here?"

I smiled, but the guard just glared at me and then looked away. This was his life. This was not a laughing matter.

"So who *is* allowed in here, exactly?"

The guard turned back and trained his watery eyes on me. Some suspicion had crept into his demeanor. "What do you wanna know for?"

"Nothing. Friend of mine wanted to meet me here after the round is all and I told him I'd check it out. See if he could."

"Well, he can't. Locker room's for players and caddies. Period."

"That's it?"

"That's it."

"No exceptions?"

"What'd I just say?" The guard rubbed his knees. "Bounced a tee-vee guy outta here just fifteen minutes ago. Forget his name, but you'd recognize him. He's on tee-vee all the time. Famous. See that tag?" The guard indicated the green tag affixed to my belt.

"Yeah."

"Without that nobody gets in, and I mean nobody. I don't care if you're Jack friggin' Nicklaus. No green tag, no admittance."

The guard straightened up, folded his arms across his narrow chest, and gave me a moment to digest the scope of the absolute power he wielded. He was proud of the rigidity of the rules, the glorious inflexibility of it all, though I would have greatly enjoyed watching him try to give the bum's rush to a tagless Jack Nicklaus.

Brad and I went out to the range and he hit two buckets of balls and then we logged a half-hour on the practice putting green. Wherever he went, people swarmed. When he smiled, everyone smiled. When he frowned, concern swept the crowd. Brad was practicing a few chip shots when I felt a hand tap me on the shoulder. It was Hank.

"How's he holding up?" he said.

"So far, so good." I nodded my chin at Hank's gallery pass. "Got your ticket, no problem?"

"Smooth as silk."

Hank had almost been left out in the cold. The fourth round of the U.S. Open had been sold out a month in advance and it had taken a half-hour of high-level deliberating the day before to crowbar one last complimentary ticket out of the Del Monte Lodge. You would have thought we were negotiating an international transference of high-grade plutonium, but eventually the tournament director gave his okay and one last precious ticket had been set aside for Hank. Now it hung from his neck, large as a dinner plate, with bright gold letters announcing Hank as a VIP guest of the Del Monte Lodge.

"I love the VIP part," he said. "You should see the looks I've been getting."

"Never mind about that," I said. "Do me a favor today and don't go roaming around. Follow our group and stick close. Keep your eyes peeled."

"For what?" Hank said. "Assassins?"

"Whatever. All I'm asking is that you stick close."

Hank nodded, watched Brad hit a chip shot. "You think he's going to go blow it on purpose?"

"Last night he said no."

"Last night was many, many hours ago," Hank said, and we dropped the subject.

Hank melted into the crowd and a few minutes later Brad

came up to me, slid the seven-iron back in the bag, and took a deep breath. "Okay," he said. "Let's do it."

We made our way to the first tee through a reverential sea of humanity. Like the day before, there were no obvious murderers among them. People reached out from behind the constraining ropes and clapped Brad on the back and shouted encouragement. Overnight, America had fallen hopelessly in love with his working-class, aw-shucks persona. They loved that he was ungrammatical and thick around the middle and the guaranteed last-place finisher in any Robert Redford look-alike contest held anywhere, anytime. The media—after ignoring him for two rounds—all of a sudden embraced his frumpy accessibility with unbridled enthusiasm. How he always ate a peanut butter and jelly sandwich between the ninth and tenth holes. His love of John Wayne movies and Dolly Parton ballads. The dog-eared Louis L'Amour paperback he carried around with him on the course so he'd have something to read when play slowed down. Even his experimental clubs contributed to the legend. They were squat and ugly and shunned by the rest of the touring pros. I had to shake my head. This was a guy who'd ceased being a household name in his own household. Now an adoring nation was ready to gather him up and plunk him down, as-is, in his own little sacred corner of the Smithsonian.

John Ratcliffe, Brad's playing partner and the defending U.S. Open champion, was already waiting on the first tee. Ratcliffe was everything Brad wasn't. Tall, handsome, aloof, British. He and Brad stiffly shook hands. In the weeks leading up to the Open virtually every sports pundit in the country had picked Ratcliffe to successfully defend his title, and—though I downplayed it with Brad—he was the last guy in the world I wanted lurking three shots back. Ratcliffe was controlled, methodical, and at his absolute best in the major tournaments. A three-shot lead wasn't much with him on your heels.

It was five after twelve. The official tee time was twelve-oh-seven and the fairway before us was empty and ready, but the starter with the microphone had no intention of jumping the gun. So we milled around the tee box and waited while the second hand slowly swept its way toward the appointed moment. I thought of other things that were scheduled right to the minute, and none of them were comforting. State-sanctioned executions. Trains under Hitler. The CBS Evening News with Dan Rather.

Both sides of the fairway were lined ten deep with people, everyone craning and stretching for a better view. Hank was out there somewhere, wearing his Del Monte ticket as conspicuously as possible and mingling with the proletarians. I hoped he would forget about being a VIP long enough to keep his eyes peeled, as I had asked.

Twelve-oh-six. Brad strolled over to my side and tugged on his golf glove, finger by finger, like a doctor preparing for surgery.

"How're you feeling?" I said.

"Like my damn zipper's come unzipped on national television."

"Your zipper's fine," I said. "Just go out and play your game. The pressure's on everybody else to catch up. It's not on you."

"Not on me?" Brad smiled genially and squinted from behind his tinted glasses in the direction of the fairway. "Appreciate the pep talk, Quinn, but that's pure-bred, Grade-A horseshit, and you know it."

I shrugged. "Can't blame me for trying."

"Anyhow," Brad said, "you remember what Lee Trevino said about pressure, don't you?"

"No."

Brad spit into his glove and flexed his fist to loosen the leather. "Trevino said pressure isn't trying to win a hundred thousand dollars of somebody else's money. Pressure's playing a twenty-dollar nassau with ten bucks in your pocket." Brad smiled again and gave me a wink. "Which I've done more times these past few years than I want to think about. Don't worry about me, Quinn. I'm gonna be okay."

Twelve-oh-seven arrived at last, and the starter flicked on his microphone and officially introduced John Ratcliffe to the crowd, ticking off the money earned, the tournaments won, the awards received. It was an intimidating litany, but despite the achievements the fact remained that John Ratcliffe had all the charisma of an ironing board and was not a crowd favorite. Rumors of an actual Ratcliffe smile sprung up from time to time, but they tended to be like sightings of the Loch Ness Monster—extremely rare, and never substantiated by hard evidence. When the starter finished, John Ratcliffe gave a curt nod to mild applause, teed up his ball, and ripped a perfect drive down the center of the fairway. Just another day at the office.

Then it was Brad's turn. The microphone clicked on, but Brad's golfing accomplishments were so bare-bones that the starter had little to say. He was forced to reach back to the long-ago college career in Texas to drum up lackluster highlights, but the crowd didn't care. They cheered wildly at every mediocre tidbit. Brad smiled self-consciously, tipped his visor, and teed up his ball.

A hush seemed to descend on the whole world. Thirty thousand people waiting, held back by ropes, watching. Even the birds fell silent in the trees. All you could hear were far-off sounds of trucks shifting gears out on the Pacific Coast Highway. Overhead the crane with the ABC camera crew was motionless, focused. Brad could quote Lee Trevino all he wanted, but I noticed he took two deep, steadying breaths before getting ready to swing. He stood over the ball, flexed his knees, took one quick look at the fairway, and let it rip. There were immediate shouts of support from the crowd, and the ball streaked away on a low line drive down the left-center of the fairway. Not as sweet and smooth as a normal Brad Helfan drive, but not a disaster either. We were off and running.

"All right!" I said, walking alongside Brad down the slope of the first tee onto the lush, wide fairway. "Good start. How do you feel now?"

"A whole helluva lot better than I felt about thirty seconds ago," he said.

I laughed and patted him on the back. "You're fine now. Just shift it into relax mode and win this thing."

There is a deceptive, roller-coaster quality to the Pebble Beach Golf Links. Just as the first part of any roller-coaster ride is a slow, comfortable climb filled with panoramic views, so Pebble Beach begins with a handful of reasonably easy holes that stay safely inland, sheltered among fragrant wooded valleys and multimillion dollar homes. But as surely as a roller coaster eventually reaches the top of that first gut-wrenching plunge, so Pebble Beach inevitably turns south and faces the Pacific. And that's when the real ride begins. Beginning with the sixth hole, the golf course becomes a frightening, buffeting, on-the-edge experience of windswept coast and jagged cliffs and blind shots over gaping canyons of rock and foaming sea.

In other words, the last thing any golfer wants to do at Pebble Beach is throw away shots at the start, because it's only going to get a whole lot tougher later on. Brad had a nice three-shot lead. Not huge, but nice. I was hoping he could start off with a couple of quick birdies, stretch the lead to five, maybe, and put the onus squarely on the shoulders of John Ratcliffe and the rest of the field. Force them to play catch-up on a course that frowns on catch-up.

But it didn't work out that way. On the first hole both Brad and Ratcliffe hit decent second shots to the center of the green, and both were left with downhill twenty-five footers to the hole. John Ratcliffe putted first. There was at least a three-foot break from right to left, but Ratcliffe read it perfectly, put a graceful, clean stroke on the ball, and rolled it directly into the center of the hole for a birdie. There was a smattering of reluctant applause from the gallery. Brad had almost the same putt, but he hung it out too far to the right and rolled his ball a foot and a half past. I bit my lower lip. Only one hole played, and the three-shot was already down to two.

Brad got ready to knock in his short putt for a par, but then backed off. Took another look at it, pursed his lips, resumed his stance. He stood over the ball a long time, much longer than necessary, gripping and regripping his club, seemingly unable to pull the trigger. I wondered what in the hell was going on. So did the rest of the gallery. The putt was eighteen inches long.

A tap-in. The kind of automatic putt a professional will make ninety-nine times out of a hundred without even trying. But Brad seemed paralyzed. Then, with a sudden spasmodic effort, he stabbed at the putt like a rank amateur and the ball jerked to the left, missing the hole entirely. The crowd gasped a collective, startled gasp. Brad's sure-thing par had just become a bogey. The round was barely under way and his three-shot lead had been cut to a single stroke.

The lead vanished entirely on the second hole, an uncomplicated par-five that John Ratcliffe routinely birdied. Brad struggled to salvage par. When Brad missed yet another eighteen-inch putt on the third hole, there was a new leader in the U.S. Open. I felt sick to my stomach. The worst-case scenario was unfolding before my eyes. Brad collapsing. John Ratcliffe playing with confidence. The gallery's enthusiasm wavering, and the most brutal part of the course just on the horizon.

On the fourth tee we had to wait for the twosome in front of us to clear out. Brad had fallen gloomily silent. His miserable start had brought other golfers into the hunt, and distant roars erupted periodically from other areas of the course, going off like depth charges, signaling someone else's spirited assault on the leader board. I took Brad aside and got my chin right down in his face. "All right," I said. "What's going on?"

"I'm kinda tense, is all," Brad said. He wouldn't look me in the eyes.

"Tense my ass! You're doing it, aren't you?"

"Doing what?"

"Throwing the tournament!"

"I'm not throwing anything."

"Come on, Brad!" I struggled to keep my voice low. "Don't give me that. You haven't missed an eighteen-inch putt all week! Not one! Today you've had two easy chances and blown them both! You weren't in the general *vicinity* of the hole!"

No response.

I leaned closer. "Listen . . . you were the one who brought up Peggy and Alison last night, so do it for them if nobody else."

"Quinn . . . "

"Pay attention to me! You can bet your ass they're in Sacramento right now watching this, cheering you on. Try to remember that the next time you stand over a simple putt!"

My locker-room-at-half-time speech was finished. I dragged the clubs away and waited at the fringe of the crowd, doing my best to look disgusted. Spectators stared at me curiously. My neck felt red, and I hoped the television cameras hadn't picked up our altercation.

I don't know whether my Knute Rockne routine worked, but on the fourth hole Brad seemed to steady himself. Good drive, good second shot, two putts for a par. He parred the fifth, the sixth, and barely missed sinking a long birdie putt on the treacherous par-three seventh. His game was coming around, but John Ratcliffe was playing just as steadily, matching Brad par for par and holding on to his one-stroke lead.

Then, on the eighth hole, the momentum reversed. Brad sunk a winding, curling, snaking forty-footer for a birdie, and the crowd exploded. The United States Open was a dead heat once again.

For the next eight holes Ratcliffe and Brad went blow for blow, swapping pars and birdies, leapfrogging each other for the lead from hole to hole. There was no more distant roaring at other ends of the course, because the U.S. Open had become a two-man race. The crush of humanity was almost too much. Play was delayed on every hole so the marshals could effect some crowd control.

As we approached the seventeenth hole, John Ratcliffe and Brad Helfan were dead even. Two holes remained to decide the new U.S. Open champion. The gallery had reached critical mass, and we nervously milled around the tee for several minutes while officials tried to clear the logjam.

The seventeenth isn't a hole you want to play with unsteady nerves. It's a brutal par-three, two hundred ten yards long, usually into the teeth of a howling ocean wind, with sand traps surrounding a narrow green and the world's largest water hazard, the Pacific Ocean, all the way down the left, and beyond.

Brad came over and stood next to me. "What do you think?" he said. "Two-iron or three-wood?"

"Two-iron. Keep it low out of the wind."

"Might not be enough club."

"It'll be enough."

Brad frowned. "I don't think so."

"If you get a three-wood up in this wind," I said, "your ball's on its way to Hawaii. Hit the two-iron."

Brad wasn't entirely convinced, but the worst thing a golfer can do is second-guess himself. He pulled out the two-iron, teed it up, and drilled a low, boring shot into the thirty-mph wind. The ball never rose above waist-level. It started a little right, slowly hooked left, hit twenty yards in front of the green, found the narrow corridor between the traps, and bounced over the ridge in the direction of the flagstick. A dull roar began to rise from the crowd surrounding the green. The roar grew louder and louder and quickly built into a tremendous crescendo. Brad's shot hit the flagstick hard and caromed off to the left, coming to rest five feet from the cup.

Ratcliffe also had a two-iron in his hands, but he wasn't quite the cool, collected customer he'd been for the first sixteen holes. I saw his Adam's apple go rapidly up and down twice while he eyeballed his target, which is the closest thing to outright panic that John Ratcliffe is ever likely to show. He waited for the crowd to settle down, then approached his ball and focused.

He hit a low line drive straight at the pin, almost a carbon copy of Brad's shot, but halfway to the green aerodynamics took over. A golf ball weighs 1.62 ounces—roughly the same poundage as a couple of toothbrushes—and when it loses momentum in a thirty-mph wind, it goes wherever the wind wants it to go. Ratcliffe's ball began to lift off like a jet reaching the end of the runway. The ball rose high in the blue sky, almost straight up, wobbled in mid-air, drifted left, then plummeted to earth like a gutshot magpie. It hit and buried in the gaping sand trap guarding the left side of the green.

The crowd didn't cheer Ratcliffe's misfortune, but they sure as hell wanted to. All around me were joy-stifled faces reminiscent of children desperately trying not to laugh aloud in church. Their hero Brad Helfan was up close for a birdie, while Ratcliffe was going to have to make a couple of great shots just to save par.

Up at the green Ratcliffe hitched his pants, took a wedge, and crawled into the sand. His ball was partially buried and he did the best he could, digging down after it and running the ball a good forty feet beyond the cup. Everyone waited while he crawled back out of the trap, swapped his wedge for a putter, and made the long walk to the back end of the green. He lagged his forty-footer up close and tapped in for a bogey. Ratcliffe's shoulders slumped. He stood there a moment, eyes shut, then he reached down, retrieved his ball, and stepped aside.

Then it was Brad's turn. He crouched behind his five-footer and stared at the sixty inches standing between him and an almost certain U.S. Open championship. Yes, he could miss the putt and still be ahead by one, but if he made it he would take a commanding two-shot lead to the final hole. Barring disaster, the trophy would be his. I squatted down behind him and looked over his shoulder.

"Left edge?" he said to me.

I nodded. "But keep it inside the cup. And not too firm. Don't hit it through the break."

Brad straightened up, pushed his tinted glasses back further on his nose, and hunched over the putt. I moved out of the way. The silence of a huge crowd waiting to erupt has its own energy, and I could feel the reined-in urge to explode whipping through the Pacific wind. Brad took his putter back, tapped the ball, and several million pairs of eyes watched as it rolled toward the left edge, hung one tantalizing second on the lip of the cup, then fell sideways into the hole. A one-second pause, then the gallery exploded. Ratcliffe lowered his head and marched toward the final tee. Brad came back to the bag on wobbly legs and I noticed his hands were shaking when he handed over the putter.

"Shit . . . " he said. "I can't take much more. Let's get this sonofabitch over with."

"One more hole," I said. "Just one more hole."

To a nongolfer, the par-five eighteenth hole probably looks like a nice stretch of manicured green acreage fronting an especially nice section of California coast. But to a golfer, standing on the tee of the eighteenth at the Pebble Beach Golf Links and gazing out toward the Del Monte Lodge in the distance is akin to being a religious pilgrim setting eyes on the ceiling of the Sistine Chapel for the first time. It is probably the most famous hole in all of golf—the most photographed, the most dramatic, the one hole almost any golfer would choose to play as a final request on the eve of his execution. For five hundred fifty yards the hole slowly bends left around rugged shoreline. Trees and luxury homes all the way down the right. Brad took a deep breath and pulled out his driver.

"Don't hit your driver," I said.

"Don't what?"

"You crazy? Leave the driver in your bag."

"What for?"

"How long have you been playing this game, Brad? The only way you can lose this thing is to put your tee shot in the ocean. So play it safe. Give up some distance and hit an iron out to the right."

"Makes the hole thirty yards longer doing that," Brad said.

I stared at Brad. He'd come down with a sudden case of brainlock. "So what?" I said. "Forget the damn thirty yards! Who cares? You don't need distance here. Par's going to win it for you. Bogey might even win it. Just don't dump your tee shot in the ocean."

Brad shook his head. "I hear what you're saying, Quinn, but I gotta play my game."

"Brad!"

He didn't allow me another word. He kept his driver in his hands, teed up, and aligned himself in such a way as to take the ball right out over the very edge of the rocky bluffs. I felt a jolt of panic go through me. What the hell? I looked around for a referee so I could call time-out, but this wasn't basketball. Before my head could clear, Brad launched his tee shot.

The ball rocketed off on the exact line he'd taken, twenty yards out over the churning blue-green Pacific. There was an intake of breath from the crowd behind me, and I felt sick inside. But then the ball started to fade right a little. Faded more. The wind caught it and blew it even further right, and it landed on the very edge of the bluff, bouncing and rolling along the precipice, coming to rest no more than a dozen yards from disaster.

The crowd cheered with relief, and Brad shook his head like that one was just a little too close for comfort. By Ratcliffe's expression you could see that he, too, was wondering what in God's name Brad was thinking of. Ratcliffe then hit a good drive safely down the right side and our group began the walk down the final fairway. I discreetly pulled Brad away from the others.

"Would you mind telling me what in the hell's going through your brain?" I said. "Sailing your ball out over the ocean like that!"

"It's high and dry, ain't it?" Brad said.

"Only because you're lucky!"

"No such thing as luck."

"Don't be stupid!" I said. "You got away with it there, but now quit screwing around with the left side. This next shot just hit an iron in the landing area to the right. Get your par. Take the trophy and put it in your trophy case. Ratcliffe's not going to eagle this thing!"

"I know what I'm doing, Quinn," Brad said, moving away from me. There was an odd inflection in his voice. He wasn't smiling.

"What are you—?"

Then it clicked. For the first time since the opening holes, I thought of Leonard and the death threat, and a twisted logic to Brad's actions began to take shape. This was Brad's way of doing two things at once. Beat Ratcliffe fair and square, and then go ahead and dump the tournament in the deep blue sea on the final hole. The death threat is adhered to, but he carries back to Palm Springs the knowledge that he's not a loser. That he could have beaten John Ratcliffe if he'd decided to. It was suddenly the only explanation that made sense. Brad had proven something to himself, and now he was going to throw the tournament. They'd gotten to him after all.

We arrived at his tee shot and waited while Ratcliffe hit his second shot straight down the middle. Then I watched in silence as Brad took a three-wood and lined up again to take his shot way out over the Pacific Ocean.

"Don't do this," I softly said.

Brad looked up at me briefly. "Trust me, Quinn."

"Don't do this."

Brad refocused on his shot. Forty thousand spectators waited. He flexed his knees, took his swing, and the ball whistled away out over the bluff, out over the whitecaps, the seaweed, the rocks. This time he was making sure the shot found the water.

Brad had swung so hard that he lost his balance and went down on one knee like a baseball player swinging for the fences. Except that professional golfers never swing that hard. Pros never fall down. But Brad knelt there a moment, still holding his club, trying to push himself up to a standing position. He pushed, but nothing happened. Something was wrong.

I took a step toward him and his face rose to meet mine. The tinted glasses were on the ground, and there was confusion in his eyes. That's when I saw the swell of red spreading near his stomach. His lips parted as if to ask a question.

"Wha . . . ?" he said.

"Brad!"

I moved to grab his arm and in the next moment the upper half of his head erupted. The force of the explosion straightened him up, lifted him violently into a standing position for a second, where he wobbled, flailed, then toppled over backwards. My hand was still outstretched to grab him, but there was nothing left to grab. His headless corpse fell to the ground like an empty coat falling from a collapsed coat hanger.

5

The official told me to sit in the reading room and not to move, so that's what I was doing. Sitting in the reading room, not moving. It was a nice room to not be moving in. Silent and peaceful, with high ceilings and dark heavy curtains. Just beyond the door, in the main lobby of the Del Monte Lodge, was utter chaos. People running. Phones ringing. A fractured montage of shock and disbelief, with guests and spectators and lodge employees milling around aimlessly, bumping into each other like dazed, confused ants who've just had their anthill kicked out from under them.

I rubbed the burn from my eyes. Short-term memory was no more than a series of unconnected freeze-frame stills, brightly lit, set against a backdrop of unfathomable black. I tried to focus on what I was sure of. Images I could trust. The three-wood shot whooshing out over the Pacific. Brad falling, then trying to get up. His face, then the sudden, violent removal of his face. More bullets ripping up the earth around Brad's lifeless body, and how I went down on my stomach and tried to pull the golf bag up and over me. But most of all I remembered the smell of the cool grass pressed into my face. That, and the muffled, hysterical screams of people in the distance.

How I got from the eighteenth fairway to the reading room of the Del Monte Lodge was more difficult, and I was trying to fill in the blanks when the door to the room swung open and a frazzled-looking man of about forty-five swept in. He was about my height, six-two, and moved with the strong, confident body language of an ex-athlete. His dark, shoulder-length hair had been combed in an unsuccessful attempt to conceal significant premature baldness up front, and a prominent, busted-up nose led down to a thick, drooping mustache. The man saw me sitting there, pulled up short, and looked down at his clipboard like a doctor who had lost track of which patient was in which room.

"You're Parker?" he said.

"Yes."

"The caddy?"

"Yes."

The man took a pen out of his shirt pocket and scribbled something on the clipboard. He wore sneakers, jeans, and a white cotton shirt rolled up to his elbows. The look was casual, but this guy was anything but. His rpm's were revved as high as they would go. He scribbled and blinked and sniffed through his nose.

"I'm Detective Lorenzini," he said. "I know it's a tough time, but I gotta ask you some questions. That gonna be okay?"

"Go ahead."

"Good."

He sat on the couch opposite me and propped the clipboard on his knees. His accent had vague echoes of the Bronx, and the general attitude was one of the street-savvy yet concerned parole officer who earns the respect of his barrio kids by being able to take a punch as well as he gives it out. The hair on his forearms was dark and simian.

"Just so we're straight," he said. "Your name is Quinn Parker and you're Mr. Helfan's caddy. Right?"

"Yes."

"And you live in Monterey?"

"San Francisco."

Lorenzini scowled, made corrections on his clipboard. "Says here Monterey."

"It's San Francisco."

"And you were standing next to Mr. Helfan when the shots were fired?" he said.

"That's right."

"How close?"

"Fifteen, twenty feet."

"As best as you can recollect, how many shots were fired?"

I shook my head. "No idea."

"Approximately."

"At least three or four."

"Could it've been six or eight?"

"Maybe."

"Twelve?"

"No."

Detective Lorenzini paused and wrote on his clipboard.

"Did you hear the report of the gun?" he said.

"I don't remember hearing a thing."

"No popping sound at all? Like a door slamming shut?"

"No."

"What about the direction of the bullets? The trajectory?"

"From the right, I think."

"Due right?" Lorenzini said.

"Somewhere off to the right, that's all. From the trees to the right."

"But definitely not from in front or behind?"

"No."

"Or from the left?"

"The ocean's to the left," I said.

"There were a dozen boats anchored out there."

I shrugged my shoulders and closed my eyes. Suddenly I was tired. Exhausted. Emptied out.

"How long have you been Mr. Helfan's caddy?" Lorenzini said.

"Four days."

The detective stopped scribbling on his clipboard. "You mean just this one tournament?"

"Right."

"Then who's his usual caddy?"

"Brad didn't have a usual caddy," I said. "He didn't play on the tour."

"He didn't?"

"No."

I wondered what planet Detective Lorenzini had been living on for the past forty-eight hours. By now half the television-viewing population of the United States knew the Brad Helfan story word for word.

"Brad got here through regional qualifying," I explained. "He's not a touring pro."

"So then you're not a full-time caddy, either?"

"No."

"What *is* your occupation?" Lorenzini asked.

I exhaled, not in the mood for the convoluted follow-up explanation I always have to give when this question is asked.

"I'm a phobia therapist."

"Come again?"

"A phobia therapist. People with phobic disorders come to me for help."

"You licensed?"

"No. I work in conjunction with a licensed clinical psychiatrist in the city who refers her patients to me when they need to go out and see if her couchside solutions are working."

Detective Lorenzini took a few seconds to chew, swallow, and digest that one. "Kind of a tag-team thing?" he said.

"That's the idea."

Lorenzini glanced back down at his clipboard and mercifully didn't pursue that line of questioning any further. Instead he asked me to recap the events of the past couple days, which I did. Where Brad and I went, who we saw. At the end of it he asked if Brad had given any indication that he might be in some sort of trouble. If there were some people who might want harm to come to him.

Lorenzini looked at me, pen poised. The second copy of the death threat was still in my back pocket. Then I remembered how Brad had leaned forward at the restaurant table in San

Juan Bautista and grabbed my arm. The panic in his face at the thought that I might bring the authorities into it. These "people" wouldn't stop with him, Brad had said. If the police were brought into it, these "people" would go straight after Peggy and Alison. And now Brad's shot-away face was too vivid in my mind.

"No," I said at last. "Brad didn't seem to be in any trouble."

Lorenzini lingered a moment, then bent to his clipboard, scribbling quickly, giving me a good look at his shiny bald head. I couldn't read whether he believed me or not.

"Which hotel was Mr. Helfan staying at?" he asked.

"He wasn't. The two of us were staying at a friend's house over in Pacific Grove for the week."

"Then Mr. Helfan's personal belongings are still at this house?"

I nodded. "Mine, too."

Lorenzini took his pen and did a small rat-a-tat-tat drum solo on the clipboard, nibbling at the end of his mustache. "We better head on over there," he said. "You can get your things and I'll take a look around. Feel up to it?"

"I feel up to being anywhere but here," I said. "Let's go."

Hank was in front of Chick's house in Pacific Grove when we drove up, pacing back and forth across the front lawn, hands shoved deep in his pockets. When our car swerved up the driveway he stopped, squinted, recognized me in the passenger seat.

"You know this guy?" Detective Lorenzini asked.

"He's a friend," I said. "It's okay."

We parked and Hank was right there at the car door. His face was twisted with pain, and he grabbed me by both shoulders, practically dragging me out of the automobile, and hugged me hard.

"Jesus Christ, Quinn! I didn't know if you were alive or dead or what!"

I tried to speak, but Hank was hugging me too hard.

"I was way the hell up by the green and couldn't see anything," he went on. "People were saying that Brad was dead and his caddy was shot, too. Jesus!" Hank released me, stared into my eyes as if to verify I was among the living, then clutched and hugged me again.

Lorenzini stood to the side, a little uncomfortable with the male affection, and after Hank had gone on for another thirty seconds or so the detective gestured at the front door.

"You got a key, right?" Lorenzini said.

"Right."

I unlocked the door. Detective Lorenzini asked Hank to wait outside because the forensic people were going to dust the place later and the fewer fingerprints mucking the works the better. Hank wasn't happy about it, but did as he was asked.

"Same goes for you," Lorenzini said. "Try not to touch anything. Just look the place over and see if everything's the way it was."

I wandered from room to room, careful to keep my hands to myself. As far as I could tell, nothing had changed from the time Brad and I had left earlier that morning. No obvious break-in. Nothing ransacked. Our dirty dishes from breakfast were still stacked on the drainboard; the faint aroma of bacon grease still permeated the kitchen. I wondered about the death threat that Brad had propped up against the coffee table the previous night. If it had been left in the house, I couldn't see it. If the note was in Brad's wallet, the authorities would discover it soon enough.

"Anything?" Detective Lorenzini said.

"No."

He exhaled and ran his fingers through his dark hair. "Then why don't you get your belongings and we'll head back. Try not to stir things up. We're still gonna dust the place anyway, just in case."

I went into my bedroom and stuffed three days' worth of dirty clothes into my single duffel bag. Detective Lorenzini tried to make it look inconspicuous, but I was never for a moment completely out of his eyesight. I zipped up my duffel bag and came back out into the living room.

"Ready?" he said.

"Yeah."

That's when I noticed the fireplace. I set the duffel bag down, stooped, retied my shoelaces, and took a discreet closer look. Atop the cold gray ashes was a charred-black, wafer-thin bit of burned paper. It was still holding its fragile shape, crisp and delicate, like one of the fleeing bodies at Pompeii.

I wanted to pick up the fire poker and crush the burned note to dust, to stir it back into the bed of cold gray ashes that was already there, but Detective Lorenzini was watching me. So I pulled the laces of my shoe nice and tight, and together we left the quiet living room.

— 6 —

The unopened bottle of champagne sat on the dining-room table in a silver bucket filled with mostly melted ice. To the left were three champagne glasses, to the right a handwritten note from Kate. "Congratulations, Brad!" the note said. "You two better save some of this for me or face the consequences! Will be home around eight-thirty. Kisses."

I set my duffel bag on the table next to the champagne and gazed out the dining-room window. The Golden Gate Bridge, three miles distant, was pale and strange in the fogless twilight, as much an apparition in clarity as when shrouded in clouds and mist. For six years now, home has been 1464A Union Street, top floor of a spacious blue-and-white Victorian halfway between Van Ness and Polk, on the western slope of Russian Hill. When I rented the apartment I didn't really care about the dining-room view. I didn't care about the four bedrooms or the wood-inlaid floors or the two functioning fireplaces, either. For me the only true requirement of a home is that it be able to slam the door on the rest of the world when need arises, and 1464A Union Street did just that. Emphatically. After dropping Hank off I'd parked the van, put the key in the front door, and climbed fifty-four steps straight up into the sky. From the dining-room window all I could see was sky and rooftops, which was fine. That's all I wanted to see.

Down the hallway I could hear Oscar the parrot squawking to be fed. Lola the cat came slinking out from behind the sofa and gazed up at me with curiosity. My family. And I don't even especially like pets.

I stared down at the champagne again. Both Kate and Carol, Hank's wife, were up in Napa coordinating a cheese-and-wine school fund-raiser. The event had been in the works for weeks, and, U.S. Open or no U.S. Open, they were committed. It was Kate's style to assume a victory party. I turned her cheerful note facedown and pushed it away.

I poured myself a severe Scotch on the rocks and drank it down like Gatorade. It hit my brain with the percussive *thwap* of a high-dive belly flop. I poured another. So many calls had come in on my answering machine that the tape had run out. I didn't listen to any of them. I turned the machine off and unhooked the phone from the wall jack and wandered back to my office at the other end of the apartment. All my books are there and I scanned the shelves until I found what I was looking for. My high school yearbook. It was back in the dustiest of the dusty corners.

I took the yearbook back out to the living room, eased myself into the deep cushions of the armchair, and slowly leafed through a strange, dog-eared, black-and-white world of very young people doing silly youthful things. Eventually I found Brad's senior picture.

Some people change dramatically as they get older, some don't. Brad was one of the don'ts. Way back in high school he had the same messed-up hair, same tinted glasses, and same shambling, good-natured smile of the man who had come within half a hole of winning the U.S. Open. Toward the back was a three-page spread of the varsity golf team, with a shot of Brad and me standing on the first tee at Harding Park golf course, smiling big goofy smiles, leaning on our clubs in a failed attempt to strike a debonair pose. I was painfully skinny, with short hair and ears big enough to jam enemy radar. The caption poked gentle fun at Brad's West Texas heritage. I closed up the yearbook and set it aside.

The empty apartment was very, very still. I sipped my

Scotch. Listened to the indifferent traffic rumble up and down Van Ness Avenue four stories below. Stared at the blank television screen. Glanced down at the remote control. Back up at the blank screen.

Unh-unh. Nope. Wasn't going to do it. I knew how the television reports would go. Somber-faced announcers warning viewers that the footage to come was graphic in nature and that parents might find it unsuitable for children. The footage, of course, was more than suitable for Nielsen-rating adults. Then a grim-faced panel of experts would sit around a table and discuss the proliferation of violence in today's society. No way. I wasn't going to have anything to do with it.

Minutes passed. My intentions were pure, but the television screen proved too blank, the remote control much too close to my right hand. I sipped more of my Scotch. Listened to the silence. Caved in.

At first I flipped from channel to channel. Predictably, the shooting at Pebble Beach dominated every news station in the Bay Area. Reporters filing live reports from the eighteenth green said that only two things were known at the moment. Brad Helfan had been killed by sniper fire on the eighteenth fairway, and the gunman or gunmen had not yet been apprehended. All else was speculation. Police were still in the process of securing the area, and the status of the U.S. Open itself was in doubt.

Finally I settled on ABC, the network that had been televising the Open. Their live camera, mercifully, had been trained on the flight of Brad's second shot, not on Brad. But the second camera had captured the murder in bright, vivid color. One could clearly see Brad take his swing, fall to the ground in a continuous corkscrew motion, attempt to rise, then take the fatal volley to the face. ABC superimposed a large white circle over Brad at the moment his head erupted into twenty tiny chunks. Thoughtful.

They showed the clip again and again and again. I stared at the television screen in a dull trance, numbed by the repetition, novacained by the Scotch. Just sat there, watching myself watching Brad die, over and over. Finally ABC moved on to other news. Live-action violence, like any other brand of pornography, quickly loses its luster.

It was a busy news night. Strikes in China, a child in Ohio who needed a new liver, and a warming trend developing along the East Coast. My eyelids started closing. They felt as heavy as poured cement, and I didn't try to stop them.

I felt her fingers on my face, and opened my eyes. The television had been turned off. Kate was crouched in front of the armchair, smoothing imaginary locks of hair from my forehead. Her eyes were red-rimmed, her face pale.

"I just heard," she said. "On the way back. We didn't have a television up there and nobody knew a thing."

She leaned into me and we held each other a very long time without speaking. Her skin was soft and her hair smelled of a day spent out of doors. Leaves and oak trees and vineyard winds. Then she released me and I gently kissed her on the lips. Tears were in her eyes.

"Are you okay?" she said.

"Yes."

"Hank?"

I shrugged. "Hanging in there."

She nodded, brushed the tears from her cheek. "Have you eaten?"

"No."

"Are you hungry?"

It suddenly occurred to me that I hadn't put a thing in my stomach since breakfast except six ounces of Scotch. "I'm starving."

Kate nodded. "Give me a second and I'll fix something."

"No," I said. "Let's go out. I need to move. Get some fresh air."

"Okay," she said. "Whatever you want. Let me pull myself together first."

She leaned forward, kissed me, then hurried back down the hall. I watched her go.

Kate Ulrich had been in my life once before, two years earlier. We'd met under difficult circumstances and tried to love each other under impossible circumstances. When a killer's bullet finally sent me to intensive care for a month, that was it. Kate stayed by my side till she knew I was out of danger, then she quietly gathered up her things and returned to her native Detroit to rebuild her life.

We kept in touch. Phone calls and letters in which we pretended that we still weren't madly in love with each other. She talked up the challenges of her new job in Detroit, and described the nice men she was seeing. I described the nice women I was seeing. She was glad for me and I was glad for her. We demonstrated a level of maturity about the whole thing that would have made a convention of marriage counselors gag.

Then one day the doorbell rang and it was Kate. My mouth fell open an inch and a half and stayed that way while she quickly and nervously went through her prearranged speech. Actually, Kate informed me, when it came to hearing about the nice women I was seeing, she wasn't glad at all. Therefore she hoped she wasn't out of line, but since there was no denying there'd been something very real between us and geography had always been our primary reason for not getting back together again, she'd decided to eliminate that lame excuse and see what happened. She hadn't called first because if we'd hashed it out by phone it never would have happened, so she'd slapped down her Visa card and hopped a 747 instead. What did I think?

I found my tongue. Did she want to come up? No, she didn't want to come up. She wanted to stay out on the front landing, all business, and hand me a piece of paper like the serving of a subpoena, listing the phone number of the hotel where she was staying. A hotel number, she informed me, that would be good for a week, starting at six P.M. that evening. If I thought there was any point in giving it another try, I should call her. If not, I shouldn't call her and she'd return to Detroit in seven days with no hard feelings.

I called that night at six-oh-one. Yes, I said. Let's do it. Kate asked if I'd hold the phone while she did a brief but meaningful headstand. I did. When her headstand was finished we began to talk specifics. My feeling was that Kate should rent her own place nearby, but she nixed that in a hurry. Unh-unh. No halfway stuff this time. She was tired of men who approached their relationships like air-traffic controllers; cautious, deliberate, anticipating problems, thinking about how to minimize damage, forever plotting out escape routes should emotional dilemmas suddenly need diverting. If my answer was a yes, Kate said, then it was a yes, and if we couldn't coexist peacefully under the same roof she'd rather know sooner than later. The live-in experiment was now in its second month, and other than a brief, bloody skirmish for bathroom shelf space, the sailing had been smooth.

Kate was back. She'd retouched her tear-streaked mascara and was wearing her coat. "Ready?"

I took a moment to look at her. She was a tall, sturdy, durable beauty, with shoulder-length sandy hair and a forthright, can-do demeanor.

"Ready?" she repeated.

"Yes," I said. "Let's go."

We walked up and over Russian Hill and down into North Beach. We found a new Basque restaurant and took a table for two at the window. There was a set menu, which relieved us of decision-making. A solid, smiling woman put a bottle of homemade wine on the table and bustled off. For a minute or two Kate and I spoke of nothing, then she put her hand on mine and looked me in the eyes.

"Do you want to talk about it?" she said.

I put my other hand on hers to hold it in place. "Can you keep a secret?"

Her face grew troubled. "What sort of secret?"

"I know who killed Brad."

Kate's eyes widened with shock. "You do?"

"Yes."

"My God, Quinn . . . who?"

"You're having dinner with him."

"What?"

"I'm the one who killed Brad."

Her expression hardened. "Not funny, Quinn."

Kate tried to remove her hand, but I held it in place between mine.

"I mean it," she said. "I don't appreciate your sense of humor."

"It's no joke." I took a deep breath, looked out the window at the dark street. "I'm not sure how much I should tell you. Brad confided some things . . . some things he wanted kept secret."

"Tell me."

"If the police ask you about it . . . "

Kate waved me off. "I'm a big girl, Quinn. I get the picture. Tell me what you know."

I did, taking my time with it, going all the way back to high school and my initial friendship with Brad and Peggy. I told her about Brad's gambling problems in Las Vegas, his life of high-stakes hustling in Palm Springs, and the typewritten death threat waiting for him in his Pebble Beach locker. I filled in as much as I could about Leonard, and why Brad was convinced that he was the man responsible for the note in the locker.

Among Kate's many gifts is the ability to listen, and she didn't interrupt me once. Our food came and she ate and concentrated intensely on what I was saying. At the end of my narrative she dabbed her lips with her napkin and poured herself another glass of red wine.

"Brad owed this Leonard fellow forty thousand dollars, right?" she said.

"Right."

"Then why would Leonard want Brad killed if he was on the verge of winning a lot of money?"

"I asked Brad that same question."

"And?"

"He brushed it off. Said it was Leonard anyway. I don't think Brad was telling me the whole story. There are too many gaps."

"What else doesn't make sense to you?" Kate asked.

"None of it makes sense. How did the death threat get into his locker? I talked to the security guard, and the only thing he lives for is to bounce unauthorized people out of there. So was it a player? Another caddy? And how did the person know we were staying at Chick's house in Pacific Grove? As far as I know, only you, Carol, and Hank knew that."

"And Chick," Kate said. "And all the people Chick might have told."

I pinched my lower lip and stared out the window. The improbabilities were piling up. So were the possibilities. "If you wanted to kill someone and get away with it," I said, "how would you do it?"

"I've never thought about it."

"In the past few hours I've thought about it a lot. You'd do it quietly, wouldn't you? Minimum of fuss. Wait till your victim is strolling down some dark alley and then pop him over the head, make it look like a robbery, slip back into the darkness. Police give it their best shot for a week or two, then put it in the unsolved file. But that's not what happened. Whoever killed Brad did it in the most glaringly high-profile way possible. On the final hole of the U.S. Open, with thousands of eyewitnesses and cameras all over the place and twenty million television viewers! Why? I mean, this is going to be headline news night after night until they find the killer. What kind of murderer would want to draw that kind of attention to themselves?"

Kate listened to me patiently. When I was finished she put her elbows on the table and rested her chin in her clasped hands. "So how come you say you were the one who killed Brad?"

"I was the one who told him to ignore the death threat."

"That's all?"

I managed a bitter laugh. "Isn't that enough, given that the people who threatened him made good on their threat?"

"No," she said. "That's not enough."

"You wouldn't say that if you'd heard me last night, Kate. It was one of my better lectures. Seize the day! Don't give in! Call their bluff! Of course, it wasn't *my* ass on the firing line. Not do-the-right-thing Parker. Brad, on the other hand, was kind of thinking that it might be a nifty idea to keep on living. I was the one who talked him out of it."

Kate turned and signaled for our bill, her face a mask of disapproval. "Let's go," she said.

We walked back to the apartment in silence. She went straight to the bedroom. I fixed myself another Scotch and went into the living room and turned on the news. There'd been a new development in the two hours we'd been gone. Brad's killer was still at large, but the police had found the weapon. A house-to-house search of the luxury homes lining the eighteenth fairway had yielded a high-powered rifle on one of the roofs. There were spent cartridges and everything, and flashbulbs popped as one of the investigating officers held the rifle high overhead at a press conference.

A few minutes later Kate appeared at the entrance to the hallway. She was barefoot, wearing a turquoise nightgown.

"They found the gun," I said. "It was on somebody's roof."

"Do you want to make love?" she said.

"Didn't you hear me?"

"Didn't you hear *me*?"

The tone of her voice got my attention.

"Do what?" I said.

"I just thought maybe a little intimacy might help both of us feel better," Kate said. "Temporary, permanent, whatever. If you're not in the mood, that's okay. But I also wanted to say one other thing tonight. Are you listening to me?"

"I'm listening."

"Could you turn off the television then?"

I turned it off.

"Thanks." Kate cleared her throat, leaned against the wall. "I hope this doesn't sound cold, but I want to know what kind of grace period you're expecting."

"What are you talking about?"

"How long are you going to do this? Everybody is entitled to a grace period, and I can handle a day or two, but after that we're going to have problems. So how long are you going to do this?"

"Do what?"

"Blame yourself for Brad's death." Kate nodded her chin at the lamp table. "Teardrops and Scotch stains on the old high school annual. How long are you going to act like you're the one who pulled the trigger just because you gave Brad a well-intentioned pep talk?"

"You're right, Kate. That *does* sound a little cold."

She shrugged. "I can't help it. I've never been able to handle strong, silent, brooding men. It's one of my character defects. I don't brood. When I have a problem, Quinn, you're not going to have to wrench it out of me. It's going to come crashing down into your lap whether you like it or not and you're going to be expected to help. For me anyway, that's what a relationship is. To relate. To establish association or connection."

We were silent awhile, Kate leaning against the wall in her nightgown, me slumped in the armchair. Then she straightened up and swept the hair from her face. Puffed her cheeks and blew out air.

"Did it again," she said.

"Did what?"

"My timing's all wrong, as usual. Your friend was killed right before your eyes a few hours ago and I'm telling you to snap out of it. I'm sorry. Sometimes I talk before I think."

"It's fine," I said. "You're right."

She nodded absentmindedly, like it wasn't really important. "Anyway," she said, "bedroom's down at the end of the hall. Offer's good for another half-hour."

She turned and left. I sat in the armchair for a while, thinking about what Kate had said. Thinking about the sniper camped out on the roof of the Pebble Beach home. I took another sip of my Scotch, but it didn't taste nearly as good as it once had.

Eventually I pushed myself up out of my seat and went into the kitchen and tossed the rest of the drink down the sink. No point in compounding things with a hangover. Then I went down to the darkened bedroom at the end of the hall. I was five minutes over deadline, but Kate proved to be flexible. Like she'd said before, everyone was entitled to a reasonable grace period.

Even me.

— 7 —

Hank's wife, Carol, often talks about how she has a hard time remembering the time before she started her family. Not that the childless years hadn't been rich and exciting and full. They had. But the advent of babies had had a curious blotting-out effect of all that went before. Month after month of diapers and squeeze toys had sandblasted away all recollection of what it was like to spontaneously go out with your spouse on a weeknight and have a carefree martini. Some events have a way of eclipsing all others.

I never fully understood what she meant until I woke up the morning after Brad's death. All shock and disbelief about the events of the day before had vanished. Yesterday afternoon it had been inconceivable that Brad was gone. There'd be no more shy smile, no more mangled West Texas syntax, no more cross-eyed squint as he cleaned the lenses of his tinted glasses. But overnight that had changed. The reality of Brad's death had settled firmly and permanently into my consciousness, eradicating every other reality in the same way baby diapers had commanded center stage with Hank and Carol. In the course of one sunset to sunrise it had become impossible to imagine a world in which Brad Helfan had *not* been murdered.

Kate was already up. She was sitting cross-legged at the dining-room table, reading the *Chronicle*, wearing the same turquoise nightgown she'd had on the evening before. The champagne paraphernalia of last night had been cleaned up and put away.

"How're you feeling?" she said.

"Better."

"Good."

I poured myself a cup of coffee and avoided a headfirst plunge into the newspaper. Peripheral vision of huge black headlines was enough.

"Hope you don't mind," Kate said, "but I listened to the phone messages. In spite of everything that's happened, I'm still in the process of looking for a job and can't function in a world where phones are yanked from their wall jacks."

"Anything important?"

"No. Reporters wanting exclusives. There were only about ten calls anyway."

"On a forty-five-minute tape?"

"The last message was from some kids and they never hung up," Kate said. "A prank thing. They played music and chatted and told jokes till the tape ran out. You need to reprogram your machine to cut people off. Know what I think, though?"

"What?"

"That one of the reporters who called earlier had their kid tie up the rest of your machine so nobody else could come in with a better offer."

I pulled up a chair and sat down. "What a cynical brain you have, Ms. Ulrich. Maybe you ought to offer your services to the Monterey police."

"No way," Kate said. "There isn't going to be any case-solving in this household. Solving cases was what helped our relationship fizzle the first time around."

I slid the headlines over to my side of the table and began reading. The lead article was a simple, straightforward account of the events leading up to the shooting. No apparent motive, but there were rumors that Brad Helfan had been associated with known organized-crime figures in both Las Vegas and Palm Springs. The mob-style professionalism of the killing had police focusing their investigation on that angle. There was a photo of Detective Lorenzini with a cluster of microphones stuck in his face. He looked appropriately grim, but—with sufficient time to prepare—had done a much more thorough job of disguising the bald spot on his head.

The reattached phone began ringing shortly after breakfast and didn't stop. Kate had things she needed to do around the apartment, so I left her to it and pulled on a jacket and took a long, brisk walk along the Marina Green. Watched the whitecaps and kite-flyers. Detoured through the chicken and vegetable section of the Marina Safeway on the way back to stock up for dinner. When I got to the apartment Kate met me at the head of the stairs. She was holding a sheet of paper.

"Ready for this?" she said. "Thirty-eight calls. Two of which you need to hear."

"Give them to me."

"We're invited to Hank and Carol's for dinner tonight. I took the liberty of accepting."

I nodded. "What else?"

"Jill somebody called. A friend of Peggy Lewis's. Brad's funeral is scheduled for Wednesday morning and it would mean a lot to Peggy if you were there."

"Where is it?"

"Sacramento. I have the directions."

I put down the sack of groceries and slowly shrugged out of my jacket and nodded. "Okay. Wednesday morning."

"Unless it's really, really important to you, I'd rather not go," Kate said. "Okay?"

"Why not?"

"I didn't know Brad. I don't know Peggy. She might want to have some private time with you . . . I'd feel uncomfortable, that's all."

Kate folded up the paper and put her hands on my shoulders. Then she slowly bent forward from the waist and kissed me on the lips. "Okay?" she said.

"Sure."

She kissed me again. This one was interrupted by the ringing of the telephone. Kate kept her mouth right where it was, planted firmly on my lips.

"More reporters," she mumbled into my teeth. "Keep kissing."

We continued the kiss for a few more seconds until Hank's voice came on.

"Are you there?" he said. "Yoo-hoo. Pick up the phone if you're there. Don't ignore me."

Kate kept her lips on my lips and shook her head no.

"If you *are* there," Hank went on, "turn on Channel Seven right now. Fast. This you've got to see."

I broke off the kiss and glanced pitifully in the direction of the television set, and Kate gave me a look.

"I defer to Channel Seven," she said. "Jesus . . . I love a man who has his priorities in order."

"I'll make it up to you."

"Sure you will."

I hurried down the hall and clicked on the television. Kate had her take-it-or-leave-it shtick down pretty cleanly, but I noticed she was right on my heels to see whatever it was that had Hank running for the phone.

It was John Ratcliffe. For a second I thought it was yet another rerun of the shooting, but then it became clear that this broadcast was live. Ratcliffe was standing on the eighteenth fairway with his caddy and a white-haired man in a red jacket.

"What's going on?" Kate said.

"I'm not sure."

I turned up the volume. The announcer was in the middle of his explanation. The United States Golf Association—in an emergency session—had determined that John Ratcliffe needed to go back out, place his ball at its original spot on the eighteenth fairway when play had been interrupted, and finish. A great deal of effort had gone into the tournament, the announcer intoned, and they simply couldn't blow the whistle because of the tragic shooting and leave the results up in the air. There was a lot of sanctimonious talk about how the show must go on, that Brad Helfan himself would have wanted it this way, that an event like the U.S. Open needed to demonstrate to the sporting world and beyond that it would not capitulate to the violent impulses of a single individual, etc. In other words, millions of dollars were up for grabs, and unless John Ratcliffe posted a final score, the lawsuits would soon be queued up around the block.

"I don't believe this," Kate said.

Ratcliffe had his arms folded across his chest and was asking the white-haired man a question. Then Ratcliffe's caddy handed over a golf ball and Ratcliffe squatted and carefully placed the ball on the grass. The white-haired man squatted with him, and they talked some more. The caddy leaned into the picture to watch. They looked like three overgrown kids trying to carefully return a bird's egg to its nest; huddled, fretful, wondering if it was going to live.

"He's not really going to play the last hole?" Kate said, mouth agape. "Not *really!*"

"Yes, he is."

"No."

"Yes."

"No!"

"Watch him."

"I'm sorry," she said. "This is too much. This is *sick!*"

Finally all parties concerned were happy with the placement of the ball. John Ratcliffe selected a club, took a couple of practice swings, and hit his third shot crisply to the green. The temporary grandstands had been disassembled and only a dozen or so stragglers were loitering up near the eighteenth green to watch. Channel Seven went to commercial, and when they came back Ratcliffe was standing on the green. He approached his fifteen-foot birdie putt, gave it a long look, then matter-of-factly knocked it into the back of the cup. For all his emotional distress and distraction, the twenty-four-hour delay might just as well have been to scoot an errant family of meandering ducks off the fairway rather than to scour the grass for bits and pieces of Brad Helfan's skull.

"Sick," Kate said. "Sick, sick, sick. This whole country needs some intense therapy."

Ratcliffe reached down and plucked the ball from the bottom of the cup. It was done. He was officially the U.S. Open champion. The USGA had not kowtowed to the violence of a single individual. Prize money could now be distributed, sponsors would be placated.

"At least he didn't smile to the crowd," I said.

"I thought you said he never smiled anyway," Kate said.

"He doesn't."

"Then who's to know?" Kate said, trailing disgust as she left the room. "Maybe he's smiling inside."

I sat in my chair and thought about it. She was right, of course. Who was to know? John Ratcliffe had successfully defended his U.S. Open title and reconfirmed his spot as the world's best player. For all we knew, his elation knew no bounds.

Brad's funeral took place as scheduled two days later on a hot, muggy, Central Valley morning. Kate exercised her option to stay home, so I headed out by myself, driving east on Interstate 80, past sprawling shopping centers and massive subdivisions that stretched all the way to Vacaville, fifty miles from downtown San Francisco. Bedroom communities for besieged families willing to spend one-sixth of their lives in an automobile rather than pay the two-hundred-sixty-five-thousand-dollar median cost of a Bay Area home.

On crisp, clear mornings, driving through the Sacramento Valley can be an uplifting experience. One's mind wanders to wholesome thoughts of egg-gathering and cow-milking, of farmers in overalls eating flapjacks and getting ready for another selfless day of feeding the nation. This wasn't one of those mornings.

The air quality diminished rapidly as I crested the coastal hills past Vallejo and descended into the bright haze of the

Sacramento Valley. The blustery freshness of San Francisco was replaced by a yellowish, burning mixture of Interstate truck exhaust, thick, drifting pollen, and billowing smoke from torched rice fields. On state-approved agricultural burn days driving through the Valley was not unlike stumbling upon the aftermath of an especially vindictive war, where the marauding conquerors had pillaged and plundered and set the vanquished ablaze.

Brad's funeral was being held at an old cemetery not far from downtown, in a run-down area of winos, boarded-up gas stations, and Salvation Army thrift stores. The graveyard itself was straight from the festered imagination of Edgar Allan Poe. Even in the summer heat, it gave the impression of mildew and soggy leaves, shifting shadows, and dank decay. Dark gray tombstones leaned crookedly beneath the clawlike branches of overgrown oaks, their inscriptions all but worn off by the ravages of time and acid rain. Behind a chain-link fence, out on Stockton Boulevard, a cluster of curious black whores wearing Spandex hot pants stared at the commotion. I sighed, took a look at the hole that had been dug for Brad. This would not be my first choice as a place to spend the rest of eternity, but Brad probably hadn't had much say in the matter.

A hundred or so people were already on hand. Three television news vans were parked outside. I milled around for a while, looking unsuccessfully for a friendly face. The mourners were all strangers. The only person I recognized was Detective Lorenzini, broken nose, droopy mustache, and all. He stood off by himself, looking fit and oddly handsome in a conservative dark suit. When he saw me he gave a slight hand signal and sauntered over.

"Quinn," he said. "Thought you'd be here."

We shook hands. Lorenzini took out a handkerchief and mopped the sweat from his face.

"Some graveyard, hunh?" he said. "I always wondered where Frankenstein spent his childhood."

"You came all the way up from Monterey?" I said.

Lorenzini nodded, scanned the crowd. "Saw too many B-movies as a kid, I guess. Remember how the killer always showed up at the funeral of the person he killed?"

"No."

"Sure you do. The guy was always out there on the fringes, slinking around."

"I don't think Brad's killer is slinking anywhere near Sacramento today," I said.

Lorenzini shook his head. "Me, neither. But I figured you'd be here and there were a couple more things I wanted to ask."

"Right now?"

"Yeah," Lorenzini said. "Do you mind?"

"Go ahead."

"I was wondering in those last two days, Saturday and Sunday, was Mr. Helfan ever out of your sight for a long period of time?"

"How long is long?"

"You know. Long. More than an hour."

I shook my head. "A few minutes here, few minutes there. Except at night when he was sleeping, of course."

"Sunday morning no?"

I shook my head. "We got up about eight, had breakfast at the house, then drove to the course together."

"You got up at eight?"

"That's right."

"Is that normal?"

"What do you mean?"

Lorenzini shrugged. "I was under the impression that caddies at an important tournament like this get up real early and check out the course first. It's part of their job."

Lorenzini was right. U.S. Open caddies traditionally rise before dawn and go out to the course to walk the dewy fairways with a pad and pencil, noting exact yardages from one place to the next, pacing off distances, scrutinizing new pin placements, and so forth.

"Normally yes," I said. "But Brad didn't operate that way."

"Why not?"

"Knowing that a pin was cut eleven and a half feet beyond

a certain sand trap on a certain hole only tensed him up. Got him thinking about those eleven and a half feet instead of the entire shot. Brad preferred to eyeball the target once, take out a club, and just hit the damn thing."

"So you got to sleep in Sunday?"

"That's right."

"Lucky you."

I shrugged, looked again at the freshly dug hole awaiting Brad's corpse. "Lucky's not a word that springs to mind these days, Detective Lorenzini."

We were silent awhile, watching the mourners streaming single file into the cemetery. Lorenzini didn't seem chastised in the least. "You heard we found the rifle," he said. "It was on the roof of one of those homes out there on the eighteenth fairway."

I nodded that I had heard.

"House was empty," Lorenzini continued. He looked at me portentously. "Been empty all week."

"You say that like it means something."

The detective lifted his eyebrows. "U.S. Open weekend at Pebble Beach? That house has gotta go for several grand a day, yes?"

"Or more."

"Or more. That's exactly what I'm saying. A couple grand a day or more. So how come it was just sitting there, doing nothing?"

"You're asking me why somebody in Pebble Beach didn't stay in their house?"

"Just seems strange," Lorenzini said. "That's all. It's not strange to you?"

"Maybe the owners aren't golf fans," I said. "Maybe they went to Hawaii for the week to get away from the crowds. Maybe they have a trillion dollars and don't need to rent out their house to strangers for pocket change."

"Yeah," Lorenzini said, unconvinced. "I thought of that, too."

"What's this about, Detective?" I said. "You didn't come all the way to Brad's funeral to ask me about why a house wasn't rented."

"No, I didn't, Quinn." Lorenzini smiled and adjusted his tie. Sweat had darkened the collar of his shirt. "If you don't mind me talking straight, I came up here because I think you're lying to me."

Our eyes locked for five seconds. "What makes you think that?" I said.

"I've had a couple days to dig around a little," Lorenzini said. "Your pal Brad Helfan had what you might call a less-than-stellar past. His present wasn't so hot either, for that matter."

"So?"

"So when I asked you back in Pebble Beach if there were people who might want to see him dead, you didn't tell me that he used to buddy up with mob figures in Vegas."

"I don't know anything about Brad and Las Vegas. We went to high school together. Period."

"No," Lorenzini said. "Not 'period.' You also were the person closest to him during the last ten days of his life. What I'm having trouble with is you telling me everything was steady-as-you-go right up to the moment he got shot."

"What's troubling you?" I said. "Specifically?"

"Specifically?" Lorenzini nodded, shoved his hands deep in his pockets, and rocked back on his heels. "Okay. You want specifically? I had a talk with the locker-room security guard and he said on Sunday, before the final round, you were standing around asking funny questions about what kind of access the public had to the locker-room area. That's one specifically. Then I went out to that restaurant you said you went to in San Juan Bautista, the Mexican place, and the waitress who'd been on duty Saturday night recognized Brad's picture and said your happy-go-lucky high-school buddy had blown a major fuse that night. Lost it completely for a couple minutes. Slammed his fist down on the table so hard it almost knocked all the drinks onto the floor and then grabbed you by the shoulder like he was going to haul off and slug you. To me, that's a funny thing to do, a guy who's out celebrating being in first place in the U.S. Open."

Detective Lorenzini paused. I didn't say anything.

"Another thing," he went on, "is that I wonder what it was that got burned in the fireplace."

"Excuse me?"

"Your friend's house in Pacific Grove," Lorenzini said. "Just when we were leaving you stooped down to tie up a perfectly tied-up shoelace, right in front of the fireplace, and I wondered why. Later on I went back out and took a look. It was all white ash in there except for one little burned piece of paper sitting neat and tidy on top. Separate."

I took a deep breath and glanced around at nothing in particular. One thing had all of a sudden become crystal-clear. I needed to quit thinking of Detective Lorenzini as a hairy-armed, busted-nose guy from the Bronx who spent his free hours in front of a mirror figuring out how to cover up his bald spot. The guy was as sharp as a stiletto.

"I've told you everything I know," I said.

Detective Lorenzini gave me a long look. A less friendly look. The expression was a bothersome stew of disappointment, anger, and don't-test-my-temper frustration. "See, Quinn. . ." he said. "My ass is on center stage with this one. Everybody's shouting at me. Everybody wants answers. This isn't some little back-street thump on the head that's gonna go away. A hundred million fucking people every morning are talking about this homicide over their bowl of Cheerios. You understand my predicament here?"

"Yes."

"I'm glad you understand my predicament. Tell you what I'm gonna do. I'm gonna go ahead and understand your predicament, too. I'm gonna assume you're still in shock about everything that's happened and give you about three more days, max, to get yourself unshocked and experience full recovery. Fair's fair. Then you and me, we're gonna sit down again and talk."

There was some commotion at the entrance to the cemetery. Two black limos rolled onto the gravel driveway and stopped. "Show's about to start," Lorenzini said. "Take care of yourself."

He strolled over to the other side of the roped-off area around the freshly dug grave, shoved his hands in his pockets, and stood there alone.

The door of the first limo opened and a woman got out. A little blond-haired girl followed her. Peggy and Alison. They were too far away for features to take shape, but Peggy looked very much as she had looked the last time I saw her, over fifteen years ago. Same petite frame. Same long, shiny, light-brown hair. Alison looked like a miniature version of her mother.

The ceremony was mercifully brief. I stayed out on the fringes of the crowd, where the killers in Lorenzini's B-movie youth always loitered. I tried to listen to the graveside words about Brad, but my mind was on the good detective. Three more days, he'd said, and then we were going to sit down and talk. Three more days. It was my week for grace periods, apparently, but I doubted Lorenzini would be as accommodating as Kate if I ran over deadline.

Suddenly the ceremony was over. The priest backed away from the gravesite and Brad's long white coffin, suspended over the dark empty hole by cranes and hoists, began to lower with a soft, mechanical whir. Peggy watched impassively. I wasn't thinking about final good-byes or good times never to come again or anything as noble as that. I was off down a gruesome mental side street, wondering how Dwyer & Sons Mortuary had dealt with Brad's disintegrated face. Had they tried to patch it up? Or had they merely gathered up the loose chunks and tossed them in? The ancient Mayans were careful about that sort of thing. They'd painstakingly reconstruct the bodies of kings who were killed and mutilated in battle. Precious stones for the eyes, embroidered cloth for the hair, the heart of a jaguar to replace the human heart that had been torn from the chest. I doubted Dwyer & Sons had done that. The jaguar was an endangered species, and these were recessionary times.

Peggy and Alison turned quickly and went directly back into the first limo. I filed out with the rest of the mourners. The whores at the cyclone fence watched us leave, hanging around just in case there might be an impulse buyer among us. Snacks always sell better when stocked near the cash register, and what the hell? Grief . . . need for solace . . . it was a natural connection. You never knew.

I got to my van and fumbled for my keys. The reception was being held at a house in the town of Folsom, just north of Sacramento. I was trying to remember the easiest way to get there when a hand was suddenly on my arm. I snapped alert. Peggy Lewis was standing beside me, a gentle smile on her face.

"Hello, Quinn."

"Jesus, Peggy!"

We embraced each other in the grimy yellow sunshine, against a backdrop of gravemarkers and disinterested prostitutes.

"Can I ride with you to the reception?" she said.

I glanced back at the limo. Peggy anticipated my question. "Alison is going to ride with my mother and father," she said. "We're covered."

"Of course you can ride with me," I said. "Hop in."

I opened the door for her and she slid into the passenger seat of the van. Then I got in beside her and started up the engine.

"I need to talk with you about something important," she said. "Just the two of us, without a bunch of people all around. Okay?" Tears were starting to form in her eyes.

"What is it, Peggy?"

"Just start driving. I'll tell you on the way."

I slipped the van in gear. Just beyond Peggy's distressed profile, silhouetted against the dark tombstones, Detective Lorenzini watched us leave.

—— 8 ——

For a minute or two we drove down Stockton Boulevard in silence. Peggy was composing herself, I was angling my van through the crush of cars leaving the cemetery. When I got up onto the freeway she finally took a deep breath and faced me.

"You look good," Peggy said.

"You, too."

"No, I mean it. You've changed a lot."

"Less hair."

Peggy smiled. "More weight. I remember you were a little on the skinny side in high school."

"'A little on the skinny side,'" I repeated. "A career in diplomacy awaits you, Peggy."

"And your ears . . . " she said.

"What about them?"

"I don't know. They've shrunk or something."

I laughed. "My friend Hank saw a picture of me from that era and said I looked like Howdy Doody at Auschwitz."

"Well . . . nobody's at their best in high school."

"Come on, Peggy," I said. "You were *terrific* in high school. You were hands-down, no question about it, the most sophisticated woman I'd ever met."

Peggy looked startled. "Go on! Sophisticated? Me?"

I nodded. "You served me my very first cup of coffee. How's that for sophistication?"

"I did?"

"You did. A fifteen-year-old boy doesn't forget something like that. Also, you spoke French and wore reading glasses and *The Philadelphia Story* was your favorite movie."

"*The Philadelphia Story*—" Peggy broke off, looked out the window. "I'd forgotten all about that movie. It *was* my favorite, too. We live most of our lives in the dark, you know that? We really do. Unless other people remind us, we forget who we are."

I studied Peggy's profile as I drove. In high school, she'd had a chipmunk quality to her face and personality—pointed nose, pointed chin, a bright, alert bundle of sudden moves, like something that should be skittering from tree to tree gathering acorns instead of studying for exams. But adulthood had softened her. There was a roundness to her features, a patience in her demeanor.

"I saw your commercial," I said.

She smiled, continued to look out the window. "My one and only?"

"I thought you gave a compelling performance."

"That makes three. My mom and dad thought so, too."

Peggy's dream all through high school was to be an actress. Nothing remarkable there. A lot of teenage girls have that dream. But Peggy had the talent and determination to give it a shot. So after graduation she'd taken a break from Brad and Texas and everything else and had gone out to New York for a couple years to see what might come of it. Peggy Lewis was Sears Roebuck catalog material all the way, wholesome and fresh, and she'd managed to parlay her Everywoman persona into—among other things—a detergent commercial that got a lot of airtime back in the late seventies. Peggy played one of two disbelieving young mothers admiring the clean laundry of a third mother.

"Why'd you quit the acting?" I said.

"Everybody kept telling me that what actors do best is

starve, so I dropped it. Smart, huh? Now I make eight dollars an hour and buy my groceries with food stamps." She cleared her throat and faced me. "I need to ask you something important, Quinn. About what happened to Brad."

"Go ahead."

"Did he talk with you before he died? About his problems, I mean?"

"Some."

"What did he say?"

"That he used to have a gambling problem, and that he was in debt to some people in Las Vegas and Palm Springs."

Peggy nodded. "Anything else?"

"No."

"Nothing about the two of us?"

I chose my words carefully. "He seemed to think there was a chance the two of you could get back together again. He felt like he'd treated you and Alison badly, and he wanted to make it up."

"Anything else?"

"I don't think so."

Peggy stared at the glove compartment. "Did you know he called me the night before he died?"

I swung out and passed a slow-moving truck. "Brad called you Saturday night?"

"Yes."

"What time?"

"Late," Peggy said. "One or two in the morning. He woke me up."

"What did he say?"

"That's what I wanted to talk to you about," Peggy said. "He acted like he knew something bad was going to happen. He told me how much he loved me. He apologized again for screwing up the marriage. It was like ... it was like the phone call of a man saying all the things he wanted to say before he died."

Peggy looked at me. Her eyes were bright and wet. "You've

got to be completely honest with me, Quinn. What else happened down there?"

"Brad got a death threat."

"A what?"

"A death threat. It was in his locker at the beginning of the third round. Another copy was waiting for us that night at the house. Unsigned, of course. Brad burned his copy in the fireplace. Mine's in the safe at home."

Peggy stared hard at me, then equally hard at the dashboard. "What else?" she said.

I tucked the van over into the slow lane, took a deep breath, and told her everything I knew. Peggy, like Kate, listened without interrupting. When I was finished she just sat there for a moment, assimilating, sorting out, connecting the dots.

"Brad made me swear to keep it quiet," I said. "He was afraid whoever was threatening him would come after you and Alison."

"They're already coming after me," Peggy said quietly.

I stole a glance at her. "What's going on?"

"There've been phone calls. I answer and a man says Brad better clear up his debts, and then hangs up."

"Brad talked about a man named Leonard."

Peggy nodded. "Leonard Novak. I know him. I mean, I don't *know* him personally, but I've heard of him. The way I understand it, he sort of bankrolled Brad's golfing bets in Palm Springs."

"Brad was convinced Leonard was behind the death threat."

Peggy shut her eyes, shook her head. "God knows. For such a sweet human being, Brad managed to make a lot of enemies. Even long after our divorce I got hate mail from someone who'd lost money on the golf course to him. How this person found my address I don't know, but he found it. Wrote threatening things about Alison and how they knew which school she went to. It was horrible. I've changed my phone number three times in the last two years."

"Do you still have the hate mail? The actual letters?"

"Yes."

"Did you go to the police?"

"No."

"Why not?"

"I called Brad and told him about the letters. I wasn't kidding myself. I knew if the police started poking around in Brad's life he could get into trouble. I just wanted him to be aware. See if he could stop it on his end."

"Did he?"

"I guess so. The letters stopped. There were only three of them, but it was scary while it was happening."

We rode in silence awhile. "Brad said he owed Leonard money," I said.

"I know all about it. Fifty thousand dollars."

"Brad said forty."

Peggy shrugged. "Fifty, forty, what's the difference? Nikki called last month demanding full payment and I explained not only that Brad and I were divorced and his debts were his debts, but that I was having enough trouble paying my own monthly rent."

"Who's Nikki?"

"Leonard's wife."

"Why would Leonard's wife be calling you?"

"Because Nikki is convinced that Brad was sending gambling money to me and Alison instead of applying it to his debt."

"Was he?"

Peggy nodded. "Some. Once or twice a month a money order would come for a couple hundred dollars. But it wasn't a big deal. Sometimes three months would go by with nothing. It wasn't the kind of money that would erase a fifty-thousand-dollar debt."

I tapped my fingers on the steering wheel. "It still seems odd to me that Leonard would have his wife calling you."

"I got the feeling maybe Leonard didn't know anything about it," Peggy said. "I don't know. Just a feeling I had. All I know is that Nikki was very unpleasant."

"You must have her address if she wanted you to send money."

"Yes."

"I'd like to get that from you before I go."

"I've got it right here." Peggy opened her purse, rummaged around for the address book, and flipped through the pages. "It's 1222 Lake Street, San Francisco."

"San Francisco?"

"That's what she told me."

"I thought Leonard was based in Palm Springs."

Peggy shook her head, closed the address book, and put it back in her purse. "Then maybe that's it. Nikki and Leonard are splitting up and the prenuptial says she gets to keep whatever Brad owed. I don't know. I don't care. I only want her to leave me alone."

We fell silent awhile, and the miles slipped by. I was thinking about Nikki and what she was doing up in San Francisco. About the hate mail from somebody Brad had cleaned out on the golf course. About whether I should attempt a small dose of honesty with Detective Lorenzini at the end of my three-day grace period. It was a lot to think about, and took us both all the way to the outskirts of Folsom.

I was born and spent the first twelve years of my life in Sacramento, and I remembered Folsom from my childhood. It was a pretty little town built above the rocky bluffs of the American River, in a rolling landscape of horse ranches and wooded hills, rattlesnakes and poison oak. I'd spent many happy Huckleberry Finn hours in Folsom, inner-tubing the river, catching lizards, gazing with fear and awe at the entrance gates to Folsom Prison, a few miles further north, where celebrity prisoners from Charlie Manson to Timothy Leary to Juan Corona had been incarcerated at one time or another.

I hadn't been back to Folsom since those childhood days, and I was surprised at the change. It existed in my memory as little more than a grocery store and a post office. The kind of place where much of the social life revolved around going to the A&W Root Beer stand and cussing out politicians. But the urban sprawl of Sacramento had completely encompassed it, and Peggy explained as we wheeled into town that Folsom was now one of the more fashionable addresses in the metropolitan area. Real estate rivaled that of the Bay Area, restaurants featuring $14.95 taco plates were the rage, and the river itself was almost un-get-to-able because of the hordes of weekend tourists.

I took the van down historic Sutter Street. I knew it was historic because about five in-your-face signs told me so. The Planning Commission had decided to make it even more historic by ripping out the original funky downtown sidewalks and replacing them with hokey wooden walkways in an effort to re-create the feel of the Old West. Bars were "saloons," food was "grub," and an "assay office" sold Folsom Prison T-shirts and made-in-Taiwan gold-panning accessories. I leaned on the steering wheel and shook my head. It was enough to make a grown child cry.

The reception was being held in the home of a family friend, and when we pulled up there were already a dozen or so cars parked on the narrow, tree-shaded street. I cut the engine and Peggy sighed.

"Don't know if I'm up for this," she said.

"What would you rather do?"

"I'd *rather* just float off somewhere far away."

I shrugged. "I know a place on the other side of extremely, excessively historic Sutter Street that used to rent inner tubes."

Peggy turned and smiled at me. "Why didn't I look at you more seriously in high school?" she said.

"Big ears and visible rib cage," I said.

"Right." She laughed. "The ears."

"And Brad."

Peggy's laughter softened into a wistful smile. She nodded and looked off into the leaves of the overhanging tree. "Yes," she said. "And Brad."

"Do you think the two of you might have given it another shot down the road?"

"No," Peggy said. "It's romantic to think so, but he had a

lot of problems, Quinn. More than anybody knew about, I bet. He was just too nice. People took advantage of Brad."

"Alison's handling all of this okay?"

"She's still awfully young," Peggy said. "And Brad left the house when she was only three years old. To her, Dad is more of a notion than a flesh-and-blood person."

We got out and locked up the van and stood for a moment in the street. The air quality out here was only marginally better than it had been in downtown Sacramento. Peggy seemed to sense what I was thinking.

"They're burning the rice fields today," she said, squinting up into the smazy sunshine. "The ash floats down this way from the North Valley and ends up in backyard pools of these three-hundred-thousand-dollar homes and the city people and the farmers scream at each other. Kind of silly, isn't it?"

"Yes."

Peggy paused. Turned to look me in the eyes. "There was something else Brad told me Saturday night," she said. "He said something big was in the works. Something that was going to make a big difference in all our lives. It was in the mail. Or he was putting it in the mail."

"Did he say what it was?"

"No. Only that it was big. Important."

I thought about it for a second. "And it was in the mail?"

"Or he was going to mail it," Peggy said. "I don't remember which. I was wakened out of a dead sleep and sort of tuned Brad out."

"Why?"

Peggy sighed. "I always ignored Brad when he got like that. He was always coming up with momentous things that were going to make everything all better, and usually it was just wishful thinking. But this time he was deadly serious, Quinn. This time I really think he meant it."

I spent an hour at the reception, mingling as best I could with people I didn't know and most likely would never meet again. Detective Lorenzini had the good sense not to crash this party, so I was spared another of his off-the-cuff interrogations. I met Peggy's mother and father. I chatted with Lauren, her best friend and owner of the Folsom house. I met Felix Stockwell, an old family friend and the creator of Platypus Equipment and Design, manufacturers of the experimental clubs Brad used. He mentioned the desire to set up a memorial tournament of some sort in San Francisco, an education fund for Alison, Brad, and Peggy's eight-year-old daughter, and wondered if I'd be willing to help out. I told him I would and he winked, said he'd be in touch later, and evaporated back into the crowd.

About midway through the hour Peggy came gliding across the living room in my direction, smiling, her arm linked in the arm of another woman. The other woman was in her mid-fifties, heavy-set, with a broad doughy face and significant girth around the middle. There was something familiar about the woman, but I couldn't place her.

"Quinn," Peggy said as she drew nearer. "Do you remember Mrs. Helfan? Brad's mother?"

Click. Brad's mother. Of course. The perennially kitchen-based woman in Brad Helfan's house who always had a heaping plate of food to serve us ravenous teenagers when we'd pile over after school.

"Mrs. Helfan," I said, extending my hand. "Of course I remember."

Mrs. Helfan ignored my hand, gave me a big, forceful hug, then stepped back to examine me. "Quinn Parker!" she said with mild wonderment. "Looks like somebody finally managed to bulk you up some."

"Your fajitas got the process started," I said.

"You ate and ate and stayed skinny as a rail," Mrs. Helfan said. "But you're right about the Tex-Mex. Fajitas. Nachos. That's all I'd fix you boys back then, way before it got fashionable."

"I'll leave you two to catch up," Peggy said. She gave my wrist a squeeze and headed back toward the living room.

"Are you still living in the Bay Area?" I said.

"Oh, God, no!" Mrs. Helfan said. "California was only for three years. My husband got transferred back to Texas, and we stayed put. Earl's been passed away now almost a year, rest his soul."

"I'm sorry."

She nodded and swallowed hard. "Lately it's been a tough go. First Earl. Now Bradley."

"None of this seems real yet to anybody," I said. "We're all still in shock."

"Bradley had a lot of problems," Mrs. Helfan said. "Got himself in chin-deep with some bad people. He never said nothin' directly, but a mother knows. He got himself going down the wrong road somehow. Don't ask me how come. He was such a good kid in high school. College, too."

"I was looking through my old high school yearbook the other day," I said, steering the conversation away from Brad's downfall. "Those were fun times."

Mrs. Helfan softly smiled. "Fun for y'all, maybe. I'm an El Paso girl, born and bred. All I remember about those Frisco years is being cold all the damn time, pardon my Latin. Cold feet. Cold hands. Middle of January or Fourth of July, didn't matter. I used to say you could put a blindfold on a person and put 'em out on the front porch all day in San Francisco and they couldn't tell you whether it was the dead of winter or the dead of summer." Mrs. Helfan shook her head at the memory. "I couldn't wait to get back to Texas."

"I remember when Brad first arrived on the scene," I said. "The rumor around the school was that the football team had finally found an offensive tackle to take us all the way to the State finals."

Mrs. Helfan laughed. "Didn't work out, did it?"

"Definitely not."

Brad's football career was, indeed, a short one. Midway through the second game of the season he picked up a loose fumble and started running with it and was immediately torpedoed by a couple of defensive linemen. One hit him high, the other hit him low, and when Brad finally responded to the smelling salts he looked up into the concerned eyes of his team-mates, wiped the mud from his face, and mumbled in his West Texas drawl, "Sorry, boys, but I think I'm gonna go find me another sport."

I recounted the anecdote to Mrs. Helfan and she grinned and shook her head. "That sounds like Bradley," she said. "Golf was more the sport for him. With his temperament, the way he kept plodding till he got something right . . . "

I nodded. "Brad's work ethic put us all to shame. I remember he used to have trouble hitting sand shots at first, so one day I casually mentioned that Gary Player wouldn't leave a practice bunker until he'd sunk ten balls out of the trap. You could see something click behind those tinted glasses of Brad's. Sure enough, that evening there he was at the course, in the practice bunker, trying to get that tenth shot to fall as the sun set in the west."

Mrs. Helfan nodded, let her gaze drift away. "He never told me any of those stories."

"I don't think teenagers ever tell their parents much."

"No," Mrs. Helfan said. "With Bradley it was more than that. He kept everything all walled up inside so nobody could help him. That was his problem."

"Why do you suppose he did that?"

"Didn't trust people," Mrs. Helfan said. "Plain as that. He never, ever did, even as a little boy. He'd get his two quarters for allowance and go out in the backyard and bury 'em in the ground. His father and I thought it was just a silly kind of thing that kids do, playing pirates, buried treasure or whatever, but even when he got older he kept it up. Wouldn't open a bank account because he didn't trust banks. He'd rather stuff the money in his mattress or put it in a hole in the ground. Post office same thing. If Bradley had a letter he thought was extra impor-tant, he wouldn't trust sticking it in some mailbox slot. He'd hop in his car and drive a couple hundred miles to hand-deliver it instead. True fact." Mrs. Helfan paused, let her gaze rest softly on mine. "Peggy said you help people with their phobias."

"Now and then."

"So what do you make of that, Quinn? A phobia where you won't even stick a letter in the mailbox?"

"Actually, Brad's paranoia isn't all that rare," I said. "Lots of people don't trust banks. Rocky Marciano was that way. When he died in the plane crash nobody could find the money he'd hidden."

"Well . . . " Mrs. Helfan looked away, swallowed tightly. "If Bradley'd only talked to some of us who loved him, told us about his problems, maybe it wouldn't have come to this. It's a terrible thing for a woman to have to bury her husband and her son, both, in the same year. It's not right. The Good Lord does what He has to do, but I don't understand it."

Mrs. Helfan broke off. Tears were close to the surface, and she was trying to fight them back. Then she held out her hand again, abruptly, and I took it in mine.

"It's good to see you looking so healthy and fit, Quinn," she said in a wavering voice. "You ever find yourself in El Paso, you look me up. I'm in the phone book. Got nobody to fix Tex-Mex for now except you."

"It's a deal," I said.

Mrs. Helfan looked as if she was about to say something else, but her throat was too tight; the well of emotion was about to overflow. She held me one last time, then turned and walked away.

After my talk with Mrs. Helfan I wasn't in the mood to chat more nonsense around the hors d'oeuvre table with half-inebriated strangers. So I took my lemonade outside to the long, sloping lawn and straddled the teeter-totter and watched the softly flowing American River in the distance—remembered the happy hours I'd spent floating its waters as a boy.

I was deep into memory when I was suddenly conscious of a person standing at my right elbow. A small person in a light blue dress. She stood next to me, silent and waiting.

"You must be Alison," I said.

She nodded, looked down at her shoes.

"Your father talked about you a lot," I said. "It's funny, but I almost feel like I know you."

"Really?" she said.

"Really."

"What did my daddy say?"

"About you?"

She nodded.

"Well . . . he said that you were a very good student."

She nodded again, waited for more. I stalled for time. In truth, Brad hadn't really told me a single specific thing about Alison. And no wonder. Brad barely knew his daughter on a day-in, day-out level. Whenever Brad Helfan spoke of his family he spoke in the most general of terms. Where they lived. How special they were. How hopeful he was that they could work things out and get back together.

"I got four A's and one B," Alison said at last.

"No kidding?"

"The B is in math."

"Math is hard," I agreed.

"We're studying division."

"Fractions are what killed me," I said. "Fractions and square roots."

"Fractions aren't till fifth grade," Alison said. "I'm in fourth."

"What's your favorite subject?" I said.

"Science and P.E.," she said. "We have a new playground this year, but I like the old one better."

I nodded, and we fell silent. Alison moved closer and sat on the edge of the sandbox, next to my perch on the teeter-totter. Our conversation wasn't exactly skipping along, but all afternoon people had been looking down at her with big sorrowful eyes and murmuring variations on "poor little thing" in her ear. She was probably glad for the chance to just sit outside and talk about school and arithmetic and why the old playground was so much better than the new one.

"You know what I did when I was in the fourth grade?" I said at last.

"What?"

"I invented a marble game with a friend. We named it

'Boorgone' and we got all the other kids in the school playing it out in the tree boxes in the recess area."

"What does Boorgone mean?" Alison said.

"Nothing. We just made it up. But you know what was really strange?"

Alison shook her head.

"A couple years ago I went back to the school, just to see it, and the kids were still playing Boorgone in the tree boxes. Even using my old rules."

Alison smiled politely.

"Thirty years later," I said. "The children were still playing my game."

Alison nodded, but my story hadn't come across. Thirty years was such a vast expanse of time it had no meaning to her, the way a layman will nod vaguely when astronomers start talking about billions of light-years. It doesn't register. It *can't* register. But Alison sensed that the story held meaning for me, so she tried to nod at the wonder of it all anyway.

"There aren't any trees in our new playground," she said at last. "They planted some but they won't grow really big for a long time."

Now it was my turn to nod awkwardly, and the silence settled in like Tule fog. Then Alison cleared her throat, tugged at her light blue dress, and looked out toward the distant river with half-closed eyes.

"My daddy's not coming back, is he?"

"No," I said. "He's not."

Her face never changed expression, then she turned and left as abruptly as she'd appeared.

I sat on the teeter-totter and watched her go. Short little steps. Blond hair bouncing on the tops of her shoulders. She'd come to me seeking comfort, and I'd told her about the marble game I'd invented. It should have been a moment where I alone among all the assembled was able to draw her out, to make her feel better, to leave her with an indelible image of the father she never really knew. I would put a poignant turn on the situation and she would walk away, sad but glowing, infused with a new understanding of life and death and rebirth. But it hadn't been that way at all. I was the strange friend of her mostly-mythical father, sitting on a teeter-totter, who'd spilled his guts about the marble game he'd invented thirty years ago. It was as if she understood my self-imposed burden to console her, to divert the flood of tears, to make it look like the sniper's bullet that tore her father's head to shreds was just one part of a great, mysterious, incomprehensible whole.

I sighed heavily, looked out at the river. It *was* a true story I'd told her, about the Boorgone game enduring through thirty years of fourth graders. From time to time in San Francisco I think of that dusty playground, imagine a new crop of eager eight-year-olds down on their knees, getting their pants dirty, playing my game. A strange kind of comfort comes with the thought. The ongoing marble game seemed a more valid kind of immortality than writing great symphonies or producing genetic offspring or signing up for one religion or another's version of eternity. I had no idea why I'd suddenly told Alison about it.

Eventually I got up off my teeter-totter and wandered back into the house and engaged in enough small-talk to not appear the brooding loner. I scanned the room, looking for Peggy or Alison or Mrs. Helfan, but they'd all disappeared. I drank the rest of my lemonade in one swallow, put the glass down on the edge of the hors d'oeuvre table, and left.

9

I spent the ninety-minute drive back to San Francisco vaguely listening to the Giants game on the radio and sifting through what Peggy had told me. Ominous premonitions, one-in-the-morning phone calls, threatening letters, the cryptic promise of "something big" that was either in the mail or about to be mailed. At the Bay Bridge toll plaza I made a decision to go directly to Nikki's house on Lake Street. Do not pass go, do not collect two hundred dollars, do not check in first with Kate. Couldn't hurt. Just a simple knock on the door, brief introduction, see what's what.

I took the Civic Center exit and headed west on Geary. I felt a little guilty, not telling Kate about my spur-of-the-moment detour, but the living of a guilt-free life is hard to come by and the best we can do is try. I decided for the sake of convenience to view my deception in a positive light. I was sparing the two of us a nasty argument.

The house at 1222 Lake Street was nice enough, in a pleasant, tree-lined neighborhood just west of Nineteenth Avenue, near the entrance to the Golden Gate Bridge. A flower-lined walkway led from the sidewalk to a high narrow door. I rang the doorbell and waited. A female voice came through the outside speaker asking who was there. I identified myself, said that I was a friend of Peggy Lewis, and that I was looking for

Nikki. Silence. Then the speaker crackled back on. She'd be right down.

Moments later the door swung open. An unsmiling woman stood firmly in the entranceway, arms folded, feet planted wide apart, her body language as warm and receptive as a javelin in the belly.

"Who're you a friend of?" the woman said.

"Are you Nikki?"

"Yeah, I'm Nikki. You said you were a friend of who?"

"Peggy Lewis."

Nikki looked to be about twenty-five years old. She stood nearly six feet tall, with long, tousled, carefully askew jet-black hair framing the kind of stunning, come-hither face you normally only see on the covers of magazines that fold out in the middle. She had a light, copper-colored tan and liquid blue eyes. Her churlish mouth was long and full-lipped. She wore a white T-shirt ruthlessly tucked into a pair of khaki L.L. Bean hiking shorts, the tuck made all the more ruthless because of an emphatic lack of bra. Her bare legs were smooth and contoured and seemed to start somewhere up around her armpits and end only because the floor got in the way. Her T-shirt was solid white except for a single word printed in black, lowercase lettering just over her heart. The word was "fuck." I read the word three times, just to confirm I was seeing what I was seeing.

"What was your name again?" the woman said.

"Excuse me?"

"Your *name*."

The combined effect of Nikki and the lowercase "fuck" disoriented me for a second. But I quickly backtracked through short-term memory and came up with both my first and last name in a matter of seconds. "I'm Quinn Parker."

"So what do you or this Peggy person have to do with me?"

Nikki glared at me. My skin-deep infatuation with the woman was wearing off already. Sensational gift-wrapping, but the voice underneath was hard and tough and ignorant, like a biker chick's.

"Peggy said you'd been in touch with her," I said. "I know all about Brad's debts."

Nikki hesitated. "So?"

"So I'd like to talk with you about it."

"What if I say no?"

"Then I'll talk to Leonard."

Nikki wasn't glaring anymore. The eyes retreated into a defensive mode. "You think you're gonna try and lean on me?"

"Not at all."

"'Cause I'd like to see you just try it. One phone call from me to one of *my* friends and the cops'd be scraping your ass off the pavement with a spatula."

I scratched the bridge of my nose, turned and looked back out at the street, did a mental count to five. "Brad Helfan owed you money, right?"

Nikki's eyes narrowed. "You got a wire on?"

"A what?"

"A wire? You wired?"

"No," I said. "I don't have a wire on."

"Why should I believe you?"

I sighed, held my arms out from my body. "Would you like to frisk me?"

Nikki smirked, shifted her weight from one foot to the other. "In your dreams."

I put my arms back. "I'll repeat my question, then. Brad owed you money, didn't he?"

"Maybe."

"Forty or fifty thousand dollars, maybe?"

"It wasn't no forty," Nikki snapped. "It was fifty. *Plus* interest."

"Okay, fifty then. Like I told you before, Peggy's a friend of mine. She's got a lot on her mind right now and I thought we could work out a deal so she doesn't have to be pestered with this stuff."

"A deal?"

Nikki stood there for a minute, suspicious, wary. She scratched a spot on her T-shirt up near the neatly printed "fuck." I put my hands in my pockets and we had a brief stare-off.

"C'mon in," she said at last, opening the door all the way and stepping back. "But try anything and it'll be your ass."

I stepped past her and continued on through a plant-infested entranceway and then down three steps into a sunken, completely windowless living-room area. The color scheme was emphatically silver. Silver floor, silver drapes, silver furniture. A gas fire burned in a silver fireplace. Futuristic metal sculpture loomed from the walls, twisted like slender, agonized fingers, reflecting the harsh light from the fireplace. I couldn't imagine someone consciously trying to create a living environment like this. It was like stepping into the guts of a butane lighter.

I eased myself down onto the couch and Nikki perched on the edge of the chair across from me.

"So what's your deal?" she said.

"Simple. I take care of Brad's debt and you leave Peggy alone."

She paused a second, then gave me that slack-jawed, don't-waste-my-time look. "*You'll* take care of the fifty thou?"

"That's right."

"Just cut a check?"

I shrugged. "Check, cash, money order. However you want it."

"I know who you are, by the way," Nikki said. "You're the caddy."

"That's right. So?"

"So I'm wondering how a caddy can take care of a fifty-thousand-dollar debt."

"My money comes from another source," I said.

"What other source?"

"Does it matter?"

"Shit yeah it matters!" Nikki barked. "If the other source is a fucking bank you just held up, I don't want your fifty thou."

"Relax. I didn't rob a bank."

"Then what?"

"Six years ago I had an accident and got a fairly big settlement."

"What sorta accident?"

"Your basic, run-of-the-mill accident," I said. "You want details?"

She nodded. "Let's have it."

"Fine. I bought a new power drill and was helping a friend fix a roof down in Redwood City and the drill blew up in my hands. Some investigating revealed that the company which manufactured the power drill knew it was defective and was trying to sneak one by. We settled out of court for a nice chunk of cash." I finished my speech. "There. Satisfied?"

"You sued?"

"Yes, I sued."

Nikki shook her head. "I don't agree with people suing everybody. Litigation is ruining this country. Lawyers suck."

I felt a headache coming on. Talk to anybody long enough and you'll eventually bump into a mix-with-water opinion. I wondered how many hours it had taken Nikki to read, learn, and commit to memory the word "litigation."

"So you were just slumming with the caddy stuff," she went on.

"Brad needed someone to pack his bag."

"That's sorta cool," she said, and for the first time a slight grin cracked the porcelain edges of her mouth.

"So what do you think of my deal?" I said.

"If the money's clean I'll take it," she said. "Why the hell not? Brad owed it, fair and square."

"You're married to Leonard, right?"

Nikki's face darkened. "What of it?"

"Don't you want to talk about this with him first?"

"What for?"

I raised my eyebrows. "He's your husband. This is a lot of money changing hands. I assume the two of you would—"

"Let me tell you something about Leonard," Nikki interrupted. "He does his thing, and I do mine. He likes Palm Springs, he can have it. I like the city, I'm gonna have *that*. He's got bucks that won't quit, but all he ever does around me is poor-mouth. He tells me okay, go ahead and move up to Frisco if that's what I want, but then I get up here, make all sorts of commitments, and what does he give me? Zip, that's what. Every time I want some lunch money I got to practically send him a fucking telegram. You notice that turd-brown Subaru parked out front."

"As a matter of fact, I did."

"Mine. All eighteen hundred bucks and thirty-day warranty worth of it. I told Leonard it wasn't exactly the kind of thing I could go driving up to the ballet in, and you know what he said. Hitchhike! That's what he told me. That I should hitchhike!"

"Why doesn't Leonard move up here, too?"

Nikki leaned back in her chair, waved a disgusted hand in my direction. "Not enough sun. He hates fog and culture and all that stuff. I mean, this is a guy who rubs his back up against a tree when he gets an itch, like Yogi Bear. Holds his fork right up near the prongs when he eats." Nikki shook her head. "All he gives a damn about is playing golf and getting a tan. I'm serious. That's it. He keeps a stopwatch out by the side of the pool so he'll know exactly to the precise second when to turn around. You should see it. All so his tan is perfect. George Hamilton's like his god."

I sneaked a look at my watch. Almost five. Kate would be wondering where I was.

"You gotta be somewhere?" Nikki said.

"Soon."

"Wanna see the pool?" Nikki said.

"Excuse me?"

"The pool. It's out back. Come on and take a look."

I followed Nikki as she pulled aside some thick silver drapes and rolled back a heavy glass door and stepped out into a smallish backyard that was totally dominated by a fifteen-by-forty-foot swimming pool.

"The whole reason I chose this house to begin with was because of the pool," Nikki said. "Leonard's a lap swimmer.

You know, one of those guys who wears goggles and every-thing and can go back and forth and back and forth for hours. He thinks I never think about his needs, but I do." Nikki folded her arms across her chest and looked out at the late-afternoon sunlight playing on the water's surface. "You swim?"

"Not like Leonard," I said. "I'm not that comfortable in the water. I'm a thrasher."

"Really?"

I nodded. "My breathing gets mixed up. The inhale and exhale. It's like that kids' game where you try to say 'toy boat' over and over."

Nikki looked at me curiously. "Toy boat?"

"You never did that?"

"No."

"Try it. Say 'toy boat' ten times in a row, real fast."

She did, and of course her "toy boat" turned into "toyd boyt" soon enough. She laughed and gave me a genuine wide-eyed look as though I'd just revealed to her one of the world's most curious phenomena.

"Anyway," I said. "That's me in the pool. Toyd boyt. Every tenth stroke or so I get a mouthful of chlorinated water. You need to get into a rhythm to swim, and I only get into a rhythm when I'm comfortable."

"Then where *are* you comfortable, Quinn?" Nikki said. She swept some hair from her face and gave me a probing look; fin-ger-to-the-lip innocent on one hand, but backed up with her own curious brand of blast-furnace sexuality. At some point even the most oblivious male will realize that he is being soft-ened up by a woman, and I was on the cusp of that realization. So I kept my mouth shut. Besides, the "fuck" on Nikki's T-shirt was starting to get to me. It massaged my libido like the sub-liminal "eat popcorn" at a drive-in movie, and despite all resolve I was getting in the mood. Not in the mood for Nikki, necessarily. But in the mood nevertheless. It was time to leave.

"Think about my offer," I said.

Her look evaporated as effortlessly as it had been turned on. And when it left, nothing else took its place. No renewed resolve. No disappointment. No anger at all that her salacious overture had fallen on deaf ears. Nikki was, above all, a practical woman. Her world was obviously experiencing a cash-flow problem, things were not terrific on the domestic front, and for a minute or two around poolside I looked like an option. That's all.

Nikki walked me to the front door and we stood there a moment. "Check, cash, or money order," she said. "Right?"

I nodded. "But I'd like to see Leonard first."

"What for?"

"There are a couple of questions I need to ask."

Nikki gave me a hard look. "Then this was all bullshit, wasn't it?"

"Pardon me?"

"I bet you don't have a nickel to your name. I bet your power drill story is a crock. You just wanted to figure out how to find Leonard."

"My offer's legitimate, Nikki. *If* you stop hassling Peggy."

"I only called her once. That's not hassling. Get yourself mixed up on the wrong side of Leonard and you'll find out what hassling really is."

"I can't get mixed up, right *or* wrong, unless you tell me how to find him."

Nikki gave me an ugly little smile. She decided maybe she liked the idea of me and Leonard knocking heads after all. "Just go to the Arroyo Seco Country Club and ask around. He practically lives out there."

"That's in Palm Springs?"

"Yeah." Nikki surveyed me again. "Hold on a second. You'll need a note to get in."

She went into a side room and came back with a pen and paper, bent over the foyer table, and began scribbling. "You know what day you're gonna be there?"

"No."

"The guards get fussy sometimes if you don't have the exact date." She finished writing and handed the piece of paper over.

"Thanks," I said. She'd put tomorrow's date on the top of the page.

"You think Leonard killed Brad, don't you?"

"I've never even met your husband," I said.

"Wanna know a secret?" she said.

"Sure."

"Last time I saw Leonard, couple weeks ago, he said he was going to level Brad if Brad went ahead and played in the tournament."

"Level?"

"Yeah. You know." Nikki made a slicing motion in the air with her palm. "Leveled. Dead."

"Leonard said that?"

"Exact words. Said it more than once."

"Any particular reason why?"

"Leonard isn't exactly Mr. Rotary Club down there in Palm Springs, you know. He was scared shitless about all the publicity if Brad did well."

"More publicity than Brad being taken out with a high-powered rifle on national TV?"

"Yeah, I know," Nikki said. "But Leonard doesn't always think things out all the way. He gets pissed sometimes and just does things. He's got a temper on him."

"Why are you telling me this?"

Nikki shrugged. "I want you to think good thoughts about me when the fifty thousand dollars comes due. And a wife can't testify against her husband in court so I'll just act dumb. We never had this conversation. But most of all I'd like to see Leonard squirm some, the cheap sonofabitch. That's why I'm telling you this. Got it?"

"Got it."

"So it was nice talking to you, Quinn. If you come back again I'll have to frisk you whether you want it or not. That's a promise."

Nikki lingered in the doorway and smiled. She tried to put on that calling-all-cars smile of hers, but it didn't work. She was the third would-be Bunny from the left in Hugh Hefner's waiting room. Nothing more.

Then she turned her back on me for the first time in our half-hour visit. Printed neatly over her back left shoulder was the lowercase accompaniment to the front-side "fuck."

It said "you."

We went back into the wall with enough force to rattle the mirror. Kate had her arms wrapped around my neck, her legs locked onto my thighs, and I was staggering beneath the passionate weight like a child lugging a suitcase. Our clothes made a sexy Hansel and Gretel trail from the top of the stairs, down the hall, and into the living room. Now there were no more clothes to trail, and Kate's back was pinned against the wall. Her mouth and teeth were all over my face, shoulders, and neck, and the mirror was vibrating like 6.2 on the Richter Scale.

Then it was over, just like that, and together we did a slow-motion sink to the rug, the sweat from Kate's back leaving a trail of moisture down the wall. We came to rest on the floor, a tangle of arms and legs and elbows, folded into each other like two collapsed deck chairs.

"Now I know how the butterflies in my old collection must have felt," Kate said.

"Dead?"

She laughed, leaned toward me so that her forehead softly clonked against mine. She kissed the tip of my nose. "No. Definitely not dead."

"Then what?"

"I don't know." She paused, brushed her lips across my cheek. "Impaled. Impaled and beautiful and admired . . . "

I held her tighter and for a minute we cradled each other in the dimly lit room. "What happened with you today?" she said at last.

"What do you mean?"

"You come up the stairs and rip my clothes off with barely a hello. I'm not complaining, mind you, but I'd hate to think attending a funeral provokes that reaction."

I brushed the hair from Kate's eyes. "Remember at dinner the other night I told you about Leonard? The guy who bankrolled Brad's gambling in Palm Springs?"

"I remember."

"I stopped by to talk to his wife this afternoon."

"Where?"

"Here in the city."

Kate leaned back a little bit to bring me into focus. She had the wisp of a smile on her face. "This wife . . . was she dumpy and buck-toothed?"

I returned her smile. "No."

"What *was* she like? I'm speaking about her superficial qualities, of course."

"Let's just say she's not the kind of woman who's going to have to wait tables to make ends meet."

"Uh-huh." Kate smoothed my eyebrows. "I *thought* the pump had been primed somewhere else."

"Kate . . . "

"No, no, no, no!" she said, putting two fingers on my lips. "Don't misunderstand. I'm not complaining. Just as long as you bring it home, where it belongs. Don't bring it home, however, and I'll be forced to see how far that loose skin around your scrotum will stretch. Deal?"

"Deal."

We kissed. A soft, prolonged, seal-of-trust kiss, reinforced by the painful image of my favorite organ turned into a flesh-tone trampoline.

"How'd you like to go to Palm Springs?" I said.

Kate did an almost imperceptible retreat. "Palm Springs?"

"Sure. Take a little break from the job search?"

Kate hesitated. She had a funny expression on her face. One I'd never seen before. Then she smiled again. It was that same smile of a moment ago, when Kate knew there had to've been a Nikki in my recent past. The sudden, disconcerting feeling swept over me that this woman would always be a step and a half ahead of Quinn Parker.

"Palm Springs . . . " she murmured. "When?"

"Tomorrow morning."

"Fly, or . . . ?"

"Fly."

Kate nodded. "You want to see Leonard, right?"

"My gate pass is only good for tomorrow."

"And what are you going to say to him?"

"I'm not exactly sure."

"Ah . . . " Kate's head went slowly up and down. "But something will occur to you in the moments before he has someone pound on your face with brass knuckles, right?"

"Something always does."

"I think you'd better think this out first," Kate said. "Get a plan."

"In Mexico they say, *'En el camino se arreglan las cargas.'*"

"Translation?"

"'The loads are arranged along the way.'"

Kate nodded. "I think I'm one translation away from knowing what the hell you're talking about."

"I'll explain it to you on the plane," I said. "In the meantime, pack whatever you normally wear in a hundred-ten-degree heat."

—10—

Our DC-10 out of San Francisco got us into the Palm Springs airport a little before noon. The Alaska Airlines logo of an Eskimo bundled against fierce polar winds looked ridiculous as we descended into the ferocious desert heat, disembarked, and walked through the muggy sunlight toward the terminal. Brad had once talked about the Palm Springs humidity. Constant irrigation of the area's one hundred golf courses created a desert microclimate unique in the world.

We rented a car and drove to our modest hotel in the center of Palm Springs. It was a blindingly white, single-level adobe structure in the Santa Fe style, with a rust-red tile roof and Indian weavings decorating the lobby. I made a harmless remark about how nice it was, but Kate only managed a tight smile. From the moment I'd mentioned going to Palm Springs the night before, her mood had taken a subtle shift toward the dark side of the moon. Something was bothering her.

While Kate took a shower I flipped through the local phone book and got the address of the Arroyo Seco Country Club. Then I went back to the lobby desk and picked up a detailed map of the area and located it. Five miles east of Palm Springs proper, sandwiched between Arrowhead Falls Country Club and a housing development called Blackhawk.

Kate came out of the shower and towel-dried her hair while

I laid out my plans. First thing I'd do was go over to Arroyo Seco and see if Leonard was even in town. If he was, I'd try to set up a meeting. If he wasn't, we'd treat this as an overnight vacation and go back to San Francisco in the morning.

Kate distractedly said she thought it was a good plan. Weather being what it was, her plans were not much more complicated than securing a tall iced tea and sitting by the pool. She might also do some mild sauntering around town, window-shopping for absurdly overpriced trinkets. There was no reason, Kate said, why women like Nikki should have a stranglehold on the superficiality market.

We exchanged a perfunctory good-bye kiss and I went out to the hotel parking garage, wondering what was going on in her brain. Kate was not a secretive woman, but she'd subtly drawn the curtains on me and was off in her own world.

The Arroyo Seco Racquet and Country Club was not hard to find. A red brick driveway led off to a little guardhouse where a pleasant, British-looking gentleman of great age sat waiting. I showed him Nikki's handwritten note and he read it carefully, peering down at it through his bifocals, using the tip of his thumb to keep his place in the wilderness of her rushed scrawl. When he fully assimilated the message he smiled, had me sign a guest register, and waved me through.

The road veered to the right, beyond a tall hedge of trimmed bushes, then emptied into a mostly vacant parking lot that fronted an undistinguished clubhouse and pro shop. Colored rock gardens surrounding clumps of cactus and desert flowers provided the bare-bones decor.

I parked the rental car and went into the clubhouse. The air-conditioning was cranked up all the way, and I wandered over to the restaurant section. There were a dozen tables on a wooden floor that you sensed doubled as a dancing section during club functions. A thirty-foot-long bar faced out on the dining area. The place was empty except for a solitary beer-sipper at the bar and two groups of drinkers off in corner tables, rolling dice and tallying golf scores.

I made it two at the bar, ordered a cold beer, and took a few minutes to get a feel for the place. The bartender was a thick, unsmiling guy in his late twenties, all tattoos and muscles, like an ex-con. He was wiping off drink glasses with intense concentration, as though unwavering attention to the task at hand was the only thing standing between him and the powerful urge to kill again. I cautiously inquired about Leonard Novak and after a long, up-and-down assessment, the bartender nodded with his chin at the floor-to-ceiling window to my left.

"That's him out on the putting green," he said.

I leaned back from the bar to see better. The practice putting green was empty except for a tall, thin character in white linen pants, white shirt, white golf shoes, and white Indiana Jones–style hat. He was hunched over his putter, stroking a set of three balls toward a hole thirty feet away. When he hit his third ball he straightened and sauntered toward the hole, twirling the putter in his hands. He seemed to float rather than walk, with his shoulder blades held unnaturally high, like a vulture.

"That's Leonard Novak?" I said. "In the white?"

The bartender nodded. "You a reporter?"

"No."

"Sure about that?"

"Positive."

"Because if you are, best to stay clear. Got it?"

I nodded. "Got it. Thanks for the beer."

I put some money down on the bar and wandered out to the putting green. Leonard had gathered his three balls together and was gazing about for a new target. He decided on a downhill, left-to-right twenty-footer. His first putt missed right, second putt hung high to the left, third putt followed the break perfectly, hit the pin with a solid metallic clank, and dropped in. I stood at the edge of the green and watched Leonard drift, hawklike, up to the balls. He noticed me and smiled a slow, sardonic smile.

"Give me three shots to get it right," he said, "and I'd set the golf world on fire."

"You and me both."

Leonard bent, retrieved his ball from the cup, and faced me straight on. Leonard had a strange face. Long, narrow, and flat, like a stretched-out pancake. His eyes were mere indentations, his mouth a tight flash of white teeth set in a permanent grin. A long nose extended from the flatness of his face. The combination was neither ugly nor handsome. Just strange. A face that would jump out at you in a crowd.

"If you're a cop," he said, "I've already talked my lungs ragged to you guys and got nothing else to say. If you're a reporter, fuck off, and you can quote me. If you're anybody else, I'm not interested in being bothered. Does that cover it?"

"I thought we might talk a minute about some money owed you," I said.

Leonard casually scanned the area for another target. "You a cop?"

"No."

"Reporter?"

"No."

"Then I guess you fall under the 'anybody else' category," he said. "In which case, beat it."

"Fifty thousand dollars doesn't interest you?"

Leonard found his hole, an uphill ten-footer. "Right now," he said, "wrapping this putter around your neck interests me."

I silently watched him methodically stroke the three balls toward his new target. The first two went in, the third burned the edge. Then he gazed around for a new challenge. Without looking in my direction he said, "Ten more seconds, pal, then you're gonna get a sand wedge enema."

"Nikki told me you had bad manners," I said. "Now I see what she meant."

The mention of his wife's name had no discernible effect on Leonard. "Oh, yeah?" he mused. "What bad manners?"

"Let's see if I can remember. She'd rather you didn't scratch your back on trees. And please start holding your fork down at the end, not up by the prongs. She thinks it shows low breeding. I'm inclined to agree."

"Anything else?"

"Those were the major points."

Leonard nodded, stroked the first ball, and waited till it came to a stop before speaking. "She tell you this before, after, or in the middle of when you were fucking her?"

"Why do you automatically assume the worst?" I said.

"The worst?" Leonard said. "You balling my wife isn't anywhere *near* the worst."

"Relax," I said. "It was a hands-off conversation. With all due respect to your wife, Nikki's not my type."

"No?" Leonard was about to stroke the second ball but instead looked up and smiled at me. "Guess what? She's not my type, either. You and me got something in common after all."

I shrugged. "Small world."

"You play golf?"

"Some."

Leonard picked up his three balls and tucked them into his white linen pants pockets. "I'm looking for a game. Feel like nine holes?"

"Don't have my clubs or shoes."

"This place is a golf course. The thing it's got most of is clubs and shoes. You feel like nine holes or not? We can talk more on the course."

"Okay," I said. "Let's play."

Leonard came up to me and held out his hand. I shook it. "Leonard Novak, but you already knew that. Who're you?"

"Quinn Parker."

Leonard smiled. "Can't believe you stood there and told me how to hold my goddamn fork."

I shrugged. "It seemed critical to the success of your marriage."

Leonard laughed. It was a good laugh. Hips thrust out, head thrown back. "The goddamn fork! And all this time I thought it was the money."

"Goes to show you."

Leonard's laugh tapered off into a smile. "You got balls, Quinn, I'll give you that. Guess I don't need to ask if you're a gambling man."

"Depends on the stakes."

"You let me worry about the stakes," Leonard said. "It'll be something you can afford, but'll hurt when you lose it."

"As a bet should be."

"Damn right. Now I gotta get you some clubs and shoes. You stay where you are and get your wallet ready."

Leonard disappeared for a few minutes and then came whipping around the corner in an electric golf cart. Two sets of clubs were strapped to the back. He braked to a gravel-skidding stop right next to me.

"Forgot to ask," he said. "What's your shoe size?"

"Eleven."

"Hold on."

The golf cart zipped away and five minutes later he was back with a brand-new pair of Etonic golf shoes, still in the box, wrapped in tissue paper.

"Try these on," he said.

I did.

"They fit?"

"Perfectly. What do I owe you?"

Leonard smiled. "Nine holes of high-stakes golf. Let's do it."

I climbed in next to Leonard and laced up the shoes while we scooted off toward the first tee.

Arroyo Seco Country Club was built in the shadows of one of the starkly beautiful mountains that line the southern edge of Palm Springs. Lush green fairways wend in and out of parched desert, tangled scrub, and dramatic outcroppings of reddish rock that protrude from the earth like silent, living things, watchful and motionless. In the crisp desert air the sky was unnaturally blue, and from my elevated vantage point on the first tee I couldn't see another soul out on the course. Not one.

"Where is everybody?" I said.

"Done already," Leonard said. "Average age out here's about ninety, and they can't take the heat. Me, I love it. Hotter the better and everyone else can just stay home."

Leonard stood on the tee and limbered up, stretching, loosening his hips, taking a series of long, fluid swings.

"So what's the handicap, Quinn?" he said. "And don't try to bullshit me."

"I don't know. Fifteen, probably."

"'Fifteen, probably.'" Leonard smirked, tossed a golf ball in my direction. "Take a practice shot and let's have a look. Give it your best."

I took a three-wood and connected. The ball rocketed two hundred and thirty yards down the center of the fairway.

"Fifteen my ass!" Leonard howled.

"That was a fluke," I said. "Not representative."

"Like hell," Leonard said, watching the ball settle in the distance. "You're either an idiot or the smoothest hustler I've ever come across. I'll give you a twelve. I'm a six. Means you get three shots for the nine. What's fair? Hundred bucks a hole?"

"That's a little steep for me."

"Hey," Leonard said. "Come on. Worst-case scenario, total disaster, you still only lose less than a grand. And you're ahead of the game already."

"How do you figure that?"

"Easy. You squeezed three bullshit strokes a side out of me and you got a new pair of golf shoes thrown into the bargain. *And* I covered the cart and greens fees. What the hell more do you want?"

"You accept Visa and Mastercard?"

Leonard smiled. "Don't worry. We'll work it out."

We hit our tee shots and climbed into the golf cart. Leonard lit up a cigarette and smoked it while we rolled over the undulating green fairway toward our shots.

"So there was some mention of fifty grand earlier," he said. "Care to elaborate?"

"How come you're pretending not to know who I am?" I said.

"I'm not pretending anything. You were Brad's caddy up at Pebble. What I asked about was this fifty-grand figure you tossed out."

"Brad said he owed you money."

"He did owe me money. So what?"

"Brad's ex-wife, Peggy, is a friend of mine. Nikki's been calling her, bugging her about payment. I'd like to work something out so Peggy doesn't have to be hassled."

We reached Leonard's drive first. He put his cigarette on the built-in ashtray, selected an iron from the back of the golf cart, and whistled his second shot to the green.

"Nikki's been calling Brad's ex?" Leonard said, climbing back into the cart.

"Yes."

"How do you know?"

"Peggy told me. Then Nikki confirmed it."

Leonard thought that one over. He didn't say another word until after I'd hit my second shot. I pulled it left of the green, into thick grass around the edge of the sand trap.

"You can cover Brad's debt?" Leonard said.

"I wouldn't make the offer if I couldn't."

"Then how come you're bitching about a hundred bucks a hole?"

"Because I don't like to be taken for a chump."

We accelerated away and Leonard drew heavily from his cigarette. "So let me get this straight," he said. "You came all the way down here to find me and cut a check for fifty thousand and go home. That it?"

"No," I said. "Brad Helfan is also dead and I'd like to know why."

"What makes you think I know why?"

"Brad was afraid of you."

This got a laugh out of Leonard. "Brad had reason to be afraid of all sorts of people. What makes me special?"

"He owed you money that he couldn't pay."

"So what was I going to do?" Leonard said. "Kill him right

when he was going to get the biggest payday of his life? That makes a hell of a lot of sense."

"For some reason it made sense to Brad."

"Look," Leonard said. "Brad had some funny notions kicking around upstairs. He was a good kid and I liked him and all that, but he had a few screws loose. That's not a knock. Some of my best friends are missing some marbles. I've got this uncle out in Utah who says he's got the finger that bombed Hiroshima."

"He's got what?"

Leonard lifted his right forefinger and flexed it. "No shit. This uncle says he worked in the mortuary where the Hiroshima bomber died and right before the burial he opened up the casket and snipped the finger off for a souvenir. Swear to God. He's got the goddamn finger in a bottle of formaldehyde down in his basement. I've seen the thing with my own two eyes. I mean, maybe it's just a finger that didn't bomb anything, but you get my point."

We reached my ball. I took out a wedge, pitched a mediocre third shot to the green, and two-putted for bogey. Leonard missed his birdie putt, tapped in for par, and we walked off the green toward the second tee.

"That was a stroke hole for you," Leonard said. "No blood."

We played the second and third holes with no further reference to Brad. Leonard was dealing with me in such a relaxed and unflappable manner that I began to wonder who was confronting who. To compound my problems, Leonard won both holes and I was two hundred bucks in the red. There was a little stucco bathroom near the tee of the fourth hole and we sat outside it for a moment so Leonard could smoke another cigarette.

"This was Brad's home course, wasn't it?" I said.

Leonard nodded. "I guess you could call it that."

"And he hustled for you."

"That's right."

"Brad said you put up the money and arranged the matches and he kept a percentage of the winnings."

"That's the way it works," Leonard said, taking a drag from his cigarette and shaking his head. "Hell of a thing, what happened to him up at Pebble. I still can't believe it."

"Most people can't believe he even got as far as he did."

"That part of it didn't surprise me," Leonard said. "Brad was a terrific player, and he could handle the pressure. Golf at that level, U.S. Open–type golf, it's almost exclusively about handling pressure."

"And skill."

Leonard shrugged. "Of course, skill. But I'm convinced that as pure shotmakers, the top thousand or so golfers in the world are virtually identical. They can all perform miracles with the ball. Absolute miracles. Work it left to right or right to left, get up and down from bunkers, make trouble shots. You and me, Quinn, we play a whole different game from those guys. That's why I've always said that if you set up a friendly round of golf, nothing on the line, just farting around, the third-best pro in fucking Finland would match up solidly against Jack Nicklaus. But tell each of them two minutes before they tee off that it's the final round of the Masters ... " Leonard shook his head, tossed the half-smoked cigarette into the grass. "You'd probably have to strap a damn oxygen mask on the Finn's face and cart him away on a stretcher."

"Brad was that good?" I said.

"Yep."

"Then why didn't he play the tour instead of hustle?"

"He was a better hustler," Leonard said. "Brad was one of the best hustlers I ever saw in my life. He had this trick shot. Number eleven here is a par three, an island hole. The green completely surrounded by water. There's a little narrow footbridge leads across fifty feet of water to the green. Brad used to bet people that he could hit a putter off the elevated tee, a hundred and fifty yards away, and guide the ball directly across the footbridge to the green."

"And he could do it?"

"Shit, yes," Leonard said. "Brad must've logged a hundred goddamn hours out there in fuckin' heat, practicing that shot. He got it down so he knew the precise slope of the tee box, how the terrain curved leading up to the footbridge. I mean *precise.* From the tee box, standing up there looking down, you'd swear on your mother's grave that no living human being could pull that shot off. But Brad got to where he could do it about a third of the time."

"Meaning he missed two out of three?"

"When you get twenty-to-one odds every time you can afford to miss two out of three. Get a pencil and figure it out."

Leonard slapped at his shirt pocket for the pack of cigarettes. He lit another, smiled at a private thought. He was warming to the subject.

"It wasn't just that Brad could make the shot," Leonard went on, "it was the way he made it look like the idea just occurred to him. *That's* what makes a good hustler. He'd knock down a few beers, stand up there on eleven tee scratching his gut, and say in that God-awful Texas accent of his, 'Tell you what, boys. I got a twenny-dollar bill burnin' its way through my back pocket sez I can putt this little ball right over that bridge down there.'" Leonard smiled. "I'm going to miss that guy. I really am."

"What about the people Brad beat?" I said. "Did they take it well?"

Leonard shrugged. "Like people everywhere. Some took it good, some not so good."

"I heard a guy from San Diego tried to kill himself."

"Like I said, some took it good, some not so good."

"What was the guy's name?"

"Graham Kirby. And he was from Marin County, not San Diego." Leonard looked over at me, and his eyes had changed. It was not a change for the better. "For someone who came down to give me some money," he said, "you sure are a curious little beaver."

"My mom always told me that's how a person learned about the world."

Leonard ignored that. He smoked his cigarette, stared off at the fourth tee.

"Know what I like best about golf?" he said at last.

"What?"

"How you get to know people. Make new friends. Like you and me, for example."

"You and me?"

"Sure. Three holes of golf and I'm feeling already that we're forming a whaddayacallit? A bond." Leonard's eyes narrowed. "So in the spirit of our newfound friendship, Quinn, I'd like to know what the hell you're really doing down here."

"I already told you."

"I know," Leonard said. "Here's fifty grand, tell your wife to quit bugging Brad's ex. But you know what I think, Quinn? What I really and truly think?"

"Tell me."

"I don't think you plan to give me a dime. I'm not even sure you have a dime to give. In fact, I think it's the other way around."

"Do you?"

Leonard nodded. "I do. I think you came down here to rattle the cage, see if any loose change falls out and rolls in *your* pocket."

"You can think whatever—"

"Let me finish," Leonard said. The indented eyes flashed in his pancake face. "I don't like you sniffing around my wife up in Frisco, and I don't like you sniffing around my friends and associates here at the club. I'm a private citizen and I got rights." Leonard paused, turned his head sideways, and called out, "Billy!"

A figure emerged from behind the stucco bathroom. A large figure.

"This is Billy Useless," Leonard said. "He'll be assisting me in my efforts to get the truth out of you."

Billy Useless was about thirty years old, six feet tall, two hundred twenty pounds. He wore a blue Izod golf shirt that hung loose and untucked over a powerful chest. His face was stupid and droopy. A doggie face. The Walt Disney dog who was the dumb bad guy and wore those ridiculous Zorro masks while perpetually burglarizing the house of the good dog. Close-set eyes, and ears that seemed to dangle. You could spread a road map out on the width of Billy's back with room to spare. He came up and stood next to Leonard and just stared at me with his cretinous, death-row eyes.

"Funny," I said. "You didn't strike me as a person who has to keep a goon stashed behind the toilets." I scratched my elbow and tried to look unconcerned. My heart was slamming against my rib cage, but sometimes you just have to brass it out.

Leonard stared at me for a second. Then he coughed out a short, disbelieving laugh and looked at me with wide, appreciative eyes.

"First of all," he said, "I'd watch how you talk about Billy here. He's an independent agent, and if you piss him off all I'm gonna do is run for shelter and come crawling out when it's over. Second, you're right, I think I could probably take you myself, no sweat. But sometimes you never know. Couple years ago this skinny little dick-high Chinaman I thought I was gonna teach a lesson kung-fooed my ass up one side and down the other. After that I said fuck it. You just never know."

Billy Useless stood there. Leonard put out his cigarette and rubbed his hands together. "So these are your choices, Quinn. Level with me right now about why you're snooping around down here before Billy introduces a few new angles to your bone structure."

"Or?"

"What do you mean, 'or'?"

"You were about to list my choices."

Leonard frowned. "Did I say 'choices'? What I meant to say was 'choice.' Singular."

I kept quiet. The silence hung, electric, on the desert air, then Leonard nodded at Billy Useless. I braced myself, but instead of coming at me, Billy walked in the opposite direction, over to the ball washer on the fourth tee. He stooped down, picked up a twig, and inserted it in the formed hole where the ball would normally go. Then he slammed down the cylinder as hard as he could and the twig snapped violently in half. Leonard turned to see what effect this demonstration had on me.

"What do you think you'll gain by breaking my finger?" I said.

Leonard looked mildly puzzled. "Finger? We weren't thinking in terms of a finger."

That evoked the first smile out of Billy Useless. I filed it as a valuable clue. There was, indeed, cognitive brain function going on in there.

"So . . . ?" Leonard said.

"Brad got a death threat Saturday morning," I said. "The threat told him to lose big or he'd be killed. Brad was sure it was from you. Just for your information, I've got the original, along with a letter detailing Brad's suspicions of you. Everything is in an envelope in the hands of a third party, with instructions for it to be mailed to Detective Lorenzini of the Monterey County Police should anything happen to me."

Leonard digested that for a minute. His demeanor grew more serious, but he wasn't concerned about me mailing anything to Lorenzini. His preoccupation was elsewhere.

"How long you going to be in town, Quinn?" he said.

"Day or two. Depends."

"We need to talk some more. There's some things you need to know about before you get your head taken off by the roots."

"My dance card's wide open."

"Then how about drinks tonight?" Leonard said. "Just you and me."

"As long as it's public," I said. "I don't want Billy coming out of the woodwork again."

Leonard nodded. He was still off thinking about something. Then, in the next moment, he dismissed Billy with a wave of the hand and his hired muscle began strolling off down the fairway in the direction of the clubhouse.

We finished up the last six holes as though nothing had

transpired. My mention of the death threat had sent Leonard spiraling off in a new, more private direction. Or maybe it was the revelation that the death threat was in my possession. Whatever the distraction, Leonard lost four of the last six holes and I won the bet. On the ninth green Leonard managed a laugh and stuffed two one-hundred-dollar bills in my shirt pocket, commenting how tough it was to play a round of golf under duress.

Then he wrapped his deadly arm around my shoulders and the two of us headed toward the clubhouse, talking about prospective Palm Springs watering holes we'd hit that night, looking for all the world like a couple of manly buddies locked in the sudsy camaraderie of a beer commercial.

—11—

Kate wasn't at the hotel when I got back. My meeting with Leonard was set up for eight o'clock, so I waited in the room till seven, then went to a restaurant down the block and ate a quick dinner of chicken enchiladas by myself. I went straight back to the hotel, and when Kate still hadn't returned by seven-fifty I left a note on the hotel bed and went out front to wait for Leonard.

The desert twilight was hot. A deep, silent purple. The mountains to the right were sharp black shapes against a darkening sky. While I stood there admiring the view a white Cadillac Coup de Ville pulled up to the front of the hotel and the passenger window came down with a steady electrical purr.

"Hop in," Leonard said.

I got in the car and Leonard pulled away from the curb. The Cadillac had a new-car smell. Retractable roof, plush white interior. After what Nikki had told me about Leonard and his tan worship, I was beginning to get the idea that the persistent white motif in his life functioned primarily as background contrast. His longish black hair was combed straight back and oiled down so that it lay flat and unyielding against his neck. He smelled strongly of cologne, and the deep tan—future skin melanoma aside—*did* give him an aura of sun-splashed good health. Leonard rummaged around below his seat, withdrew a pistol, and matter-of-factly handed it to me.

"What the hell's this?" I said.

"A gun. Can you stick it in the glove compartment for me?"

I took the gun and placed it carefully in the glove compartment. "Do you always carry a weapon?"

"Always," Leonard said.

"Is that legal?"

"Misdemeanor. Which to me is the same thing as legal. Protection's worth an occasional small fine." Leonard smiled. "Speaking of which, I still can't believe you took two bills from me out there on the course today. The hustler got himself hustled."

"Duress, like you said."

"*Me?*" Leonard laughed. "Duress? *You* were the one about to get flattened by Billy Useless!"

"Who won't be joining us tonight, I trust?"

"Nope," Leonard said. "It's just you and me, kid, like we agreed. Just you and me."

We tooled out into the golden dark and turned east on Highway 111, going away from downtown Palm Springs, toward Palm Desert, Rancho Mirage, Indio, and the vast empty reaches of the Mojave Desert.

"Where are we going?" I said.

"Gotta check on some business stuff first," Leonard said. "Only take a minute. That okay with you?"

It was a rhetorical question. Unless I felt like disembarking the automobile at sixty mph, Leonard's errands had better be okay with me. So I settled back and watched the flickering lights of the desert towns. Even after dark we had the windows up and air-conditioning on. Beyond the tinted glass, absorbed heat from the hundred-ten-degree day seemed to flow upward from the four lanes of pavement in rippling, visible waves, like the depiction of departing spirits in a low-budget ghost movie. They spread thickly into the evening sky, released, diffused, blurring and warping the canopy of early stars overhead. A top-forty music station was on the Cadillac radio, and Leonard absentmindedly tapped his forefingers on the steering wheel in time with the music.

Palm Springs receded behind us and we drove through relative emptiness for a while. Sand and cactus and ill-lit auxiliary roads leading off to God knew where. Then a cluster of bright lights suddenly brimmed on the horizon and Leonard reached down to snap off the radio.

"This is it," he said. "Cathedral City."

We got off 111 in the middle of town and zig-zagged around through a series of back streets before ending up at a small neighborhood bar at the end of a scruffy residential block. A neon sign announced the bar as the Lone Star Saloon, featuring billiards and beer. Leonard parked out front and cut the engine. "Let's go," he smiled. "Enough of this country club shit. It's high time you saw a different slice of desert life."

A dusty sidewalk led to a dusty three-step walk-up to an even dustier porch area. A snag-toothed cur was stretched out near the entrance door, head resting on its paws, giving us the evil eye as we approached. The entrance door itself was a patchwork of signs specializing in "no." No shoes, no shirts, no service. No minors allowed. No spitting. No guts, no glory. Leonard pushed open the door and together we walked in.

Upon occasion I have a vivid flash of what women mean when they sometimes talk about the male race as a perilous and menacing species, driven by impulses of violence and conquest, unfairly given superior physical strength with which to assert their questionable will. This was one of those flashes. Eight pool tables stretched away from us in two rows of four. Lean young toughs wearing baseball caps and jeans and T-shirts filled the room. They moved in predatory fashion through a haze of cigarette smoke, swaggering, assessing their shots, swigging beer from the bottle.

There was nothing so highfalutin as air-conditioning in the Lone Star Saloon, and I felt the sweat immediately begin to bead and roll down my sides. A jukebox was off to the left, playing a mournful country and western ballad of a guy whose wife had run away with his best friend and now all he could do was sing the faithfulness of the bottle. To the right was a kind of half-assed, makeshift bar, and a man stood behind it with both palms flat on the counter, watching us. He was about fifty years old, with the puffy, misshapen face of an ex-prizefighter. His thin gray hair was combed straight back and lacquered into place with industrial-strength styling gel. He had big dangly ears and curiously delicate lips that were pinched and unrelaxed, as if they'd been stretched at the edges and then glued together. Little piggy eyes gleamed out from the doughy folds of his face. The man wore a black T-shirt with large white lettering that said, "If It Ain't Texas, It Ain't Shit!" The T-shirt fell several inches short of completely covering his fish-white beer gut.

"Torp!" Leonard called out. "What's up?"

"Nothin'," the bartender said.

Torp looked at Leonard with an element of fear and apprehension. Leonard plunked himself on one of the two stools in front of the bar. Torp leaned down and dug out a beer from the cooler without Leonard having to ask.

"Same for my friend, here," Leonard said.

Torp wordlessly pulled out a second beer and set it in front of me. The effort hiked his T-shirt up another couple of inches, exposing a navel filled to overflowing with moist black lint. It wasn't a sight to aid in the digestion of chicken enchiladas, so I turned my head away.

"Haven't seen you around much," Leonard said.

"There a problem?" Torp said.

"That's my point," Leonard said. "Let's say there *was* a problem, you wouldn't know about it. *I* wouldn't know about it. Not with how scarce you've been keeping yourself."

"Things've been busy," Torp said, nodding in the direction of the pool tables. "School's out."

"School?" Leonard said with a disgusted laugh. "Your customers haven't seen the inside of a school since third grade."

"School's out," Torp repeated. It sounded weak, but it was the only thing going for him.

"That's not the only thing out," Leonard said tersely. "Your brain's out, too. Out to *lunch*."

Torp didn't push the "school's out" strategy anymore. Little droplets of hair goo began to streak down the side of his face. Leonard got up off the stool and looked at me.

"I gotta go out back and discuss something with Torp here," he said. "You want another beer, just reach down in front and help yourself. That's okay if he does that, right, Torp? That he should just help himself if he wants another beer?"

"Sure," Torp mumbled. Then he and Leonard disappeared behind a small door at the end of the bar.

I sat by myself and nursed my beer. Some of the young roughnecks playing pool snuck glances at me in between swigs of beer. They squinted unpleasantly through the cigarette smoke, spoke in voices that seemed unnecessarily loud, as if making primal claim to this dubious turf of theirs that I was violating. They shouted vulgar insults at each other. Delbert could suck on this. Dwayne could bend down and kiss that. Ralph wouldn't know a pussy if it came up and hit him in the face.

Delbert, Dwayne, and Ralph. The children of Cathedral City were not named after the colors of the rainbow or Mayan gods or birds in flight. They were the sons of fathers who poured swimming-pool cement and of mothers who served deep-fried restaurant food out on Interstate 10. And I was perceived to be from the other world, the world of people who swam in the pools their fathers built and made fun of the food their mothers served. I was the enemy.

I sipped my lukewarm beer and watched the second hand sweep across the overhead clock. Eight-thirty. Then the door behind the bar suddenly opened and Leonard came back out alone.

"Let's do it," he said.

"Everything okay?"

"Everything's perfect. Just had to iron out my differences with Torp, is all."

We got back in the car and drove in silence awhile. A light

sheen of sweat covered Leonard's face, and he was breathing deeply. The ironing out with Torp had taken some physical exertion.

"Torp . . . " I said, just to be saying something. "Strange name. Is it short for something?"

"Yeah," Leonard said, pausing to glance at the rearview mirror. "It's short for stupid, lard-ass motherfucker. Listen, I'm feeling juiced. Let's go have our drinks somewhere wild and woolly, okay?"

The question was framed as an announcement. It had been a hairy-chested kind of evening up till now, what with weapon-fondling and beer-swilling and the roughing-up of bar owners, so I figured it would not look good for me to start mewling now. Sure, I said. Wild and woolly sounded great. I was being dragged along on Leonard's nightly errands for a reason. I'd continue to ride shotgun till I got a better handle on the reason.

Out on 111 we took a right, drove a few more blocks, then pulled into a small but crowded gravel parking lot in front of a run-down wooden building. A large whitewashed plywood sign hung over the door, announcing the establishment as the Foxy Female. I thought the name was straightforward enough, but the bottom two-thirds of the sign was devoted to a crude drawing of a naked, large-breasted woman dancing among cactus, just in case potential customers hadn't figured it out.

We got out of the car and went to the entrance and paid the cover charge. A chalkboard at the door showed three dollars, marked down from five. Not an auspicious beginning. The dance area was to the left, a bare wooden stage with a glistening vertical fireman's pole in the middle. Bar to the right, three rows of smallish tables bunched up around the dancing area. "Cherokee Nation" was blaring out at the half-empty room, and a woman with long, imitation blond hair and a few thousand bucks' worth of breast implants was twirling around the fireman's pole. She wore a cream-colored cowgirl outfit, with a button-down vest and boots with spurs and flashing tassels. Dale Evans on helium. Leonard and I took a table toward the back.

"This is a pretty classy joint, actually," Leonard said.

"My thoughts exactly."

"No, I mean it," Leonard said. "You see that three-dollar cover at the door, you're thinking visions of cellulite, right? Well, forget it. Best-looking women in the Springs dance here, and that's a fact. Bartenders don't water down the drinks. Good music. And the minute one of these hayseed assholes gets out of line? Boom! Their butts get bounced pronto. Besides, I figure if you have the choice to unwind where beautiful women keep their clothes on or where beautiful women take their clothes off, who in their right mind would chose clothes on?"

There was something wrong with his logic, but whatever the fallacy was, it temporarily escaped me. We ordered drinks from a scantily clad waitress and settled back.

"So what do I need to know about Brad?" I said over the din of music.

Leonard shrugged. "What do you *want* to know?"

"Out on the course today you said I might get my head 'taken off' without the full story. By the roots, I think was the way you put it."

"That's right," Leonard nodded. "You might. By the roots."

"So . . . ?"

Our drinks came quickly. A beer for me, double vodka-tonic for Leonard. He twirled his swizzle stick, clinking the ice, distractedly watching the cowgirl up on stage. She was down to her silver spurs, and not much else. But Leonard wasn't focused on her. He was sorting out what he was going to tell me and what he wasn't.

"Did Brad ever talk to you about how he ended up in Palm Springs?" Leonard asked.

"He said he had some problems in Las Vegas, gambling and drinking problems, and that he went to California to get his life in order."

Leonard arched his eyebrows, took a slug of his vodka.

"Is that wrong?" I said.

"Not wrong," Leonard said. "Just tidied up. What happened was he got himself in very hot water with Jerry Kerrigan in Vegas. Name mean anything to you?"

"No."

"Well, go ahead and believe me when I tell you Kerrigan's bad news. Drugs, prostitution, money laundering. Mid-level mobster type. Not big enough to be on the tip of everybody's tongue, but you'd still end up in a car trunk if you crossed him. Brad was part of Kerrigan's stable."

"What do you mean, stable?"

"Hustling," Leonard said. "Golf hustling, like he was doing here. And I guess he was doing okay for Kerrigan, except for those other problems you mentioned. Too many twenty-four-hour blackjack tables in Las Vegas for a guy like Brad. My understanding of the situation is, Brad got the hell out of Vegas before Kerrigan had him waxed."

"Why would Kerrigan want Brad dead?"

"Maybe it wouldn't have been dead," Leonard said. "It might've just ended up being sort of temporary crippled. But it would have been something. Brad got in debt with Kerrigan, just like he did with me. It was a pattern with Brad. No matter how much he made, he always found some way to piss it away."

"Did Brad do well with you?" I said.

"Are you kidding? He did great! There were some dry spells, sure, but Christ Almighty . . . There'd be weeks his share of the take would be ten grand. Averaged out, I bet he cleared close to a hundred thou a year. Nontaxable."

"Then where did it all go?"

Leonard shrugged. "Who knows? Brad claimed he had the gambling problem licked, but maybe not. He still drank some, but nobody can drink up a hundred thousand bucks worth of booze a year. You know, all the money he was making, him living out there in that piece of shit RV for practically free . . . I *still* had to front him cash. All the fucking time. Five hundred here. A thousand there. It kept getting more and more outta hand, so I finally had to pull the plug."

"How did you do that?"

"Paraded Billy Useless out in front of him, just for show,

like I did with you today. I explained to Brad that he was a good guy and all that, but the honeymoon was over."

"When did this happen?"

"Month ago. Month and a half. It rattled him good. That's probably why he said I was the one who wrote the death threat. Billy Useless was too fresh in his mind."

"But you didn't?"

"Didn't what?"

"Write the death threat."

Leonard gave me a disappointed look, like how could I think such a thing, then went back to his drink. The cowgirl had finished her routine to rousing applause and was reattaching her bra. Then she came down off the stage and moved from table to table, bending forward to accept the tucked bills in her manufacturer's-guaranteed cleavage.

"What does any of this have to do with me having my head taken off?" I said.

"You ask that question, Quinn, because you don't know Jerry Kerrigan. The police are crawling all over this case and it's just a matter of time before Kerrigan's name gets smeared all over the front page. So all I'm doing now, tonight, is warning you about Kerrigan. Take my word for it. Stroll into Vegas and mouth off to *him* on the practice green, he's not going to be as compassionate as me. That's all."

The cowgirl reached our table and stood there in front of us for a second.

"Hey, guys," she said.

"Hey," Leonard said.

"Having a good time?"

"Don't know yet, honey. Just sat down."

She hovered over us for a long five count. "Like my show?" she said.

"Loved it," Leonard said.

Another five count. A sliver of irritation invaded her coquettish demeanor. "You boys believe in tips?"

"Sure," Leonard said. He took a puff of his cigarette, squinted through the smoke. "Unsolicited tips."

"What's that mean?"

"It means I don't give money to people who shove their foot in my door."

The stripper pushed at her upper lip with her tongue. "Hey, you guys enjoy yourselves tonight."

"Already are."

"Good." She gave Leonard a kiss-my-rectum look and angled over to the next table.

"Cunt," Leonard muttered, just loud enough for her to hear. She twirled and glared daggers at him.

"Take it easy, Leonard," I said.

"What for? 'You boys believe in tips?'" he mimicked. "I hate that shit. Most've the girls here aren't like that. I take you here and brag it up and then something like that happens, right off the bat. Pisses me off."

The next dancer was up on stage and the music changed. Donna Summer's "She Works Hard for the Money." The woman was introduced as Lilah, a feisty, high-energy Hispanic, and the theme was high-class street hooker. Heels, nylons, bump-and-grind.

"So the real mystery seems to be where all Brad's money went," I said.

Leonard shrugged. "Who the hell knows. Maybe he stuffed it in a mattress somewhere. Maybe he had a woman on the side. Nikki sure doesn't have any problems figuring out ways to spend *my* money. When we first got married and moved into the new house, the one here in Palm Desert, she drove all the way to this special store in Beverly Hills to stock the kitchen. The only thing this store has is kitchen stuff. One of those. Won't stock anything unless it's imported from fucking Sweden or somewhere. That woman spent sixty-eight hundred bucks in *one* afternoon on pots and pans and gadgets! Sixty-eight hundred bucks!"

"Nikki didn't strike me as a woman who spends a lot of time tinkering in the kitchen."

"You got that right," Leonard said. "She tried to cook something once. A chicken dish . . . "

"Bad?"

"First bite, I almost threw my back out."

"Why did she move up to San Francisco?" I said.

"Because she all of a sudden refuses to live in Palm Springs, that's why."

"What's wrong with Palm Springs?"

"Who the hell knows? She thinks Sonny Bono for a mayor is tacky, that's why. Not enough operas down here for her cultured tastes." Leonard took a disgusted, angry gulp of his drink and shook his head. He sniffed and stared down at the table, unfocused. He suddenly looked a little inebriated, and I wondered if he'd been drinking earlier in the day. "Not enough operas," he mumbled. "This from a woman who ... She has one of those things. What're they called? You stick it in a baby's mouth to shut it up."

"A pacifier?"

"That's it. A fuckin' pacifier. I wouldn't kid you about this, Quinn. One month after we're married. We're sittin' in the nicest restaurant in Palm Springs, sitting there at the table with our drinks, full house, and all of a sudden Nikki goes diggin' through her purse and pulls out a *pacifier!* Put the thing in her mouth right there at the fucking table, like it was the most normal thing in the world for a grown-up to do! And this from the lady who thinks Sonny Bono for mayor is tacky!" Leonard shook his head. "Go figure. She can stay up in Frisco for all I care. Less grief for me."

"Nikki said she doesn't have the money to stay there."

Leonard shrugged. "So she doesn't have the money. Do you think I give a rat's ass?"

"I'll guess that you don't."

"Damn right I don't. But she'll stay there. Nikki'll hold on somehow. That woman, she's got a will harder than an old maid's dreams."

"Can I ask a favor?"

"Fire away."

"Will you ask Nikki to quit calling Peggy about the money?"

"Who's Peggy?"

"Brad's ex. Remember?"

"Oh, yeah," Leonard said, nodding. "You changed the subject and threw me off. We're back to the purpose of your visit. That fifty thousand you were talking about."

"Will you tell Nikki?"

"Yeah. I'll tell her to knock it off."

"And as far as the money goes—"

"Forget it," Leonard said. "I don't want the fifty grand, and don't give it to Nikki, either."

"Why not?"

"One, the IRS is camped out on my front doorstep these days waiting for me to fuck up. Two, I don't think you're really going to cut a check anyhow. Three, I always allow for bad debt expense in my business. As far as I'm concerned, the Brad Helfan account is closed."

Lilah had finished her dance and was going table to table just as the cowgirl had done before her.

"Now *she* deserves a tip," Leonard said. "*She* was good!" He shoved his hand in his pocket and fished around.

Lilah got to our table and winked at Leonard as he tucked a five-dollar bill in her cleavage. She had a nice face. A nice smile. I could easily picture her in a non–Foxy Female environment. As a single mom, maybe, doing this to support a five-year-old at home, with Grandma doing the late-night babysitting. You could never picture the long, blond, tip-begging cowgirl that way. Leonard followed Lilah's five-dollar bill up with a rolled-up twenty.

"My friend here could use a table dance," he said to her. Lilah looked over at me and smiled again.

"Sure thing," she said.

"I'm fine," I said.

"No, he's not," Leonard said. "Make it a good one, Lilah."

"Just sit back and enjoy yourself," Lilah said to me. "Only thing is don't touch, okay? House rules."

"Don't worry."

A new song came on and Lilah gave me my table dance,

straddling the chair I sat in, undulating, gyrating, bringing her damp breasts right up into my face. I sat there as stone-cold motionless as a root-canal patient beneath the dentist's drill. When the song ended she tweaked me on the cheek, told me I was a sweetheart, and moved to the next table.

"Okay," Leonard said. "Party's over. Let's get out of here."

I paid the bill over Leonard's objections and we wandered back out into the parking lot. It was completely dark now, a million stars in the deep blue sky, a soft balmy breeze coming in from off the Mojave Desert. Leonard was fumbling with his car keys when I became conscious of a disturbance at the other end of the lot, near the Foxy Female entrance. Boozed up or not, Leonard had a faster reaction time than me, and he whirled quickly. A hard-looking guy in his twenties was striding after us with anger and purpose. He wore blue jeans, cowboy boots, white T-shirt, and flaring sideburns.

"Hey!" he shouted. "Hold it right there, asshole!"

"I'm not going anywhere," Leonard said. "What's your problem?"

Leonard's eerie calm caused the guy to put on the brakes and take a couple seconds to reassess. Then the door to the Foxy Female swung open and the cowgirl stripper hustled up to where the man stood fuming. She wore heels and had an overcoat wrapped around her body. Bare legs flashed, and the phony blond hair sparkled artificially beneath the parking lot floodlights.

"That him?" the man said.

"Let it go, John," she said. "Come on back in."

"I said is that him or not?"

The stripper positioned herself in front of John and began pushing. He didn't budge an inch.

"*Is it?*" he shouted.

Leonard cleared his throat. "If you mean am I the guy who called this cunt a cunt," he said, "the answer's yes."

John's eyes went wide. Even the stripper turned around for a second, jolted by Leonard's brazenness. Then she turned her back on us again and began pushing.

"Forget it, John!" she said. "Can't you see he's drunk? Leave him alone!"

"I'm gonna teach you some manners, buddy," John said. "*Nobody* uses the 'c' word with my girlfriend!"

Leonard looked over at me as if to verify what he'd just heard. "The 'c' word?"

"That's it!" John exploded. "Your ass is *dead!*"

The door to the Foxy Female burst open again and two other men charged out. John clones, right down to the flaring sideburns. They marched up and flanked him on either side and glared at us.

Leonard surveyed the situation, meandered over to the Cadillac, opened the passenger door, and took the gun from the glove compartment. He held it in the air for all to see and released the safety catch.

"If it's going to be three against one," Leonard announced to the assembled throng, "then the rules change."

"Oh, shit!" the stripper moaned, starting to cry. "Shit, John! He's got a goddamn gun! Don't do this! Don't! It's not worth it!"

"Put the gun away, Leonard," I said.

He kept his eyes on the three men in front of him. He was very calm. "Stay outta this, Quinn."

"Put the gun away or I'll take it away."

Leonard shifted his focus from John to me. A smile creased the corners of his mouth. "How do you figure you're gonna do that?"

"You're too drunk to stop me."

"Care to put a bet down on that?"

"You've lost two hundred dollars already," I said. "Today's not your day."

The stripper wailed again and pulled on her boyfriend's arm. John tried to give the impression of being anchored, but this time he yielded pretty easily to her tug, eyes fixed on Leonard as he let himself be dragged back in the direction of the Foxy Female.

"We're not finished!" John yelled as a parting shot. "Next time I'll bring *my* rod!"

Leonard wasn't listening. He was still looking at me, wondering if I really would've made good my threat to disarm him. Then he turned, got into the car, and put the gun back in the glove compartment, and we drove silently back into Palm Springs. He pulled up alongside my downtown hotel and left the engine running.

"Helluva Thursday night, hunh?" he said.

"This your typical day?" I said.

Leonard just smiled, trailed his fingertip along the bottom of the steering wheel. "Can't imagine we'll be seeing each other again, Quinn," he said. "So take care of yourself up north. And a word to the wise. Never mind my bitching tonight. If Nikki ever kicks the thermostat up, looks you in the eyes, and says yes, you say no. Kapeesh?"

"You need to understand something, Leonard," I said. "I'm not interested in Nikki. I'm interested in finding out what happened to Brad."

Leonard blew air through his nose. "Forget about Brad. He's dead, he's gone, it's over."

"I can't."

"You'd better."

"I was the one who told him to ignore the death threat."

Leonard continued to play with the steering wheel. The quiet seconds ticked off. "So that's what this is all about? The tough talk. The fifty grand. You feel guilty?"

I didn't say anything. The silence in the car went on for a while. A stretch limo went by. Then a police car.

"Let me tell you something, Quinn," Leonard said. "One night when I was a kid back in Illinois, five or six years old, I heard this sound coming from the backyard. It was a terrible sound, almost like a kid screaming, only quieter. I told my folks and they told me to shut up so I went outside to see for myself and looked through a hole in our fence and there was this kitten. At first I couldn't tell what the problem was, but then I saw the snake. A snake had the kitten in its mouth, swallowing it down whole. The kitten was screaming and scuffling and slipping back an inch at a time, but there was nothing I could do about it. The snake would've got me, too, so all I did was watch. In my whole life I never forgot the look on that kitten's face while it got sucked down the snake's throat." Leonard paused, looked over at me. "There wasn't a damn thing anybody could do. That kitten was doomed from the moment it was born. Just like Brad. He got gobbled up by a big old snake, too, and if you keep poking around, Quinn, it's gonna keep on eating. It'll grab your arm and won't stop till you're as dead as Brad is. Have a good trip back home, and don't say I didn't warn you."

—12—

Kate was waiting in the hotel room, stretched out on the bed fully clothed, watching television. When I came in she clicked the TV off with the remote control and gave me the once-over.

"Everything still seems to be intact," she said.

"Just barely."

"What does that mean?"

I sat on the edge of the bed and kissed Kate. A strong, up-and-down-and-all-around kiss.

"You haven't answered my question," Kate said, a little dazed, surprised by the intensity of my affection. "How come you're just barely intact?"

"Because Leonard Novak is, hands-down, the most on-the-edge adrenaline junkie I've ever met. Either that, or he went to an awful lot of trouble staging scary stuff for my benefit."

"For instance?"

"We'd barely said our hellos out on the practice putting green when he threatened to perform some amateur proctology work on me with his sand wedge. Then we played nine holes for a hundred dollars a hole and halfway through the match Leonard's Cro-Magnon sidekick came out of the bushes and did the usual Cro-Magnon stuff. Scowl, crack knuckles, glance at the boss for permission to tear me limb from limb. Then the two of them demonstrated what a ball washer could do to one of my appendages. What else? This evening Leonard roughed up some bar owner in Cathedral City, then he capped off the night by almost getting us into a thirty-eight-caliber shooting match with a gang of rednecks outside a strip joint."

"Strip joint?"

"Leonard's choice, not mine."

"I *thought* something had put a little starch in your testosterone." Kate sighed, sat up in bed. "When I said back in San Francisco that it was okay if somebody else primed the pump from time to time, I didn't mean *all* the time." Kate leaned forward and gave me a kiss. She let the kiss linger, then broke it off in slow motion and looked me straight in the eyes. "Don't abuse the privilege."

"Wouldn't dream of it."

"Good." Kate moved to the bedside chair and began pulling on her shoes. "So what's your take on Leonard, then? For a guy who does such horrible things, you sure seem to hang out with him a lot."

"Glutton for punishment."

"Answer my question. Was Brad's hunch right? Do you think Leonard might have killed him?"

"If you mean did Leonard Novak stretch out on the roof of that house on the eighteenth hole and pull the trigger, no. Whether he hired somebody to pull the trigger is a tougher call."

"Why?"

I shrugged. "Leonard says he doesn't know anything about anything."

"And you believe him?"

"I don't know. Despite everything else, Leonard doesn't strike me as a liar."

"But a killer maybe?"

"Maybe."

"What about the money Brad owed him?"

"Didn't seem to be that big a deal."

Kate frowned. "A forty-thousand-dollar gambling debt is no big deal?"

"Fifty thousand, but Leonard acted like it was chicken feed. A write-off. Apparently Brad had some earlier trouble with a mobster type named Jerry Kerrigan over in Vegas, and that's where Leonard was trying to steer my suspicions. It's hard to know what to believe, Kate. The only thing I'm truly convinced of is that Brad didn't tell me everything that was going on."

"Why do you say that?"

"According to Leonard, Brad made some serious money hustling golf. I mean serious. Averaged a couple thousand dollars a week, free and clear. He apparently lived in a recreational vehicle somewhere, so his expenses were nil. But up at Pebble Beach the guy didn't have enough spare change to buy thirty minutes of metered parking. If what Leonard says is true, I wonder where all the money went."

We were silent awhile, then I put it out of my mind, focused instead on Kate. "Enough about me. What did you do all day?"

"Nothing as exciting as your day," Kate said. "But I did see this half-tacky, half-swanky bar a couple blocks down the street. Buy me a drink there and I'll give you the hour-by-hour breakdown."

"Deal."

So we walked arm-in-arm through the warm dark to half-tacky, half-swanky Charlie L's Bar and Grill. My personal ratio would have been seventy-five–twenty-five in favor of tacky, but Kate is a generous woman. Besides, coming on the heels of the Lone Star Saloon and the Foxy Female, I was in no position to nitpick.

The place was busy. We were led to a table for two in the back. The decor was New Orleans cathouse: dark, heavily varnished wood, red velvet curtains, the kind of sumptuously padded booths that whoosh like air brakes when you first sit in them, then take several seconds to allow you to come to a complete stop. Framed black-and-white photographs covered every available inch of uncurtained wall space. They were mostly of marginal Hollywood celebrities, circa early sixties, all signed with varying degrees of fondness to "Charlie." Our waiter was about a hundred years old with a long, droopy, bloodhound face. He wore a lumpy toupee of such size, shape, and age that a peek underneath might very well have revealed the remains of the Lindbergh baby.

Kate decided on a Beefeater martini, straight up, one olive, and so dry she expected to see a fine powder of martini dust at the bottom of the glass. It was not a drink order to be improved upon, so I followed suit. The waiter nodded, vaguely irritated by all the specifics, and disappeared into the darkness. Kate sat there for a while, scanning the walls, going from photograph to photograph, reading the inscriptions.

"You don't have the market cornered on intuition," I said. "Something's on your mind. Something's been on your mind ever since I mentioned Palm Springs yesterday. What is it?"

The ghost of a smile crossed Kate's face. She continued to examine the portraits. "Give me a couple of minutes, okay?"

"Take as many minutes as you want."

Kate nodded, retreated further into her silence. After two months of living together I was beginning to understand some of her idiosyncrasies. This particular one she happened to share with Brad. The need to take a few silent minutes to order things in the brain before speaking. It reminded me of a story I once heard about Pablo Casals, the great Spanish cellist. Casals was nearing the end of an hour-long concerto in Paris when a woman in the audience began a fit of uncontrollable coughing. Casals kept playing for a minute or so, but when the hacking continued he abruptly pulled back his bow and stopped his performance, sitting quietly on stage in the hushed auditorium until the noise had subsided. When the woman's coughing jag finally ended, he patiently readjusted the cello against his body, cleared his throat, and started the concerto over again. From the beginning. From the very first note.

That was Kate Ulrich when she was immersed in this kind of silence. An interruption, a break of concentration before she'd finished the reasoning process, and the whole cardhouse would come tumbling down and it'd be back to square one.

Finally she cleared her throat and looked me in the eyes. "You're not going to let go of this, are you?"

"Let go of what?"

"Brad. The murder. You're going to keep turning over rocks till you find something, right?"

"I doubt it."

"How about this as an alternative plan?" Kate said, leaning forward. "Let the police find out who killed Brad, then they can tell you all about it. That way there's less chance of having some thug shove your penis in a ball washer."

The heavily toupeed waiter was standing next to our table with the martinis. The penis-in-the-ball-washer remark stopped him for a second, but only for a second. After thirty years at Charlie L's, he'd overheard just about everything there was to overhear.

"I know some things the police don't know," I said.

"Then tell them."

"We've been over this before, Kate. I can't. It involves Peggy—"

"—and her daughter," Kate said with exaggerated patience. Then she exhaled deeply, stared down at her martini glass. "I have this sort of half-baked theory, Quinn, that successful relationships fall into two general categories. Honest and not so honest. I think a couple should decide which it's going to be before they set up house. Both categories work, but it should be one or the other."

"What do you think ours is?"

"That's what I'd like to nail down here at Charlie L's Bar and Grill in Palm Springs, California."

"Okay," I said. "In your mind, what's the difference between honest and not so honest?"

"Nothing esoteric," Kate said. "Not so honest means that if from time to time you do something you think your partner isn't going to like or approve of, you keep it quiet. You tell little white lies to keep the good ship *Lollipop* on an even keel. I'm not condemning it. Some cultures have made an absolute art form out of it. The discreet affair. The secret rendezvous. It comes, it passes, nobody blabs and nobody's ever the wiser.

Life and love and the pursuit of happiness continue on like nothing ever happened."

"And honest . . . ?"

"Honest means just that," Kate said. "Honest. Like when you put your hand on the Bible in court. Full disclosure all the time, no exceptions, and let the chips fall where they may."

"Which do you favor?" I said.

"I favor honest."

"Then honest it is."

"Good!" Kate drank from her martini as if toasting our new resolve. "Then you don't have to keep telling me that you're on the verge of quitting this private investigation of yours. Because you're not, are you?"

"No," I said. "I'm not."

"Excellent!" Kate said. She paused, looked down at her knuckles. "See how much better this is. Now it's my turn. I was going to tell you on the plane down, but . . . "

"Tell me what?"

Kate hesitated. "This is where the Prince and I spent our honeymoon."

"Palm Springs?"

"In a little hotel about a block and a half from this table."

"You're kidding?"

"Nope."

The Prince was our nickname for Kate's ex-husband. I'd never met him and his name was not a subject that came up with us often, but it now explained why Kate had been acting so funny ever since I brought up the Palm Springs trip.

"Why did you feel like you couldn't tell me that?" I said.

Kate kept her gaze averted. "Full disclosure, right?"

"Right."

"I didn't want to tell you because six months ago I met the Prince out here again."

The silence between us thickened. Kate took a nervous sip from her drink.

"Six months ago?"

"Over the Christmas holidays."

"Why didn't you tell me?" I said.

"There was no reason," Kate said. "You and I weren't together anymore. Not romantically, anyway. My life in Detroit was turning into a dead end and a job opportunity came up for me to move back to New York, practically next door to where the Prince was working. He got wind of it somehow, from my folks probably, and called me in Detroit. First time in three years I'd heard his voice. You know how it can be. Time passes and you forget all that was bad and start to concentrate only on what was good. He said he still loved me, asked me to forgive him, blah, blah, blah. The next week there was a round-trip air ticket to Palm Springs in the mail with a wonderful note saying that we owed it to ourselves to give the relationship another chance. Rekindle the flame. If it worked out, terrific. If it didn't, we'd go our separate ways, no hard feelings." Kate paused, gave her shoulders a small shrug. "So I did it."

"And . . . ?"

"Obviously, it didn't work out."

We were silent for a long time, then Kate finally exhaled and finished off the rest of her drink. "Well, now I've told you and I feel better. No reason for it, but the whole incident made me feel like I'd been unfaithful to you."

"You just said it yourself, Kate. We weren't even seeing each other then."

"I know," she said, running the tip of her finger along the edge of her glass. "Funny thing was, the Prince and I never even made love once during this big reunion."

"You don't need to justify anything to me, Kate."

"I know, but can you imagine it? Here he flew all the way out from New York and me from Detroit, prearranged get-together in a romantic French restaurant at the stroke of what-ever, and nada. Zip. I thought we were going to. I mean, the dinner was warm and affectionate. Nice talk. Hand-holding. Back at the hotel I went in the bathroom and got myself pre-pared and everything, but when we got into bed together it was suddenly so wrong. I think he had good intentions. We both did. It just didn't work out, that's all. The Prince felt terrible, rolled over onto his side of the bed. He wouldn't hold me so I held him and he was just like ice. Like glass. He went back to New York, and I went back to Detroit and we didn't try that anymore."

"You're sure it's over?" I said.

Kate looked up at me softly. "It is now."

I paid the bill and we walked back to our hotel and made love with curious urgency in the large bed. She stretched her body beneath me, reached far back with her arms till she grabbed the wooden headboard and held on to it tightly while I kissed her lips, ears, neck, breasts. I ran my tongue along her body as a soothsayer will tenderly run his fingertips along the shape of a crystal ball, and Kate's nipples lengthened beneath my touch as flowering roses do in time-lapse photography.

When it was over she fell immediately asleep in my arms. I wanted to drift off with her, but my mind was filled with other things, other concerns. Blended with images of lovemaking were images of a more disturbing nature. My last conversation with Brad. My talk with Peggy. The encounters with Nikki and Leonard. Something didn't fit. There was another voice tugging at the sleeves of resistant consciousness, standing on tiptoes and whispering muffled sounds in my ear. I couldn't make out the words, but the tone was ominous. I strained to hear, to understand fully, but couldn't.

Finally I slid out from under Kate's draped left arm and went to the bathroom to pour myself a glass of water. I studied my face in the mirror and took a quick inventory of what I knew with certainty. Facts that were not put together with baling wire and supposition.

One, Brad was threatened.

Two, Brad was convinced Leonard was behind it.

Three, the killing itself was done with chilling perfection. A professional hit.

Four, Nikki claimed that Leonard said he would "level" Brad if Brad went ahead and teed it up in the Open.

But what about the Vegas connection? Jerry Kerrigan? What

about the guy who was cleaned out by Brad and sent hate mail to Peggy? What did Leonard say his name was? Graham Kirby? I drank the water, turned off the bedroom light, and left my reflection in there to brood by itself. I needed sleep.

Kate had shifted under the single sheet and now lay on her side, facing the wall. Moonlight fell through the half-opened window and gently illuminated her face, her shoulder, the sensuous curve of her hips beneath the fabric.

I stood there for a second and watched her. Thought about the reconciliation-that-wasn't with the Prince. The hope against hope that had brought her all the way out from Detroit to give it another shot, just as she'd come all the way out to San Francisco to stand on my front porch and give *me* another shot. Anyone else, you'd start to think desperation, but not Kate. It was her willingness to go the extra mile, to go the extra several *thousand* miles, before acknowledging defeat and tossing in the towel.

And while I stood there watching her, another thought slipped in and took hold. Maybe the coincidence was even more complete than simply the two of us coming to Palm Springs. Maybe I had inadvertently booked us into the same hotel where she and the Prince had had their Christmas rendezvous. Kate herself had said that it was a block and a half from Charlie L's. This hotel was a block and a half from Charlie L's. Hell, maybe this was the very same room. The very bed. The same lamp, the same sheets, the same wedge of moonlight slanting in through the street-level window. And perhaps the bathroom behind me was the room where she'd prepared herself for the anticipated lovemaking. The place where she took care of that tedious, annoying, pharmaceutical business so that when the fire began to build, it wouldn't have to be interrupted. I imagined how she must have felt, when the Prince turned to cold glass and turned away. The acidic guardians of the uterus, all poised for battle with no war to fight. Dying on the darkling plain as each of them eventually tumbled into an argumentative and defeated sleep.

It was almost a sad enough image to drive me back into the bathroom to spend more time with my reflection. But there were no answers waiting in there, either, so I went to the bed, pulled back the single sheet, and put my body right up next to hers, where it belonged.

—13—

Our Alaska Airways flight got us back into San Francisco at eleven the following morning. Kate and I didn't say much to each other during the return trip. She read a paperback and I stared out the window. Kate's curiosity about Leonard and company—limited to begin with—was now apparently exhausted, and no reference at all was made to the failed Christmas reconciliation with the Prince. Honesty pact or not, I had the distinct feeling Kate regretted ever telling me about it, and our silence on the subject swung mightily overhead, whooshing close to our ears every now and then like Poe's pendulum.

Back on Union Street Kate unpacked while I checked phone messages, went through the mail, and gave Lola the stomach-rub she demands if she's been left alone for any length of time. There was a note from Mrs. Sorenson, our downstairs pet baby-sitter, saying Oscar was almost out of parrot seed.

The answering machine held few surprises. More reporters wanting to talk to me. A message from Carol asking us over for lunch. Felix Stockwell, the Platypus owner who'd talked to me at Brad's funeral reception, had called to say the memorial tournament was coming together quicker than he'd anticipated and he'd like to talk to me about coordinating the San Francisco portion. I should come out to the Platypus factory in Walnut

Creek and take a look for myself. He left directions.

An overnight letter had come from Peggy, thanking me for coming up to Sacramento and listening to her problems. Stapled to the note were photocopies of the three threatening letters she said she'd received from the man who'd been cleaned out by Brad. They were signed with the initials "G.K.," which fit in nicely with the name Graham Kirby and the Marin County location that Leonard had spoken of. I read through them quickly. The first was merely unpleasant. The second nasty. The third frightening, with a not-so-veiled threat toward Peggy's daughter Alison. Peggy didn't have the original envelopes anymore, but she said all the letters had been postmarked out of the Bay Area. The first had been received in mid-January, the other two in April, one after the other.

I went back to my office and dug out the Marin County phone book and started looking. I didn't have to look far. There was a listing for Graham C. Kirby in the town of Ross, fifteen miles up the highway. I wrote down the number on a scrap of paper and tucked it in my wallet.

Kate finished the last of the unpacking and wandered into the office. "Just talked to Carol," she said. "The lunch invite is still valid if we want it."

"I want it."

"Then let's do it."

We hopped in the van and drove across town to Hank and Carol's. They live in a nice house in a nice, family-oriented neighborhood, on a shady, tree-lined street that more or less dead-ends into the western slope of Sutro Forest. When we drove up Carol was sitting out on the front porch with Cort, her younger son. They were reading a book together, and when I pulled the van up Carol waved and Cort saw his opportunity to bolt and scampered back into the house to the easier demands of television. Carol stood, leaned against the porch rail, and watched us as we climbed out of the van.

"All right," she said. "I'm already sick with envy, so we might as well go all the way. Let's see the Palm Springs tans."

I held out my arm. Kate hiked up her skirt.

"No contest," Carol said. "Kate wins."

I climbed the steps leading up to the porch, mumbled excuses about my pale Danish heritage, and gave Carol a kiss. Born and reared in a four-room apartment above a pasta joint on lower Grant Street, the former Carol Scardino was San Francisco to her fifth-generation North Beach bones—a dynamic, five-foot-six bundle of gesturing hands, spirited laughter, and take-no-guff energy. She had a compact, athletic body and vibrant, close-set eyes that locked on to you and wouldn't let go. Her jet-black hair was cut fashionably short, and made her look younger than her thirty-three years. Carol and I had known each other since college and had even dated briefly years ago. Back then we could never seem to sort out exactly what it was we felt for each other. At times it seemed to be romantic, but we never shifted it into romance. There were occasional nights when it skimmed the edge of becoming sexual, but we'd always drawn the line at serious kissing. Our compatibility factor was off the charts, yet we never once entertained notions of getting married, settling in, and growing old together in matching his-and-her rocking chairs. I brooded on it from time to time, wondering if I was being blind to generous destiny, but then one afternoon nine years ago I casually introduced Carol Scardino to Hank Wilkie and that, as they say, was that. The two of them sorted out *their* threads in no time at all and were married six months later.

"Hank's in the back bedroom," Carol said, "trying to install the satellite dish."

"Uh-oh."

"I know. If he's electrocuted himself, just drag the body onto the back porch till I can get to it. And please excuse the mess in the living room. Cort had a birthday party yesterday—an intimate little soiree for thirty-five of his very closest runny-nosed friends—and we still haven't recovered."

I stopped short. "Cort's birthday was yesterday?"

"Number six."

"Why didn't you remind me?"

"You've had a lot on your mind," Carol said. "I've had a lot on *my* mind. Besides, you were at the other end of the state."

"You should've called me anyway."

"Don't worry, Quinn. He's so buried in presents he hasn't had time to sort out who didn't kick in. Surprise him with something later."

"I will."

Kate and Carol sat together on the front porch swing and I went down the hallway to the bedroom. Hank was sitting cross-legged on the floor in front of the television and a small black satellite box. He held a remote control programmer in his right hand and was snapping it in the direction of the black box. A silent television screen showed a religious revival meeting in an enormous auditorium.

"Lost the audio," Hank said.

I crouched down on the floor next to him. "How's the dish working out?"

"I wish I'd never won the damn thing."

Several months ago Hank and Carol had entered some raffle at the grand opening of a new electronics store in San Francisco and, to the shock of all concerned, had won a parabolic satellite dish, complete with installation, remote-control box, and descrambler. At first all Hank could talk about was the two hundred and fifty-seven channels he'd be able to plug into, but now the thrill was gone.

"I thought the factory was supposed to install this," I said.

"They did."

"Then what's the problem?"

Hank leaned up close to the black box, punched in a couple of numbers on the machine. "The problem is two days ago Carol came in here and our two darling, innocent little boys were perched on the edge of the bed watching the Triple-X-stacy channel. God knows how they found it. Carol heard this moaning and groaning coming from down the hall and went to check it out. She thought the kids were sick or something. Unh-unh. There, in bright vivid color, were two naked women out on a beach having sex with a guy with a shlong the size of a jumbo kielbasa."

"That explains the moaning."

"No kidding. And sitting right there were Cort and Matty, just camped out on the end of the bed, taking it all in. I was out in the front yard and Carol screamed so loud I thought she'd stepped on a goddamn nail."

"What did the kids say?"

"Nothing. They probably thought it was just a very, very offbeat cartoon."

"Keep telling yourself that," I said. "Anyhow, don't they have parental locks on these things?"

Hank stopped, gave me an exasperated look. "What do you think I'm trying to do now? I get the code numbers locked in okay, but when I do it kills the audio."

I watched Hank punch numbers into the machine. Nothing happened. Just the soundless preacher in a flashy white suit yelling into a microphone, stage littered with discarded crutches and abandoned wheelchairs.

"Let me try it," I said.

"You've done this before?"

"No, but I have a knack for this sort of thing. Come on, let's have it."

Hank gave me a look. "I don't know . . . "

"You don't trust me?"

"Quinn . . . with the possible exception of microwaveable sausage, I trust just about everything. But we're talking about four thousand dollars' worth of system here."

"Gimmee."

Hank sighed, handed over the remote control, and moved over so I could take his position in front of the television.

"So the kids didn't have any comment at all about what they'd seen?" I said.

Hank shook his head. "No. The four of us sat down that night to discuss it, but they didn't know what all the fuss was about. They were ready to move on to the next thing. I don't think it made much of an impact, but still . . . six and eight years old. Where is the first flush of romance going to be for them? After the lady and donkey show where's the charge in holding hands at the school dance?"

"The charge'll still be there."

"I hope so," Hank said. "Otherwise my kids are going to skip the prelims and head straight to bondage." Hank paused, watched me fiddle with the controls. "I guess you found this Leonard character?"

"Does it show?"

Hank made a slashing sign of the Z on his forehead. "You have three huge stress wrinkles right there."

"Only three?"

Hank peered, recounted. "That's all. But they're deep and nasty and I think maybe permanent."

"Thanks."

I fiddled with the parental lock and briefly brought Hank up to speed with events in Palm Springs.

"Leonard sounds like somebody to avoid," he said when I'd finished.

"That's why I flew all the way back here to fix your satellite dish." I handed over the controls with a flourish. "Done. There won't be any more beach orgies in your bedroom unless you and Carol want them."

Hank grumbled, set the controls aside, and muttered something to the effect that he'd been on the verge of getting the job done himself when I came in.

"Can I use the phone?" I said.

"Help yourself."

I took Graham Kirby's number from my wallet and dialed. A woman answered on the second ring. I asked for Mr. Kirby and she hesitated.

"You want to speak to Graham?" she said.

"Please."

More hesitation. "Can I ask who's calling, please?"

"Quinn Parker."

When nothing came back to me, I decided to cut right to it. "I was a friend of Brad Helfan's," I said. "I believe Mr. Kirby had some business dealings with Brad earlier in the year."

"That's old business," the woman said. "I don't have any more to say about that to anyone."

"Is this Mrs. Kirby?"

"Yes."

"I think it might be easier all the way around if you let me speak to your husband," I said.

"Whatever you intend to say to him can be said to me."

"Fine. I have some letters in my possession that your husband sent to Peggy Lewis, Brad's ex-wife. Are you aware of the existence of these letters?"

Silence.

"Mrs. Kirby?"

"I'm still here," the woman said. Her voice was flat and defeated. "What do you want?"

"I'd like to talk to Mr. Kirby."

"What for?"

"I've got a few questions."

"Ask your questions now."

"I'd rather do it in person," I said.

"I don't care what you'd rather do. You have no right to be calling me like this. Bothering me."

"Would you rather I bothered the police with this instead?"

More silence. I hated putting the thumbscrews to the poor woman on the other end, but she was leaving me no choice.

"I'd rather bother the two of you with this first before turning the letters over to the police."

"You've got the address, right?" she said at last.

"No."

Mrs. Kirby gave it to me. "Come over right now or don't come at all," she said. "I want to hear what you have to say."

The line went dead. I returned the receiver to its cradle and Hank gave me a funny look. "I've never been one to pry . . . " he said.

"Feel like a field trip?" I said. "Celebrate your children's return to innocence?"

"I'll get my jacket," Hank said.

Carol and Kate were still sitting in the front porch swing when we came out.

"You wouldn't object if Hank and I took a little drive, would you?" I said.

"Just the boys?"

"Just us."

"I thought after Leonard you'd have had your fill of male bonding," Kate said.

I shrugged. "Hank doesn't pack a weapon."

"Let them go," Carol said to Kate. "We can always sit here and compare soap opera notes, right?"

"Hadn't thought about that," Kate said. She was smiling, but her eyes were boring into mine to see what in the hell I was cooking up now. "You two'll be careful, right?" she said. "No girls or ice-cream cones?"

"Perish the thought."

"Don't be too long," Kate said. "I need to get home and work on my job resumé some more."

"An hour," I said.

Kate looked at her watch, held her hand up like a race starter, then let the hand drop. "Go!"

——14——

Traffic was sluggish going northbound across the Golden Gate Bridge. A hard cold wind was blowing in off the Pacific, and a solid line of stalwart tourists, bundled and miserable-looking, walked in both directions across the length of the span like refugees confused as to which direction led to the Promised Land. By the middle of the bridge I'd slowed to a twenty-mph crawl.

"What now?" Hank said. "Accident?"

"Can't tell yet."

Hank stretched, yawned. "Okay, refresh my memory. We're out here on the bridge fighting bumper-to-bumper traffic in gale force winds for *what* reason?"

"To visit Graham Kirby in Ross," I said.

"Graham Kirby being?"

"A golfer. More specifically, a *gambling* golfer. *Most* specifically, a gambling golfer who last year lost everything he owned to Leonard and Brad in a high-stakes hustle in Palm Springs."

"Uh-huh," Hank said warily. "Which of course makes him your latest candidate to be the sniper on the roof."

I gave Hank a look. "Wrong. Just to get your head clear on this issue, I don't think the person or persons who wanted Brad dead were anywhere near the roof. I think whoever pulled the trigger was a professional assassin doing it strictly for cash and probably didn't know Brad Helfan from Wayne Newton."

"Fine," Hank said. "Which still brings us back to why we're chasing after Graham Kirby."

"It may lack a certain flamboyance, Hank, but I think people murder other people when there's a motive involved. From what I gather, Leonard and Brad combined to do a pretty good job of ruining Graham Kirby's life. Took his money, his house, car, business, everything. Couple weeks later, Graham Kirby ate a pile of sleeping pills and had to have his stomach pumped."

"How long ago did this happen?"

"Over the Christmas holidays. Six, seven months ago."

"And you think he still harbors the kind of grudge that would want Brad dead?"

"Why not? This guy didn't just lose some pocket money. He was fleeced down to his last cuff link. After Graham Kirby got out of the hospital he started sending threatening letters to Peggy in Sacramento. Hate mail, promising revenge. And he wasn't even subtle about it. Signed his initials and probably mailed the things from his local post office. Like he wanted Peggy to know who they were from."

"Still seems like kind of a stretch to connect him with what happened in Pebble Beach," Hank said.

"Why?"

"If Brad was a professional hustler, there must have been a lot of Graham Kirbys who got cleaned out and a lot of them must've been unhappy. I'd think after-the-fact threats would be a common occupational hazard."

I reached into my shirt pocket and handed Hank a copy of the final letter Peggy'd received. "Read the last paragraph," I said.

Hank unfolded the paper and began reading out loud. "'School's in session tomorow and I know where your sweet little girl goes. Oakwood Elementary. This is no joke.'"

"See how he spelled 'tomorrow'?"

Hank refocused on the letter. "It's misspelled. So what?"

"It's spelled with one 'r,' the same way it was misspelled in the death threat to Brad."

Hank stared at me, expectantly, as though I'd just uttered six words of a twelve-word sentence. "And?"

"Don't you find the coincidence a little curious?"

"That the killer is a poor speller?" Hank said. "Come on, Quinn. These are the nineties! Poor spelling as a clue narrows our list of suspects in the continental United States alone to about one hundred fifty million."

"Never mind," I said. "Give me the letter back."

Hank handed it over and I tucked it back in my shirt pocket. Traffic slowed to almost a standstill near mid-span, and up ahead I could see the problem. Bridge workers were sandblasting one of the support towers below and swirling wind was blowing debris up and into the car lanes. We were silent awhile.

"Know what I did yesterday?" Hank said.

"What?"

"Played a round of golf. First time in my life."

"No kidding?" I said. "Where?"

"Little public course over in Mill Valley."

"And?"

"I liked it. No. I *more* than liked it. The first few holes I missed the ball a lot, but then I got my timing down."

"We'll go to a driving range one of these afternoons," I said. "I'll give you some lessons. There's a place right here in the city, south of Market, a three-tiered range with wine and beer and coffee. From what I hear, it's the hottest singles spot in San Francisco."

"You're on."

We fell silent again. Our twenty-mile-per-hour crawl was down to a ten-mile-per-hour creep.

"I've been thinking," Hank said at last. "Screw the satellite dish. Parent lock or no parent lock. When we get back today I'm going to pull it off the roof and sell it. Carol never wanted the damn thing to begin with, and now with the kids dialing up *Debbie Does Barnyard Animals . . .* "

"What about your two hundred and fifty-seven channels?"

"I'll make do," Hank said. "Besides, what's so special about instant accessibility? Remember when we were kids and *The Wizard of Oz* only came on once a year? Remember what a thrill it was?"

"I remember."

"That's what I'm talking about. Scarcity is what gives a thing its value."

I put the van into neutral, rested my wrists on the top of the steering wheel. I somehow knew that it would eventually happen one day. Gridlocked on the bridge, water to the left, water to the right, no way out, and Hank about to launch into one of his speeches.

"It's like Cort's birthday yesterday," he went on. "One of the kids gave him a complete boxed set of baseball cards."

"Nice."

"No," Hank said. "That's just the point. It's *not* nice."

"Why not?"

"Because the whole fun of collecting baseball cards is saving up your allowance and going down to the store and buying a couple of precious packets and then unwrapping them with your heart pounding and wading through a pile of Marv Throneberrys hoping to find a Mickey Mantle."

"Terrific fun," I said, "unless you never find a Mickey Mantle."

"If you don't, you don't," Hank said. "Fate. You take what's given to you, just like in real life. I remember when I was in the fifth grade there was this rich kid named Ronnie Brothwell. Creepy little jerk who never had any friends. He used to pick his nose and roll it into a little tiny ball and flick it off his desk at people. Anyway, one day his dad gave him a wad of money and he bought all the cards in town just so he'd be assured of getting a Mickey Mantle. He thought that would make him king of the hill, but none of the rest of us kids would trade cards with him. Know why?"

"I'm on pins and needles."

"Because, wise-ass, his Mickey Mantle didn't count. The

whole idea of trading was that the person you were trading with valued terribly what he was about to part with. Ronnie Brothwell's Mickey Mantle was worthless. It was acquired with too much ease. He hadn't sweated out the anguish of wading through ten Marv Throneberrys to find his Mantle."

Up ahead the gods intervened. The bridge workers turned off the sandblasting machine and traffic began to move once again. The remainder of Hank's lecture on the virtues of scarcity would have to wait for another time.

The town of Ross sits between San Rafael and San Anselmo in northern Marin County. Like most of Marin, Ross is a woodsy, upscale, pleasant place to live. Mrs. Kirby's directions took me up the side of a hill just off Sir Francis Drake Drive, into a neighborhood remarkably well-heeled for a man who had supposedly lost his last nickel on earth only six months ago. I wondered what had changed Graham Kirby's fortunes.

The address Mrs. Kirby gave me was a two-story wooden structure built along the slope of a very steep hill, with twenty-foot-long stilts propping up the portion of the house that jutted out over the canyon. The home was painted pale yellow and was nicely landscaped. A black late-model Jeep Cherokee was parked in the open-air garage, and I tucked my van in behind it. Hank peered at the front door of the house.

"Tell me again why I can't wait out here in the car," he said.

"Because if Graham Kirby is planning an ambush it'll be harder to pull off with two of us to deal with."

"Oh, yeah," Hank said. "Now I remember."

We locked up the van and rang the doorbell and stood there. The spot was very private, very rustic. No visible neighbors and no traffic. Just tall, shady pines, birds chirping in the fragrant heights, and lizards scrambling through the brambles below. My ambush comment to Hank was a joke, but as I stood there waiting a little genuine paranoia began to creep in. Then I heard approaching footsteps from inside the house, and in the next instant the door swung open and I was face to face with Mrs. Kirby.

Our phone conversation hadn't been warm and cuddly, so I was braced. But the woman didn't seem particularly angry or upset. Just the opposite. She radiated utter harmlessness; the blond, diminutive, no-red-meat personality perfectly consistent with a certain brand of young, sporty, California female. She wore a visor and tennis whites and her hair was cut fashionably short.

"I'm Mrs. Kirby," she said.

"Quinn Parker. This is my friend, Hank Wilkie."

She nodded, opened the door wider. "Come on in."

We went into the large, airy living room and Mrs. Kirby indicated a couch for us to sit in. Hank took one end, I took the other. Art books were stacked evenly on the coffee table in front of us. Expensive-looking landscapes hung from the walls. A grand piano anchored the room, and beyond the piano were floor-to-ceiling windows that opened up a tree-crowded vista of the canyon below. The room smelled of leather and propriety and the impossibility of a rash or hasty decision ever being made there. A clock ticked. The bookshelves oozed mustiness. I had that bad feeling you get as a child when you find yourself in a dull museum where rules about talking and touching are strictly enforced. It was hard to reconcile this calm and reasoned living environment with a man who would recklessly gamble away everything he had on a golf course.

Once Hank and I were settled, Mrs. Kirby perched on the edge of a chair facing us. The way she sat, I got the feeling this was not going to be a long visit.

"So what do you think you're going to get out of me?" she said.

"Pardon me?"

"What you're attempting to do is criminal," she said. Her voice was calm, even. "If you think you're going to extort any money out of me, charges will be filed. That's as direct as I can say it."

"Maybe we'd better back up," I said. "My name is Quinn Parker. I was a friend of Brad—"

"I know who you are," she snapped. "You were a friend of

Brad Helfan's. You were his caddy. None of that changes what I just said."

I paused. "Maybe if I could talk to Mr. Kirby directly. He would know—"

"You're talking to me now," Mrs. Kirby said.

I sighed, reached into my pocket, and withdrew the photocopied letters Peggy had sent. "You're aware your husband sent these to Brad's ex-wife, aren't you?"

Mrs. Kirby continued to stare at me. There was enough concentrated loathing in her eyes to ignite dry leaves. When I pushed the letters at her she leaned forward, took them, and set them in her lap. The whole time she never took her eyes off me.

"Read them," I said.

She did. Quickly, practically skimming the words, turning the pages around to see if anything was scribbled on the back. When she was finished she refolded them and disappeared into another room and when she came back out a minute later she didn't have the letters.

"I have other copies," I said.

"Those are for me," she said. "As evidence for when I have you thrown in jail."

"Your husband didn't send those?"

"My husband sent the first one. He's already admitted that. And if you'll read it carefully, you'll see there was nothing threatening in it at all. Graham only felt that Peggy Lewis should know what her ex-husband was up to."

"What about the other two letters?"

"Why don't you tell me?" Mrs. Kirby said.

"Tell you what?"

"Why you wrote them."

"Why I—?"

Hank and I exchanged looks, and Mrs. Kirby pointed at the door. "I want the two of you out of my house, right now."

"Mr. Kirby's not here?" I said.

"No, he's not. Leave. Now."

Mrs. Kirby made a funny kind of whistle and a Doberman Pinscher big enough to run in the Preakness trotted around the corner from the hallway. It didn't growl and bare its teeth, but we got the picture. Hank slapped me on the side of the leg. "Let's do what the lady says."

We carefully stood and walked in as unthreatening a manner as possible to the front door, stepped outside, and closed the door behind us. Halfway to the van I heard the door open again and Mrs. Kirby came out, arms folded, jaw set. The Doberman wasn't with her.

I turned to face her and she strode briskly along the walkway, past the Jeep Cherokee, hugging her bare arms against the shadowy chill of the canyon.

"Did Peggy Lewis say when she received those other letters?" Mrs. Kirby asked.

"April," I said. "Middle of April."

"Both of them?"

"She said they came within two weeks of each other."

"My husband committed suicide in February," she said.

I blinked. "Graham Kirby's dead?"

"He killed himself on February eleventh," she said. "After the first letter that he *did* write. Before those other two that you concocted. Next time you plan to extort money from somebody, do your homework."

Standing there under the fragrant trees in her tennis whites Mrs. Kirby didn't seem at all like the kind of woman who'd suddenly haul off and slug you very hard in the face without a word of warning, but she was, and she did. In one motion she squared, planted her feet, and threw a short, sweet right cross—the ten-inch kind Joe Louis used to let go when a burly heavyweight needed stretching out. Zero to sixty in a fraction of a second. Shortest distance between two points. It caught me flush in the mouth and my head snapped a full one-eighty.

"That's for Graham!" she said, beginning to sob, face contorted. "That's for all of you sonofabitches who helped kill my husband!"

I was able to stay upright, but just barely. Mrs. Kirby's face was flushed, her chest heaving.

"If you ever bother me again," she said, "and I mean *ever*,

I'll see that you're thrown in jail for the rest of your life! I'll scream rape! I'll put drugs in your house! I'll lie until I can't think of any more lies to tell! Whatever it takes!"

Mrs. Kirby stood there a moment as if actually expecting a response. She didn't know how preoccupied I was with watching how the world was going up and down at the edges. Up, down, up, down.

Then she pivoted and stormed off back to the house, leaving me to deal with my consciousness or unconsciousness in whatever way I saw fit.

——15——

I located the driver's side door to the van and crawled in behind the wheel. Hank was already barricaded inside, window up, door locked. Only a lack of tail spared him the further humiliation of having his tail between his legs.

"Just so you don't get the wrong idea," he quickly said, "I wouldn't have let her pound you to pulp."

"Thanks."

"I mean it. I was ready to jump in if she got you into real trouble. Together I know we could have taken her."

"You're a regular profile in courage, Hank."

"Wow." Hank softly whistled. "She really popped you. I didn't see that coming at all."

"Neither did I." I put the van in gear, then paused a second to rotate my jaw. "Blood?"

Hank peered at me. "No. But you might be getting a visit from the tooth fairy tonight."

"Terrific."

Back on Woodland Avenue I went in to fetch Kate while Hank sat to confer with Carol about his decision to dismantle the satellite dish. We said our good-byes and Kate and I headed back toward Russian Hill. As we edged crosstown through the red-light, green-light, Kate asked how things had gone in Ross.

I gave it to her straight, except for the part about getting punched in the mouth. I left that out.

"So let me get the chronology right," Kate said. "Graham Kirby tried to kill himself after the match with Brad, but he survived and instead wrote a letter to Peggy telling her what a scumbag her ex-husband was."

"Correct."

"And this was in January?"

I nodded. "Late January."

"Then in February he tried to commit suicide again and succeeded."

"Correct again."

Kate spread out her right hand and absentmindedly concentrated on the fingernails. "So the two letters that showed up in April had to be forged. Somebody wanted Peggy to think Graham Kirby was hounding her again."

"Not only that," I said, "but the tone of the letters was much more threatening. They mentioned money. They mentioned the abduction of Peggy's daughter."

"And give it to me again about the misspelled word."

"'Tomorrow' was spelled with one 'r' on both the Pebble Beach death threat and the last letter to Peggy."

"Which is supposed to lead one to think that both letters came from the same person?" Kate said.

"It leads *me* to that conclusion."

Kate was silent. I looked over at her.

"You don't agree?" I said.

"A lot of people don't know how to spell," she said.

"That's Hank's theory, too."

I would have spent more energy trying to make Kate see my side of things, but when I turned the corner on Polk and Union, something else got my attention. I recognized him instantly. Detective Lorenzini, sitting on the top porch step in front of my apartment building, long legs stretched out, a paperback in his hands, bright sun shining off his bald spot. He saw us coming from fifty feet away and put the book to the side and waited for us without standing up.

"My seventy-two hours aren't up yet," I said.

"I know," Lorenzini said. "I had to accelerate the schedule some."

"Why?"

"This morning we found the guy who shot Brad Helfan."

For a good ten seconds the three of us were as motionless as figures in a photograph. Then Lorenzini looked at Kate. "Detective Lorenzini," he said. He stood and held out his hand, and Kate, after a moment's hesitation, shook it.

"I'm Kate Ulrich," she said. "Why don't you come up, I'll get some coffee going."

"Sounds good," Lorenzini said.

We marched up the stairs and when we got to the living room Lorenzini sat on the couch and I took the overstuffed armchair near the fireplace.

"Jesus," he said, gesturing in the direction of the stairs. "That's a hell of a hike to make ten times a day. No wonder you're in good shape."

"How do you like your coffee, Detective?" Kate called from the kitchen.

"Black is fine."

Kate came back in the room and handed the cup and saucer to Lorenzini. He thanked her and she nodded and for five seconds we sat around while the detective blew steam from the surface of his coffee. The game apparently was for me to demonstrate my guilty nervousness by prompting Lorenzini into speaking. I was too weary to call his bluff, so I went along with my part.

"You said you'd found Brad's killer."

"That's right," Lorenzini said, as if the fact had slipped his mind in the past few minutes. "Eight o'clock this morning. Two hundred miles south in San Luis Obispo. Quiet little apartment in a quiet neighborhood."

"Who is it?"

"Well . . . " Lorenzini said. "He's Randall Smisak. He's also Roger Schenke and . . . " Lorenzini reached into his pocket and withdrew a small notebook. ". . . Roy Smith and Richard Simpson." He put the notebook back. "In other words, what we found was a guy who liked the initials 'R.S.'"

"Where's he now?" Kate asked.

"Now?" Lorenzini sipped from his coffee. "Now he's on a slab somewhere being dissected like a frog."

"You mean dead?" she said.

"For his sake, I sure hope so. They found him out on his back patio, and he wasn't breathing. Our forensic entomologist says judging by the insect infestation our shooter's been dead two days, minimum. Pretty messy."

"How did he die?" I said.

Lorenzini lifted his right hand, extended the forefinger, and methodically tapped himself four times in various spots on his forehead. "Shot. Somebody stitched a little low-caliber connect-the-dots design from one end of his forehead to the other."

"You're sure this is the guy who killed Brad?" I said.

"Yep. Matched some fibers from the Pebble Beach roof. Even found a phony U.S. Open caddy tag in his drawer." Lorenzini nodded. "This is the guy. No doubt about it."

Kate came over and stood with her back to the fireplace, hands behind her hips as if warming them to nonexistent flames. "Why did you come all the way up here to tell us that?" she said.

"Primarily because Mr. R.S. wasn't a stranger to law enforcement officials, ma'am. He was a guy who was known to do dirty work for various organized crime types. Free-lancer who shopped out his services. Killer, breaker of thumbs, gouger of eyes . . . whatever the want ads listed for that week. During the period when our shooter called himself Roy Smith he did a lot of these odd jobs for a Palm Springs lowlife named Leonard Novak. Ring a bell?"

Lorenzini paused, took another sip of his coffee, settled back in the couch. Kate put her hand on my shoulder.

"You don't need to audition, Detective Lorenzini," I said. "You've got the part."

"What's that supposed to mean?"

"It means you know full well that Leonard Novak rings a

bell so I wish you'd get on with it and tell us what's on your mind."

Lorenzini's expression hardened. "What's on my mind is whether Leonard Novak rings a good bell or a bad bell. Or whether the two of you jump to the same bell."

"I'm not following you."

"You'd follow me better if you told the truth for a change." Lorenzini's eyes went cold and flat. "You'd follow me better if you quit pretending you're just some dumb-shit caddy who got caught in the crossfire. Because quite frankly, Parker, I don't know what to make of you. I *know* you're lying to me. That I'm not confused about. You and Brad had an argument at the restaurant in San Juan Bautista and you won't tell me what it was about. You asked the security guard about getting into the Pebble Beach locker room, and now we find a phony caddy tag next to the body. I don't know what it was you burned in the fireplace in Pacific Grove, but it wasn't a grocery list. Then at the funeral you play kissy-face with Brad's ex and the two of you drive off together to God knows where."

"We drove to the reception," I said.

Lorenzini kept right on going. "The same ex, I might add, who now that Brad is dead stands to collect over a half-mil in insurance payoffs. Then the very next day you're down in Palm Springs playing golf and knocking down Mai-Tais with Leonard Novak."

"You're way off base," I said.

"Am I?"

"Yes."

"Then point me in the right direction," Lorenzini said.

"I can't. But I *can* tell you one thing. Peggy and whatever insurance money she has coming has nothing to do with it. I didn't even know Brad had a policy payable to her until just now."

"Three policies," Lorenzini corrected. "Two-fifty, one-fifty, and one-fifty. And what was I to think? You two looked pretty tight there at the funeral before you both went disappearing." His eyes flashed briefly up to Kate.

"I think it's time for you to leave," I said.

"You're right," Lorenzini said. "I've got a full day ahead of me. We can talk about Palm Springs another time."

"Am I under surveillance?"

"Surveillance?"

"You seem to know my itinerary better than I do," I said. "If you're not a psychic, I assume you've got somebody watching me."

Lorenzini smiled. "Mr. Parker, trust me. Right now whether you're under surveillance should be the least of your worries." He paused, put his hands on his knees, and slowly pushed himself to a standing position. "There's going to be a press conference at six o'clock to announce the discovery of Mr. R.S. This is the last chance you'll have to tell me anything I should know about before it all hits the fan. If I've got anything wrong, feel free to correct me now."

"Only that Leonard Novak and I weren't drinking Mai-Tais down in Palm Springs."

"No?"

"No. It was beer for me, vodka tonics for him."

Lorenzini nodded, pursed his lips. "I'll see that my notes are changed. And you just keep right on digging your own grave, Parker. Saves me the trouble. Thanks for the coffee, Miss Ulrich. I'll show myself out."

—16—

Platypus Equipment and Design occupied a small corner of a sprawling industrial park complex on the outskirts of Walnut Creek, thirty miles deep into the eastern suburbs of San Francisco. The complex was called Westwind Centre. The Platypus office was like all the offices in the park; a low, sleek, black-mirrored module, glistening futuristically in the bright California sun. The architectural intent evidently was to convey the image of unbridled success to prospective tenants, but the vacancy rate said otherwise. Even from a distance you could see that most of the shining modules were unoccupied.

I was coming out to visit Felix Stockwell out of a sense of both duty and curiosity. Despite all else, I'd given him my word at Brad's funeral reception that I would help with the memorial tournament he was organizing. Now he was counting on me, and I had to deliver. But I was also curious. Part of the short-lived Brad Helfan mania was due to the clubs he used. They were odd-looking things, as if the woods and irons were held over a smelting pot where they melted, warped, and then were removed to cool. The kind of clubs Salvador Dali would have played with. The woods were broad and flat, rounded in front, tapering away in back like the webbing of a duck's foot. It was an aerodynamically effective design, dramatic and revolutionary, but no matter which way you cut it, the club was ugly as hell. Clunky. Unpleasant to gaze upon. The company decided the best marketing strategy would be to go ahead and admit the obvious and use something equally ugly as its emblem. The Duckbilled Platypus seemed to fit the bill, and Platypus Equipment and Design was born. Brad told me that the club's design had only recently been sanctioned by the USGA after two years of legal squabbling. He was utterly convinced that once the general public tried them, Platypus would take the golfing nation by storm.

The front door of Felix Stockwell's office did not allow automatic entry. A small sign indicated the button that I should push, so I did. A buzzer sounded and an attractive middle-aged woman on the other side looked up from her desk, smiled, and pushed the lock-release beneath the drawer. The door clicked open and I walked into a room where the air-conditioning was kept hovering at a comfort zone designed for polar bears.

"Can I help you?" she said pleasantly.

"Is Felix Stockwell here?" I said.

"Your name, please?"

I gave it to her and she wrote it down on a piece of paper.

"Hold on just a sec. I think Mr. Stockwell's out back."

The woman left her desk and disappeared behind a pink door next to the water cooler. She wore a light, sleeveless blouse despite the frigid temperature. I twiddled my thumbs and waited. The reception area was antiseptically clean. Bright white carpeting. Modernistic chairs facing a rectangular glass table in the waiting area. Walls decorated with muted watercolors of nineteenth-century golfers playing famous British golf holes.

Moments later the door opened and Felix came into the room, the receptionist following close behind. He was dressed casually in baggy white trousers and an untucked blue golf shirt. A light coating of wood dust covered the hairs of his muscular forearms.

"Quinn!" he said. "You got my message!"

"I was out of town for a couple days. Hope it's okay to just drop in like this."

"Of course it's okay." We shook hands. "I appreciate you coming all the way out here. I know it's a haul. I commuted this SOB back and forth to the city for a year and a half. Come on back a minute while I finish up."

We went through the pink door and into a dark, high-roofed work area. Three young men sat at three separate work-tables, each filing and sanding a wooden golf club that was held in place by clamps. They acknowledged my arrival in the room with quick glances and quicker smiles, then went back to their jobs.

"The nerve center," Felix announced with a grin. "As nerve centers go, not big, but a nerve center nevertheless."

Felix took me around to the first table and attempted to explain what the worker was doing. The talk was highly techni-cal. Wind resistance and destabilized air and the aerodynamic balancing of power and speed. Felix explained that Platypus clubs were designed with the good player in mind, profession-als and low handicappers.

"Look," Felix said, signaling me to get down close. "Now this is a driver. See how small the clubhead is?"

I bent down to look. "It's even smaller than what Brad used."

"That's the idea," Felix said. "Whittle it down, smaller and smaller."

"Why?"

"Most designers design for the average duffer and they keep going for bigger and bigger clubheads, trying to expand the sweet spot. That's fine and good, but what happens when you get a huge clubhead is you slow the swing down. The prin-ciple is no different than what you find in motor racing. In fact, one of the people I consult with now and then is a guy who designs Formula One racing helmets. That's what Platypus is all about. Smooth air flow and no buffeting. Gives you a quicker, more consistent swing, which is critical for good golfers. We assume someone who plays at that level knows how to hit it on the sweet spot with regularity. Our concern is increasing club-head speed through the ball to achieve more distance."

"Are there enough golfers good enough to merit a club like this?" I said.

"Are you kidding?" Felix said. "We'll have them lined up. The growth of this sport is going right off the charts, Quinn. Not just here, but worldwide. In the United States alone they'd have to built a full-length eighteen-hole golf course every single day of the year, weekends and holidays included, just to keep up with the escalating demand. A course a day. That means there are a lot more golfers out there who are getting good and are serious enough about their game to invest in getting better. And anyway, a lot of so-so golfers are going to buy these just for snob appeal, or to make themselves look better than they are."

I ran my fingers along the smoothly varnished wood. "Strange-looking club. It *is* legal, right?"

Felix nodded. "Took a while for the USGA to come around, though. Innovation scares them to death."

"Why?"

"Oh, who knows? They're afraid some genius is going to figure out a way to build a club that will suddenly make this game easy. That one day everyone's going to go out and shoot sixty-two and make a mockery out of the sport."

"Is that genius out there?"

"If he was, he'd be me," Felix said with a wink. "But to answer your question seriously, no. Okay, maybe the equipment is better today and we're hitting the ball farther, but the courses are longer and tougher, too, so things even out. The point is, Quinn, I don't know why the officials get so worked up about club innovation. Nothing dramatic is going to change the face of golf unless they change the golf ball itself."

"Why's that?"

Felix rolled his eyes. "If you think the technology *here* is advanced, you should go take a look at Titleist's research and development department. A buddy who works there took me once. You walk in the door and there's fifty engineers from

Hong Kong sitting around computers and space-age wind tunnels. You think the best minds of our generation are out there trying to solve world hunger? Hell, no! They're trying to come up with better dimple configurations on golf balls!"

"Makes you think, doesn't it?"

"Not really," Felix said. "There's a lot more money in manufacturing golf balls than ending famines. Twenty years ago Titleist figured out that an icosahedron pattern of dimpling worked better than the standard octahedron pattern, and they've been riding the crest ever since."

"English, please."

Felix smiled. "Never mind. It has to do with drag-to-lift ratios and turbulence blankets and all sorts of technical stuff. The point is, if one company can figure a way to squeeze an extra thirty-six inches out of the average drive, it can mean tens of millions of dollars in additional revenues. *That's* why you see a room full of Ph.D.s spending the bulk of their productive lives analyzing spatial relationships among golf ball dimples. Crazy world."

We went back out into the main office. Felix asked his receptionist if she could drop off a packet to a client in Concord and she said of course. Felix pulled a folder out of a file cabinet, handed it over, and told her to go ahead and take the rest of the afternoon off. She said of course to that as well. As soon as she was out the door Felix switched on the telephone answering machine, then went over to the thermostat and jacked the temperature up out of the blue zone.

"Eileen's going through the change," Felix said. "Major heat flashes. You should see my utility bills. If ice isn't forming on the water cooler the poor woman about dies out here. I always thought this hormone talk was just an excuse for women to be pains in the ass, but I guess it's for real. Another one of the million things men'll never understand about the fairer sex."

Felix took another folder out of a different file cabinet and motioned for the two of us to sit at the rectangular glass table. He eased himself down into the chair and softly laughed at a private joke.

"What's the matter?" I said.

"Oh, this air-conditioning business with Eileen just got me thinking about a restaurant in Palm Springs that used to be there years ago. First time I stepped inside the place I couldn't believe how damn cold it was. The kind of cold that goes right to the bone. There was absolutely no way to get the food out of the kitchen and onto the customer's table without it cooling off completely en route. Cold potatoes, cold vegetables, cold everything. And this was an expensive place, Quinn! At the time maybe the priciest joint in all of Palm Springs. I was a much younger man then and my date was a rather fetching lady from Los Angeles who wasn't happy, so I complained to the waiter about maybe turning the air-conditioning down. He hemmed and hawed and finally came out with it. They *had* to keep it cold as hell! It was restaurant policy to keep it frozen! Know why?"

I shook my head.

"It was the only place in Palm Springs where society women could go out to dinner and show off their furs!" Felix threw his hands up. "True story, Quinn! I wouldn't make a thing like that up!"

Felix continued to shake his head at the memory while opening the folder and spreading the contents out on the table. The benefit golf tournament was officially being called the Brad Helfan Memorial Tournament. Felix had several printed-out lists. Competitors who had signed up to play in the tournament at a thousand dollars a pop. Corporate sponsors. Anonymous donors. The television and radio stations that had offered to provide free promotion of the tournament. Felix had done a yeoman's job in organizing the benefit in a very short amount of time, but problems remained. A number of Bay Area sports celebrities had committed to participate, and there was some squabbling from the thousand-dollars-a-ticket peons about who would get to play with which celebrity. Not only that, but the host Olympic Country Club in San Francisco was having serious second thoughts as more and more information came out about Brad's past. Propriety and decorum ruled the day at the exclusive Olympic Club, and some of the members were not at all pleased to be hosting a tournament to honor the memory of someone who'd apparently been gunned down by mobsters. I decided to not tell Felix about Lorenzini's imminent press conference. He had headaches enough.

"Do all these participants know about Peggy's insurance payoff?" I said.

Felix glanced up from his papers. "Her what?"

"Rumor is that Brad left a half-million in life insurance, with Peggy as sole beneficiary."

Felix blinked. "That's news to me."

"I'm only thinking that the newspapers might have a field day with it if they find out," I said. "An education fund tournament for a little girl who's about to cash in big time."

Felix plucked at his lower lip, slowly nodded his head. "I see what you're saying."

"We ought to figure out some way to defuse that."

Felix continued to nod. "Maybe we ought to make it a general education fund, then. A scholarship thing for a lot of kids, not just Alison."

"That might be smart."

We set aside that possible snag and spent about twenty minutes sorting out the rest of the business. I quickly scanned the list of those who had signed up to play in the tournament. No Leonard Novak. No fellow professionals from the PGA tour. Felix Stockwell's own name was down there, conveniently paired with Willie McCovey. Organizer's prerogative. Down near the end of the list one other name jumped out at me. Jerry Kerrigan, the Las Vegas character that Leonard told me to watch out for.

"You and Brad go back a ways, don't you?" I said.

"Years."

"Before Palm Springs?"

"Oh, God!" Felix leaned back, linked his hands behind his head. "*Way* before Palm Springs. Before Las Vegas, even. I met Brad and Peggy when they were first married in El Paso and he was working as an assistant club pro. I went to Alison's baptism."

"So you must have known some of the people the newspapers have been mentioning."

"I knew them all."

"Leonard Novak?"

"Especially Leonard Novak."

"What's your take on him?"

Felix kept his hands linked behind his head, puffed out his cheek, and slowly exhaled. "My take on Leonard Novak ... that's a tough one, Quinn. The correct answer, of course, is to say he's a lousy, miserable, two-faced sonofabitch. He's a crude, vulgar, dangerous hothead. Personally, just between the two of us, I also think he's got some kind of drug problem going. Likes to dip into the nose candy, if you know what I mean. But you know what? I always kind of liked the guy in spite of everything. Ten, fifteen years ago, we used to have great times together. Those were super days in the Springs. Great weather, pretty women, money falling off the trees. And for a golfer, heaven. Absolute heaven. The entire area down there is a monument to golf. The only school of golf course management in the entire country is in Palm Springs. Anyway ... I guess I always liked Leonard's devotion to the game."

"So you liked him because of the golf?"

Felix looked a little pained. "Not only because of the golf. Leonard was one of those guys who had the cards stacked against him early but overcame adversity. I'm a sucker for those kind of stories. Horatio Alger. He grew up in Granite City, Illinois, which was pretty tough sledding, from what I gather. The way he talked about the old gang was that you drove a truck, guzzled beer at the local dive, and beat up your wife. That was all his old buddies back in Granite City wanted out of life. But Leonard had something extra. It's like in roller derby when one skater breaks out of the crowd and speeds on ahead and wins points for everybody else back at the hangout. That was Leonard. By Granite City standards, Leonard Novak was the best and the brightest. I admired the gumption it must have taken to bust out of that."

Felix paused, a smile flickered across his features. "A long time ago Leonard was married to this debutante type for about six months. Total mismatch, but who knows? She was a rebel and enjoyed shoving Leonard in her parents' faces. He wanted the Dom Perignon. Whatever the reason, they lived for a while in a condo right off the fifth fairway at the Thunderbird Country Club. Back in those days the Thunderbird was restricted, and Leonard, being Jewish, wasn't allowed to play there. Now he could, but not back then. So he said he'd go out in the early morning two or three times a week and stuff a bagel in the cup of the fifth hole. Whenever a stray ball would sail into his yard he'd take this Star of David stamp he had made and brand the golf balls before throwing them back out onto the fairway. Things like that . . . I don't know. I always sort of liked him. He had spirit, and he didn't take things lying down."

"Brad hustled for Leonard, didn't he?"

Felix nodded, his smile evaporating. "Yes."

"High stakes?"

"High enough," Felix said. "I don't really know. That aspect of life around Arroyo Seco I stayed away from."

"Did they have a falling out?"

"Leonard and Brad?" Felix pursed his lips, thought about it. "Not that I know of."

"I ask because the papers are hinting around that Leonard might have had something to do with Brad's death."

"The papers can hint all they want," Felix said. "I don't think anybody has the first clue about what happened out there."

"Did you ever know a man named Graham Kirby?"

"Graham Kirby . . . " Felix scrunched his forehead and thought about it.

"Brad took a lot of money from him last Christmas," I said. "Then the guy tried to kill himself."

"Yeah, yeah, yeah," Felix said, remembering. "Sure. The stomach pump thing. I *did* hear about that. Never met the guy, though."

"How about Billy Useless?"

Felix gave me a curious look. There was an odd mixture of

surprise and respect in his eyes. "You certainly get around, don't you, Quinn?"

"In Billy's case, he got around me."

Felix didn't press for details. "Yes," he said, "I know Billy Useless."

"Is that his real name?"

"Nickname."

"Why? Is he useless?"

"No," Felix said. "When the smoke clears, other people are. All those nice things I just said about Leonard? They don't apply to Billy Useless. He plays by a different set of rules. The rumor is he once blinded a pimp in Tijuana with his bare hands. Broke both the guy's eye sockets and then shoved his thumbs all the way, as far as they would go."

"Jesus . . . "

"Like I said, just a rumor."

We sat there together contemplating the Tijuana rumor for a moment or two. Then Felix suddenly slapped his hands together and flashed a big smile. "Enough of that! You're a golfer, aren't you, Quinn?"

"Used to be."

"You got an extra few minutes?"

"Sure."

"Then come on out back with me. I want you to try something."

Felix gathered up his folder and put it back in the cabinet and we went through the pink door again. Felix went past the three workers who were still bent to their tasks and opened a closet at the far end of the workroom. A dozen wooden clubs were mounted vertically inside, like guns in a gun rack.

"You're a tall guy," Felix said, stroking his chin and gazing at the clubs like a sommelier in the wine cellar. "And I imagine you're pretty strong . . . Here. Why don't you use this one."

Felix selected a driver and handed it to me, then chose one for himself. Then we went out another door into the bright sunshine. A long, undeveloped dirt field stretched out for a good quarter-mile before us. Facing the field was an improvised two-mat driving range.

"Our testing facilities," Felix said with a smile. "This industrial park, when it first opened, they thought they were going to set the world on fire. You couldn't even apply to get leasing space here without going through about five review committees to see if you met their exacting standards. Somebody forgot to tell these people that there's a recession going on, so now they've got twenty percent occupancy and are practically going door-to-door like Jehovah's Witnesses, begging for tenants. They'll take an extra dime wherever they can find it, so for an additional two hundred bucks a month I get to whack golf balls all over their high-priced acreage."

A bucket of balls was waiting for us on the tee, and Felix gestured for me to step up and hit one. I stretched for a minute, then put a ball on the rubber tee. The Platypus club design was definitely peculiar, and I understood why Felix and Brad had initially been subjected to such ridicule. The clubhead was barely wider than the ball itself, and the sensation was one of getting ready to hit a golf shot with an extremely long-handled hammer. I swung and hit a solid line drive, low and slightly left, about two hundred and fifty yards into the unrented dirt field of Westwind Centre.

"Wow," Felix said. "First swing, right out of the blocks! Are these clubs good, or what? Here. Hit another one."

I did. Then I hit a third and a fourth and a fifth. As I got accustomed to the feel of the club, each shot went a little farther and a little straighter.

"What's your handicap anyway?" Felix said.

"Fifteen."

"What'd it used to be?"

"Two."

"That's what I thought. How does the club feel?"

"Great."

"The DX series," Felix said proudly. "This is going to be the design to put us over the top."

I hit one more drive, then stepped aside so Felix could take some swings. He whistled his first tee shot straight and true and long. He had the compact, flawless swing of an accomplished golfer.

"So what's *your* handicap?" I said.

"Five. But that's because I'm old and creaky and spend too much time with business. A little serious work and I could get it down to a one or two. In my heyday I played scratch."

"You ever think about turning pro?"

"Oh, I thought about it," Felix said, drilling another drive straight down the middle. "But I could never make that leap up to the next level of ability. You can go from fair to good and from good to great, but that last leap, from great to unreal . . . " Felix shook his head. "No way. This world is jammed full of sensational amateurs who think they're going to be the next Arnold Palmer. Only a handful per generation ever make it."

"They don't want to put in the work?"

"Putting in work's not the problem," Felix said. "When I was young I used to hit golf balls till my hands bled. It's something else. I don't want to get mystical about it, but I used to walk around with Brad when he played and tried to mimic the whatever you'd call it he had. Attitude. Rhythm. Crazy, hunh?"

"Not so crazy," I said. "In college a friend of mine wanted to write like Hemingway so he typed *The Sun Also Rises* from start to finish."

"What for?"

"He thought his fingers would memorize how to hit the keyboard in a Hemingwayesque manner and then carry right on through into his own writing."

Felix laughed, put another ball on the tee. "Now I don't feel so bad."

He ripped another drive and paused at the end of it and took a deep breath of the late-afternoon air. Then he leaned on his driver. There was concern in his expression, hesitation on his lips. A reluctance to broach a subject. Then he sighed a what-the-hell sigh and looked me straight in the eyes.

"Can I tell you something in absolute confidence, Quinn?"

"Of course."

"Brad called me the night before he died. Must've been one in the morning. Woke me up."

"What did he say?"

"He said he'd gotten a death threat." Felix paused, assessed my reaction. "I'm not telling you anything new, am I?"

"No."

"Didn't think so. You saw it, then?"

"It was in his locker before the third round. Another one was waiting back at the house."

Felix nodded. "I had to ask. To make sure. Sometimes Brad got paranoid for the strangest reasons, and he had a way of bending the truth."

"What else did Brad say?"

"That was it. He wanted to know what I thought he should do. I'm not much of a role model, but Brad always treated me like his father anyway."

"What did you advise?"

"First of all, I didn't know if this was even real. I mean, one in the morning? Secret death threats? First thing that went through my head was that he'd been drinking, celebrating or whatever, and I told him so. The only advice I gave him that night was that if he was hung over the next morning to drink a couple of stiff Bloody Marys before teeing up. I told him to go out there on Sunday and win the damn tournament."

"Why are you telling me this?" I said.

"I had to make sure this death threat business wasn't just something Brad cooked up," Felix said. "That, and some detective from Monterey came by yesterday and leaned all over me."

"Lorenzini?"

"That's him. He been bothering you, too?"

"Yes."

"This Lorenzini guy got my phone number off the long-distance records and wanted to know what Brad was doing calling me in the middle of the night."

"Did you tell him about the death threat?"

Felix didn't answer right away. He winced as though in pain, shook his head. "No. On the phone that night Brad made me swear not to say anything about this to anybody. *Especially* to the police. He had a notion about who the death threat was from, and he was afraid that they'd go after Peggy and Alison if the authorities got involved. But if this detective comes back with court orders or something ... I'll admit it, Quinn. I'm scared. Never mind these characters play with guns. Fact is, this company's about to make some money finally after years of waiting, and trouble with the law could wreck it for me. But at the same time I feel like I need to protect Peggy. Honor Brad's request. Hell, I don't know ... "

Felix trailed off, looked down the dirt field littered with little white golf balls.

"Who did Brad think left the note?" I said.

Felix shrugged. "He wouldn't say. But I could tell from his tone that he knew who it was, and that it was serious."

"Any ideas of your own?"

"Yes and no. Yes, because taking people's money away from them on a golf course for a living can earn you a big pile of enemies in a hurry. No, because everybody really seemed to like Brad in spite of what he did. As far as I knew, he didn't have an active enemy in the world."

I wanted to ask Felix about Jerry Kerrigan and the trouble in Las Vegas, but the sun was fading and I needed to get back to San Francisco in time to watch Detective Lorenzini's news conference. Besides, Vegas was a whole new can of worms and I wasn't in the mood to dig around. Not today.

We took our respective clubs back into the building and hung them up in the closet and went into the main office area. The chat was over and Felix walked me to the front door.

"One last question," I said. "At the funeral Peggy told me something. She said Brad also called her that last night and said he had sent her something important. Or was going to send something to her. Do you have any idea what he might have been talking about?"

Felix had started nodding halfway through my sentence.

"She told me the same thing. The thing that was going to change their lives forever."

"No ideas?"

Felix shrugged. "Maybe he was talking about the life insurance. A half-million dollars could sure make a big difference in their lives."

"Life insurance would change *her* life, not *theirs.*"

"You got me," Felix said. "Unless he'd been squirreling away money on the side. He did that, you know. Brad had this trailer way out in the middle of nowhere, and I mean *nowhere.* Go out there and you'd find fifty-dollar bills in the damn sugar bowl. He didn't trust banks. Maybe all this time he'd been putting aside a wad of money."

The office phone rang and the answering machine picked it up. Felix and I listened. It was from an especially insincere-sounding man who was inquiring about the Platypus golf line. He left a number where he could be contacted, then hung up. Felix shook his head.

"Ever since Brad died that damn phone's been ringing off the hook," Felix said. "These same assholes who wouldn't give us the time of day before. It's a damn shame Brad isn't alive so he could hear this. He'd love it. After all he'd been through, he'd sit here in this office and laugh his big West Texas butt off. It's a tragedy he couldn't see this day. Sometimes this old world just doesn't play fair."

We stood there silently, contemplating the unfairness of the world, when the phone rang again. Felix shook his head and looked at me. "Here we go again."

Only this time the voice froze us both in place. It was Peggy Lewis. Her voice was thin and frightened. Tentative.

"Felix . . . " she said. "I don't know if you're there. I don't know how much to say . . . "

Felix moved quickly to the desk and snatched up the phone. I only heard his half of the conversation. It sounded bad. Finally he told her not to move, not to go anywhere, he was on his way. Then he hung up and stood there a minute, looking down at Eileen's desk trinkets, dazed.

"What is it?" I said.

"Somebody tore Peggy's house apart," he said in a robotic monotone. Then he lifted his eyes to meet mine. "The guy beat her up and took Alison."

"Took Alison!"

The fog was clearing for Felix, just starting for me.

"I've got to go now," he said.

"I'll go with you," I said.

Felix thought about it for a second, then rapidly nodded his head. "Yeah," he said. "That'd be good. Let's go."

—17—

I followed Felix's coal-black Jaguar in my rusty, dented-up Volkswagen van as best I could. I kept the pedal to the metal all the way, but Felix would sometimes forget and rocket far ahead of me, out of sight, then have to chug along in the slow lane at fifty miles per hour until I caught up. We did this tortoise-and-hare routine all the way from Walnut Creek to Fairfield, and then into the valley toward Sacramento, and I could feel his reined-in frustration to go faster every inch of the way.

It was late afternoon by the time we got to Peggy's house. She lived in a somewhat down-at-the-heels area of Sacramento, a couple blocks off Marconi Avenue in the north of the city. Clusters of dilapidated, 1950s-style houses with untended yards and cars parked up on the sidewalks. Peggy's home was a lime-green, single-story affair midway down a block of identical homes. The only thing to distinguish it from its neighbors was the flower garden out front. A lot of care, energy, and expense had been put into the yard, and it gave the modest little house a sense of coziness that its counterparts lacked.

Felix parked first and hit the pavement running. He rushed up to the screen door and barged right in without knocking. I took it a little more cautiously. Parked the van. Locked up. Faked a casual whistle in case the neighbors were peering from behind parted curtains. Seemed to me Peggy would want to downplay whatever had happened, not make it look like the Eyewitness News van was about to come roaring around the corner.

I was able to maintain my casual facade all the way to her half-opened screen door. Inside, Peggy and Felix were standing together in the middle of the living room, holding each other, rocking slowly like a couple of marathon dancers in the wee, wee hours. Peggy was crying. Her house—what was left of it— had been ripped and shredded from one end to the other, as though it were flesh and blood to a pack of frenzied wolves. Every drawer was yanked from its spot and overturned on the floor. Silverware lay strewn on the kitchen tiles. Razor blades had been taken to every single piece of upholstery, and the stuffing now lay like billowy tumbleweeds on the wall-to-wall carpeting. Even the carpeting itself had been torn up at the edges.

Peggy saw me, left Felix, and half-fell into my arms. Felix's face was very, very pale, and he looked at the destruction with a combination of repulsion and fascination.

"I hope it's all right that I came," I said.

"Of course it is," she cried, her face in my shoulder. "I'm glad you're here."

Then she gathered herself quickly, pulled away from me, swept her hair back with two hands, and did her best to rub the redness from her eyes. I noticed some discoloration at the edge of her mouth. What looked to be dried blood on her bottom lip.

"I'd offer you some coffee," she said, "but . . . "

Her laughter was false, quickly died, and she didn't attempt to lighten the situation again. Felix came up behind her and led her to the one chair in the house that still looked as though it might support human weight.

"Jesus Christ, Peggy," Felix said. "How long have you been here alone?"

"I don't know," she said. "I called you right after he left. Whenever that was."

It was a small house, and I took a quick look down the hall, peeked into the two bedrooms. It was the same as the living room. A complete and savage disruption of everything. The pink dresser in Alison's room was missing all its drawers. It sat there with five dark rectangular holes where the drawers used to be. The gaps looked like crude dental extractions. I wandered back into the living room. Felix was handing Peggy a glass of water and she nodded gratefully.

"Tell us what happened," Felix said. "Exactly. Nothing left out."

Peggy shut her eyes. "I was out in the backyard watering the plants, and when I came back in, he was right there in the kitchen. He just grabbed me from behind. He wore wool gloves. All I remember at first was the smell of wool in my face and eyes. I dropped the pail of water and it spilled everywhere."

"What time was this?" I said.

"About three. I'm always here to meet Alison when she walks home from school."

"What did he do after he grabbed you?"

"He . . . he dragged me over to the couch and got his face right down next to mine and said he'd kill my daughter if I made any sound at all. Then he let go of me and I just sat there while he tore the house to pieces. I couldn't believe what was happening. It wasn't me. It was somebody else this was happening to."

"What did this guy look like?" Felix asked.

Peggy shook her head. "He wore a ski mask."

"Was he big?" Felix said. "Small? Medium?"

"Big. Not real tall, but very strong and broad through the shoulders."

My mind flashed for a second on Billy Useless, strong, not real tall, broad-shouldered. Then I pushed the thought away.

"After the man finished tearing up the house," Peggy went on, "he told me to listen carefully. He said he knew that Brad had mailed something up to me, and he wanted it. I told him I didn't know what he was talking about. That's when he hit me the first time."

I could see Felix's jaw tighten, his knuckles go white.

"Then what?" I said.

"I started to get a little hysterical, I guess. I told him he could hit me all he wanted, Brad hadn't sent me anything. He hit me again, harder, and when I still didn't tell him anything I think he finally believed me."

"Did he say what Brad was supposed to have mailed?" I said.

She shook her head. "I don't know if he even knew himself. He said that, okay, I might be telling the truth. It might still be in the mail, on its way. He said that if I were to get anything from Brad, or anything without a return address, I was to give it to him, unopened. He made a big point out of it needing to be unopened. He said if I gave it to him opened, it would be the same thing as not giving it to him at all, and he would kill Alison." Peggy's voice suddenly clotted up, unable to continue.

"Where's Alison now?" Felix said softly, putting his hand on her knee.

Peggy answered haltingly, crying again, difficult to understand. "I don't know."

"No more," Felix said. "No more questions."

"What's going on?" she shouted through her tears, enraged, cornered, furious. "Won't somebody tell me what's going on!"

Felix moved and knelt beside Peggy and they held each other awhile. He stroked her shoulder. Whispered reassurances. For several long minutes the three of us just stood there like that, in the silent wreckage, then Felix asked if she'd called the police. Mention of the police snapped Peggy alert in a hurry, just as it had with Brad at the long-ago dinner in San Juan Bautista.

"No police!" she said, desperation in her voice. "The man said that. Any police and Alison is dead. That's exactly what he said. Swear to me now that you won't contact the police."

Felix and I both swore that we wouldn't. Again, almost Brad's words exactly. The same dread of police involvement. The same implanted fear.

"The man said if the neighbors wondered what was going on, to tell them that this was a burglary," Peggy said. "He had it all worked out. It was so *cold*. He said that if people won-dered what happened to Alison, that I was supposed to tell them that her father's death, plus this burglary, it was too much for her, so I sent her to spend a few weeks with relatives out of state. That's what I mean about it being planned. It was all thought out." Peggy looked at me, eyes pleading. Clutching at straws. "You know what I think, Quinn?"

"What?"

"I think it has something to do with those threats from the guy Brad beat in golf. He mentioned Alison in one of his let-ters, remember? About how he knew which school she went to?"

Felix looked puzzled. "What's this?"

"Graham Kirby," I said.

Felix still looked blank.

"The guy we talked about earlier," I said. "The one Brad cleaned out last Christmas who tried to kill himself."

"Okay," Felix nodded. "That guy. He sent threatening let-ters?"

"Three," I said. "The last one mentioned the possibility of doing something to Alison. Only problem is, Graham Kirby gave suicide another chance in February and that time suc-ceeded. Somebody else wrote the last two letters. Not him."

It was too much information to add to the pile. Peggy shook her head. Felix's eyes stayed clouded.

"What happens if nothing from Brad ever comes?" Felix said, refocusing on Peggy. "Did this guy have an answer for that? What're you supposed to do if it turns out Brad never mailed anything?"

"The man said he'd call every afternoon at three-thirty sharp. I'd tell him if anything arrived and he'd let Alison talk for a second so I'd know she was okay."

Peggy hadn't answered Felix's question. Maybe the answer was too grim to contemplate. I changed the subject by asking Peggy if it would be okay if I took a stroll around the neighbor-hood, ask if anybody had seen anything. I'd only say that there'd been a burglary, mention nothing about Alison. Peggy thought it over for a second, then nodded. All right. She didn't see how that would hurt. As long as I just kept it a burglary, and didn't say a word about involving the police.

I left Felix and Peggy where they were and walked back out into the late-afternoon warmth and surveyed the street. It was a densely packed little neighborhood, and I had a hard time believing nobody would have noticed a big guy in a ski mask abducting a little girl as she walked home from school.

Surprise, surprise. Nobody knew a damn thing. Of the closest ten homes, six were either empty or not answering the doorbell. The other four would barely crack their doors for me, mumbling variations of the "get lost" theme before I could get in a complete sentence. I felt my fist clench in my pockets. Hoped for their sakes that one of their children was never snatched away in bright daylight.

Back in the house, Peggy and Felix were making plans. He was going to spend the next few days in Sacramento with Peggy. They'd take rooms in a nearby hotel and he'd stick around until things started to settle. Peggy said she felt good about that. Every afternoon at three-thirty they'd come back to the house to wait for the phone call.

For my part, I told Peggy that she knew I was always there to help when I could. Any business with Brad or the insurance company or nosy reporters could be deflected my way and I'd handle it. I confirmed that she had my Union Street phone number, then we hugged, kissed, said good-bye. Hugged again.

Outside the house Felix caught up with me and together we walked to the van, speaking in hushed tones. Felix was concerned about how in the world we were going to be able to keep the police out of it.

"We'll just follow Peggy's wishes," I said. "It was a burglary. Alison went to spend part of the summer with relatives out of state. The only thing that matters now is that little girl's safety."

"I know," Felix said, nodding rapidly. "You don't think I know that? I've watched Alison grow up. I saw her the very first day she was born, for Christ's sake. What I'm saying is, the police find out we've been covering things up, not telling them the truth . . . it could come down on the two of us. You and me. *We* could be the ones with our butts on the hot seat."

I stopped at the front door of the van and reached into my pocket for my keys. "What are you suggesting? That we tell them anyway?"

"I'm not suggesting anything," Felix said. "It's just that I've got that Lorenzini character closing in on one end, and now this . . . I've got a life, too. I have things I need to think about."

I flipped through my keys. Yes, Felix Stockwell, you have a life. More importantly, you have a business that looks to be on the crest of making a lot of money as long as there are no more inconveniences. Like murder. Or kidnapping. Or friends who have mob connections. It's the kind of thing that could greatly interfere with one's ability to play golf with Willie McCovey at benefit tournaments.

"Let's do what she wants," I said at last.

"I agree," Felix said. "We'll do it her way."

He'd tested the waters to see if I might be inclined to blow the whistle, and when I said no he automatically said no as well. I found myself not liking Felix Stockwell as much as I had when we were out at the industrial park, hitting golf balls.

"You have my number," I said, climbing into the van. "Give me a call tonight to tell me which hotel you'll be in."

"Will do," Felix said, and he gave me the thumbs-up, like we were in this thing together, like we were of one mind.

—18—

Hank, Carol, and the kids were waiting with Kate back at the apartment when I returned. Lorenzini's news conference in which the public was informed of the discovery of Mr. R.S. had come and gone. I'd completely forgotten about it. Hank and Carol had picked up some Thai food on the way over, and the original plan was for us to have dinner together and watch what Detective Lorenzini had to say. By the look on Kate's face I remembered I'd forgotten something else. To call. They'd been waiting three hours for me to return from my quick jaunt out to Walnut Creek.

"Sorry I'm late, folks."

"Traffic?" Hank said.

I nodded. "Like you wouldn't believe."

"I was just telling them about the traffic across the bridge today," Hank said. "Remember?"

"I remember."

"Middle of the day. Bumper to bumper. It's not worth owning a car anymore."

I could feel Kate's eyes on me. She wasn't buying the traffic jam excuse for a minute, but was holding her tongue till we could talk privately.

"I heard the kids on the way up," I said.

"They're in the guest room," Carol said. "Trying to figure out how to play Monopoly."

I went back down the hall to the guest bedroom and stood at the opened door. "Hi, guys," I said.

Cort and Matty looked up, said their perfunctory "Hi, Uncle Quinn," then moved to the business at hand. How to play Monopoly. Cort is six and Matty is eight, a little young yet to understand high finance and price gouging and setting up deadly series of hotels so as to bring your competitor down in misery and ruination. So I crouched down and spent a few minutes illustrating a variation on the game, rolling the dice and chasing each other around the board until somebody went to jail. They loved it, asked me if I wanted to play, and I told them some other time. I watched their little heads bent over the game, improvising rules. I had a new and jarring appreciation for children who were not being held hostage by ski-masked strangers. I thought of Alison. Wondered where she was this night.

Then Hank and Carol and Kate were all calling for me to hurry back to the living room. The local news was showing a tape of the "late-breaking" development in the Brad Helfan shooting.

"This is what they showed earlier," Hank said. "Watch."

Detective Lorenzini stood on a platform and spoke into a beehive of microphones while cameras flashed furiously all around him. They lit the podium with a strobe-light effect, emphasizing the sheen of sweat on Lorenzini's face, the brightness of his eyes, unnaturally animated in the excitement of the moment. It reminded me of old black-and-white newsreels of Adolf Hitler, raving fanatically from a balcony.

Lorenzini had nothing new to add to what he had already told Kate and me privately earlier in the day. The body in San Luis Obispo had been firmly linked with the Brad Helfan murder. The forensic entomologist placed the time of death as roughly forty-eight hours earlier, Wednesday morning. The day of Brad's funeral. The victim and suspected killer had gone by many aliases, but was known to law enforcement officials in three states as a professional hit man with direct ties to several organized crime figures.

Lorenzini finished reading from his prepared statement and reporters immediately began shouting questions from off-screen. Which organized crime figures? How did they know for sure that this man was Brad Helfan's killer? Had Brad and his killer known each other from Palm Springs? Las Vegas? Was it a kill-for-hire thing?

Lorenzini patiently weathered the barrage, then politely declined further comment. He had made his triumphant declaration to the cameras, and now it was time to shift into the role of prudent homicide investigator who is reluctant to jeopardize other aspects of the investigation by speculating on what may or may not be.

"That was it," Kate said, turning the television off. The four of us just sat there with our elbows on our knees, looking at each other.

"Forensic entomologist . . . " Hank wondered aloud. "What exactly is that?"

"A person who tries to establish the time of death by analyzing the type and extent of insect infestation in a corpse," Kate said.

Hank made a face. "That's what I thought it was."

"So what if this guy in San Luis Obispo is the one who pulled the trigger," Carol said. "Isn't the more important question who hired him?"

"I think that's why Lorenzini came by to visit us today," I said. "He knows this man they found in San Luis Obispo is only the first step."

"Who in God's name would want to grow up to be a forensic entomologist?" Hank said. "Where in one's hopelessly diseased childhood would forensic entomology crystallize as a career goal?"

"It didn't crystallize for you," I said, "so don't sweat it."

"Because it had to've been a deliberate decision," Hank went on. "There you are one day, sitting in high school, a vast array of career options to choose from, and what do you come up with? Archaeologist? Dentist? Painter? Lawyer? Unh-unh. Nothing feels right. Then suddenly it clicks! Hey! I know! Forensic entomology! The study of insect infestation on rotting corpses!" Hank was growing more alarmed by the second. "Christ! What kind of human being willingly *does* that?"

Knowing when to tune Hank Wilkie out is an acquired skill critical to all those who spend significant time with him. So while he was off on his maggot-scrutinizing-as-vocation tangent, Kate, Carol, and I shifted to other, more mundane topics. What the kids' school netted from the Napa fund-raiser. How parking had gotten even worse in the city now that the crush of summer tourists had hit full-force. Then Carol brought it back to the primary subject by suggesting that maybe the person found in San Luis Obispo *was* a lone wolf killer after all and not on anybody's payroll. It was a convenient way of looking at things. That way the Brad Helfan tragedy would be finished. Done. Finalized. A poetically just, live-by-the-sword-die-by-the-sword conclusion to a terrible episode in all of our lives.

But we all knew that wasn't the case. Mr. R.S. was a hired gun, and he had not died forty-eight hours ago slipping on a bar of soap in the bathtub. His four-bullets-to-the-head execution sounded as cold-blooded and competent as his own rooftop execution of Brad had been. Besides, the image of Peggy's ravaged house in Sacramento was too fresh in my mind. The mystery was widening, not narrowing.

When the small talk was at last exhausted, Carol started gathering up the cartons of Thai food, dumping the remaining food into one large carton. "Tomorrow's kiddie lunch," she said. "Thai goulash."

Carol finished her consolidation of the food and then sat back down on the edge of the couch. She sighed and looked at me. "What do you think, Quinn? What's your gut-level reaction to all this?"

I tried to think of how I could answer without revealing what I'd seen in Sacramento. "I don't have any outlandish theories," I said. "My opinion is that Mr. R.S., whoever he is, was

hired by somebody who wanted Brad killed in a clean and professional manner, and then this same person turned around
and killed Mr. R.S. for whatever reason. So he couldn't talk or
he wouldn't have to pay him off. Both reasons, probably."

"Who do you think hired him?" Carol said.

"Leonard Novak."

The abruptness of my answer stopped all three of them for
a second.

"Why?" Kate said. "Just because Brad thought Leonard
wrote the death threat?"

"Brad didn't think it," I said. "Brad was absolutely convinced of it. There wasn't an element of doubt in his mind at
all. He *knew* the death threat came from Leonard."

"That doesn't mean he was right," Kate said.

"There are other factors," I said.

"Such as?"

I held out my right hand and began counting off fingers.
"First, there's what I just mentioned. Brad's utter conviction
that it was Leonard. Don't discount that. Brad knew a hell of a
lot more than he told me over a couple margaritas, more than
any of us know, and whatever he knew convinced him that all
roads led to Leonard Novak. Second, a Brad Helfan victory in
the Open would have stimulated a lot of unwanted, prying
interest in Leonard's activities in Palm Springs."

"And having Brad shot to death on the eighteenth hole
wouldn't!" Kate said. "Come on, Quinn!"

"Okay, so reason number two has some flaws. But let me
finish. Three, Leonard's wife, Nikki, said that on several occa-
sions Leonard told her he'd 'level' Brad if Brad went ahead and
played in the tournament. Four, Nikki—and I'm betting with
no small amount of prodding from Leonard—has been pester-
ing Peggy about repayment of the fifty-thousand-dollar gambling debt. Why would they do that? Why come after Peggy?
The woman's a part-time bookkeeper in Sacramento, living on
food stamps and scraping out an existence about a half a step
away from the welfare rolls. What could have possibly invaded

Leonard and Nikki's collective brain to think Peggy Lewis could roust up fifty thousand in cash?"

"I give up," Carol said. "What?"

"Maybe they had a funny feeling her fortunes might change," I said. "Like perhaps Peggy Lewis might soon be in line to collect a half-million bucks from a cluster of surprise insurance policies. Five, it'd take an extraordinarily ballsy and erratic guy to even *conceive* of a killing like the one out there on the eighteenth at Pebble Beach, let alone see it through. Leonard's got both the balls and the erraticism. I had a chance to see that close up for myself in Palm Springs. If Leonard Novak has the choice between quiet and loud, he'll always go for loud. He also had the kind of money it must have taken to hire Mr. R.S. for such a risky assignment."

The fingers of my right hand were used up, so I raised my left thumb.

"And six, according to Lorenzini, this killer they just found in San Luis Obispo has worked for Leonard in the past. Definite link. They knew each other. Leonard would have had no problem getting in touch with him."

My six-point program to arrest, try, and convict Leonard Novak was over. Kate and Carol sat and thought about it for a while. They saw it, but they didn't like it. Too many thick veins of illogic were wrapped around the frail stem of logic.

"Ronnie Brothwell," Hank said suddenly, breaking the troubled silence.

Carol looked at him. "What?"

"Ronnie Brothwell. Remember, Quinn? The kid I told you about who bought all the baseball cards and nobody'd trade for his Mickey Mantle?"

"What about him?" I said.

Hank nodded to himself, happy with his realization. "I bet *he* grew up to be a forensic entomologist. Now that I think about it, I can't imagine Ronnie Brothwell as anything *but* a forensic entomologist."

Carol rolled her eyes, gathered up the large carton of Thai

leftovers, and announced it was time to get Hank home. The kids had started their own variation on my variation of Monopoly, which consisted of throwing clumps of play money up in the air and then pretending it was snow. Carol insisted they reassemble the game so it was in the shape they'd found it, and she stood there in the doorway for a good five minutes till it was done. Then the Wilkie family traipsed down the stairs with over-the-shoulders good-byes.

That night Kate wrapped herself in a blanket and curled up on the living-room couch and announced that it was nothing personal, but she was going to keep her nose buried in her novel for the rest of the evening. I built a fire in the fireplace for her, she called me over couchside, kissed me warmly on the lips.

"What happened today?" she said.

"You mean why was I three hours late getting home from Walnut Creek?"

Kate nodded. "Some couples still don't know each other at their thirtieth anniversary. But you . . . I've been able to read you from the first moment you came to my apartment in Carmel. So let's have it. Stop with the traffic story and tell me where you've been."

So I told her. All of it. Thankfully Kate was not overflowing with questions or suggestions. She listened quietly, nodded, and at the worst of it closed her eyes against the nightmare.

"Kiss me again," she said at the end of it, and I did. The kissing might have gone on for a while, except Lola the cat chose that moment to slither past me on her way to the kitchen, rubbing her soft fur against my ankles. Lola only gives me the fur-on-the-ankles treatment when she wants something. Kate nodded permission with a tight, difficult smile, and I went in to check the milk bowl. Almost empty, and what was left was borderline sour. Lola looked up at me with big pitiful eyes. I rinsed the bowl out in the kitchen sink and filled it with the last of the fresh milk. This presented a cream-in-the-coffee problem for the next morning, but I'd deal with that crisis then.

That night while Kate quietly read I went back to the office and called Chick Bratton, the woman whose house Brad and I had rented in Pacific Grove. After the standard opening of my God, Quinn! how are you? what's happening? isn't it awful? and so forth, I asked if her most recent phone bill had arrived yet. The question caught her off-guard, but yes. She said the bill had just come that day. There was the rustling of papers and opening of drawers over the phone as she dug around for it.

"You don't owe me any more money," Chick said. "House rental comes with phone privileges."

"We made some long-distance calls."

"Don't sweat it." Chick paused, another drawer opened, she dug around some more. "Well, okay. If you talked to your long-lost cousin in northeastern Malaysia you'll owe me money. But otherwise . . . "

"No calls to Malaysia," I said. Then I thought about the level of Brad's phone activity that last night. "At least, I don't think so."

"Here we are," Chick said at last. "Found it. Let's take a look . . . nope. No Malaysia. No Europe. No Africa. You're off scot-free. I'm covering the bill, Quinn, and I refuse to stand here and argue with you about it."

"Fine," I said. "Here's the deal. Just read off the itemized long-distance calls for Thursday through Sunday, that's the eleventh through the fourteenth, and I'll gladly let you pay for the whole shebang."

She did. I held the phone between my shoulder and my neck and wrote down the information on a piece of scrap paper. The only calls Thursday and Friday were made by me, to Kate at the Union Street number. But late Saturday night and into the early hours of Sunday morning Brad had been a busy man. The first was a one-minute call to Palm Springs shortly before midnight, followed immediately by a three-minute call to San Francisco. This was followed by another one-minute call to the first number in Palm Springs. Then there was a nineteen-minute call to Walnut Creek, a ten-minute break, then a thirty-three-minute call to Sacramento. Next was a three-minute call to San Jose. Brad's evening of around-the-state dialing concluded with another one-minute call to the Palm Springs number he'd already called twice before.

I thanked Chick for her trouble, hung up, and stared down at my hastily-scribbled notes. The Sacramento number was Peggy's and the Walnut Creek number was undoubtedly Felix's, so I dialed Palm Springs directory information and asked for Leonard Novak's number. Naturally, there was no listing under that name. I then dialed the number Chick had given me and got a scratchy, metallic recording of a male voice telling me I had reached the Novak residence and that if I would please leave a message . . .

I hung up and tried the San Francisco number and—no surprise—discovered that I had just reached the Novak residence again, only this time with Nikki's sultry voice on the answering machine. Finally I dialed the San Jose number. It was an outfit called Burke Aviation. Sales leasing, private charters. The man on the other end asked how he could help me. I considered for a moment, then simply said that I must have dialed the wrong number and hung up.

I sat at the desk and tapped the pencil on the tablet and reconstructed how it might have gone. Brad calls Leonard in Palm Springs. One-minute call, or fraction thereof, so he probably wasn't there. Or was dead asleep and had the answering machine on. Brad then calls Nikki, has a three-minute chat in which she probably chews him out about interrupting her sleep and perhaps takes the opportunity to bug him about the gambling debt. Final word is she doesn't know where the hell Leonard is and doesn't give a goddamn. So Brad tries Palm Springs again. Nada. Leonard's unaccountability at this point must have fueled Brad's anxiety. If Leonard wasn't in San Francisco or Palm Springs, where the hell was he? In Pebble Beach, preparing to make good on his threat? Brad then called Felix to tell him of the death threat, maybe to see if he had a handle on where Leonard was, perhaps seek a little counseling along the way. No help there. Felix thought Brad was in the grips of a paranoid drunk and told him to sober up, drink a few Bloody Marys the next morning, and win the tournament. Brad must have been going silently crazy, hunched beside the bedroom phone, running his hands through his hair, me sleeping peacefully in the next room. Then the long, thirty-three-minute call to Peggy, telling her of the "something big" that was either in the mail or about to be put in the mail. Next the call to Burke Aviation. Was he trying to find some way of getting down to Palm Springs in a hurry? I remembered what his mother had told me at the funeral reception, about how Brad didn't trust the mails. How he'd drive an important letter across the state to hand-deliver it. For some reason Burke Aviation didn't pan out. Then one last desperate call to Palm Springs.

While I sat there stewing about it the phone rang and Felix Stockwell was on the other end.

"Glad you made it home okay," he said.

"Why wouldn't I?"

"Shit," he said. "I've got the jitters so bad I almost ran me and Peggy off the road getting to the hotel. Here's our number."

He gave it to me, along with the address and a paging number where he could be reached during the day.

"Did you catch the news?" he said.

"You mean Lorenzini and the guy in San Luis Obispo?"

"Yeah. What do you think it means?"

"I'm beyond thinking about it right now," I said.

"You and me both," Felix said. "And I've called off the memorial tournament, obviously."

"Just now?"

"Two hours ago. Finished, done, kaput. Things were shaky enough as they were, but now with this guy they found shot up down south, plus what's happening here? No way. The Olympic Club didn't take the news real hard, anyhow. They and the sponsors both were trying to wriggle out of it. They think this might be some sort of Mafia gang war and don't want to attach their names to anything until the police figure out what the hell's going on."

"This John Doe they found in San Luis Obispo," I said. "Did you know him?"

"Hell, yes," Felix said. "He was a fixture for a while down there in Palm Springs. His name was Roy Smith back then. Very nasty person. Certifiable killer sociopath. Nothing he wouldn't do if the price was right, and I mean *nothing*. Roy Smith and Billy Useless got hatched out of the same black egg."

"Were Roy Smith and Leonard Novak close?"

This got a laugh from Felix. "Close? They practically took bubble baths together. Yes, you could say they were close. Damn it all to hell anyway, Quinn. This whole thing's going to get real ugly real fast. Strap on your helmet."

"How's Peggy holding up?" I said.

"Not so hot. I got some sedatives from a doctor friend in town and she's conked out right now. It's going to be a tough night."

"Anything happens, any hour of the day or night . . . "

"I'll call you," Felix said. "And I'll definitely call tomorrow to let you know how the three-thirty call pans out. I think just hearing Alison's voice, knowing she's okay, will help Peggy get through this."

I returned the phone to its cradle. I hadn't said anything to Felix, but I doubted the "something big" was going to be arriving in the mail. Brad's call to Burke Aviation had nixed that.

I stood, stretched, wandered down the hall. Out in the living room Kate had fallen asleep in the couch with the novel lying open, facedown, on her lap. Lola had taken the opportunity to jump up onto her chest and plunk her furry face down between Kate's breasts.

I stood and watched them for a moment. The steady rise and fall of Kate's breathing, how it gently lifted Lola an inch up, an inch down, as if she were gently bobbing in the gentlest of seas. Then I took a blanket from the guest bed and draped it across the two of them. Kate never moved, but Lola lifted one eyelid briefly, before going back to sleep.

—19—

When I got up the next morning Kate was in bed next to me, having wandered from her couch sleep at some point in the night. Over time I'd noticed that Kate had the curious habit of often falling asleep wherever she happened to be the most tired at any given time. Usually she would eventually find her way back to the bed, but not always. I'd seen her spend entire nights sprawled in sofas, curled up in chairs, and even stretched out on the living-room rug with a makeshift pillow stuffed beneath her head, like a child.

I quietly gathered up my clothes, showered, and got dressed out in the living room where I wouldn't disturb her. Lola had the chair all to herself now, and she stretched and yawned and watched me balance on one leg and then the other, pulling on my trousers.

The morning beyond my dining-room window was obscenely beautiful. Too beautiful to be gracing a world where a little girl was taken from her mother. The overhead sky was absolutely cloudless, the bay below a deep rich cold blue, already dotted with sailboats even at this early hour. Directly underneath the Golden Gate Bridge a low blanket of thick fog, billowy and painfully white, slid toward the city.

Watching it all, I was suddenly sick to the core with having my days consumed with looking beneath this rock and that, trying to figure out which lowlife was responsible for what rotten deed. I felt the sudden and urgent need to dispel, once and for all, the image of Brad's head coming apart like a burst watermelon. Of Alison, wild-eyed, trying to scream through her gag. I needed to spend a happy, carefree day beneath the warm summer sun. Roust Kate from bed and the two of us take the ferry over to Angel Island for a picnic. Forget about Brad and Leonard and Nikki and Felix and Mrs. Graham Kirby. The hell with all of them. Kate and I needed to spend a few hours stretched out in some meadow somewhere, feeding each other peeled grapes. But that wasn't going to happen. There would be no more carefree days until Alison was home and safe.

I got some coffee brewing, thought over the picnic possibilities that might have been, then went down the stairs and out into the bright fresh sunshine of Union Street. I needed to restock the milk Lola had lapped up the night before. I was curious to see how the *Chronicle* covered the discovery of Mr. R.S.'s body in San Luis Obispo.

As I crossed Van Ness and began angling toward the Silver Platter market, a dark blue Mercedes with tinted windows pulled alongside me. The slowly turning wheels kept pace with my walk for a few seconds, and when I finally glanced over the car accelerated a bit past me and braked, and a large blond man immediately stepped out from the passenger-side front seat. He planted his sturdy body directly in my path.

"Get in," he said, opening the back door and holding it. "And don't give me any trouble, buddy. We don't want any scenes."

I hesitated. A voice came to me from inside the car. "Have a seat, Quinn. You're not going to get hurt. Promise."

I considered my options. Blondie, leaning forward to keep the car door open, was momentarily vulnerable. One swift kick to the groin would drop him and then I could make a run for it. Run? Run where? Become the first phobia therapist on record to outsprint a Mercedes? And what for? Whoever these people were, they knew where I lived and they'd be back, and the notion of dealing with a post-swift-kick Blondie was not a comforting thought.

All this passed through my brain pan in a fraction under three seconds. I nodded, ducked into the backseat, and Blondie closed the door behind me. The Mercedes eased away from the curb and we began accelerating up Van Ness Avenue.

The man sitting next to me in the backseat was in his early fifties, casually dressed in slacks and a sports shirt, legs crossed in a feminine manner and body turned sideways to face me. He was tan and trim, the skin on his skull and cheekbones unnaturally taut, like maybe he'd ordered up one too many facelifts over the years. Little tiny ears, a whittled-down nose, and cold thin lips rounded out the curiously androgynous persona. Behind large rimless glasses the man had perhaps the hardest and grayest eyes I'd ever seen affixed to a human head. Shaved ice, with a pupil in the middle.

"Somebody mind telling me what's going on?" I said.

"I apologize for the melodrama, Quinn," the man said, "but I needed to talk to you in a controlled environment. An environment I control. So I thought we would perambulate around a while and chat. You're not going to be hurt."

"Perambulate where?"

"Around."

I looked into his distant gray eyes. Forget it. No admittance signs everywhere. "Who are you?" I said.

"Jerry Kerrigan." He watched me closely for signs of recognition. "You've heard my name before?"

"Sure," I said. "I read about you in the paper."

"I'm not talking about the papers," Kerrigan said. "I'd hazard a guess that you've bandied my name about over golf or drinks or maybe watching strippers at the Foxy Female. With Leonard Novak maybe."

Kerrigan and Blondie both had their eyes on me. Blondie had turned almost completely around in his front seat so he could glare at me properly. He was of your standard Neanderthal variety—the type who loafs around on the fringes, chewing on his cuticles, waiting to be called in if gentlemanly deliberations should break down. He was not that tall, but strong. Broad-shouldered. The thought crossed my mind. The Filipino driver was a nervous little ferret with a pointed jaw, bony shoulders, and a prominent Adam's apple. He had dark oily hair pulled back into a three-inch ponytail and equally dark eyes that darted up to the rearview mirror constantly. He wore black gloves when he drove. The gloves business did not help to put me at ease.

"So what's all this about?" I said at last. My throat was very dry. Difficult to talk. "We drive out to some abandoned warehouse where you interrogate and then kick the shit out of me?"

"No," Kerrigan said, softly smiling. "It's not about any of that. I already told you that you weren't going to be hurt, and I'm a man who keeps his word. But this isn't going to be any question-and-answer session, either. Not from your end. If you *are* hooked up with Leonard Novak, then all you're gonna do is lie to me now to save your own skin. No. This is going to be a me-talk-you-listen session. Got it?"

"Hooked up with Leonard how?"

"I asked if you got it."

"Sure. I got it."

"Good." Kerrigan linked his hands around his right knee. His speech was as unnatural and calculated as the cosmetic sculpting of his face. He had the big words and phrases down. His "perambulates" and "bandied abouts" and "hazarding of guesses." But from his lips they sounded contrived, like the regurgitation of impressive legal terms an ex-con might have memorized from lawbooks in the prison library while doing his eight-to-ten stretch for armed robbery.

"This can be a real short drive," Kerrigan said. "Just tell me what were you doing with Leonard Novak down in Palm Springs."

"Brad Helfan was a friend of mine."

"What kinda answer is that?"

"I want to know who killed him," I said.

"They already found out who killed him," Kerrigan said.

"It was that poor sonofabitch down in San Luis Obispo. Butkiewitz."

"Butkiewitz?"

"Paul Butkiewitz. That's his real name," Kerrigan said. "The police'll have it figured out by later today."

"You knew him?"

"He worked for me." Kerrigan paused, then made an elaborate display of slipping his fingers up under his glasses and rubbing his cold gray eyes. "Maybe we'd make better progress if you told me exactly what you *do* know about me, Quinn. What you *think* you know."

"Only what Leonard told me."

Kerrigan laughed. "This oughta be good. I can't wait."

"He said you're based in Las Vegas. That Brad used to do some golf hustling for you, the same as he's been doing for Leonard in Palm Springs. He says Brad got into some serious trouble with you, money troubles, and had to leave Vegas."

"*Had* to leave Vegas? Why did Novak say Brad Helfan *had* to leave Vegas?"

"I think the phrase he used was that you were going to have Brad 'waxed.'"

A smile tugged at the edges of Kerrigan's cold, gray lips. "Have him waxed?"

"That's what Leonard said."

"That I would've killed him, you mean?" Kerrigan said.

"Or hurt him."

Kerrigan shifted his narrow butt on the leather seat, looked off out into the traffic on Van Ness and shook his head. "'Had him waxed.' That's a good one."

"You wouldn't have?"

Kerrigan faced me. "First of all, do you think that if I wanted Brad 'waxed' I couldn't have figured out how to drive down the highway to Palm Springs and get it done? Or take care of it in Vegas? I mean, it's not like he skipped town and ran off to fucking Burma and vanished. Is that logical?"

I nodded. It was logical.

"Brad's problem in Vegas," Kerrigan went on, "was that yeah, he did some hustling for me like he did for Leonard in the Springs, but he had a gambling problem. A bad one. Drank like a fish too. He got into me for seventy grand so I sat down and had a little talk with him. You need to understand, Quinn, I liked Brad. Always did. *Everybody* liked Brad. He was like this little immature boy who charmed everybody anyway. But seventy thousand is seventy thousand and there was nothing on the horizon in Vegas that showed me he was going to be able to make any kind of dent in his debt. Not as long as there were casinos on every fucking street corner. So we made ourselves a deal. He gets out of Vegas, gets a handle on his gambling, drinking, whatever other vices were sucking up his money, sets up some sort of payback schedule, and sticks to it. Simple. I didn't even charge the sonofabitch interest! It was me who practically handed Brad over to Novak so he could keep making money doing what he was doing for me."

"Did Brad make his payments?"

"To me? Hell, yes. That was the deal."

"Never missed a payment? Not once?"

"Twice, but that's only natural in the hustling game and I was understanding."

"Why is it natural?"

"Usually the money is steady," Kerrigan said. "Usually you fleece whoever you're hustling. That's what a hustle's all about. A guy like Novak, he'll do a dozen things to make sure he wins a bet."

"For example?"

"Oh, all sorts of things. Get the marks laid and boozed up the night before. They get to the course the next day in what you might call less than a hundred percent condition. Or Novak's guy'll have all sorts of trick shots, and the junk bets start slipping in along the way. Whatever. I'm not criticizing. That's what keeps the money steady. But sometimes you run up against a mark who isn't such a mark. The guy might be as tough as you are. Won't drink or get distracted. Those are the ones you have to beat flat, and sometimes you're the one who gets beaten. That's when the money's not so steady. So Brad missed two payments. No big deal. It's all part of the game. You need to get beat once in a while anyway to keep up the credibility."

"How come?"

Kerrigan shrugged. "Slot machine that never pays off gets left alone after a while. That's why casinos put the best slot machines right up near the entrance, so everybody walking by can hear the coins pouring out. So when Novak lost, he didn't really lose because he made sure everybody heard about it. He was the slot machine at the door. Lured more people in."

"How much was Brad giving you?" I said.

"I made it more than manageable," Kerrigan said. "Not a dime for the first six months so he could get on his feet, then five hundred a week once he was up and running. That made it what? A five-year payback schedule? If I 'waxed' him like Leonard's saying then I'm out seventy grand and I feel lousy on top of it because Brad was a kid I genuinely liked. Where's the logic to that?"

The Filipino driver had driven past the Opera House and the Civic Center and was nearing the intersection of Van Ness and Market. He looked into the rearview mirror for instructions from Kerrigan. Kerrigan made a circular motion with his forefinger and the driver nodded.

"So, Quinn . . . " Kerrigan said. "I've been Mr. Information here. Now it's your turn. What do you know that I should know?"

"I don't know anything."

He got a pained look on his face. "Aw, Quinn . . . "

"I mean it. Leonard Novak and I aren't 'hooked up' in any way, shape, or form, except that I have a vested interest in nailing his ass to the wall if it turns out he was responsible for Brad's death."

Kerrigan considered me for a second. "You wouldn't be fucking with me, Quinn?"

"I don't have the energy."

Kerrigan stared at me, long and hard. I didn't like his turn toward the blunt vernacular. I preferred his memorized, poly-syllabic persona. It also seemed an awful long time since he'd assured me I wouldn't be hurt.

"Okay," he said at last. "I believe you. Don't ask me how come, I just believe you. And you're not going to make me look like an asshole because I believe you, right?"

I shook my head that I wasn't.

"Because if you *do* make me look like an asshole, I'll come back here and put a bicycle spoke through your neck." Kerrigan never changed expression. "This is business, Quinn. I don't fuck around with business. Now what I think, deep down inside, is that you're probably a regular Joe who happened to caddy for a guy who happened to get murdered. I really honestly do. Ninety-five percent of me thinks that you're on the level. This conversation we're having right now is to wise you up in case it's the other five percent that might be stupid enough to be forming alliances with Leonard Novak."

"Why would I want to ally myself with someone like Leonard?" I said.

"Watch it," Kerrigan said with a smile. "I'm someone like Leonard."

"Sorry. Bad choice of words."

"But to answer your question," Kerrigan said, "I'd say money, but you look like you're pretty well-heeled already, so I don't know. All I know is suddenly my life in Vegas, my opera-tion, everything, is coming apart at the seams because of this Brad Helfan killing. Every time the goddamn phone rings it's some lawyer telling me one more way I'm front-center in this thing. What I think is that Novak is trying to set me up and then move in on my action in Vegas. Because we *do* overlap in our business interests. Novak is a small-time operator out there in Palm Springs who'd love to quit being small-time. With me in jail or the cops watching my every move, the opportunities for him open up a lot."

The driver had gotten on to Franklin where the lights are timed and we were heading back toward the Union Street apartment in triple time. The Mercedes pulled up alongside the

Silver Platter on Van Ness and Blondie got out to open the door for me. Strong, not-especially-tall, broad-shouldered Blondie. Jerry Kerrigan leaned forward to have a final word.

"I don't see any reason for us to talk again, Quinn," he said. "And if anybody asks about this little chat this morning, hey. I'm just a respectable private citizen who came all the way from out of state to take part in a memorial golf tournament that got canceled out from under me. Don't do anything stupid."

——20——

A steelier man than I, one with colder blood and stouter heart, might have disembarked from Kerrigan's car, readjusted his collar, and continued on with the business of acquiring milk for the coffee, chatting with the Silver Platter grocer, digging through his pockets for pennies to make the change come out nicely. But my brain was elsewhere. Jerry Kerrigan's bicycle-spoke comment superseded my earlier focus on restocking dairy products, so I drifted back to the Union Street apartment in a distracted fog, milkless, empty-handed. Kate was waiting for me at the top of the stairs. She was just out of the shower, steamy and fragrant and toweling her hair dry.

"I heard you leave this morning," she said. Then, seeing that I had neither food nor newspaper, "What have you been doing?"

"We agreed in Palm Springs on total honesty, right?"

Kate's eyes narrowed. "Right . . . "

"Honesty no matter what, right?"

Kate stopped toweling her hair. The eyes narrowed even more. "What is it, Quinn?" Another pause. "Are you having an affair?"

I looked up at the ceiling, did a slow count to five, then said, "Between eight-oh-five and eight-twenty-seven in the morning? No, Kate. I'm not having an affair. What happened was, I got picked up in a blue Mercedes and taken for a drive down Van Ness by a Vegas mobster and his two goons."

"Is this a joke?"

"No joke. The mobster's name is Jerry Kerrigan, and Brad used to hustle for him in Las Vegas before he went to Palm Springs. Leonard warned me about him."

Kate nodded, looked off back toward the bathroom door as if thinking something over. It wasn't an angry or disgusted nod. It was a resigned nod. The whole thing was starting up again.

"Your friend Bill Prescott called while you were gone," she said at last.

"Just now?"

"Ten minutes ago."

Bill Prescott is my stockbroker and a licensed financial analyst with one of the bigger securities firms in the city. "What did he say?"

"Just wanted to touch base. The two of you haven't talked since Pebble Beach and he wanted to say how sorry he was. Nothing critical."

I nodded, filed the information, and poured myself a cup of creamless coffee. Then I sat at the dining-room table, watching the Golden Gate Bridge, thinking about Felix and Peggy back in the Sacramento hotel room, counting down to three-thirty. Then I wondered who was going to be handling Platypus now that the phone was ringing off the hook. One mild curiosity led to another till I finally put down my cup of coffee and leaned back in my chair and called to Kate down the hall.

"Was he at home or at the office?"

Kate wandered out of the bedroom. She was in her bra and panties, still toweling her hair. "Who?"

"Bill Prescott."

She shrugged. "He didn't say."

I went back into my office, flipped through the Rolodex, and dialed Bill's home. He was still there, in the middle of breakfast, with a mouthful of ham and eggs. I said I'd call back but Bill said no-no-no-no, it was okay, that I should hold on just a second. In the background was a clatter of utensils, then Bill was back on the line.

He fumbled around for a few minutes trying to let me know how gosh-darn sorry he'd been about what had happened at Pebble Beach. He'd tried to call a few times earlier to offer whatever help he could, but the dang phone was either busy or out of order. I told him how much I appreciated his concern, then moved on to what was bothering me.

"What sort of access do you have to financial records of other companies?" I said.

"If they're public companies, practically complete access. Private companies are trickier."

"Tricky but doable?"

"Uh-huh," Bill said knowingly. "Let's have it, Quinn. What do you want?"

"I'm wondering if there's any way you could poke around for some information on Platypus Equipment and Design Company out of Walnut Creek."

"How do you spell that?"

I spelled it for him. "I'm not looking for anything specific," I said. "Just whatever you can drum up. General overview. Prospects. Estimated worth."

"Oh," Bill said sarcastically. "That's all you want?"

"That's it."

"Call me at the office in two hours," he said, and with one last audible swallow of food, hung up.

I didn't have the chance to make the call. Ninety minutes later the phone rang and Kate answered it. She talked, nodded, talked some more, then hung up.

"That was Bill," she said. "He's too busy to talk right now, but he says he has the information you asked for about that golf company and you should meet him at the casting pools in Golden Gate Park at eleven this morning. Otherwise he'll get together with you later this evening."

"The casting pools?"

"You haven't been there?"

"No. Where are they?"

"Far west end of Golden Gate Park," Kate said. "Take Geary all the way out to the Great Highway and make a left into the park just before the windmill. The road veers right, but don't take that. You want to bear left. It's—" Kate stopped, sighed, shook her head. "It's complicated."

"Draw a map."

"Even a map'll be complicated." Kate thought about it a moment. "Give me a half-hour and I'll drive you over myself."

"No need to do that."

"Yes there is," Kate said. "Your solo jaunts don't seem to be working out so well today. Just sit tight and don't argue. We'll go together."

Kate was right about the location of the casting pools. They were hidden away at the extreme northwestern corner of Golden Gate Park, out near the ocean, sandwiched between the golf course and a tulip garden and a hill with bison roaming about. The Casting Pools/Angler's Lodge sign off John Kennedy Drive was easier to miss than not miss, but Kate drove with a sure hand and the confidence of someone who had been there many times before. She had put on her L.L. Bean best for the occasion: plaid wool shirt, jeans, sturdy hiking shoes.

"How did you know about this place?" I said.

"Used to date a guy who was a hardcore fly fisherman."

"You did?"

"Yes."

"No kidding?"

Kate gave me a look. "Why so thunderstruck?"

"It's just that I never knew that about you."

"I know it's hard to imagine, Quinn, but I've been wandering the earth for over three decades now and there are a great many things you don't know about me. This is no slam against you personally, but I've somehow managed to have the semblance of a life even before Quinn Parker entered my world."

"Never," I said. "I refuse to believe it."

She nodded. "It's true. Mother, father, sister, friends. Guys of the male species who've kissed me right on the lips and everything."

"So what happened to the fisherman?"

"Craig?"

"Excuse me. What happened to Craig?"

"Oh, nothing. We had your basic superficial, fun-filled six-month affair, then he packed up his tackle box and moved to Montana." Kate softly smiled. "You would've liked Craig. He was a very attractive man. Not exactly rocket scientist material, but a very attractive man."

"Dumb, in other words?"

"No," Kate said. "*Not* 'dumb, in other words.' I don't date dumb men."

"Then what was superficial about the relationship? Lots of lighthearted sex, or Craig's brain?"

"Craig had a good brain," Kate said.

"For fishing."

"For lots of things."

"Like what?"

"He was terrific at Jeopardy, for one thing."

We fell silent. Jeopardy. A ridiculous jealousy rumbled around in me for a moment or two. The absurd resentment that a romantic partner has had the audacity to have lived a life before you. In truth, everything about the current conversation was silly. I began to wonder if this was the mind's way of focusing on harmless events rather than harmful. Brad dead, Alison kidnapped, Peggy slugged in the face, Kerrigan and his bicycle spoke with the promise of more to come. Of course we were arguing about Craig. To argue about anything else would have made no sense at all.

"So what constitutes a very attractive man to you?" I said at last.

"Pardon me?"

"You just said that Craig was a very attractive man. How come?"

Kate paused and peered off into space, like she'd never

before really given serious thought to the actual components of Craig's attractiveness. "What made Craig attractive . . . ?" she mumbled to herself. "That's a tough one to answer. I don't think women usually break these things down the way men do."

"Can you try?"

"Sure."

"Thanks."

Kate thought some more. "Well, physically he was a knockout. That's for starters. Rugged. Outdoorsy. Kept himself in great shape. Nice legs and great tush. I've always liked a man who takes pride in his appearance. And with Craig, when you were talking to him, he had this wonderful way of looking at you . . . "

"What wonderful way was that?"

"Hard to describe. His eyes would just sort of . . . gather you in," Kate said. "And for those few moments while you were talking to him, no matter what you were saying, he had a way of making you feel like you were the most important person in the world."

"I'm sure he did."

"Hey, don't trivialize it," Kate said. "Most men don't listen to women at all. They half-listen, and spend the other half thinking about what they're going to say." Kate paused again, held her right hand up in the air, balled it into a gentle fist. "Craig was just . . . a real *man*." At the word "man" she opened her fist, as if to release and distribute all Craig's musky maleness into the car.

"Well, that's the job of men who fish and hunt," I said, folding my arms across my chest. "To be real men."

Kate looked over at me, a smile on her face. "Are you jealous, Quinn?"

"Of course not. It just disappoints me to see a bright woman like you harboring a double standard."

"Oh, really?" Kate cocked her head and looked at me. "And what double standard would that be?"

"Just listen to yourself. Imagine if I was describing a

woman to you the way you just described Craig to me." I shifted my voice to imitate Kate's. "Well, first of all, she's a knockout, physically. Great legs, terrific ass. I've always admired a woman who knows how to strut her stuff."

"I never said Craig strutted his stuff."

I plowed on, still imitating Kate. "And when a man is talking to her, she just kind of . . . gathers him up with her eyes and for those few minutes she makes him feel like he's the most important person in the whole wide world."

"I also didn't say 'whole wide world.'"

"Come on, Kate," I said. "Admit it. If I talked that way about an old girlfriend you'd laugh and say, 'What a bimbo!'"

"Men have lots of double standards," Kate said. "Women are allowed a couple. Besides, I think this has nothing to do with double standards and everything to do with you being jealous. It's fine, Quinn. I like it that you're jealous. It's flattering. It lets me know you care."

"Trust me, Kate," I said. "Before I even had my first cup of coffee this morning a Las Vegas mobster threatened to stab me with a bicycle accessory. I am *not* wringing my hands about past fishermen in your life."

"Good," Kate said. "Then we'll drop the subject of Craig altogether."

"Fine."

She adjusted the rearview mirror, dabbed the edge of her mouth. I'd never known Kate to leave me the last word yet, and she didn't disappoint now. "And we won't talk about Craig's terrific tush anymore, either," she said.

We pulled into the parking lot and tucked the van in beside a Volvo and an Oldsmobile, both of which had Angling Club stickers on the back windshields. Kate cut the engine and made an elaborate display about handing over the keys.

"One last Craig question, if I may," I said.

Kate shrugged. "Go ahead. You're the one having trouble with Craig, not me."

"If he was such an attractive, attentive, terrifically tushed guy, how come you didn't follow him up to Montana?"

"I wasn't invited," Kate said. "Not that I would have gone anyway."

"Why not?"

"It wouldn't have worked out."

"How can you be so sure?"

Kate exhaled. "I told you he was good at Jeopardy, right?"

"I remember."

"Well, I'm not so bad myself. You've seen me. But whenever we watched the show together, Craig would cheat. He'd *never* state his answers in the form of a question. Never, ever."

"Excuse me?"

"You know. When the answer pops up you're supposed to say, '*What is* the Ottoman Empire?' or '*Who is* Benjamin Spock?' Well, Craig wouldn't do that. He'd just sit there in his chair and blurt out 'Ottoman Empire!' while I was still doing the 'what is?' part, and that'd be it. Wasn't fair."

"I'm surprised you were able to stay with the relationship as long as you did."

"Piss off."

On that note we got out and climbed a series of steps up to the Angler's Lodge. It was a cozy stone structure with steep roofs and a large fireplace, evoking the mood of a creekside lodge deep in the pine forests. A plaque on the wall next to the front door informed visitors that the lodge had been built in the 1930s. Kate led me around the back of the lodge, and three casting pools came into view. Two small ones flanked a very large one. The water was crystal clear and there were partitioning squares painted on the pool floor. There were also a dozen or so round plastic tubes of various colors floating at staggered distances in the water. Two narrow concrete walkways separated the small pools from the big pool, and I could see Bill Prescott standing on the walkway to our right.

From a distance he looked like the big, stout, corn-fed country boy that he was. Thick-soled shoes, jeans, Pendleton shirt, and weather-beaten gray hat pulled low to keep the cool, late-morning sun from his broad pale face. He was waving his casting line rapidly back and forth over his head, trying to get the feel, the line whistling and snapping like a lion-tamer's whip. Then Bill let the line fly and it hissed through the crisp morning air at a yellow plastic target seventy-five feet away. It fell short and to the right and Bill glumly reeled the line back in, shaking his head, chewing on his lower lip. Kate and I went down the hill and out onto the concrete walkway to join him. When Bill saw us coming his face brightened.

"Hey!" he said. "You made it!"

"Kate blazed the trail."

Bill pushed his hat back a little, leaned down, and gave Kate a kiss on the cheek. Bill Prescott has been my financial adviser for six years, ever since the settlement from my power-drill accident had given me an unexpectedly large sum of money to either fritter away or build on. Until the accident I'd always functioned on a net worth of about two thousand dollars and didn't have a clue as to how to invest my unexpected windfall. A friend had recommended Bill, saying to not let the rustic, toothpick-in-the-side-of-the-mouth demeanor fool me. Bill Prescott possessed one of the sharpest financial minds in the Greater Bay Area. His instincts were great, his track record astonishing.

So I'd given Bill a call and we made arrangements to go out on his boat one afternoon to fish for steelhead and get to know each other. Fishing was Bill Prescott's one true overriding passion. It had nothing to do with the romance of the Man and the Rod and the Beast below. He didn't give a damn for any Zen-like drivel about the Inner Fisherman. Bill Prescott simply loved the water and the talk and the bringing home of fresh fish for dinner. And though Bill could untangle the most perplexing theory of macro-economics, my ongoing ability to resist the temptations of fishing was a mystery he simply couldn't begin to comprehend.

"First time out here?" Bill said to me, getting a snag out of his line and preparing to cast again.

"First time."

"Well, that doesn't surprise me a bit." He smiled. "Hardly

anybody knows about this place. Most peaceful two and a half acres in the whole blessed city. Look at it. We could be out in the middle of Alaska."

"Do you have to be a member to use the facilities?" I said.

"Nope. These pools are open to the public. Come one, come all. If you want to join the Angler's Lodge you can, but that's just icing on the cake."

Bill lifted his rod, went through his over-the-head whipping motion again, and cast out for the distant yellow circle. Still short and to the right.

"Damn!" he muttered, reeling the line in. "My release is all screwed up."

"Kate said you came up with something about Platypus," I said.

"Sure did," Bill said. "But it wasn't easy."

"Why not?"

"These companies involved with design and development are all as skittish as a newborn horse. Paranoid up the kazoo. Any time you get into things like engine design, cars, computers, pharmaceutical drugs, it's tough. They keep everything under wraps because they think the rest of the world is trying to steal from them."

"*Is* the rest of the world trying to steal from them?"

"Damn straight!" Bill laughed. "I'd be paranoid, too. But it makes it more of a pain in the butt to find out stuff from these companies."

"What *did* you find out?"

"Fellow by the name of Felix Stockwell is the brains behind the whole schmear. Founder, creator, original money man, everything. He used to be the whole ball of wax, but designing and manufacturing golf clubs is an expensive business, so when he got in a cash problem a few years back he started selling shares in the company. Five percent here, three percent there, another two percent over there. Now Felix Stockwell owns only sixty percent of Platypus, though there are worse fates in life."

"Why do you say that?"

"Because it looks like Mr. Stockwell is about to become a very wealthy man."

"How so?"

Bill licked his lips, gave me his this-is-no-joke look. "I had to cash in on some long-owed favors for this one, Quinn, so keep whatever I'm about to tell you under your hat."

"Done."

"But I mean seriously. This information leaks out for *any* reason whatsoever, my big blond goose'll be cooked. This goes for you too, Kate."

"I'm not even listening," Kate said. "I automatically tune out when men get together to talk about the big, complicated world."

"Okay, then," Bill said. "Here's what's happening. A major sporting goods conglomerate out of Chicago whose logo you've seen a thousand times but which will remain unnamed for the duration of our little talk is about to make a seven-figure bid for Platypus Equipment and Design Company. A *high* seven-figure bid. Fine print's still being haggled over, no ink on any dotted lines yet, so until things're finalized it's hush-hush."

"High seven figures . . . "

"My source said seven or eight million."

"Did this buyout interest perk up because of what happened at Pebble Beach?" I said.

Bill shook his head. "That's what I thought at first, but no. This deal's been in the works for months. Top secret, of course. The fact that your buddy did good in the Open may have upped the buying price some, that I have no way of knowing, but the wheels've been in motion on this one since way back in at least February."

We were silent a moment. I calculated what sixty percent of a high seven figures would be. Felix Stockwell wouldn't have to worry about his office air-conditioning bills anymore.

"Can I try casting once?" Kate said.

Bill looked at her, surprised. "You really want to try?"

"Is it okay?"

To ask Bill Prescott if it's okay to try your hand at fishing is like asking a ten-year-old Little Leaguer if he'd mind showing you his baseball card collection. Bill's face lit up.

"Where in the hell did you find this woman!" he said.

The fortunes of Platypus and Felix Stockwell took an immediate backseat to the business at hand. Bill got behind Kate and demonstrated to her how one properly grips a casting rod. He talked about the wrist movement, her stance, when to release, the way to reel it back so you wouldn't snag the line. Kate listened and nodded and when Bill was confident she had a good grip she mimicked Bill's over-the-head lasso motion and cast out. The line hit the yellow plastic marker absolute, no-doubt-about-it dead center. There was a moment of stunned silence.

"I'll be goddamned!" Bill said under his breath. "You nailed it! You nailed that sucker first try!"

"She used to date a fisherman who cheated at Jeopardy," I explained.

Bill wasn't listening to me. He was telling Kate to reel it in so she could give it another shot. They went through the whole rigmarole again and she let it fly, this one turning out almost as good as her first. It hit the outside edge of the tube. Bill just stood there, agape, hands on hips.

"Close your mouth, Bill," I said. "That's how flies get in."

He blinked twice, looked over at me and said, "She dated a fisherman who cheated at what?"

"Never mind."

You could see that Bill would have loved nothing more than to make it a best-of-thirty casting contest with Kate, but the shock slowly wore off and he said he had a lunch meeting downtown and had to get back to the office. So the three of us walked together up past the Angler's Lodge and into the parking lot, Bill talking excitedly to Kate the whole way, about how they'd definitely have to schedule some time and do this again. I straggled along while they figured out dates and times.

"The other forty percent of Platypus," I said. "Who did Felix Stockwell sell it to? The general public?"

Bill was in the middle of disassembling his rod and reel and had to think for a second to remember what I was talking about. Then he shook his head. "The other forty percent," he said. "No, it went to one member of the general public. Guy by the name of Leonard Novak."

I could feel Kate's eyes suddenly on me. Bill paused briefly and watched the reactions of the two of us. "Why do I get the feeling you've heard of him?" he said.

"I've met him."

"Really?"

"Down in Palm Springs."

Bill nodded, disassembled the last of his rod and reel, and put them in the trunk of his car. "I read about him, too. The newspapers say he might have had something to do with your buddy's death."

"He might've."

"Seems like a guy you'd want to be careful around."

"Does the company making the bid for Platypus know about Leonard Novak?" I asked.

"Yes."

"And that he has links to organized crime?"

"Yes."

"Didn't Novak's financial interest in Platypus cause them to rethink?"

Bill nodded. "According to my source, this company in Chicago has been doing nothing *but* rethink from the moment the bullets started flying at Pebble Beach. The money's all there and it looks like it's a go, but my source thinks the deal is also hanging by the thinnest of threads."

"Because of Leonard Novak?"

"Because of all of it," Bill said. "Blood and bullets and murder. Nasty stories about mobsters and hit men. It's not really the image this unnamed sporting goods company would like to convey. Apple-pie citizens at their leisure is what they want to convey."

"I thought corporate America didn't worry about morality when it came to the bottom line," Kate said. "I mean, look at the U.S. Open itself. Because of sponsor money they carted away Brad's body and practically finished the tournament over the police chalk marks."

"I'm with you there to a point, Kate," Bill said. "And fifteen years ago I would've been with you all the way. When I was first getting into this racket I would've told you that it didn't matter a whit to the purchasing company whether Platypus was owned by Mother Teresa or the American Nazi Party. I used to think that the only relevant fact about any business deal, Platypus or whatever, is that the people doing business were going to make money. Period."

"You don't think that anymore?" Kate said.

Bill shook his head. "Nope."

"What changed your mind?"

"Too many times in these past fifteen years I've seen companies walk away from lucrative deals because there was something unsavory whipped into the mix." Bill leaned forward and gave me an elbow in the side. "That's how come I'm such an optimistic guy. Contrary to widespread belief, the almighty dollar doesn't call *all* the shots. Not yet, anyway."

Bill slapped his hands clean and reiterated how late he was for his downtown appointment. He impressed upon us again the confidential nature of what he'd been able to unearth about Platypus, and then took a half-minute to drive home to Kate the extraordinary potential she showed as a fisherperson and the incalculable loss the sport would suffer if she did not pursue this obvious God-given talent. Then Bill got into his car and rolled down the driver's window.

"I give nonfinancial advice, too," he said to me. His expression was serious.

"Let's have it," I said.

"Friend to friend, Quinn. The papers really do say this Leonard Novak is a pretty rough character."

"The papers are right."

"Then keep your head low, all right? My talk about corporate morality doesn't apply to the criminal element. This deal with Platypus is a big one. Eight million dollars up for grabs, with some rough people grabbing for it. If you keep poking around with a stick somebody's liable to hand you your butt on a plate. There's too much money floating around on this deal for anybody to let a guy like you muck it up. Hear what I'm saying?"

"I hear."

"Good."

Then Bill put his Volvo into gear and pulled out of the parking lot.

—21—

While Kate turned on the car radio and drove back toward town, I sat in the passenger seat and played with Bill Prescott's information like a child digging a spoon in the mashed potatoes. Heap it on, hold it high, let if fall, watch it splat. You never know. Sometimes you see shapes in the mess, faces form in the tumble and billow of passing clouds.

At first I decided just for the hell of it to be mule-headed stubborn and cling to my original conviction that Leonard Novak had ordered Brad's killing. Never mind that Bill's source claimed Brad's death had put the takeover bid—and Leonard's forty percent of the potential millions—on thin ice. Bill's source might not have the whole story. The deal to take over Platypus had apparently been dragging along since at least February. So who was to say that the offer to purchase wasn't waffling anyway, long before events at Pebble Beach? An old advertising axiom states that there is no such thing as bad publicity, and Leonard may have gambled that a dramatic, coast-to-coast killing of Brad Helfan in front of twenty million potential consumers—gruesome as it was—might be a fresh transfusion to waning corporate interest. The Platypus Company would boldly scorch its name into the public mind in a way five years' worth of full-page color ads in *Golf Digest* never could. Didn't Felix himself say that the phones at his office hadn't quit ringing since Brad's death? Weren't other investors now clamoring over each other to grab on to Platypus's tainted coattails?

"Talk it out, Quinn," Kate suddenly said, turning off the radio.

"What?"

"All this teeth-grinding up front is drowning out my music. Let's have it. What's on your mind? And if you say Craig's tush you can get out right here and walk the rest of the way home."

"No," I said. "That crisis has passed. I'm at peace with myself over Craig's tush."

Kate softly smiled. "Good."

"I'm looking for some way to keep thinking of Leonard Novak as the bad guy."

"Why would you want to do that?"

"Because all roads lead directly to Leonard's doorstep except this one, and it's bugging the hell out of me."

"Any success?"

"No. I was just thinking that Brad's death might heighten the interest in Platypus and maybe create a bidding war, which Leonard would want. But it doesn't wash."

"Why not?"

"A U.S. Open victory with Platypus clubs by a folk hero in the making would be all the boost any golf equipment company would need. Leonard didn't need to look for another angle. Certainly not one that involved murder."

"True," Kate said. "But you still think it's Leonard anyway, don't you?"

"I don't know what I think anymore. I need to get back to the basics."

"Which are?"

"The note," I said. "The death threat in Brad's locker. That's as basic as it gets, and the note told Brad to lose big. Not to be edged out and finish in second place. Not to make a respectable run at the title before fading in the end. The note quite specifically told him to lose *big*. In other words, collapse. Flop. Nosedive. Shots to the right, shots to the left."

"Make Platypus look bad, maybe?"

"Exactly. America loves winners and hates losers," I said. "Simple as that. Maybe whoever wrote that note wanted Brad—and his clubs—to be branded as losers. Pull the rug out from under his mystique. Reveal him to be just a blue-collar player with some funky equipment. Neither, as it turned out, up to the task of coming through when it counted."

"But if Brad lost big," Kate said, "Leonard and Felix would lose big, too."

I nodded. "Probably. If negotiations with this unnamed big company were stalled anyway, a prime-time collapse by Platypus's primary spokesman might be the final nail in the coffin."

"Which is another road leading away from Leonard as guilty," Kate said. She took a deep breath, winced as though the intake of breath had hurt her. "But to have killed him in the brutal way they did . . . "

"It was the only way *to* kill him."

"What do you mean?"

"Don't you see? A discreet broken neck in a remote location wouldn't serve the purpose. Brad refused to lose. He was out there on the eighteenth fairway, a three-wood, wedge, and two putts away from claiming the biggest title in golf. If the ultimate plan here was to somehow sabotage Platypus, then what else could be done? I'll tell you what. Gun him down, live, in front of twenty million people."

"I'm still not with you."

"Like this, Kate. If you wanted to bury Platypus Equipment and Design, what more horrific stamp could you put on the company? How could sporting-class America ever be able to look down the shaft of a Platypus driver after that without seeing bloodstains?"

Kate drove, thought for a while. "The roads leading away from Leonard are wide and many," she said at last.

"I know."

"Who'd stand to gain the most from Leonard losing millions of dollars?"

"I can think of a couple. Mrs. Graham Kirby, for one."

"The wife of the man who sent the letters to Peggy?"

"Sure. Once upon a time Leonard and Brad combined to ruin his life. Maybe she was deeply, madly in love with her husband. Maybe she's convinced he killed himself because of Brad and Leonard. This would be a way of getting revenge on both of them at the same time."

"How does a suburban housewife go about hiring a professional killer?"

"If somebody wants something badly enough, they'll find a way."

"I don't know . . . " Kate said. "And how would Mrs. Kirby know about the corporate interest in Platypus? Or that Leonard owned forty percent of anything?"

"We know, don't we?"

"Good point," Kate said. We idled at a red light, waited for it to turn green. "So who else had it in for Leonard besides Graham Kirby's widow?"

I glanced at my watch. Quarter to noon. "Do you mind making a little side trip on the way home?" I said.

Kate glanced warily at me. "How little?"

"Little."

"If you mean Palm Springs, forget it."

"You'll never have to leave the city limits. A right turn on Gough and then a left further on will be sufficient."

"Further on . . . ?"

"Turk Street."

"The Tenderloin?" Kate said.

"Just for a few minutes."

She arched her eyebrows. "If this is a ploy to make Palm Springs look better . . . "

"Just drive."

The Tenderloin District of San Francisco really isn't that bad if you can ignore the whores and the peep shows and the drug paraphernalia in the gutters and the occasional derelict taking a long, wine-induced piss against the wheels of your car. Kate had a hard time ignoring all that. She parked her spiffy new

Honda a half-block up from Newman's Gym and sat there a moment, reluctant to leave.

"How long is this going to take?" she said.

"Assuming Roscoe's even there, just a couple of minutes."

"Maybe I should wait in the car."

A drunk weaved by, shouted something incomprehensible at a telephone pole. The telephone pole apparently answered back, because the drunk took extreme offense, put his nose an inch from the wood, and let the telephone pole have it, but good.

"You sure you want to wait out here by yourself?" I said.

Kate rethought that option. In years past the Tenderloin used to be merely down-at-the-heels. But when California ran into budget problems, one of the first things the political brain trust in Sacramento did was empty out the state-run mental hospitals, and now the Tenderloin had a dash of psychopathy added to the stew. Danger was in the air. The sense that anything could happen at any time.

"I don't want to leave this car just sitting here," Kate said. "I mean, my heart bleeds liberal blood as much as the next person's, and I feel for the people who have to live here, but the cold hard facts are that I have four more years' worth of payments on this vehicle and I'd rather not have it trashed."

"Then why don't you head on home?" I said. "I'll grab a taxi."

Kate thought about that for a second. "You don't mind?"

"No. This way I can take my time with Roscoe. Works out better."

"Okay," Kate nodded slowly. "I will. While you and Hank were in Ross, Carol and I talked about the two of us catching a matinee some afternoon. Maybe today's the day."

"Do it. Just leave a message on the machine if you're going to be late."

Kate nodded, blew me a kiss good-bye, and accelerated away through the cluttered street. I turned in the other direction and walked the half-block up to Newman's.

San Francisco hasn't been much of a boxing town since the

early days of Gentleman Jim Corbett, but those who fight and train and call the city home these days usually do their sparring at Newman's. It is as grimy and smelly as you would expect a boxing gym to be. Except for an aberrant period several years ago when boxing became the temporary rage among yuppies, the clientele at Newman's tend to be young tough Hispanics and blacks, interspersed with the occasional thirtyish white-boy dabbler like me. We get along fine. The serious fighters don't pay much attention to me. They've got ambitions. They're focused on their dreams.

The gym, usually a hub of activity at any time of the day or night, was oddly quiet. Two scrappy Hispanic bantamweights in the back were hammering away at a couple of speed bags. A bigger black guy was skipping rope off to the right. A sluggish white kid thumped away on a heavy bag in the corner, flat-footed, dull-eyed.

Ritchie Dalgiacomo was sitting on a stool up alongside the apron of the first of Newman's three boxing rings. He was reading a boxing magazine, and when I walked in he opened his mouth wide in a caricature of bowled-over surprise.

"Well, whaddaya know!" he said. "Look what the cat drug in!"

"Hey, Ritchie," I said. "How's our boy?"

Over the last two years Ritchie Dalgiacomo and I have had perhaps thirty opportunities to greet each other, and it has always gone the same way. Look what the cat drug in. How's our boy.

"Our boy's lacing up," Ritchie said. "We was wonderin' if you was gonna drop by or not."

"Did you honestly think I wouldn't?"

"How the hell do I know?"

Ritchie Dalgiacomo has been a fixture at Newman's for over thirty years. Fat, chain-smoking, reeking of Brut 33 from the squeeze bottle, Ritchie wanted nothing more in life than to have the kind of money to be able to walk into a Las Vegas lounge with a big-busted redhead on his arm and have the owner oil up to him. To Ritchie, that would be heaven. To be on a first-name basis with people he considered big shots. To that end he wore leisure suits and gold necklaces and—though he could smarm with the best of them—never could quite figure out why his dream wasn't crystallizing yet. I'd only seen Ritchie in the company of true big shots once, at a cocktail reception before a heavyweight title fight at Caesar's Lake Tahoe, and he drank too much and stood too close and laughed too hard at their jokes. The big shots cringed and tolerated him because he was affiliated with Roscoe, but that was it. At the first opportunity they excused themselves and went elsewhere, leaving Ritchie standing there wondering what went wrong, trying to figure it out.

Actually, Ritchie *had* figured it out. He'd figured it out a long time ago. Nothing compensated for a lack of social polish like money, lots of money. And since Ritchie Dalgiacomo wasn't a likely candidate to climb the executive ranks at General Motors, he focused on what he knew best. The fight game. For three decades he'd staked out Newman's Gym with the hope that a Sonny Liston might come shuffling in off the streets, a pugilistic diamond in the rough, with the heart of Jack Dempsey and the speed of Muhammad Ali, needing only guidance and training and someone to give fifteen percent of his future millions to. "Our boy" in the back lacing up was Roscoe Laughinghouse, my old goofing-around sparring partner and Ritchie's last best chance to swagger into the Mirage Hotel and Casino with cash in his pockets and cooing redheads in tow.

"I need to talk to Roscoe for a minute," I said.

"Talk all you want," Ritchie said. "Long as you don't think you're gonna do any sparring."

"You think I'm crazy?" I said.

"Do bears shit in the forest?"

In the early days—before Roscoe Laughinghouse became an undefeated professional with increasingly frequent appearances on ESPN—I used to come down to Newman's a couple times a week to spar with him. We never pretended it was a fair match. We never pretended it was a match at all. Roscoe Laughinghouse is two hundred tightly muscled pounds of ferocious fighting machine. I boast arms that usually start trembling around the tenth push-up, and have developed a chicken-shit backpedaling motion in a boxing ring so effective that other fighters have been known to stop whatever they were doing to come over and marvel. But Roscoe liked to spar with me anyway because of my height, quickness, and three-inch reach advantage. In return for a solemn promise not to hurt me, he'd practice against my size and speed in preparation for the bigger and meaner heavyweights waiting for him out there.

Roscoe and I don't spar anymore because Ritchie won't allow it. The last time we spontaneously mixed it up, a year earlier, things got out of hand. I inadvertently made a comment that Roscoe misinterpreted and caused him to temporarily forget his promise not to hurt me. In desperate, flailing, let-it-all-hang-out self-defense I actually managed to land a hard combination and dropped Roscoe momentarily to his knees. My lucky left-right didn't improve his mood. He got up with renewed purpose and drilled me, and for ten or fifteen minutes the rafters of Newman's Gym came alive with planets and suns and multicolored giraffes nibbling on comet dust. While I sat in the corner watching the constellations form and re-form around zoo animals, Ritchie clawed his way into the ring, screaming, a vein the size of the Mississippi River forming on his forehead. That was the last time Roscoe and I have ever thrown a punch at each other, whether in play or in earnest.

"How's the phobia racket these days?" Ritchie said.

"Terrific," I said. "The world's a scarier place than ever."

"You're telling me?"

"How's life in Vegas?"

"All the action a guy like me can handle," Ritchie said. "My kinda place. My kinda town."

Six months earlier Roscoe was supposedly served up as out-of-state black fodder for a hotshot white fighter from Utah and he stunned the hometown Salt Lake City crowd by icing the local favorite in the first minute of the first round. The boxing world took notice, and immediately after that fight Ritchie and Roscoe moved from Newman's to Las Vegas. More opponents, better training facilities, closer to the spotlight. Roscoe was only back in San Francisco for a couple weeks, training for a special nationally televised fight at the Cow Palace featuring all Bay Area fighters.

"Cupie!"

I looked up and Roscoe was walking up to me, a big smile on his face, hands already strapped into red eight-ounce gloves. He held up his right glove and we touched fists.

"Didn't know if you was gonna show, Cupie," Roscoe said. "Been holdin' on to your free tickets a week. Give him the free tickets, Ritchie."

Ritchie was back to his magazine. "Don't got 'em on me."

"Where are they?"

"Back at the hotel."

"The *hotel*?" Roscoe said. "Aw, man . . ."

"Would you fuckin' relax?" Ritchie said. "They're at the hotel right in the drawer. He'll get 'em."

Roscoe turned back to me. "You got two free tickets to watch me take out Johnson. Third row, ringside."

"I'll be there."

"Tell you what. When I knock out his mouthpiece, I'll try to aim it over your way." Roscoe smiled. "Souvenir."

"Appreciate the thought," I said, "but go ahead and aim Johnson's mouthpiece somewhere else. And what's with the hair?"

Roscoe rubbed his head with his glove. In all the time I've known Roscoe Laughinghouse he's always shaved his head and buffed it to a fine polish. At a Halloween party one year he painted a white "8" on the back of his skull and came as a billiard ball. Now a rough, inch-long stubble covered his head.

"I was thinkin' about it," Roscoe said. "Shaved head makes it look like I'm *tryin'* to be mean, you know? Bein' fussy with it, standin' in front of a bathroom mirror all morning like an old lady gettin' ready to go to a garden party. That ain't me. A junkyard dog don't have no time to do nothin' except be mean. If I come in lookin' just normal, scruffy-like, makes the other guy wonder."

"You're thinking about it too much," I said.

"Are you kiddin'?" Ritchie mumbled, lighting a cigarette and squinting down at the magazine. "All this guy *does* is think about his image. Should be thinkin' about his weight."

"Ritchie don't understand about image," Roscoe said with a smile. "Course, not his fault. Way he looks, image wasn't never an issue in *his* life."

Ritchie ignored that.

"And anyway"—Roscoe nudged Ritchie's shoulder—"what was that thing you told me the other day?"

"What other day?"

"The other day! The funny thing that baseball player said. Who was it?"

"Yogi Berra," Ritchie said.

"Right!" Roscoe said. "How was it again?"

Ritchie yawned, turned the page of his magazine. "Ninety percent of baseball is half mental."

"That's it!" Roscoe said, looking at me. "Boxing's the same way. This guy I'm fighting Thursday, Johnson, you know what he told the newspapers today?"

"What?"

"He said he *likes* to get hurt! He says one of his favorite things after a fight is to watch himself heal! He's doin' a psych job on me, so I gotta psych him back. Ritchie don't understand that."

"Sigmund fucking Freud," Ritchie murmured.

That stopped me for a second. Ritchie Dalgiacomo knew who Freud was? Ritchie Dalgiacomo knew Freud had a first name, and how to pronounce it?

"Hey," Roscoe said, expression sobering, "I'm sorry about all that shit that came down at the golf thing. Really. I was gonna call you up and say, you know, how sorry I was . . . "

"Thanks," I said. "As a matter of fact, I have a question to ask you about that."

Roscoe's face grew puzzled. Ritchie looked up from his magazine.

"About the golf?" Roscoe said.

"About somebody my friend Brad might have known in Las Vegas."

"Who?"

"A guy named Jerry Kerrigan."

I suppose if I'd dropped my pants and defecated on the floor while sucking my thumb the moment might have been more awkward, but not by much. Roscoe stared at me, Ritchie stared at Roscoe, my gaze went from one to the other. Three gunslingers facing off in a Sergio Leone movie, lacking only an Ennio Morricone soundtrack.

Then Ritchie folded up his magazine and announced that we'd been farting around long enough. Fuck it. This wasn't a high-school PE class. It was time for Roscoe to get to work, f'chrissake! He got up off his stool and went around back where the slack-jawed white guy was still pounding on the heavy bag.

"Wilson!" Ritchie shouted to the white guy. "Let's go! Enough of this crap! Let's get to work!"

Roscoe took the opportunity to sidle up close. "Ritchie don't like this shit," he said.

"What shit?"

"He don't approve of this Vegas underworld talk. He's afraid I'm gonna get corrupted or dump him or something. Kerrigan manages some fighters too. Ritchie's an asshole, man. You know it, I know it. But I gotta play the game right now."

"Can you answer one thing? Do you know Kerrigan?"

"Yeah, I know him. Not personally, but . . . " Roscoe looked over his shoulder. Ritchie was marching back with the white guy shuffling along behind. "You gonna be home tonight?"

I nodded.

"What if I come by around seven?" Roscoe said. "Easier to talk then, though I really don't got much to say."

"Seven o'clock," I said. "I'll be there."

"Good."

The white guy climbed into the ring and Roscoe did the same, waving a good-bye to me with his gloved right hand. The two of them began shadowboxing, warming up, and

Ritchie cupped his hand beneath my arm and walked me to the door, like a teacher hauling a bad student off to the principal's office.

"Been good to see you again, Quinn," Ritchie said, pushing open the entrance door and half-pushing me into the Tenderloin's soiled sunlight. "And I hope you don't take this the wrong way, but I don't want you comin' around Newman's again. Not while Roscoe's training."

"Take it easy, Ritchie."

"Don't tell me how to take it."

"I'm not here to cause trouble."

"Well, you're causin' it anyway. Look!" Ritchie put a pudgy finger up in my face. "You know as well as me our boy's got a focus problem. From day one he's got a focus problem. Before I came along he was just another wannabe in this dump, goin' nowhere fast. Under me he's beat twelve chumps in a row so he thinks it's gonna be straight chumps all the way up the line. Johnson's no chump. Last guy Johnson fought got his cheekbone cracked, here to here." Ritchie drew a line across the length of his face.

"Get to the point, Ritchie. And take your finger out of my face."

"My point is, this fight's gonna be a sonofabitch. When Johnson knocks people out they go to the hospital. He knocks out Roscoe next Thursday, our boy's gonna have a nice long rest of his life unloading orange crates in the Alameda dockyards. So butt out with this talk of who knows who in Vegas."

Every once in a while Ritchie looks like he might back up a threat with his own fists, overweight chain-smoker or not, and this was one of those times.

"I'm Roscoe's friend," I said. "I'll be his friend whether he's heavyweight champion of the world, or unloading orange crates in the Alameda dockyards, which is more than you'll ever be to him. You're his trainer. I'm his friend. Don't tell me how to behave around my friends."

"There's only one part of this conversation that matters," Ritchie said. "And that's that you stay away from the fuckin' gym till the Johnson fight is over with. I'll Fed Ex your fuckin' tickets to your house," he said. "So don't show up anyhow saying all I came for was the tickets. Do, and you're gonna hit the sidewalk face-first. No offense."

Then Ritchie whirled and headed back into the gym. The exit line had to be his, so I let him keep it. But if he'd stuck around I would've told him that there was no offense taken. There never was around Ritchie Dalgiacomo. Except for his cologne, of course. Offense always was, and always would be, taken there.

——22——

It was a long, slow crawl to three-thirty P.M. I grabbed a taxi back to the Union Street apartment, threw together a sandwich of sorts from leftovers in the refrigerator, fed the cat, fed the parrot, took a quick, remote-control spin through the wasteland of daytime television that left me feeling dirty and ashamed, then finally opted to lose myself in a paperback.

At a quarter to four the phone rang. It was Felix. The news was reasonably good. The abductor had called Peggy's house at the precise time he said he would. Peggy had talked tearfully with Alison for only a matter of seconds, but in that brief time it was obvious that Alison was all right. She was comfortable, she was eating, and whoever had taken her had not mistreated her. The bad news was the lack of anything from Brad arriving in the mail. Peggy had even spoken to the mailman, asking if he could check at the main post office if something might have been misplaced. Perhaps whatever it was had arrived in a box, or special delivery, and a minor glitch had it sitting in a back room somewhere. The mailman said he would do what he could.

I fought off the urge to ask Felix about Leonard's forty percent ownership of Platypus. To ask him why he hadn't volunteered the information the day before, when we were out being confidential with each other at the driving range in back of

Platypus's offices. I knew what he would say, anyway. Having Leonard Novak as your business partner isn't something you trumpet to the world. Felix needed money to keep his business going and his old golfing buddy Leonard wanted in. Simple as that. And then Felix would want to know how I found out about Leonard. Bill Prescott said the deal was at a sensitive stage and had asked us to keep our mouths shut. It hurt, but I kept my mouth shut.

Shortly before five o'clock Kate called and asked about Alison and I told her what Felix had just told me. Her guarded relief mirrored mine. Kate said that she and Carol had spent the afternoon at the zoo with the kids, and now were about to shift into adult mode. The boys had been deposited with Hank and the women were going on the town by themselves. Dinner, movie, two or three après-cinema cocktails somewhere. Assuming she didn't run into Mel Gibson along the way, Kate said I should expect her to come wobbling up the stairs no later than midnight.

After Kate's call I still had two hours to kill before Roscoe was due to show. I went back to the paperback but couldn't concentrate. I wondered if Roscoe would have any light to shed at all. Other than Mrs. Kirby, Kerrigan was the only person I knew of who would prosper by Leonard Novak's slow sinking in the west. Maybe Roscoe could fill in a few of the blanks—*if* Ritchie let Roscoe out of his sight long enough for us to get together at all.

Then my mind wandered and I thought about Johnson and the cracked cheekbone of his last opponent. Happy thoughts. It is madness to initiate a serious bout of worrying without a tequila in your right hand, so I tossed the paperback aside, pulled on my jacket, and walked five blocks down Union Street to the Bus Stop for a fortifying drink.

A hard, cold fog was blowing off the Pacific. Sometimes the foghorns in San Francisco Bay sound as polite and cute as manicured geraniums, tooting on schedule for the delight of the tourists. But in this thick gray twilight they seemed dead serious, booming urgent warnings into the dense mist. People hustled along the sidewalk, coats clutched tight, eyes watering in the wind. Just another balmy summer afternoon in everybody's favorite city.

I ducked into the warmth of the Bus Stop and took my usual stool at the bar. It'd been almost a month since I'd sidled up to the old watering hole, but nothing had changed in my absence. Time marches on, but at the Bus Stop it marches in place. A couple of well-dressed couples sipped Irish coffees at tucked-away tables. Flanking me at the bar were the standard half-dozen beer drinkers, augmenting their guts, watching the Giants-Cardinals game on the overhead television. It was a warm and sultry evening in St. Louis, the way summer was once described to me by ancestors who knew of such things. The camera zoomed in on the pitcher mopping sweat from his brow. I envied his muggy discomfort.

The cold walk and the impending talk with Roscoe got me out of the tequila mood. Suddenly I was craving something hot and nonalcoholic. Warm me up, keep my head clear. Roger came out from the stockroom and when he saw me he stopped, clutched his heart, and leaned against the cash register for support.

"I can't believe it!" he gasped.

"Save the theatrics," I said. "It's been a tough couple of weeks. Get me a cup of tea."

"A cup of what?"

"Tea. You make it with hot water and green leaves that look like oregano."

Roger leaned close and peered into my eyes. "You can't fool me. I saw *Invasion of the Body Snatchers.* How do I know you're the real Quinn Parker and not a pod person?"

"Roger . . ."

"I'm serious."

"Then ask me a question. A question only Quinn Parker would know the answer to."

"Okay." Roger leaned even closer. "What's my mother's maiden name?"

"I have no idea."

Roger relaxed, though his eyes showed he still wasn't com-
pletely convinced. "Okay. You dodged that bullet. The real
Quinn Parker didn't know my mother's maiden name, either.
So it's tea you want?"

"Please."

Roger put his hands under his apron and swiveled about,
mildly disoriented, doing a full three-sixty while scanning all
the bottles on the shelves. He was from Los Angeles and had
the looks, attitude, and general worldview of a dedicated
surfer. Mid-twenties, handsome, sculpted body, sun-bleached
hair, and a smiling, boyish, well-tanned face. Seemed like
everybody I was meeting these days had a glorious tan. Roger
lived a spartan life on a small sailboat over in Sausalito and
saved his money to go on mythic voyages in search of the perfect wave. His love life was said to be positively Bunyanesque,
the stuff of legends, though Roger made a game of modestly
pretending otherwise. Our enduring inability to find a single
common reference point was one of the most interesting things
about our friendship.

"Tea . . . " he mumbled. "Tea, tea, tea, tea, tea."

Roger disappeared around the corner and came back a
minute later with the tea, complete with saucer and dainty stir-
ring spoon. "Snuck a look at the bar book," he said confidentially. "What you do is let it just sit there for a couple minutes
and then take that little soggy bag out."

"Thanks for the technical information."

"Where's Hank?"

"Babysitting."

"Hey, listen." Roger cleared his throat, uncomfortable. "I've
been meaning to say . . . I was watching TV when that terrible
thing happened to your friend. I'm really sorry, you know . . . "

"Thanks."

"Because it must've been horrible."

"It was. But thanks."

Roger nodded, relieved that the ordeal of broaching the
subject was over. I sighed and looked down at the steam
swirling up from my tea, did a mental count of how many

acquaintances I hadn't seen yet who would have to fidget their way through the same thing. A stiff shot of Cuervo 1800 was sounding better all the time.

"How's the love life?" I said.

"Ah!" Roger winked at me, snapped his fingers, pointed. "Glad you asked. I got a present for you."

He ducked back into the stockroom and emerged a few seconds later with a paperback in hand. A romance novel, *Moon Flames*, with boilerplate cover art of a cleavaged female and steroid-freak male swooning into each other.

"I know you're a big reader," Roger said. "So here's something to stick on the old bookshelf!"

"*Moon Flames?*" I said.

"I'm dating the author!"

"Epiphany Daniels?"

"That's not her real name." Roger opened the book and pointed to the copyright information. "Lisa Wallace."

"I don't know how to thank you, Roger."

He lifted his palms to shoulder level. "Hey! What are bartenders for?"

I whiled away an hour at the Bus Stop, dividing my attention between watching the Giants game and scanning the turbulent sexual adventures of Epiphany Daniels's heroine, an overheated little number named Regan Trembly. A little before seven I paid my tab, thanked Roger again for the book, and headed back toward the apartment.

I was hoping Roscoe might already be out front, waiting for me, but he wasn't. I put the key in the door and marched up the stairs and it wasn't till I reached the first landing that I realized something was wrong. The front door lock hadn't snapped back when I'd turned the key. Somebody'd already opened it.

I looked up and saw Billy Useless standing twelve steps above me, at the top of the stairs, leaning on the banister.

"Keep on coming," he said.

His legs were crossed casually at the ankles, and I didn't hesitate. I whirled around and vaulted back down the stairs toward the front door, legs moving as fast as I could make them go without tumbling head over heels. It would have taken at least a couple of seconds for Billy to disentangle his ankles and start after me, but I was not aware of any pursuit from behind. He was letting me go. For some reason Billy Useless was allowing me to escape.

The reason was waiting for me at the bottom of the stairs. Another man had slipped in behind me from the street and was standing in front of the closed door, waiting. This man I hadn't seen before. He was wide and dark and had his feet planted as I descended the stairs, just in case I tried to batter-ram the two of us out the door and onto the street.

It was a good thing for him to have anticipated, because that's precisely what I did. I propelled myself headfirst from the fifth stair at top speed and slammed into him with a full-body block. No matter how big you are, how wide, how strong, how braced for impact, one hundred ninety airborne pounds hitting a stationary human target will cause the stationary target to go backwards. I heard the man grunt with pain. He grabbed my shoulders, but the momentum of my dive carried the two of us back anyway. Our combined weight of four hundred pounds hit the entrance door full-bore and it went away in a hail of splinters and we fell and rolled out onto the cold and windy front porch.

Whatever advantage I had was lost at that point. The dark man, still wheezing from the collision, grabbed me by the neck and dragged me back through the broken door to the foot of the stairs. He positioned himself above me, turned me onto my stomach, using his weight to hold me down, pressing my face into the carpeted stair. Billy Useless was on his way down in a hurry. I could hear the rapid thump-thump-thump-thump of his footsteps as he hustled sideways down the stairs, one step at a time. I waited till the thumping was almost on top of me, then instinct took over. I lurched up with a sudden twisting motion, broke momentarily free of the dark man's grip, and at the same time threw a blind uppercut to a spot I roughly calculated Billy Useless's testicles might be occupying.

I guessed right. There was an unpleasant little sound like a cockroach crunching underfoot, then a second of incredulous silence, then Billy Useless let out a howl that must have carried out the door, down Van Ness Avenue, and halfway to the Opera House. His mouth formed a tiny, fragile O and he went straight down in a crumpled heap, clutching his groin. His knees were clamped together and he just rocked back and forth, making strange high whimpering noises.

The dark man jerked me upright and spun me around. "You sonofabitch!" he yelled.

I never saw the punch coming. The fist hurtled out of the darkened air and caught me flush in the face. There was no pain. At least, not at first. There was only the overwhelming sensation of impact, the brutal slam of thing against thing that in the world of nature usually results in deep and permanent craters. I hit the wall hard and sank to a sitting position. Liquid bubbled from my mouth.

The dark man left me like that and hunched over Billy Useless. Billy still had a death grip on his balls, clutching them with both hands as though that was the only thing preventing them from falling to the ground and rolling out onto the front porch and bouncing down the stairs. His whimpering had stopped, though. Now he was merely breathing rapidly, a little hysterically, like a woman in the throes of childbirth, all the while trying to make his vocal cords function so he could let me know what he was about to do to me. The syllables didn't run together right, but I got the idea. It wasn't going to be good. I tried to move, but my head stayed flush to the wall as if cemented there with Super Glue.

The dark man left Billy's side and came over to me and matter-of-factly gave me a hard elbow to the jaw, just in case I'd forgotten that I was in the process of having the shit beaten out of me. My teeth rattled, but his elbow also woke me up. My head came unglued from the wall and I tossed a punch in his direction. It missed badly, and the dark man slugged me in the stomach, took me by the neck, and drove my forehead into the opposite wall. I heard a crunch. Bone or tissue or plaster, I couldn't tell. I just felt the light of the world ebb away, and my pain was replaced by fear. This wasn't getting beaten up. They were killing me. This is how I was going to die.

I slipped in and out of consciousness. Billy Useless was up now, still in serious pain, but furiously kicking me in the stomach anyway, shouting obscenities. That went on for a while, then both men had me by the arms and were dragging me up the stairs.

I felt my heels dragging along the hallway floor, then we were in the waning light of the living room. Billy Useless and the dark man let me drop hard on the wood floor, and Billy gave me another kick, this one to the face. It didn't even hurt. I was beyond hurt. All it did was move my head a few inches and give me a different angle on the ceiling. After the kick Billy clutched his testicles, doubled over in pain, and moaned a guttural moan.

Then the dark man took Billy aside and I could hear them arguing. The dark man was telling Billy to cool it. That if I ended up dead there'd be trouble from Leonard. I was only supposed to be hurt, not killed! Billy Useless told the dark man he didn't give a shit about what Leonard wanted. For a minute they argued whether I was going to live or die.

The dark man said no fucking corpses. If I *did* have the goods, they'd never find it with me dead. Billy Useless finally said okay, fuck it. He wouldn't kill me. At least not on this night. But he sure as hell was going to crush my balls permanently. The dark man said fine, crush his balls, but no fucking corpses. Billy got up and hobbled toward me. My head slumped to the side. Jesus.

I've heard and read many accounts of people who have died momentarily on the operating table and then come back to life with strange and vivid images of what it was like on the other side. Some talk of a bright warm light. Others of a tunnel, with a person dressed in white at the other end, beckoning them to enter. But none of them, to my recollection, ever mentioned having a vision of a two-hundred-ten-pound thug suddenly doing a mid-air cartwheel over a couch and landing headfirst into a dining-room table. But that's exactly what Billy

Useless proceeded to do. The angle of trajectory was a little different, but the dark man followed suit, launched like a clown from the circus cannon, crashing into the bookshelf.

I tried to lift my head, but the neck muscles wouldn't respond. So I simply lay there with my eyes on the ceiling, sensing the violence all around me. Feeling the vibration of the floor. Watching mayhem shadows on the ceiling. It didn't last long. A couple of sickening crunches of flesh against flesh, and then a different hand was under my head, lifting me up. Roscoe's eyes were wide with concern.

"Good God, Cupie!" he said. "Christ Almighty! Say something!"

I pushed the thick liquid away from my lips with my tongue. "Thanks for being punctual . . . "

"Oh, *man!*" He almost looked ready to cry. "What the hell happened to you? Who *are* these guys?"

"Sit me up," I mumbled. "But if I say stop, stop."

"You got it."

Roscoe put his hands under my arms and gradually hoisted me to a sitting position. I expected to hear my ribs rattle like a belly full of loose change, but there was no pain at all. An initial swell of nausea swept through me and I leaned over to gag, but then the feeling passed. Once the dizziness subsided, I actually didn't feel all that bad. Numb.

Groans emanated from the other side of the room. Roscoe scooted me along the floor so that I was propped against a chair, then he went out of sight. The floor vibrated twice, and the groans stopped. Roscoe came back.

"I gotta get you to a doctor," he said.

A distant siren wailed down Van Ness. It grew louder and louder and then came to an abrupt stop on Union Street, right outside. Roscoe ran down the hall, ran right back.

"Shit!" he said. "It's the police!"

"Good," I said.

"No it ain't good!" Roscoe said. "It's *bad!* I'm a pro fighter. Know what that means?"

"What?"

"I get in a fight with my fists outside the ring, it's a fuckin' felony!"

"No . . . " I mumbled.

"Think I don't know what I'm talkin' about?" Roscoe said. "There goes the Johnson fight! There goes the whole goddamn career! Shee-it! Ritchie's gonna die! Ritchie's gonna have a cardiac arrest for sure!"

Roscoe crouched next to me, rapidly rubbing his chin, thinking. I didn't have the energy to argue with him. Boxer or no boxer, how could self-defense be a felony? How? Then Roscoe got up and marched out of sight and the next thing I saw he was dragging Billy Useless in one hand and the big dark man in the other over to my section of the living room. They were groggy but conscious and looked atrocious. Bleeding, bruised, hair matted with sweat and saliva and whatever else. My stomach went cold thinking I might look like that, too.

"Okay, listen up!" Roscoe said. "There ain't much time and you better hear good. I never touched you guys." Roscoe pointed at Billy Useless and the dark man. "I never laid a fuckin' finger on either one of you. My buddy Cupie here's the one who did it. Me, I come up here to visit and all this here'd already happened."

Billy Useless didn't answer right away. He swished his mouth around like gargling with Listerine and spat out blood. "Fuck you, nigger," he said.

Roscoe leaned close to him. Put his mouth right up next to Billy's ear. I couldn't hear what he said, but Billy's eyes went a few millimeters wider, and when Roscoe backed away and restated the question as to who had trashed them, Billy glanced in my direction and nodded.

"Good," Roscoe said. "Keep it like that and all this ass-kickin's gonna come to a stop. Don't, and both of you crackers are gonna be shoppin' at Dentures R Us tomorrow."

I saw the gun first, the black, lethal piece of forged metal peeking around the hallway wall, held straight out with both hands. Then the policeman's arms came into view.

"Nobody move!" the cop shouted. Both the gun and the

command were directed at Roscoe. "Hands out away from your sides. Do it now! Out, where I can see them! Now!"

Roscoe held his hands carefully out away from his body like someone walking a tightrope. Another cop slid rapidly past the first one. He also had a gun. The officers were strung as tense as piano wire, both of them. You had the feeling one ping from an egg-timer in the kitchen and there'd be a blood-bath.

"Take it easy, officer," Roscoe said. "Nobody wants no trouble."

"On the floor!" the first cop shouted. "Now! Stomach down! Hands behind your head!"

Roscoe did as he was told, and while the first cop kept the gun on him, the other cop knelt and did a quick frisk and nodded that it was okay. Roscoe was clean. Then the cop checked me, the dark man, and Billy Useless. He pulled a far more serious-looking gun than their police issue from Billy's shoulder holster and immediately wrenched Billy Useless to the floor and held him there with his boot while completing the frisk. Billy Useless groaned. "I gotta license," he muttered.

"Shut up!"

"My balls're killing me."

"I *said* shut up!"

The second cop went over Billy Useless twice, carefully, then quickly released his boot and stepped back when he was satisfied Billy could inflict no more damage.

"What the hell's going on here?" the first cop said. It was the first sentence he hadn't shouted at the top of his lungs.

"I don't know what's going on," Roscoe said. "I just got here myself."

"You just *got* here?" the second cop said.

"Half a minute before you guys. Swear to God!"

The second cop looked at Billy Useless, the dark man, and me. "That right?"

The three of us nodded in unison. The two cops looked at each other. What the hell *was* this?

"I'm losing my patience fast," the first cop said. "Looks like someone tossed a goddamn hand grenade in here. I want the straight story and I want it now!"

"This is my apartment," I managed to say. "I caught these two guys robbing me."

The first cop waved his gun at Billy Useless and the dark man. "These two guys?"

I nodded. Closed my eyes against the pain of nodding.

"What happened?" the cop said.

"I stopped them."

"*You* stopped them?"

The cop sized up Billy Useless and the dark man, then looked down at me again. "You took out both these gorillas and their fucking nine-millimeter semiautomatic all by yourself?"

"Yes."

The cop looked at Billy Useless for confirmation. Billy wiped blood from his nose and nodded. The cop sighed, looked back in my direction.

"How'd you manage to do that?" he said with a smirk. "Throw pieces of your broken teeth at them?"

Nobody said anything. The first cop nodded his chin at the dark man. "What about you? That the way it happened? This guy half-dead on the floor caught you robbing his place and took you out?"

The left side of the dark man's face was swelling rapidly. Blood seeped between his clenched teeth. He looked first to Billy Useless, then back to the cop and nodded. The two cops looked at each other, relaxed their grips on their weapons. The first cop hooked a thumb in Roscoe's direction. "What was this guy for?" he said to me. "To mop the sweat off your brow once in a while?" Then, disgustedly, to his partner. "Better get an ambulance over here."

A second siren came wailing up to the doorstep fifteen minutes later and two white-suited paramedics trundled up the stairs with stretchers and carted the three of us out, stepping gingerly through the remains of my front door. A small crowd had gathered out on the sidewalk, braving fog and cold to watch the festivities.

I tried to tell the paramedics about my broken door, about how much easier it was for strangers to gain access to my apartment if there were no front door, about Lola the cat who might slip down the stairs and go racing out into the dark night forever. Sonia would never forgive me if I ever lost her cat that way. The paramedics needed to know about Sonia, poor dead Sonia, consigned prematurely to an endless darkness of her own, but there was something seriously wrong with my tongue and no more words would come. I closed my eyes, and the world folded in on itself like the shutting of a half-finished book.

—23—

Given the ferocity of the attack, I escaped with a minimum of damage. My injuries were not the sort that have you jumping up out of bed the next morning, a little stiff but rarin' to go, but neither were they especially serious. The doctor at S.F. General's emergency room clucked his tongue and pronounced me lucky. I had a mild concussion, bruised ribs, a lacerated tongue, and a half-dozen other minor but painful dents to the corporeal Quinn Parker.

I spent the first day in bed, being spoon-fed Jell-O by Kate. Hank and Carol visited briefly, bearing gifts of Godiva chocolates. Others tried to visit, but Kate screened them. The first time I hobbled to the bathroom I noticed someone had taken down the mirror. I asked Kate to please get the bathroom mirror out of hiding and reattach it. She did, reluctantly, and I took some time to stand there at the sink and assess the damage.

My head was shaped like an onion, purple and green and criss-crossed with a series of crusted abrasions. Two small lumps over my left eye. A nasty red welt on the tip of my chin. Kate's early-morning bandaging of my forehead had come loose and begun to unravel. I looked horrible. A bedraggled foot soldier from the Army of the Potomac, bruised and beaten and fed up with marching in the cold.

Kate's face appeared in the reflection, looking over my shoulder.

"If it's any consolation," she said, "you look much, much better than you did last night."

"Really?"

"*Much* better."

"Jesus . . . " I rubbed my cheek. "And you still love me?"

Kate stood on tiptoes and kissed the nape of my neck. She'd found the only spot on my body that didn't hurt. Or maybe it was the kiss.

The walk to the bathroom was about all the physical exertion I could handle for one morning. I groped my way back to clean sheets and warm covers and Kate sat on the edge of the bed and ran the tips of her fingers along my arm. Because of my presumed fragility, nothing had been said about the fallout from the attack. But the Words Not Spoken had gone on long enough.

"How's Roscoe?" I said.

Kate sighed. "The doctor said you shouldn't—"

"Never mind about the doctor. How's Roscoe?"

"Roscoe's fine."

"The police believe his story?"

"No."

"Is he in trouble?"

"Only with that disgusting manager of his. The police know he's lying, but there's nothing they can do. Everybody involved said Roscoe didn't have a thing to do with the brawl, so he's home free."

"He saved my life."

Kate nodded. "I know."

"What about the two guys who attacked me?"

"They're in jail."

"Both of them?"

"I think so."

I nodded, let my head sink further into the pillow. "And the door downstairs. You took care of it?"

Kate rolled her eyes in mock exasperation. "Yes, Quinn. I

took care of the door while you were asleep. I also took care of the dining-room table and the bookcase and the broken coffee maker."

"Coffee maker?"

"Somebody fell on top of it."

"Is it fixed?"

"It's in the garbage. I bought a new one. State-of-the-art. You program it the night before and the next morning it does everything but brush your teeth for you."

I nodded dully. It hurt to think of the old coffee maker gone. I'd had it for a decade. We'd kept each other company through some pretty rough times, me and that coffee maker. Kate could see I was taking it hard.

"There were heavy casualties among *all* the kitchen appliances," she said. "My juicer and brand-new food processor got taken out, too."

"I loved that coffee maker."

"I know you did."

"I've had it longer than Hank and Carol have been married. That coffee maker'd been to Mexico and back with me."

"And if this apartment came with a garden," Kate said, fluffing my pillow, "I would have dug a little hole out back and given it a proper burial. But for now I'm declaring an end to this absurd conversation. Close your eyes and get some more sleep."

I did. The afternoon and early evening blurred together in a montage of bandage changes, consumption of various soups and multiflavored Jell-O, and occasional creaky visits to the bathroom. The loss of my coffee maker took its natural place in the scheme of things. Ashes to ashes, dust to dust, grounds to grounds.

Then it seemed I slept a particularly deep sleep: long, hard, dreamless. An anesthetized sleep so the body could put the finishing touches on the healing process, and when I awoke I knew I was over the hump. Silence filled the bedroom. Horns honked below on Van Ness. Sunlight slanted through the bay windows and formed a perfect parallelogram of brightness on a patch of floor near the closet. Lola the cat was stretched out in the small expanse of warmth, sleeping. I closed my eyes. The world was beckoning to me. I was going to be okay.

I went out into the hallway to brag to Kate of my recuperative powers, then pulled up short. She was standing at the top of the stairs, talking to Detective Lorenzini. They were in the process of having a mild disagreement about something, and when I appeared on the scene they fell silent and looked at me. Kate gave me a you-blew-it look. Lorenzini smiled.

"He *is* awake," Lorenzini said. "Your girlfriend just told me you took a couple of knockout drops."

"Are you hungry?" Kate said, deflated.

"A little."

"Want to try some solid food?"

"Sure."

"I'll fix something while you talk to the detective."

Kate went off into the kitchen and I spent a few minutes in the bathroom sprucing up, thinking of what I was going to tell Detective Lorenzini. My face didn't look *that* bad. It had a burnished look, red and shiny from various ointments, but otherwise things weren't so awful. I looked like someone who'd accidentally driven past the microwave factory with the windows rolled down, that's all. The only thing that still really hurt was my tongue. Big black Frankenstein stitches ran the length of it.

Lorenzini was relaxing on the couch in the living room when I came back out.

"Great woman you've got there," he said, nodding his chin in the direction of the kitchen. "She shooed me away yesterday, twice, and was going to do it again just now. If my wife was that protective of me, my life'd be a hell of a lot easier than it is. My wife's thinking is, whatever mess I cook up, I'm in charge of uncooking it."

"You said you had a few questions."

"Only one question, really. But I'm willing to trade. Are there any questions you have for me?"

"Why so cooperative all of a sudden?"

Lorenzini smiled, leaned both elbows on both knees and

steepled his fingers. "I'll fess up, Parker. For a long time there I figured you were mixed up in this murder somehow. I *knew* you were lying about Brad and whatever got burned in the fireplace and you seemed all cuddly with the widow over in Sacramento at the funeral. Then the next thing I know you're in Palm Springs knocking down cocktails with Leonard Novak. I mean, come on. You can't blame me for thinking something was screwy. I thought you were in it up to your neck. But I don't think that anymore."

"No?"

Lorenzini shook his head. "No."

"What do you think now?"

"I think you just decided to strap on a six-shooter and be Wyatt Earp and got your clock cleaned for your troubles. Tell me I'm right."

"You're right."

"Good. Now that you're innocent and I know you're innocent, let's swap information. First me. Anything you want to know?"

"The two guys who beat me up," I said. "Kate said they were in jail."

"They are. One's going to be in for a while. The other's getting ready to post bail. He'll be out by tomorrow morning."

"Which one's going to be in for a while?"

"Gentleman by the name of William Hall. Everybody knows him as Billy Useless, though."

"Why isn't he going to post bail?"

"Two things," Lorenzini said. "The original charge is just robbery and assault. But Billy Useless had a modified semiautomatic weapon on him. That made his bail about fifty times more expensive than the other guy's. That's one. Two, Billy's still in the prison hospital. Seems you gave him your basic five-knuckle neutering job. They had to do some delicate surgery where you belted him, and now Billy Useless really *is* useless. No offspring for that guy."

"That's a shame," I said. "He would have been a terrific dad."

Lorenzini laughed. "Hey, he had a lock on my vote for father of the year! Anyway, he'll be out of commission for a while. But keep alert. When he gets out, he may harbor some bad feelings toward you. If you hear a squeaky little falsetto voice creeping up on you from behind, better assume it's Billy."

"Thanks for the warning. Now I'll tell you something. Jerry Kerrigan's in town."

"We know," Lorenzini said. "He have a talk with you?"

"Yes."

Lorenzini smiled. "Thought he might. If he looks you up again you can tell him he's not at the top of the suspect list anymore."

"Why not?"

"We've tied these two goons who beat you up directly to Leonard Novak and might have enough to move. That's the good news. Bad news is, we're not sure right now where Novak is. I was wondering if you had any thoughts."

"Did you try the Arroyo Seco Country Club in Palm Springs?"

Lorenzini nodded. "He's not there. Leonard Novak's all of a sudden dropped out of sight. Not that we've set up any kind of dragnet for him. It's just that my connection in Palm Springs says he hasn't been around the last couple of days, haunting his usual haunts. We think he might be up here, in the city."

I shrugged. "Your guess is as good as mine."

"That's it?"

"Sorry."

Lorenzini considered that for a while, nodding, pursing his lips. Then he abruptly pushed himself up to a standing position and exhaled. "If you come up with a guess that might be better than mine, give me a call, okay?"

"Okay."

Lorenzini walked over, leaned his head in the kitchen, and said good-bye to Kate. Then he winked at me and headed on through the hallway and down the stairs. When Kate heard the bottom door open and slam shut, she ventured out of the kitchen holding a cup of coffee.

"I don't like that man," Kate said. "Pushy."

"He's just doing his job."

"Listen to you," Kate said, putting the coffee down in front of me. "The new, compassionate Quinn."

"Getting kicked in the head would soften anybody up."

"Bill Prescott called earlier," Kate said. "He said you should give him a buzz when you're feeling up to it."

"Did he say what it was about?"

Kate shook her head. "Only that it was important."

I took a look at my watch. Almost eleven.

"Why don't you use the phone in the kitchen," Kate said. "I want to straighten up a little out here."

I went into the kitchen and dialed Bill's office number from the wall phone and leaned against the refrigerator while his secretary put me through. The new coffee maker was down at the other end of the drainboard, black and sleek and evil-looking. We stared at each other for few seconds. The thing didn't know it was only a coffee maker. It sat there with the arrogance of sculpture. We were going to have to get used to each other.

Then the line clicked and Bill was on the other end. We spent the requisite couple of minutes rehashing the terrible ordeal I'd been through, and how damn happy he was that I'd come out of it okay, and when that had been dispensed with I asked him what news he had.

"The vow of silence I extracted from you about Platypus is off," Bill said. "It's now public knowledge. Ameritime Sporting Equipment of Chicago, Illinois has just purchased Platypus for an undisclosed sum of money. Would you like me to disclose it anyway?"

"Disclose."

"Fourteen point nine million."

I took a second to let it sink in. "I thought the figures were more like seven or eight million."

"They were," Bill said. "I hate to admit it, but I think your theory of Brad getting killed to start a bidding war was dead-on. Even my source didn't know it, but under-the-table interest in Platypus absolutely skyrocketed after Pebble Beach. Ameritime had to throw another six mil over and above their original offer just to stay in the Sweepstakes."

"Fourteen point nine million . . . " I said.

"Firm. A done deal. Breaks down to roughly nine mil for Felix, six mil for Leonard." Then Bill sighed a disgusted sigh. "And me with my big speech about the ethics of business! Shoot, Quinn. I'm gonna take that dumb-ass optimism I was telling you and Kate about and dump it over the side of my boat the next time I go fishing. I'm just gonna give it the heave-ho and watch it sink. An honest man can't win in this world anymore. An honest man better learn to just bend over and take it."

——24——

After my talk with Bill I went straight back to bed and lay there awhile, hands linked behind my head, staring at the ceiling. It was amazing how many winners there were in this tragedy. Felix and Leonard were rich beyond their wildest dreams. Nikki wouldn't have to beg for Big Mac money anymore. The heat was off Jerry Kerrigan so he could turn his attention back to making dirty money in Vegas, and Mrs. Graham Kirby had experienced the joy of having landed a solid right cross on my overly inquisitive face. John Ratcliffe couldn't complain. One squeeze of the trigger had turned his second-place U.S. Open finish into a first-place U.S. Open finish. CNN had a solid week of terrific ratings. And somewhere in Chicago, high in a skyscraper with a glorious view, the executives at Ameritime Sports were doubtlessly clinking champagne glasses at a deal well-consummated. The only loser was Brad, and the loved ones he left behind.

I drifted into a troubled sleep, remembering the slow-motion images of Brad's actual death, replayed endlessly on national television. The millions of words printed for an insatiable public, and how faded the incident had already become in the public's eye.

I was tired. My eyes were heavy. I thought of Billy Useless and how his real name of William Hall made him sound so harmless. I wondered about the "something big" Brad had talked about, how it was supposed to have changed all their lives so dramatically. Money? If so, where was it now? Not in the mail to Peggy. It would've arrived by now, and Brad wouldn't have been calling private air charters at two in the morning. Was it stuffed in a mattress, like Leonard thought? And then there was Leonard himself. He'd sent his thugs up to pound on me, then dropped out of sight. Where was he hiding? Had he found a mattress of his own to crawl inside of? Or had someone given him a burial of his own?

These thoughts finally ushered me into a deep and dreamless sleep. I don't know how long I was out when I felt Kate nudging my arm. I struggled to open my swollen eyes, looked up into her face.

"Sorry to wake you," she said.

"It's all right."

"There's a man on the phone. He said he needed to talk to you. That it was urgent."

The cobwebs cleared in a hurry. I pushed myself up in bed and Kate handed me the bedroom phone. The man on the phone was Felix Stockwell, and he was in the throes of a full-blown panic. He went straight to the point without bothering to ask how I was feeling. Alison's kidnapper hadn't called for two days in a row, and the last message, right before the calls stopped, had been ominous. When they told the kidnapper that nothing had come from Brad, he got angry. Threatening. He said that he didn't believe Peggy knew nothing about what Brad had mailed. He said he was going to give Peggy three more days to come up with Brad's gift package or he was going to send Peggy "something" from her daughter to show that he was serious. Now two of the three days had already passed.

"What did he mean by 'something'?" I said.

"Use your imagination!" Felix said. "I wasn't going to stand there with Peggy and start wondering out loud if it was going to be a finger or an ear or a lock of hair, for Christ sake!"

"He wouldn't do that," I said.

"Why not?"

"If a severed finger shows up on Peggy's doorstep he knows all bets are off. The police and FBI will be crawling all over the case. He'll be finished. He's just trying to scare you."

"Well, it's working," Felix said. "Peggy's about to lose her mind over here. I vote for bringing the police into it now. Right now!"

I thought about what Felix had said. There was no good reason why the kidnapper wouldn't call as scheduled. He had everything to gain, nothing to lose. Unless, of course, he was sitting in a prison cell, waiting to post bail.

"You still there?" Felix said.

"Yeah, I'm here." Another pause. "Listen, the guy said we had three more days, right?"

"If we want to believe someone who's a kidnapper and a thug, yeah."

"Then we should wait the full three days. Buy as much time as possible."

"Why?" Felix pleaded. "Buy time for what?"

"Because police involvement could almost certainly mean Alison's death. These same people threatened Brad and made good on it. They're not going to get timid now. After three days I agree with you. We let the authorities know as quietly as possible."

There was a brooding, troubled silence on the other end. Felix didn't like it, but he saw the logic. He ran through his inventory of exasperated noises, then finally grumbled something about how I better be right, and hung up.

Kate came into the room after the phone call and sat on the edge of my bed. "What is it?" she said.

"Alison's kidnapper is upping the stakes."

"How?"

I told Kate the gist of the conversation with Felix. She nodded grimly, looked down at the floor.

"What do you think?" I said. "Do you agree with Felix? Do we go to the police right now?"

She thought for a while before answering. "No," she said at last. "I think you're right. If he promised three days, wait the three days. A little girl's life is at stake, after all. The worst thing to do would be to hit the SOS button ahead of time."

"There's something else," I said.

"What?"

"When I was getting beaten up, when I was stretched out on the floor in the living room, I heard Billy Useless and the other guy having an argument. Billy wanted to kill me and the other guy said something. I don't have it exactly clear in my head, but it had to do with Leonard, and how unhappy he'd be if I were killed before they found out where to get the goods. Something like that."

Kate's eyes locked onto mine and didn't let go. "These men thought if Peggy didn't have whatever it was, maybe you did?"

"That's how it looks to me."

Kate paused. "You don't, do you?" she said.

"Don't what?"

"Have whatever it is of Brad's that everybody wants?"

I sighed, let my head sink deeper in the pillow. "No, Kate. I don't. If I did, I'd've given it to them the moment Alison was taken."

"Okay," Kate said. "I just asked."

We were silent for a good half-minute. City sounds drifted in the window. Then Kate looked at me and said, "What else?"

"What else what?"

"There's something else on your mind," she said. "I can see it."

"Going back to sleep is on my mind," I said.

Kate didn't believe it, and she didn't appreciate that I was being less than completely honest with her. We'd made a vow back at Charlie L's in Palm Springs, after all. She gave me another minute or so to confess, and when I kept quiet she stood and went out of the bedroom without another word.

I listened to her footsteps go down to the end of the hall. Then I heard the living-room television click on. If my ears were sharper I probably could have heard her throw herself angrily into the overstuffed armchair and mutter a few choice deletable expletives under her breath. Seeing as how I was up to my neck in it anyway, I picked up the phone and dialed Hank. Asked if there was any way he could hop in the car and come over for a chat. He said he was on his way, and I hung up.

I leaned back in bed and closed my eyes. Kate, of course, was right. There *was* something else on my mind, a plan taking form, but I needed to share it with Hank. Share it with Kate and I might end up with tranquilizers in my tea and leg-irons in my bedroom.

Half an hour later I heard Hank coming up the stairs. He lingered outside the bedroom door for a moment, talking with Kate, then he came in by himself.

"You're looking better," he said, scooting the chair near the fireplace up toward the head of the bed and easing down into it. "A *lot* better."

"That's what Kate says."

"You should've seen yourself yesterday."

"Don't tell me."

"Scary. The Phantom of the Opera would've gotten more dates than you."

"I asked you not to tell me."

Hank smiled, started digging in his back pants pocket. "I've got a legal question for you."

"I'm not a lawyer."

"Doesn't matter. Can I get in trouble for withholding evidence from a crime scene?"

"Which crime scene?"

Hank looked at me. "Which crime scene? The one just a couple days ago that started on your front porch then crashed into the street and then went up the stairs and down the hallway and then went back and forth between your living room and the dining room. *That* crime scene."

Hank pulled a paperback from his back pocket. It was Roger the bartender's gift copy of *Moon Flames*, bursting cleavage, rippling biceps, and all. Hank set it on the foot of the bed.

"Didn't think you'd want friends, loved ones, or business associates to see this lying around the house," Hank said. "Your secret's safe with me."

"It was Roger's," I said wearily. "He gave it to me."

"Roger?" A momentary hitch as Hank tried to compute the information. "Are you talking about *our* Roger?"

"The same."

"Surfer Roger?"

"Yes."

"And he owned a book? The kind with words instead of pictures?"

"He's dating the author."

Hank looked dubious. "What you mean is, he's dating the bombshell who modeled for the cover."

"No. I mean he's dating the author."

"I'll be damned." Hank picked up the book, gave it another thumb-through. "Roger's moving up in the world. Next thing you know, he'll be going out with women who can do long division and everything."

"Let's not expect too much too soon. Did you give the book a try?"

Hank nodded. "I did like Samuel Goldwyn. Read part of it all the way through."

"And . . . ?"

"Not bad, actually," Hank said. "Kind of surprised me. The hero's this former space shuttle pilot who goes into politics. His name is Keldon Bannister. Tall, dark, handsome. Charisma that won't stop. Whenever he makes a speech his very presence is enough to excite all the women in the audience to instant sexual readiness. I mean it. One glimpse of his chest hair and the waterworks start from one end of the room to the other like a remote control sprinkler system."

"Sounds like a must-read." I yawned. "What else have you been up to? Is that sunburn I see on your face?"

Hank nodded. "I'm hooked, Quinn. I've got the bug."

"What bug?"

"Golf. It's all your fault. I took your advice and have been spending a lot of time out at the driving range and it's paying off. The game's really starting to come around. I've been out to Lincoln Park three times this week already."

"How can you afford to play golf three times a week?"

"The Tripple-Flipple people back in Wisconsin love my bubble-gum humor, that's how. They ordered up fifty more jokes at a hundred bucks per. That's five grand! Besides, Lincoln's a public course. Doesn't cost that much."

Hank then proceeded to launch into a blow-by-blow description of his last nine holes. Every putt that rimmed the cup. Each drive that found the fairway. He never swung and completely missed the ball anymore. He always made contact. Even his worst shots went at least twenty or thirty yards. I closed my eyes and listened and then cut him off when he began to describe the nine holes he'd played the day before.

"This is riveting," I said. "But I need to talk to you about something more important than your golf swing."

Hank got a hurt look on his face for an instant, then folded his arms across his chest and looked at me as if to challenge such a claim. "Fire away," he said.

"A few days ago Brad's daughter was kidnapped," I said.

Hank's whole body snapped alert. He sat up straight and his eyes went wide. "My God! Is she ... Do they still have her?"

"Yes. I can fill in on the details later, but I have an idea of who may have kidnapped her."

"Who?"

"I don't know his name, but I know what he looks like and I know where he is right now."

"Where?"

"At the city jail waiting to get out on bail tomorrow morning. He was one of the two guys who pounded on me."

The two of us fell silent. Hank picked up the thread and followed it without me needing to walk him through it.

"You'd like to see where this guy goes after he's sprung?" Hank said.

"Exactly. I don't know how well I can drive in this shape. But if we could do it together ... "

"It's done," Hank said. "No need to say any more."

I smiled. "Good."

"I mean, we're not going to go in shooting up the joint or anything, right? We just follow this guy and see what's what."

I nodded. "That's all."

Hank hooked his thumb toward the bedroom door. "What did Kate have to say about this?"

"I haven't told her yet."

Hank put his hand to his chin and mulled that one over. "Can I hang around tonight to watch you and Kate have your knock-down-drag-out?"

"No," I said. "Why don't you head home now and swing by here tomorrow early."

"How early?"

"Seven."

Hank winced. He is not an early riser. At all. He believes early morning is a cruel hoax perpetrated on man by a taunting and ruthless God. "Seven?"

"I don't know what time they start releasing bailed-out prisoners," I said. "I don't want to miss this guy. We'll only have one shot at it."

Hank saw the logic, reluctantly, and headed out the door. After he left I logged some time strategizing the presentation of my plans to Kate. All it did was lead me to the painful conclusion that there *was* no strategy. There was nothing to do but to just go out there and announce how things had to be and weather the storm.

I stood up and practiced my look in front of the closet mirror. I was seeking a delicate blend of pathetic and healthy. Healthy so Kate would realize I was fit enough to go driving around with Hank, pathetic so as to keep her from inflicting too much physical and emotional harm on me if my proposal struck her wrong. I'd been a bachelor for a long, long time, had grown unaccustomed to seeking the permission and blessings of others before acting. I didn't like it.

As it turned out, I couldn't have underestimated the fallout with Kate. I went out to the living room and announced my proposal with no formal lead-in. Kate took a momentary break from the television show she was watching, nodded at the end of my speech, said I could do what I wanted, then went back to the TV. My chest was all puffed out, but there was no battle to fight. I turned and wandered back to the bedroom, scratching my head.

The rest of the evening we avoided each other, but at night, in bed together, I was tired of the silence. A car roared up Union Street, the headlights forming fast-shifting designs on the ceiling above us.

"Why did you acquiesce so easily today?" I said.

"About what?"

"Me going out tomorrow with Hank. I was expecting more of a fight. I thought you'd be dead-set against it."

"I am."

"You hide it very well."

Kate shifted in bed, propped herself up on one elbow, and faced me. My eyes had gotten accustomed to the dark, and I could clearly see the features of her face. The hollow of her neckbone. The soft swell of her breasts beneath the sheets.

"I hope we live together for a long time, Quinn."

"So do I."

"Forever."

"Me, too."

Kate paused. Her eyes were bright and alive in the shadowy bedroom. "I think if two people decide to live together, they need to make sure their world keeps expanding."

"Pardon me?"

Kate shifted, sat up straighter. "When I was a little girl, dressing up and playing house, I did it because it made my world bigger. But then when I really *did* grow up and got married, my world didn't get bigger. It got smaller. It shrunk a tiny bit, every year. Every month. It happened with the man I lived with before the Prince. It happened with the Prince. It even happened with Craig, great tush or not. I don't want it to happen with us. This whole business with Brad . . . you need to do what you need to do without worrying about some scowling fishwife waiting for you at home with a rolling pin in her hands."

"Thanks."

"You don't need to thank me," Kate said. "All I ask is to be given the same parameters."

"You've got them."

She smiled, touched the tip of my chin, leaned down close and kissed me. "Then there's no reason why we shouldn't live together forever, is there?"

"None."

The sheets fell aside and Kate carefully, carefully eased herself atop me and lowered her body onto mine.

"How's that?" she said. "The doctors said we shouldn't do this for a while."

"Doctors used to think leeches sucked out bad blood."

"Then I'm not hurting you?" she said.

"We can work around the pain," I said.

And we did.

——25——

ank and I were entering hour number three of waiting
in the cold morning fog when I saw him. It is very tax-
ing on the eyes to scrutinize every single person coming
out of a busy building for three hours, and I was beginning to
doubt my ability to pick my own mother out of a crowd, let
alone a man I had only seen once, and even then from the
wrong end of his fist.

But there he was. The dark man, coming out of the swinging glass doors at the top of the steps leading to the city jail. He
walked with a slight limp, carried a paper sack, and wore a
square adhesive bandage on his face. He was alone, and he
stood for a second in the muted morning light as if to get his
bearings before descending the stairs.

"That's him," I said to Hank.

"You sure?"

"Positive. Go get the car, quick."

There was no three-hour metered parking around the city
jail, so we'd been forced to put the car in a garage around the
corner. The dark man hobbled down the stairs and stood on the
side of the street, maybe fifty yards away, peering past me.
Hank disappeared around the street corner. I felt my heartbeat
quicken. We couldn't let him slip away now, not after all this.
Then I saw the dark man take two steps into the street and start

waving his hand. A taxi darted out of the flow of traffic, pulled over to the curb and, after a brief discussion, the dark man picked up his paper sack and climbed in the back.

Damn! I tried to get the number of the taxi, but he was too far away. I looked back to where Hank had disappeared. Back to the taxi. They were still idling at the sidewalk. I could see the silhouette of the dark man leaning forward to say something else to the taxi driver. They both nodded, and the taxi accelerated from the curb and stopped at the first red light headed north, toward downtown.

Then there was a squeal of tires behind me and Hank was fishtailing around the corner at high speed. He braked for me, almost putting two wheels up on the curb, and I hurried to the passenger door.

"He's in that taxi," I said. "And try not to kill any pedestrians in the meantime, okay?"

"Piece of cake," Hank said, but I noticed he had the steering wheel gripped like Mario Andretti going into turn three at Indianapolis.

There was no need for any further stunt driving. The taxi took things slow and peaceful and we were able to lag back a safe distance all the way to my neighborhood of Russian Hill. The taxi stopped at Pacific and Larkin, only four or five blocks from my apartment, and let the dark man out. Hank and I drove casually past, tucked the car into a red zone in the next block, and waited.

The dark man looked around, fumbled in his pockets for some keys, then opened the door to a blue Ford Ranger pickup. He climbed in, slowly, gingerly, then without a moment's hesitation fired it up and roared away down Larkin, spewing exhaust in our faces.

I thought we might have a fairly long drive ahead of us and had insisted that Hank top off his gas tank the night before. I was right. The blue Ranger went out onto the Golden Gate Bridge, all the way up Highway 101 to the Blackburn Point cutoff, and then northeast, following the outermost perimeter of the bay toward Vallejo and the linkup with Interstate 80. I wondered if we were going back to Sacramento.

We weren't. The blue Ranger did indeed pick up Interstate 80 going east, but thirty miles later turned off on 505 going north, toward Redding, Mount Shasta, and the Oregon border.

"Jesus . . . " Hank mumbled. "I hope I have enough gas."

"We have more gas than he does," I said. "We'll be fine."

A dozen miles north on 505 the dark man made another turn, left, going back west on a two-lane road that passed through the town of Winters and then continued on to Lake Berryessa. I'd been on this road only last year, during one of Bill Prescott's failed attempts to turn me into a fisherman.

We eased through Winters, a summery little town of barefoot kids and hamburger stands and bait shops and John Deere tractors parked on Main Street. The blue Ranger continued through town and then picked up speed as the highway widened to Lake Berryessa.

"He knows we're following him," Hank said at last.

"Why do you say that?"

"I just know it. He's leading us way out into the middle of nowhere where he can quietly kill us and feed our bodies to wild boars."

I was about to answer Hank when the brake lights went on in the Ranger up ahead. He slowed almost to a stop, then made a sharp left turn onto a dirt road.

"I'm not following him up there," Hank said. "Unh-unh. No way."

"Keep going straight," I said. "Slowly. Let's find a place to park."

There was a turnout a quarter-mile further and we pulled the car in there. Hank cut the engine and looked over at me. "Now what?" he said.

"Let's walk."

"Up that dirt road?"

"Where else?"

"Come on, Quinn," he said. "You're in no condition to take

a hike. What if that road goes another five miles up the mountain?"

"Then we stop walking. I'm betting wherever our buddy is going is very close to the main road. There was a mailbox out there on the highway."

Hank shook his head. "I don't like it."

I opened my door and stepped out. "Then you stay here. I'll be back in a half-hour."

I began walking down the road back to where the blue Ranger had turned off. Hank was right on my heels. "Don't be ridiculous," he said. "I'm coming, too, goddamnit. Let's just not do anything stupid. Promise me that. We won't do anything stupid?"

"We won't do anything stupid."

"Can you put some sincerity in your voice?" he said.

"We won't do anything stupid," I said sincerely.

"Thanks," Hank grumbled. "I feel so much better."

I was right about the dirt road. We'd only gone a couple hundred feet when a single cabin appeared through the trees. The blue Ford Ranger was parked out front. We stopped short, crouched down in the brush.

A minute passed. No sign of life. The cabin was built in a clearing on a ledge. The shelf of the ledge extended about fifty feet, then sloped down to a scraggly canyon of weeds and rocks and what was probably a decent-sized stream during the rainy season. Behind the cabin was more forest. Dense, uncleared, rising gradually to become part of the small mountain range surrounding Lake Berryessa. There were no other houses in sight. The dirt road dead-ended at the cabin.

"I'm going to take a look," I said. "You wait here."

Hank groaned. "You told me we were just going to follow him."

"That's what I'm doing," I said. "Following him. Sit tight. If anything goes wrong, run like hell back to the car and get the police."

"Great," Hank said. "Just great."

I stood up straight and moved slowly along the tree line

toward the cabin. The ground beneath my feet was dried dirt, soft, smooth, and I was able to walk in virtual silence. I worked my way around to the back of the cabin and then took a second to lean against the wall, shut my eyes, and let my pulse rate return to only twice its normal speed. I could hear a funny sound from inside the cabin, but I couldn't place it. A familiar funny sound. Music, but not music.

I looked back to where Hank was waiting. I couldn't see him. Could only see the section of tree and brush where I knew he was crouching. I gave a reassuring wave anyway, then slid around the side of the cabin toward the front, my back pressed against the wall.

The curious musical sound got louder as I edged toward the front of the cabin. A window just to my left was cracked open a little, and I slowly ventured a peek inside. The dark man was in there. He had his back to me and was leaning forward in a chair, eyes riveted on the television screen before him. As far as I could tell, he was alone, a can of beer to his right, some potato chips to his left. The dark man was playing a Nintendo game. I got a flashing image over his shoulder of a yellow creature jumping from cloud to cloud, avoiding missiles, then I pulled my head back. There was something else in the room. Draped over the back of the chair was a black ski mask.

Five minutes passed. Seven. Eight. Then I heard the sound I was waiting for. The Nintendo music fluttered down in an electronic signal of defeat, and I could hear the dark man shift in his seat.

"Shit!" he said. "This goddamn motherfucker . . . "

I took another quick peek. He hadn't moved from his chair. He reached to his right, took a long slug of beer, shrugged some of the video-wars tension out of his shoulders, belched loudly, and started up a new game. Back to level one. If the dark man was anything like Hank's kids, he was going to be totally focused on demons and clouds and launched missiles for a good solid ten minutes.

I went back around to the other end of the house, tried to

force open the two windows but couldn't do it. They were locked securely from the inside. There was a flimsy-looking back door that didn't appear to get much use, and I tried that as well. Also locked, but barely. It was one of those doors that have a little button on the doorknob that you twist to lock and unlock. The kind of door juvenile delinquents can spring open in two seconds with a laminated driver's license.

It took me a little longer—twenty seconds, maybe—but the lock easily gave way beneath the edge of my Visa card and I softly opened the door. I was in a tiny room, seven feet by seven feet, that functioned as the laundry area. A mid-sized washer and drier to the right, wooden shelves hammered into the wall on the left. The shelves were filled with old rags, odd socks, plastic bottles of detergent and bleach, great handfuls of colored lint scraped from the dryer filter but not thrown away. An open door directly in front of me revealed a hallway, and at the end of the hallway I could see the flickering light from the video game and the stretched-out legs of the dark man. The left side of the hall was just flat, unadorned wall. To the right, halfway between the laundry room and the living room, was another door.

I eased down the hall, holding my breath, taking five seconds between steps. Blood pounded in my temple, bringing with it a headache that was gathering force like an avalanche. My lacerated tongue throbbed. I kept my eyes on the dark man's outstretched legs. The video game beeped and burped and rewarded points.

The door to the right opened easily, and I slipped inside. The curtains were drawn, but in the dim shadows I could make out the figure of a small girl hunched on the floor at the foot of the bed. She was utterly motionless, a gray cloth hood covering her head and neck. Her wrists were bound together behind her back, ankle cuffs clamped over her right foot and hooked onto an old-style metal radiator attached to the wall. She lay prone on the hard wooden floor, apparently asleep. There was a strong smell of feces and urine in the room.

I willed myself to be calm, to think logically. Outside the

door the Nintendo game droned on. I needed to wake Alison up soundlessly, keep her from screaming. I knelt down to her face, very gently lifted the edge of the hood, then quickly, roughly, shoved my right hand up and over her mouth. I felt the muffled scream in my hand, and I pulled the hood off of her head in the same motion. Alison's eyes were filled with terror. She looked up at me blindly, seeing and not seeing, jerking her head violently from side to side to escape my grip. I leaned my weight down on her so she wouldn't break free and scream, then put my mouth down so close my lips touched her ear.

"Alison!" I whispered. "Listen to me. Listen. I'm not going to hurt you. My name is Quinn Parker. Do you remember? I'm a friend of your mother's. We met at your father's funeral in Sacramento and talked about what subjects you liked in school. Do you remember?"

She quit fighting me, but the terror didn't leave her eyes. Her small body was absolutely rigid.

"You need to listen to me very, very carefully," I continued. "Are you listening?"

Nothing.

"Are you *listening?*"

She nodded twice.

"Good. The bad man who did this to you is in the other room. He doesn't know I'm here. I sneaked in. I'm going to rescue you. Do you understand what I'm saying?"

Alison nodded, but I kept my hand over her mouth nevertheless. "I want to let go of your mouth now, but you have to promise not to say anything. Don't make any noise at all, or the bad man in the other room will hear us. Okay?"

She nodded, but something in her nod didn't convince me.

"Do you want to see your mother today?" I said.

This time the nod was real. Urgent, desperate, yearning.

"Good," I said. "If you stay very quiet when I let go of you, you'll be having dinner with your mother tonight. That's a promise. Now, I'm going to count to five. When I reach five, I'm going to slowly take my hand off your mouth. Do you understand?"

She nodded again. I smiled down at her reassuringly. "You've been an extraordinarily brave girl," I said. "Are you ready?"

She nodded, and I counted slowly to five. At "five" I eased my hand off her mouth, ready to slap it back down if she panicked. But she didn't. Alison just stayed frozen where she was, looking up at me as if waiting for further instructions.

"Good," I said, forcing myself to smile even more. I began untying her hands. "Good! Now I need to ask you some questions. Okay?"

"Okay," she whispered, her voice surprisingly firm. She was ready to do this with me.

"Is there more than one bad man, or just him?"

"Just him."

"Good," I said. "He put handcuffs on your foot. Do you know where he has the key to get them off?"

She shook her head, and her lower lip began to tremble.

"Don't cry," I said. "Please don't cry. He might hear you. When we're on our way to see your mother you can cry your eyes out, okay? You can hold your mother and cry together."

She fought back the tears, nodded.

"Try to think, Alison," I went on. "When you talked to your mother on the phone, did you call from this house?"

"Yes."

"And he took the cuffs off your ankle so you could go to the phone?"

Another nod.

"Do you remember where he went to get the keys? Were they in his pocket? Did he go to another room, or look in a drawer?"

The lower lip started to go again. "I don't know," she said. "I'm scared!"

"Okay," I said, putting my hands on her shoulders. "You've helped me a lot. No more questions for a while. Stay here while I think how to get the cuffs off you. No more talking."

I got behind Alison and examined the anklecuffs. They were serious. A Visa card wasn't going to open these. I stayed down in my crouch and thought. The cuff was latched onto the metal pipe that came out of the floor and into the radiator. With a wrench I might be able to disconnect the pipe from the floor and slide the anklecuff off.

A wrench. There was a lot of junk in the laundry room. I hadn't seen a toolbox in there, but I hadn't been looking for one, either. I bent close to Alison again and tried to paint my face with optimism.

"I need to go to the next room down the hall—"

I got that far when she started violently shaking her head. The tears erupted. Chest heaving. "Don't go!" she said, loudly. Far too loudly. I clamped my hand over her mouth again and she silently wailed into my flesh. I stayed very still. Down the hall the video game continued to diddle along. Yellow cloud creatures dodging the missiles. The game would be ending soon. The dark man might take a break to come check his prey. I needed to hurry.

I put my mouth to Alison's ear again and this time I didn't try to sugarcoat it. I told her if she made any sounds the bad man might hear us and if he did she might *never* see her mother again. Her eyes went wide and I felt horrible to the core for scaring her, but it worked. When I took my hand from her mouth she barely dared to breathe.

I stood, carefully made my way across the darkened bedroom to the door, and cracked it open. I put my head out and took a cautious look down the hallway. The television still flickered the oranges and greens and reds of intense video combat. Electronic squeaks as more missiles were fired. I took a half step out into the hallway, then every nerve ending stood on end. Something was missing. The stretched-out legs weren't there. The dark man wasn't in his chair.

This realization hardly registered when there was sudden movement to my left. I ducked instinctively and felt something shatter just above my head, and then the dark man was ramming himself into me, smothering me, overwhelming me, taking me down hard onto the floor with all his weight.

Alison screamed. I felt sharp, stabbing pain all up and

down my back, moving like a line of fire from my left hip to my right shoulder. Broken glass. The dark man had his face inches from mine, and he was using his left forearm in an all-out attempt to crush my larynx. I fought his superior strength, trying to keep my own arm wedged between his elbow and my throat. He grunted, wheezed, pushed with all his might to get my arm out of the way. He was winning the battle. I felt his lethal strength easing down on me, a millimeter at a time. Behind me Alison screamed and screamed and screamed.

Then there was a hard, sharp crack and the dark man's face moved abruptly a half-dozen inches to the left. He looked confused for a moment, then fell off to the left and rolled away and lay there, very still.

Hank stood above me, still holding the heavy wooden cutting board in both hands. The dark man groaned and Hank smacked him on the head again, almost fearfully, the way you stomp on a scorpion two or three times to make sure it's dead.

"I heard screaming . . . " Hank said.

I nodded, closed my eyes, took great gulps of air. "Don't kill him," I said. "We need him awake."

Hank nodded, the chopping board poised overhead anyway, ready to let it come down again if the dark man made a threatening move. I dragged myself to my feet, held my head with both hands to stop the pain. I could feel the small rivulets of blood running down my back from where I'd been crushed into the broken glass.

The dark man was on his back, gurgling nonsense, trying unsuccessfully to right himself. He reminded me of a drugged rhinoceros. Hank looked from me to Alison and back to me.

"Now what?" he said.

"If he tries anything, smack him again," I said.

I got down on my knees and frisked the dark man for the gun that I knew wasn't there. If he'd had a gun he would have used it. Then I went into the laundry room and rummaged around through a few drawers till I found some loose pieces of extra clothesline. Back in the bedroom I rolled the dark man onto his stomach and bound his hands fast behind his back, then wound it down to his ankles and yanked it up all in one tight bundle, the way you'd rope a steer. Then I rolled him around again so we could be face to face. His eyes were clearing. He was suddenly aware of his predicament.

"Where are the keys to the anklecuffs?" I said.

The dark man looked up at Hank, then at me. "Fuck you."

"Where?"

"Fuck you and your mother both. I'm not telling you shit."

I grabbed him by the collar and jerked his head up so that it was close to mine. "There's no way we're leaving here until you tell us where the keys are. There isn't a single thing I won't do to you to get that information out of you, understand? Nothing."

"I never been so scared in my life," the dark man said with a smirk. Now that I could see him close up, could hear his natural voice, I was aware of how young he was. Nineteen or twenty, no more.

I stood up, leaned over, grabbed him by the neck, and dragged him out of the bedroom and down the hall into the living room. The video game had come to an end and was prompting the player to hit the start button to begin again. I dumped the dark man on the rug and stood over him.

"I dragged you out here because I don't want that little girl to see what's going to happen to you," I said. "She's seen enough these past few days."

"I'm real scared," the dark man repeated, but his voice had changed.

I turned to Hank. "There's some bleach in the laundry room," I said. "Can you go get it?"

"Sure thing," Hank said, and off he went.

The dark man glared at me. I leaned down again and got close. "I am absolutely dead serious," I said. "I'll do whatever I need to do to get those keys. You grabbed an innocent girl and terrorized her. You left her up here for two days alone, chained to a radiator, a hood over her face, no food, no water, letting her crap her pants. Then you come back and pop a beer and start playing a video game while she's in there huddled in her own urine. So to start we're going to hold your eyes open and pour concentrated bleach into them. If that doesn't get you to talk, we'll have to sit down and drum up some more painful ways to get through to you."

Hank came into the living room with the bottle of bleach. I told Hank what we were going to do and Hank gave me a startled look. "Bleach in his eyes?" he said. "Jesus, Quinn. That'll blind him permanently."

"He's done some permanent damage to that little girl in there," I said. "This will even up the score."

"But concentrated bleach . . . "

I held out my hand. "Give it to me. I'll do it."

I snatched the bleach away from Hank and opened up the bottle, and the dark man suddenly fought against his binding, wriggling on the floor like a fish pulled from the water.

"The keys're in the goddamn refrigerator!" he yelled. "Jesus Christ! What kinda psycho *are* you? Put bleach in somebody's eyes!"

"Where in the refrigerator?" I said.

The dark man was hyperventilating. "In the baking soda."

I went into the kitchen, sifted through the half-full box of baking soda, found the key. Then I went straight into the bedroom and uncuffed Alison. She instantly grabbed on to me and wouldn't let go. Her frail body was trembling and I held her while she sobbed and wailed a deep, to-the-bone wail. After a minute I took her by both shoulders and looked her in the eye and told her she was safe. She'd be with her mother in just a few hours. Alison nodded, tried to rub away the tears.

"I had an accident in my pants," she said.

"It wasn't your fault," I said. "We'll get you some new clothes first, on the way to your mother."

She nodded again and I told her to go into the kitchen and get some food and wait for us there, that we'd be ready to go in a couple of minutes. I led her to the kitchen, shielding her from the sight of her tormentor now hog-tied on the floor. I found some leftover pizza and a Pepsi and she greedily began to wolf it down.

Back out in the living room Hank and I dragged the dark man back into the bedroom and anklecuffed him to the radiator proper, not the pipe, so there'd be no way of breaking free.

When we were done I stood and slapped my hands and looked down at the dark man. "One more question," I said. "Who put you up to this?"

"Nobody."

"Independent operator?"

"You got it."

I sighed, looked over at Hank. "Better go get the bleach again."

"It's a guy named Leonard Novak," the dark man said. "Shit, man! What more do you want outta me?"

"Leonard Novak?"

"That's what I said, didn't I?"

"Where's Leonard now?"

The dark man forced out a short, hysterical little laugh. "Where *is* he? How the fuck do I know where he is?"

I glanced over at Hank.

"*I don't know where he is!*" the dark man screamed. "That's the truth! I never even met the guy! Billy set it up. Billy's the one who brought me in! All I know is Leonard's behind it. Put that shit in my eyes and I swear to God I'll come find you and kill you both!" The dark man was crying now. Big, blubbery, hysterical tears.

"I believe you," I said. "The police will be showing up here in a while. We might wait a day or two, though. Let you work up a little hunger. Some thirst. Give you a chance to wet your pants and get in touch with the child inside you."

The dark man wasn't listening. He was still trying to stem the tears, to dissipate the bowel-emptying fear of being blinded by maximum-strength Clorox. I signaled for Hank that it was time to leave and we shut the door behind the dark man. Out in the kitchen Alison had already demolished the pizza and was picking through the refrigerator for more.

"Let's go," I said. "We'll get you some clean clothes, call your mother, and get a hamburger and fries to go."

Alison didn't smile with joy. She started quaking again, cupped her hands over her face, and almost doubled up with the force of her weeping. I thought she would come to me, but she staggered over to Hank instead and buried her head in his stomach. He stroked and smoothed her hair and I could see the emotion rise in his gorge as well. This traumatized little girl could be one of his boys. For this moment, she *was* one of his boys. Children and parents recognize each other all over the world. They share a bond the rest of us don't.

I left them to it and went out into the bright sunlight and tried to ignore the pain of the broken glass in my back. I looked at the blue Ranger. Went over, released the hood catch, and tore a half-dozen wires and plugs and hoses from where they were and tossed them into the trees. Just in case.

Finally Hank came out of the house, carrying Alison, and I said I'd go bring Hank's car around. He set her down momentarily and dug around for his keys.

"I've got to ask you something," he said quietly.

"What?"

"Would you really have poured bleach in that guy's eyes?"

I thought about it a second. Looked back at the house itself. "No," I said. "I wouldn't have."

"Good," Hank said, handing me the keys. "We'll be waiting right here."

—26—

I n the town of Winters I placed a phone call to the hotel in
Sacramento, and Felix answered on the first ring.

"This is Quinn," I said. "Alison's safe."

A momentary silence. "What?"

"Alison's with me and she's okay. I can't talk long. This is
what I want you to do—"

"Wait wait wait," Felix said. "She's with you? Alison's with
you right now?"

"Yes."

"Good God! What . . . what happened? Who had her?"

"I can tell you all about that later," I said. "Right now I
want you to listen to me. Is Peggy there?"

"No," Felix said. He was still a little dazed. "She's downstairs having lunch."

"Tell her to get in her car and drive up Interstate 5 to the
Chevron station in Arbuckle. That's about fifty, sixty miles
north of Sacramento. She can't miss it. Tell her I'll meet her
there."

"You want her to come alone?" Felix said.

"That would probably be better."

Silence. Felix's mile-a-minute excitability stopped on a
dime. When he spoke again, he was almost whispering. "Are
you talking freely, Quinn?"

"What?"

"Is somebody there, making you do this?"

"No," I said. "This is no trick. If you want to come with her to make sure, that's okay, but trail up in your own car. She needs to bring a car for herself. Understood?"

"Sure," Felix said. "Understood. Jesus, Quinn! It's just now starting to sink in. This is terrific news! Wait till I tell Peggy. She's going to come apart at the seams."

"Tell her to keep from coming apart till she gets to the Chevron station in Arbuckle. Tell her I'll see her there in an hour."

I hung up and then the three of us went to a clothing store and bought Alison some underthings, a pair of jeans, and a white, summery blouse. I picked up an unbloodied shirt for myself. The elderly woman running the store watched us warily. Alison changed and cleaned herself up in a gas station restroom, then we were on our way, north on 505, to the rendezvous with Peggy in Arbuckle.

Peggy was there waiting for us when we turned off Interstate 5 and swung around to the back of the Chevron station. Felix was with her. For some reason I'd foolishly imagined how I would recap the details of the rescue for Peggy, and how she would listen and nod her head and ask for Alison to stay quiet a little bit longer while Uncle Quinn was talking. Nothing of the sort happened or was ever going to happen. Peggy and Alison rocketed toward each other like heat-seeking missiles and collapsed, literally, in a wild embracing pile of kisses and hugs and feverish stroking.

Felix came over and hugged me. He didn't know how I'd done it, but I'd done it, and that was all that mattered. I introduced him to Hank and explained that Alison wouldn't be here without him, so Felix went ahead and hugged him, too. Hank smiled sheepishly. Said something about danger being his middle name.

Then I took Peggy aside and told her what I wanted her to do. She and Alison were to get in her car and drive somewhere that would be completely safe. She wasn't to tell anybody where she was going. Nobody. Quinn Parker included. I pulled my wallet out of my back pocket and gave her some money. I also gave her Detective Lorenzini's card from Monterey.

"This is the only person I want you calling," I said. "The *only* person. He's the homicide detective working on Brad's case."

Peggy nodded that she remembered. He'd come to Sacramento once to talk to her about Brad.

"Then you know he's a little rough around the edges," I said, "but you can trust him. Check in with him every other day or so. He'll let you know when it's safe to come back."

"It's not safe now?" Peggy said.

"No."

"But I thought you got the kidnapper."

I exhaled. "There are others involved."

Peggy nodded, looked over at Alison. "I don't care if others are involved," she said. "I've got my daughter back. Nobody is going to take her again. They'll have to kill me first."

Then the three of us split in separate directions. Peggy turned north on Interstate 5, toward Oregon, Washington, Canada, the far, far reaches of the Yukon. Felix headed back to Sacramento. Hank and I got on 505 for the two-hour return trip to San Francisco.

We stopped along the way, at a medical clinic in Fairfield, so a doctor could dig the broken glass out of my back. He did his job in silence, nurses looking in from time to time at the desperate character who'd come off the highway with a banged-up face and taped ribs and bits of Pepsi-Cola glass embedded up and down his back like they were pellets shot out of a scatter gun. I paid my bill and Hank and I got back in the car and drove away. As we left the parking lot I could see the white-jacketed doctor standing at the window, watching us go. Taking down a license number, no doubt, just in case.

In the city I directed Hank to drop me off where my van was parked, around the block from my apartment.

"You going somewhere?" Hank said.

"Yes."

"You've got to be kidding. Where?"

"Let's just say an interested party."

Hank glanced over at me. "What about the interested party waiting for you back on Union Street?"

"This visit won't take long."

Hank pulled alongside my van and I got out. "Can I tell Carol what happened today?" he said.

I thought about it. "Sure. As long as it stays between the two of you."

"Would it be okay if I tell her that I took out that monster with my bare hands instead of hitting him from behind with a cutting board?"

I nodded. "If danger is your middle name, that's the way it should be. Your secret will be safe with me."

"Watch yourself," Hank said, and then he drove away.

I was parked out in front of 1222 Lake Street for almost an hour waiting for her. I'd just made a decision to give it ten more minutes and then go home when I saw a silver Lexus turn off Nineteenth Avenue, head directly for me, then swerve sharply into the driveway.

Nikki popped out, locked the door, and hustled up the walkway, looking sexy and windblown in a tight short skirt and heels. She was carrying a Nordstrom's shopping bag and seemed to be in a big hurry.

I watched her go into the house, let another five minutes tick off, then eased out of the van. This was a long shot, but one worth taking. Leonard had dropped out of sight in Palm Springs. If he'd gone anywhere it was reasonable to assume that he might have come to San Francisco. Check up on his blushing bride. Maybe stick around long enough for a conjugal visit. Lorenzini had probably already checked it out, but the good detective hadn't said a word about Nikki, ever, and the possibility existed that he actually might not know at all about her second residence here in the city. I took a look at the Lexus as I walked by. Brand-new, right out of the showroom, the list of dealer options still taped to the inside of the window. I rang the doorbell and waited.

No intercom this time. Nikki swung the door wide open like she was expecting somebody. When she saw me her face fell, and the door halfway closed.

"Hi, Nikki."

She took a look at my face. "What the hell happened to you?"

"Your husband's business associates like to settle things with their fists."

The right side of her mouth went up in a smile. A head-cocked-to-one-side smile. "Told you, didn't I? About what'd happen if you messed with Leonard."

I looked back at the Lexus. "Nice car. What happened to the turd-brown Subaru?"

"I traded it in."

I nodded. "That was a hell of an upgrade. You expecting a turnabout in your fortunes?"

"I don't have to stand here and listen to this," she said.

"Then why don't you invite me in?" I said. "You can stand inside and listen to this."

She smirked. "If you thought I was serious about giving you a frisk the next time you showed, you're wrong. Loosen up with some of that fifty grand you were going to give me and go hire a pro."

"Where's Leonard?"

Nikki let her mouth fall open and her head nodded up and down as if bouncing on a spring. "Hey, who are you? You think we know each other? You think you can just—"

My courteous approach wasn't working, so I tried something a little more direct. I lowered my left shoulder and went hard into the half-opened door and practically bowled Nikki over. She staggered back three steps and I slammed the door behind me. Her face was bright red with fury and fright.

"You better have a damn good lawyer!" she muttered under her breath. "Because you're in a *shit*load of trouble!"

"I thought you were the one who hated litigation, Nikki."

She kept backing up and I kept moving forward. But I wasn't going to push it. This was a woman who'd keep a loaded gun in the silverware drawer.

"Where's Leonard?" I said again. "And quit moving backwards. Stay right where you are."

She stopped. "Touch me and you're dead," she said.

"Get it through your head," I said. "I don't want to touch you. Ever. A little girl's just been through something no child should ever have to go through and I'm sick to death of your lies and your cut-rate imitation of a sex kitten and your 'fuck you' T-shirt. Leonard's in a lot of trouble and I want to know where he is."

"Leonard's been in trouble all his life."

"Unh-unh. This time he's gone over the edge. He ordered the kidnapping of a little girl, and the people involved have already named Leonard. Protect him now and you're going to be thrown in jail, too."

Nikki stood utterly motionless. She was thinking it over. "Leonard called me this morning," she said at last.

"Where was he?"

"Shit, I don't know where he was. Palm Springs, I guess. That's where he usually is. I mean, Leonard doesn't call me up and say, 'Hi, darling, I'm in Palm Springs as usual.'"

"What did he call about?"

"You saw it parked out front. He told me to go ahead and get the car I wanted."

"What else?"

"Nothing else."

I'd gone as far as I could with Nikki. I waved her off, disgusted, and marched out of the house and toward my van. She came out on the porch and yelled some obscenities at me. A couple of the conjugations I'd never heard before. The neighbors must have been delighted when Nikki Novak took up residence on Lake Street.

"And what about the fifty grand you said you were going to hand over?" she shouted after me. "What about that, you lying piece of shit!"

I kept walking. Got in the van, turned the key, and got the hell out of there as fast as I could.

27

Kate wasn't home when I got back to the apartment. I went to my office and sat down at the desk and hung my head. All of a sudden my whole body ached. I got out Detective Lorenzini's card and tried his office in Monterey. A woman said he'd gone home for the day so I gave his personal number a ring and he picked up the phone in the middle of the second ring. I identified myself and Lorenzini expressed mild surprise to be hearing from me at home. He asked what was up and I told him. The abduction of Alison, her rescue, the dark man up there in the cabin in Winters, handcuffed to the radiator.

"Sonofabitch!" Lorenzini said at the end of it. "And this guy fingered Leonard Novak?"

"That's right."

"Sonofabitch . . . " Lorenzini said again.

"Do you know where Leonard is?"

"No," Lorenzini said. "But with this information we have enough to quit farting around and move. I'll formally charge him and then we'll have an easier time lifting up the rocks to see where he's hiding. If he's still alive, that is."

"His wife said she talked to him this morning."

"She could be lying. You're talking about that Nikki broad, right?"

"Right."

"That woman's already lied to me so much I don't know if I'm coming or going," Lorenzini said. "I wouldn't believe a single thing that ever came out of her mouth. If she said he called her, he didn't. If she says he's alive, he's dead. I mean, we've been looking for Novak pretty seriously and haven't come up with diddly. When people disappear that thorough, it usually means they're at the bottom of some lake."

"This guy in the cabin," I said. "He let Peggy's little girl sit there on the floor in her own urine, no food, no water, while he slugged down beer and played video games. I was hoping you could indulge my childish wish and let this guy sit there for a day or two."

Lorenzini laughed. "Appreciate the sentiment, Quinn, but no can do. We'll send somebody to pick him up right now. I'll make sure he has a rough night in jail, how's that?"

"Suppose it'll have to do."

I hung up and walked slowly to the kitchen and dug around the refrigerator for leftovers. I was picking at some questionable meatloaf when the phone rang. It was an Officer Orwood from the Indio city police. He said they'd spoken to Brad Helfan's widow the day before and were given to understand that I was authorized to handle some of Brad Helfan's affairs in Palm Springs. At least, she had given them this number. I told them yes, that I was helping Peggy through this difficult time, and Officer Orwood said that Brad had parked a recreational vehicle on city-owned property and the vehicle had to be moved immediately or be impounded. Normally they would just have the vehicle towed away, Officer Orwood said, but this was a special case. There'd been a murder involved, and the police had gone through the RV. The law now required that either Peggy or some other authorized person had to come down, look at the vehicle, and sign a statement that the police had not stolen, damaged, or in any other way altered the vehicle illegally while it was in their custody. The officer sighed. It didn't used to be like this, but with all the suing going on, this was the only way the police could not be held liable later on. I

asked if there was a deadline and Officer Orwood said the
sooner the better. The city of Indio would like it off the property within the next couple of days, anyway.

I asked him to hold on a minute. I held the receiver in my
lap and thought about it. Why not? This was the perfect excuse
for me to take one more quick trip down to the desert. Ask
around at Arroyo Seco. The Foxy Female. Torp's pool hall in
Cathedral City. Just a day or two. See what was what.

I got back on the phone and told Office Orwood I'd be
down to take care of Brad's vehicle either tomorrow or the day
after. Orwood said what I should do was go to the vehicle first,
look it over, then come down to police headquarters and sign
the release of liability form. He gave me directions to both
Brad's Airstream and the police headquarters in Indio, told me
he appreciated the cooperation, and hung up.

An hour later I heard the door downstairs open and Kate
came trudging up the stairs. She was carrying two sacks, one
large, one small. She set the bags on the dining-room table and
came over to where I was sitting and held my face between her
hands and gave me a long, slow, delicious kiss.

"Hank told me all about it," she said. "You found that little
girl."

"You're not mad?"

Kate smiled, stood up, and went over to the large paper
sack. "Dinner for two from Stars," she said, pulling out a couple of styrofoam containers. Then, from the smaller sack, a bottle of Mumm's. "Champagne for two from Kate Ulrich."

She set the table and lit a candle and we ate watching the
sun set behind the Golden Gate Bridge. The champagne didn't
last long, so Kate got up and rummaged through the closets
and came back with a bottle of wine.

"You mean all I have to do is rescue innocent children from
the clutches of evil men and I get this kind of treatment?" I
said.

"That's all it takes," Kate said.

I picked up my wineglass, clinked it against hers. "How
about if I return the favor?"

"What do you mean?"

"The Indio police called earlier this evening. They need me to come down and get Brad's Airstream off the property. I thought maybe you, Hank, Carol ... the four of us could go. Make it kind of a mini-vacation."

"Quinn ... "

"No, wait a minute. There's a sumptuously tacky hotel in Palm Desert where we could stay. Palm Desert. That's a good fifteen miles from Palm Springs so you don't have to have any memories or associations with the Prince. It has a spa. Tennis. You and Carol'd have a ball. It won't be like when we went down before, with you sitting around a hotel room by yourself, remembering how the rendezvous with the Prince flopped. Come on. What do you say?"

Kate smiled, put her hand gently on top of mine. "I say your idea is wonderful. You should call Carol and Hank tonight and invite them. But I can't go."

"Why not?"

"Because I have three important job interviews lined up, beginning tomorrow."

I slouched back in my seat. "Can't you line them up another time?"

"Don't pout," Kate said. "You know full well this is what I have to do. Now, here." She reached back, picked up the kitchen phone, and set it down in front of me. "Call Carol and Hank. My mundane need to find honest employment shouldn't get in the way of the rest of you having some fun."

"Be honest with me, Kate," I said. "Do you really have a job interview tomorrow, or is this a way of begging off Palm Springs?"

"It's real," Kate said. "Bowles and Melton Advertising Agency. Nine-thirty sharp. Mr. Herbert Thompson, director of personnel."

"What's the position?"

"Assistant to one of the VPs."

"Secretarial?"

"No. Supposedly I'd be out there in the field, selling the

people of America things they don't know they need yet."

"I thought you disliked advertising," I said.

"I do. But I dislike sitting around even more and in six months all my savings are going to be gone and I'm not the kind of woman who'd be comfortable asking you for an allowance." Kate sighed. "The position pays well, and it'd be nice to make some decent money for a change, too. I've done the other. Waitressed in Key West. Manned a cash register in Stowe. Sold homeopathic medicine in a head shop in Colorado because I believed in it. Who knows? Maybe I could bring a soul to the advertising world. Probably not. If I sound confused, Quinn, I am."

There was a moment of silence, then Kate waved off her confusion like it wasn't worth the fuss. She picked up the phone and plopped it a couple inches closer to me. "So call!"

I did. Hank and Carol had nothing lined up for the next couple days, and they jumped at the invitation. Their two boys had just started a summer arts and crafts program up in Mendocino and would be gone camping for a week, so this would be the perfect time to steal away for a little trip.

I hung up and looked at Kate. "Done."

"As it should be," she said. "Just remember to send postcards."

─28─

The Alaska Airlines flight out of San Francisco was the same one Kate and I had flown on earlier. Same bundled-up Eskimo painted on the tail, same rushed snack and beverage sequence, same arrival time in Palm Springs. The broiling heat awaiting us hadn't changed, either. Midmorning or not, you could still feel your eyebrow hair crackle and singe.

We rented a car at the airport, jacked up the air-conditioning as high as it would go, and drove to the Marriott's Desert Springs Resort and Spa in Palm Desert. The hotel is substantially bigger than the Palm Springs airport terminal, runway and all, with a rain-forest motif gone amok. The ten-story-high lobby features splashing waterfalls, screeching parrots, and tangled vines hanging from the roof like high-voltage wires left dangling after a storm. Little concrete streams zig-zagged through the lobby, past cubbyholes where guests sipped cocktails, eventually cascading down an extended series of concrete steps and emptying into a greenish lagoon.

"This isn't a hotel," Carol said, turning three hundred sixty degrees to take it all in. "It's a theme park with rooms!"

She was right. One half-expected to see monorails and guides and booths selling cotton candy. In the green lagoon at the bottom of the lobby the motif shifted from Brazilian jungle to Italian waterfront, with several parked gondolas manned by brightly uniformed gondoliers whose job it was to ferry guests across hokey manmade waterways to their rooms. In and around the lobby itself were garish stores selling every kind of kitsch imaginable. Trick tennis balls that disintegrate on contact. Head-to-foot red plastic cowboy outfits for little children. Atrocious paintings of full-busted Indian women direct from the Raquel Welch gene pool, clad in deerskin miniskirts, gazing off across purple landscapes of tepees and buffaloes.

"This is *so* horrible!" Carol said, a wide grin on her face.

"You want to go somewhere else?" I said.

She whirled on me. "Absolutely not! This is the place. When you said 'tacky' back in San Francisco, I never imagined anything so . . . "

"Tacky?"

"Exactly! This is more than I could ever possibly have hoped for."

"All this running water . . . " Hank said ominously. "How do the guests keep from wetting the beds?"

We registered and signed up for adjoining rooms on the seventh floor, and the young woman working the desk seemed surprised when we chose to walk to our rooms rather than endure the canopied boat ride. The gondoliers were probably not required to sing Venetian boat songs while poling us slowly through the parched desert air, but one can never be too sure.

I took a quick, cool shower. Hank and Carol opened their suitcases just long enough to extract bathing suits, and they were off to the pool. I said I'd be joining them later, then got in the car and headed back toward Palm Springs proper and the Arroyo Seco Country Club.

It wasn't until I eased into the red-brick driveway past the Members Only sign that I remembered I didn't have a permission slip this time from Nikki. Damn. I slowed down to try to formulate a seat-of-the-pants strategy. Maybe I wouldn't need a permission slip this time. Maybe the pleasant old man with the kind manner and thick bifocals would remember me from before and dispense with formalities.

No dice. A different guard was manning the checkpoint,

and he was all business. This guy was tall, strapping, and handsome, with shaggy blond hair, pale eyes, and a full, sensual mouth turned south at the edges in a smoky frown. He bent down to my window, stared at me like I'd just been the guy fingered from a child-molestation lineup, and asked me to "state my business." No hi, howdy, or kiss my ass. State your business.

"I'm looking for Leonard Novak," I said. "My name's Quinn Parker."

The guard went back into his little booth and scanned a sheet of paper. He came back out, bent down again, shook his head. "Nothing here."

"I realize that," I said. "He's not expecting me."

The guard just looked at me.

"Is Mr. Novak here?" I said.

"We aren't authorized to give out that information."

"You can't even tell me if he's here or not?"

"No."

I rubbed my chin, looked grimly at the steering wheel. The guard kept staring at me with his vacuous pale eyes. "This is bad," I said. "I don't know what to do."

"What's the problem?"

"There's been a medical emergency with his wife in San Francisco and I urgently need to get in touch with him."

Shameless.

"A medical emergency?" the guard said. "Mrs. Novak?"

"She's still alive, but . . . oh, never mind. I understand your predicament. Policy's policy. But if Mr. Novak *does* come by, could you please, *please* tell him I'm staying at the Marriott over in Palm Desert? It's very critical."

The guard stayed in his crouch, thinking about it. "What happened to Nikki?"

"You know her?"

"Yes."

I bet he did. "Car accident," I said.

He gave me the once-over. "You in the car, too?"

"Yes," I said. "But I was wearing my seat belt, thank God."

"Hold on a minute."

The guard stood, went back into his booth, turned his broad back to me, and picked up a phone. I took a deep breath. Jesus. Every year it was getting harder and harder to go where six-dollar-an-hour people didn't want you to go. I thought of the teenage stockboy guarding his Dumpsters against illegal french fries. The bony character at the Pebble Beach locker room, bragging how he'd keep out Jack frigging Nicklaus if he wasn't sporting the required little green tag. People like that forced honest, upright citizens of faultless reputation, like myself, to invent lies.

I could see the jaw muscles going as the guard spoke into the phone. Maybe he was calling Leonard. Then it struck me that Nikki's San Francisco number might be on file, and the guard could well be checking to see if there really *was* an emergency. In which case he'd be making a second call, for backup security to hustle my scheming butt off the premises.

The talk went on for a while, then an extended period of silence, then more talk. I was about to ease the car into gear and quietly motor away when the guard hung up and came back out to crouch down at my window.

"The reason I called is because I've been on vacation," the guard said. "The guy who was taking my place says Mr. Novak hasn't been at the club for the past couple days."

"Not at all?"

"Nobody's seen him."

"Okay," I said. "Thanks a lot for your help, anyway. This'll mean a lot to Mrs. Novak."

I smiled a brave smile and the guard gave me an expressionless half-wave. I waved back and layered on another coat of heartfelt appreciation. When a brittle prig actually shows some flexibility in the face of regulations, you need to encourage it.

I did a U-turn away from the Arroyo Seco Country Club and gave passing thought to going out to Indio and giving Brad's Airstream a look. But the midday heat was cranking up and it would involve about a fifty-mile round trip. I had told the Indio cop that I'd get to it today or tomorrow. I decided to relax a little and make it tomorrow.

Back at the Marriott Desert Springs I went to my room, took another cool shower, checked my bodily damage in the full-length bathroom mirror, then changed into light cotton desert wear and took the elevator down to the lobby.

I'd asked Hank and Carol to come with me to Palm Desert for several reasons. One, they were my friends. Two, after Billy Useless and the dark man had pounded on me, Carol stayed with Kate every minute of the first twenty-four hours, answering phones, running errands, taking care of the day-to-day. Three, Hank and Carol were coming off the roughest period yet in their marriage and seemed on the brink of turning a new, brighter corner. Four, they had a ninth anniversary coming up in July. This trip would be a thank-you and celebration of all the above, wrapped into one. Consequently, I wanted the dinner I was treating them to tonight to be warm and romantic and special.

I went up to the reservations clerk and asked his advice on where we should have this dinner. I was quite specific regarding the requirements of this meal. The food had to be excellent, with price no object. Great atmosphere. Dark and romantic, but with a minimum of pomposity. A place with waiters whose first names remain a mystery for the duration of the meal. Absolutely no employees singing Happy Birthday to the patrons at tableside, and no tropical-fish aquarium in the waiting area.

The clerk was with me all the way until the part about the waiters and their first names, but no matter. Expensive and great atmosphere already had him locked on the Marriott's own Lake View Restaurant. I tactfully indicated that we would prefer to dine elsewhere. He understood. The place we wanted was Maison d'Epicure, he said confidentially. That was the restaurant for a special occasion. Even movie stars went there, he added, under his breath. Through a separate entrance on the side.

So Maison d'Epicure it would be. I called the restaurant

from the lobby, made reservations for nine o'clock, and then headed back to the elevators. Usually I'm not so fussy about the process of putting food in one's stomach. On the contrary, one of my enduring irritations with San Francisco has always been the feverish intensity with which people there discussed the presentation of poached salmon at one place or another, and how stampedes regularly formed, season after season, to beat down the doors of the latest establishment serving four grilled shrimp and three slivered carrots on an oversized dinner plate. But on this occasion I would have to rise above petty bias. This dinner was for Hank and Carol.

Back in my room I pulled my cream-colored, White-Man-in-the-Tropics suit from the closet and set it out on the bed. I stared at it, and a bad feeling started to take hold. I know nothing about fashion—zip, nada, zero—yet even *I* had an inkling that perhaps I hadn't made the right choice. Maison d'Epicure was French, dark, romantic. Suddenly I pictured myself in this suit, loping past the valet parking like a grinning conventioneer in search of Margaritaville.

There was a tap on the door, and then Carol's voice on the other side. "Anybody home?"

I opened the door. Carol stood there, smiling self-consciously, holding her arms out away from herself so I could see.

"How do I look?" she said.

"Good Lord!"

She wore a light-brown jumpsuit with matching jacket. The top was low-cut, revealing a swell of olive-skinned, fullish breasts. Her shoulder-length dark hair was pulled back and she wore long, ornate silver earrings. Her face was relaxed, full of poolside sun.

"You look . . . terrific," I said.

"Thanks." She stepped into the room. "I don't have all my makeup on, but you get the idea. Notice the single pleat and reasonably flat tummy? Not bad for someone who's popped two big boys, huh?"

"Not bad at all."

"This is a Givenchy," she said, waiting for me to react.

"I've heard the name. I assume it's good?"

"Good? It's *great!* Obscenely expensive, but look here." Carol lifted her arm, leaned closer to me. "This little part of the seam right here, that you can't even see, it's not exactly straight."

"Looks straight to me."

"That's just it! Nobody's going to even *see* it, but it's considered a manufacturer's defect anyway. Plus this is last year's model, so guess what I got the whole outfit for."

"I don't know."

"Guess."

"Two hundred bucks."

"Don't be ridiculous," Carol said. "Nothing's two hundred. I got it for three fifty!" Carol stood there a moment, waiting for me to be as stunned about that as she was.

"That's good?" I said.

"That's *amazing!*" Carol said. "Three hundred fifty dollars! A Givenchy! Normally you'd sit down and decide which you wanted, a Givenchy or maybe a second family automobile. Hank bought it for me last month. I told him even three fifty was too much for us right now but he did it anyway. Said all it cost was three and a half bubble-gum-wrapper jokes."

"Did Hank try the pool?"

"Are you kidding? He gave it ten minutes, then went back and changed and he's been out on the driving range ever since, hitting golf balls. He's turned into a fanatic, Quinn. I thought he was going to get heatstroke. I'll prepare you right now. He's insisting on a round of golf tomorrow at someplace famous."

Carol's face was filled with more than mere sunshine, and Hank had been doing more than just hitting golf balls. When I'd come back from Arroyo Seco there'd been a Do Not Disturb sign hung on their door, and I suspected at least a portion of their afternoon had passed in a more pleasant fashion than mine.

"You *did* say we're eating fancy tonight, right?" Carol said.

"French. Movie stars slip in through the side door."

She nodded, stole a glance at my Miami Beach outfit on the bed. "You're going to wear that?" she asked diplomatically.

"I was thinking about it."

"What else did you bring along?"

"What else?"

"Another suit?"

"Nothing," I said. "This is it."

Carol nodded some more.

"I screwed up, didn't I?"

"Well . . . " A smile creased her lips.

"I always screw up when I try to dress myself," I said.

"The trick is to think James Bond, Quinn. What you ask yourself is, would Double-O Seven wear a suit like that to an elegant French restaurant?"

I sat down on the edge of the bed and sighed. "So what do we do?"

Carol hesitated, folded her arms across her chest, and looked down at me. "We don't have to do anything so fancy. Hank and I would be just as happy eating at a more informal place."

"No way," I said. "We're eating at Maison d'Epicure and that's that. The evening is not negotiable."

"Reservations are for when?"

"Nine o'clock."

Carol looked at her watch. "That's five hours. Did you bring your credit cards?"

I nodded.

"Then throw on some clothes while I change back into something casual. We're going suit shopping."

The two of us drove around Palm Desert until we found an upscale men's clothing store on the main drag through town. Julian Cubblefield, Clothier. The sign outside announced they had been "purveyors to gentlemen" since 1948, and had branches in Beverly Hills, San Francisco, Seattle, Santa Fe, Puerto Vallarta, and Palm Desert. We parked out front and Carol sensed my natural instinct to flee in the face of imminent purveyance, so she put a hand on my knee and assured me things were going to be fine. All I had to do was try on a few things and she'd give thumbs-up or thumbs-down. Simple. It was like getting a flu shot at school. A moment of pain, just a pinprick, then it was over.

We spent the first thirty minutes at Julian Cubblefield's deciding on a basic clothing strategy. Color, style, price. I went through my paces dutifully. Trying this on and that, turning around when Carol asked me to turn around, suppressing homophobic flinches whenever the salesman ran his hand up my leg to demonstrate fabric characteristics to Carol. From time to time the salesman and Carol would back up and scrutinize me as though I were as perplexing as an Escher painting, huddled together, fingers to chins, speaking that curious language of fashion. Finally the two of them decided on a brown linen suit, on sale and moderately priced, that was neither trendy nor stodgy. The salesman was delighted. He disappeared in search of a matching shirt and tie.

"I think we did well," Carol said. "How do you feel?"

"Like I've spent the past half hour sitting in the wrong end of a zoo."

Carol laughed. "It was worth it. This is a good suit. Nice, but not so dressy you only wear it once a year. This suit you can wear a lot."

We sat together in the plush couch beside the mirrors. "Kate won't be mad we did this, will she?" Carol asked.

"Why should she be mad?"

"I don't know. A suit's kind of a personal thing. Maybe she'd like to pick out your clothes."

"I'll tell her it was an emergency."

Carol nodded and we fell silent. The two of us have moments of awkward intimacy from time to time, and this was one of those times. The salesman had referred to us as husband and wife from the moment we walked in, and neither of us had corrected him. Now we were sunk together in the large soft couch, shoulder to shoulder.

"That really is a nice suit," Carol said again. "At that price I should bring Hank in here before we go."

"I need your advice on something else," I said.

"I mean, a classic suit like that doesn't go on sale very often."

"Carol . . . "

She blinked, refocused on me. "Argyle," she said, smiling.

"What?"

"Argyle socks. I've always been partial to argyle socks."

"I'm not talking about clothes anymore," I said. "This has to do with what happened to Brad."

"Brad?"

"And it may change your mind about whether you want Hank playing golf with me tomorrow."

Carol's expression darkened. "What is it?"

"This thing isn't over with, you know."

She nodded her head. "I know."

"Leonard's still out there and now he knows that I know a lot. Too much."

"Hank said he might be dead," Carol said.

"Could be. But even if he's dead, it means somebody killed him, and that somebody might not be finished tidying up yet. To tell you the truth, I'm a little scared. You might not want to have Hank hanging around me too much down here. Maybe we could do our golf another time."

We were suddenly interrupted by the salesman, who appeared before us with three shirt-and-tie combinations he thought would work with the brown suit. Carol managed to shift focus and go over to the table where he had laid them out for contrast and comparison. They spoke, nodded, pointed, and then Carol was on her way back to the couch.

"Let's let Hank decide," she said. "He's a big boy. He knows the risks."

I nodded, and that was the last word on the subject. Twenty minutes later, after socks, cuff links, and affiliated items had been decided upon, Carol announced that our shopping spree was complete. The trousers seemed fine to me, but both Carol and the salesman insisted they needed a little alteration here and there. The salesman understood the time frame I was dealing with and said that the suit would be ready within an hour and would be hand-delivered to my room at the Marriott Desert Springs.

As I started driving back I began to regret even bringing up the Brad Helfan business with Carol. This was their weekend vacation. My treat. But a sense of unease now permeated the automobile. My words had cast a pall on the spontaneous shopping spree. So I tried to lighten the mood by describing to Carol some of my more serious sartorial gaffes over the years. It worked. She smiled at first. Then laughed. Then really laughed as the anecdotes grew more and more ridiculous.

To someone standing alongside the highway, watching us drive by, you'd think we were a delighted couple on their vacation of the year. We looked as if the world was our oyster. As if we weren't expecting anything bad to happen at all.

——29——

I woke up the early the next morning with only a mild hangover. I sat on the edge of my bed and rubbed my eyes and avoided direct sunlight.

After a rocky start, our evening at Maison d'Epicure had turned into a success after all. The maître d' at Maison d'Epicure had taken one look at my damaged head and—new brown linen suit or not—tried to hustle us off to a remote table so close to the bathrooms you could hear the toilets flush. I declined his choice of a table, asked for a different seating arrangement, and—after an icy three seconds—the maître d' begrudgingly complied.

That was round one. Round two was our waiter. A small, red-faced man with little pink pouches under his eyes, he spent the first half-hour pacing sullenly around us, like a Reno pit boss at the two-dollar blackjack table who resents having to wear a toupee. The years had taught him to sniff out middle-class stiffs out on a biannual splurge, wearing defective Givenchy outfits bought with bubble-gum jokes, and people like that always cut costs at the end of the meal by shaving on the tip. Three times he tried to push a menu on us, and three times I politely told him we were going to relax with a cocktail first. Grumble, mumble, more pacing. A few barely veiled disgruntled words with the maître d'. The hurry-up offense on the part of Maison d'Epicure's staff only encouraged me to order an appetizer and another round of slowly sipped drinks.

When the appetizer came and the waiter all but launched it onto our table like a harried waitress in a truckstop diner, I excused myself from the table and strolled into the kitchen to have a few words with him. The cooks were startled at my sudden appearance back among the pots and pans. The waiter blinked and started to splutter about insurance regulations, but I cut him off.

First of all, I told him that impolite as a response to polite was one of those things that always ticked me off, and he should brush up on his manners. Then I asked him if he'd ever read *The Old Man and the Sea*. The waiter's vocal cords still weren't functioning properly, so I took a minute to explain to him the parable of Hemingway's giant fish strapped to the boat and how his precious catch was taken apart, piecemeal, by the sharks as the old man tried to get back to shore with his treasure. I explained to the waiter that his eventual tip was something like Hemingway's giant fish. Impressive at the start, but getting more and more chewed away by the minute. This was a very special occasion for my friends, and I'd walked into Maison d'Epicure in an expansive mood, thinking an automatic twenty percent. But the menus jammed in our noses had dropped it to fifteen and the appetizer plate that rattled to a stop on our table had brought it down to ten percent. In other words, his tip at our particular table was now in a state of free-fall. If the waiter wanted to work for free, that was his business, but one more unpleasant moment during the course of our dinner and he would also be the subject of a long and detailed letter to the owners of Maison d'Epicure.

The dining experience went much better after our stoveside literary chat. It turned into a long and sensuous exercise in totally unjustifiable indulgence. We all laughed and told stories and Hank and Carol leaned into each other and kissed and I sat there, the third wheel, topping off the wineglasses and suddenly missing Kate ferociously.

At one point Hank asked which golf course we were going

to play the next morning. I told him I had to check out the Airstream first. Hank said yeah, that was fine, but after the Airstream, which championship golf course were we going to play? I glanced at Carol and she gave me a lift of the eyebrows. Do what you want to do, the look said. I told Hank we might give Indian Wells a try. It was close to Indio, where the Airstream was parked, which meant we wouldn't have to drive all the way into Palm Springs. But was it famous, Hank wanted to know. Of course it was famous, I said. They played the Bob Hope Classic there every year. The Bob Hope Classic! Hank almost jumped up and down in his chair.

Our evening ended with Hank rubbing his hands together and Carol trying to buck herself up and feel optimistic. The waiter even came by with a complimentary round of Remy Martin for the three of us, along with apologies. I was so impressed I bumped his tip back up to twelve percent.

But that was last night. Now my head hurt. I wasn't going to make the hangover go away by sitting on the edge of the bed, so I hauled myself to my feet, took a shower, changed into clothes suitable for golf, and went over to knock on Hank and Carol's door. I'd told him the night before that we were going to hit the road at eight A.M. sharp and Hank said that would be no problem at all.

The door swung open and Hank was right there, wearing a bright yellow golf shirt with a bright yellow golf hat and beige slacks. The color combination didn't help my hangover.

"Let's do it!" he said.

Over his shoulder I could see Carol still stretched out in the king-sized bed with the covers pulled up. She drowsily lifted a bare arm and waved good-bye to us and then turned away, clutching her pillow, burrowing further into the sleepy warmth.

The morning desert sun was bright and fresh as we loaded up the trunk with our rented clubs and turned east, toward Indio.

"I can't wait," Hank said. "This is the first time I've ever played a real, legitimate golf course. They really play the Bob Hope there?"

"I'm not sure we can even get on, Hank, so don't get your hopes up."

"But we'll play somewhere famous, right?"

"There are one hundred golf courses in the Palm Springs area," I said. "We'll play somewhere."

"Famous?" Hank said.

"Famous," I said.

I followed the directions to Brad's Airstream exactly as Officer Orwood had given them to me. We went through the blue-collar city of Indio, past several mobile home parks, and then we were out in no-man's-land. I was just about to turn around and see if I'd made a wrong turn somewhere when I saw the glinting silver of an Airstream a half-mile to my left.

"That must be it," I said.

"This is where Brad lived?" Hank said.

"Apparently."

"Jesus . . ."

I turned off the rutted county road I'd been on and began to go practically cross-country on a line for the Airstream. The terrain got worse and worse. Heavy-needled cactus and broken beer bottles and jagged rock hidden beneath a thin cover of light-brown sand. In the distance were the low whitish mountains that separated California from Arizona. There were miniature rolling hills out here, surrounding the Airstream like a papier-mâché scale model of a mountain range, the highest of which was perhaps fifteen feet tall. They almost looked man-made. A row of palm trees, twenty or thirty of them, went on a straight line directly behind the Airstream. Again, the work of civilization, as though intended at some point in the past to be a windbreak. The Airstream itself was under the shade of a large, leafy tree. I hadn't seen anything resembling a stream or other water source in a long while, but Officer Orwood said the vehicle was parked on city property. Maybe some sort of irrigation had been put in once upon a time. There were three or four other structures out near the Airstream, small one-room wooden shacks, boarded-up, windows bashed out and criss-crossed with nailed two-by-fours. The whole area had the feel of a grand plan from a decade or two ago that didn't pan out. Then I remembered. Of course. El Dorado Estates. The luxury development that had belly-flopped.

There was more debris as I closed in on the Airstream. Crushed beer cans, bleached to colorlessness. Broken glass. Cigarette butts. Drained whiskey bottles. Discarded condoms. This was obviously where the young people of Indio came to discover the mysteries of romance and upchucking booze. I stopped the car two hundred yards from the Airstream and cut the engine.

"What're you doing?" Hank said.

"I'm not in the mood to change a flat tire," I said. "Let's walk."

Hank groaned. "How long did you say this was going to take?"

"I didn't say."

"So it's open-ended?"

"I need to look around, Hank. You knew that before we came down, so don't start giving me a hard time. Jeez, you're as bad as Cort."

"I'm just thinking about the golf," he said. "It's not getting any cooler."

"Tell you what," I said, reaching under the steering wheel and springing the lock on the trunk. "Why don't you take a five-iron and a couple of balls and smack them around while I'm going through the Airstream. Practice your sand shots."

Hank perked up a little. "You know, that isn't a half-bad idea."

"Just be careful for rocks," I said. "Those are rental clubs and we're responsible."

I got out and started walking toward the Airstream.

"Hey!" Hank called. "Watch this!"

I turned, put hands on hips, and watched. Hank stood over the ball, took an amazingly fluid swing, and the shot rocketed off into the pale blue desert sky. Damn. He *was* getting good. He turned to look at me and I gave him the thumbs-up. He started marching off into the desert, in the opposite direction, taking practice swings at cactus tips as he walked.

I went up and tried the door of the Airstream. It had been violently chiseled open. I stepped inside and surveyed the damage. It was a smallish Airstream, with a kitchenette and little two-person table for eating and a couch facing an ancient ten-inch television with rabbit ears on top like the televisions of the early black-and-white era. Two steps beyond the couch was a bathroom. No bedroom, so I assumed the couch folded out at night. Of course, I was imagining all of this as it might have looked before the place had been thoroughly gutted. I don't normally think of an inanimate thing being disemboweled, but Brad's Airstream had been eviscerated. No other way to describe it. The drawers hadn't merely been rifled through. They'd been yanked out, their contents strewn all over the floor. Every cushion from the couch had been slashed open and half the stuffing had been hurled about the interior, exactly as it had been at Peggy's house in Sacramento. Even the metallic floor beneath my feet had been hacked at, as though the intruder had been searching for a false bottom. The fixtures were missing. No faucets in the sink, no flush handles on the toilet. It was hard to distinguish what had been ransacked by Leonard and company and what had been the result of youthful vandalism. I spent fifteen minutes sifting through the wreckage. This had been the home of somebody making a hundred thousand dollars a year, tax-free?

Brad had built a small, elevated wooden terrace leading off the back door of the Airstream and had made a sad attempt to spruce up the low-rent ambience with some potted flowers, a small barbecue, a lounge chair facing east toward the dust-blown wastes of the Mojave. I went out onto the terrace and stood there a moment. Even the plants had been ripped from their clay pots, the dirt scavenged through as though a dog had been frantic for a misplaced bone.

The questions promenaded past me, one after the other, like beauty contestants walking down the runway: mocking, delicious, distant, untouchable. Who did this? Leonard? An emissary of Leonard's? Kerrigan? Were they successful? You see a trashed house, a room turned inside-out, and you tend to assume nothing was found, that it had been an exercise in frustration. But maybe not. Maybe the intruder had found what he wanted and was off to the nearest Swiss bank.

I sighed, looked out across the flat, monochromatic desert. No, whatever had been hidden was still hidden. Had to be. The upping of the ante in Sacramento had been a result of not finding anything down here. I felt it. The police had all the time in the world to go through the Airstream with the finest of fine-tooth combs. If the "something big" had been hidden here, it would have been discovered by them. Unless, of course, the something big wasn't as blatant as a suitcase full of hundred-dollar bills. Maybe it was something the police wouldn't have paid much attention to even if they'd picked it up and held it in their hands.

Okay, Parker. Stop. Back up. New approach. If you had something very secret and very valuable, where would *you* stash it? The bank, probably, behind one of those time-locked vaults. But Peggy said the police and insurance people had already checked all the banks for other holdings and found nothing. Cross-checks of social security numbers had turned up nothing. It was always possible Brad had used a phony name, a trumped-up social security number for secrecy purposes, but I doubted it. Brad was too simple a guy for such John le Carré machinations. Besides, didn't his mother say at the funeral reception how much Brad hated banks? From the time he was a kid, he didn't trust them. To hell with savings accounts and accrued interest. Little Brad Helfan preferred to take his chances burying his allowance money in the backyard.

A breeze came up off the desert, dry and warm. A tumbleweed rolled a bit and stopped. I felt a tingling at the base of my spine.

The backyard . . .

I leaned forward, looked out onto the sandy expanse of land leading back to the palm trees, then the desert off and beyond. Fragments of conversations came back to me. Leonard at the Foxy Female, saying Brad was the type to stuff his money in a mattress. Kate trailing her fingernails along my arm, saying that she would have given my broken coffee maker a proper burial if my apartment had only come with a big enough garden. There was plenty of room out here to bury things. Something small. Or something big.

I stepped down from the terrace and wandered the dusty area behind the Airstream. Slowly at first, then more hurriedly as my conviction strengthened. But there were no dramatic dissimilarities in the texture of the earth anywhere. I came to a stop. Fences didn't bind this property. A hundred miles of desert stretched away.

I went to the end of the line of windbreak palm trees and began walking slowly east to west, hands behind my back, staring hard at the shaded earth at the base of the trunks. Halfway back to the Airstream I noticed a weather-beaten sign, gritty with sand and sun, hammered crookedly into the earth. The metal face of the sign had been pocked with BB-gun fire, and you could barely read the letters. The sign announced the spot as El Dorado Estates. The light-brown earth at the base of the sign was mixed with a slightly darker soil, gently mounded.

I went back to the Airstream and rummaged around until I found a dented soup spoon on the floor next to the kitchenette. Then I went back out to the sign, got down on my knees, and started digging. My heartbeat was quickening. I could feel the dry heat on my back as I worked. Calm down, I told myself. You're probably excavating goldfish bones.

After two minutes of digging I hit something solid. I got down on my knees and scooped the dirt away with both hands. It was an old-fashioned Dutch Masters cigar box, the wooden kind. My last thrust with the spoon had cracked the top, and dirt was seeping in. I worked the cigar box free, lifted it out of the ground, and set it next to the discarded spoon. The painting of the Dutch Masters on the top had grown faded with exposure. The splintered wood perfectly decapitated them along the edge of their neatly bearded heads. I took a deep breath, lifted the lid.

The first thing I saw was money. A thick stack of hundred-dollar bills held together by a rubber band. I picked it up and flipped through to see if they were all hundreds. They were. Maybe seven or eight thousand dollars' worth. I put the money aside. In the corner of the cigar box was a key chain with a half-dozen keys attached. Two were car keys, with a Ford Motor emblem stamped on them. The other four were of standard size, not the kind that would fit a conventional bus locker or bank safety-deposit box. But that's not what had my attention. In the middle of the cigar box was a five-by-eight manila envelope, unsealed, clasped together by a string. I opened it and pulled out the contents. A legal-looking letter on expensive stationery, with dozens of vouchers stapled together and paper-clipped to the letter. I read the letter. Scanned the vouchers. And as I read, I knew why Brad had died. I also knew who had hired Paul Butkiewitz, aka Mr. R.S., to do the killing.

The realization insulated me from everything else. I wasn't aware of the heat of the desert, or the Airstream, or the warm breeze wafting in from the Mojave. I'd found the "something big" Brad had wanted to send to Peggy before the sniper's bullet cut him down. I was not even aware of the human forms closing in on me, rapidly, from behind.

——30——

Stay in that crouch just a few seconds longer," the voice behind me commanded. "Good. Now bring your hands out to your side and stand up very, very slowly."

I did as I was told. Felix Stockwell moved into my line of vision from the right. Leonard Novak was with him. Leonard didn't look good. He was pale, sleep-deprived, the eyes in his long, flat face so sunken you could barely see them. Felix was dragging a shovel in his left hand. In his right hand he held a pistol. Both hands were gloved.

"I didn't hear you drive up," Felix said. "What'd you do? Walk?"

"Car's parked by the main road."

Felix moved to the side, squinted, saw it. "Oh, yeah. I see it now."

I glanced at Leonard. "What's going on?" I said. He didn't answer.

"You don't strike me as the gun-toting type, Quinn," Felix said, "but I have to make sure." He moved close and slapped my arms, chest, and legs, quickly, nervously. Satisfied, he backed away and nodded. "Go ahead and put your arms down. I don't think we've been properly reintroduced," Felix said. "We spoke on the phone a couple of nights ago. Officer Orwood of the Indio police department, remember?"

With one eye on me, Felix moved sideways, knelt down, and picked up the cigar box. He leafed through the vouchers, shook his head. "Buried in the yard," he said. "All this time, it was buried in the backyard. Brad was such a simple guy, bless his heart. Buried nine million bucks in a cigar box! One good rain and the whole thing would've turned to mold."

The nine-million figure was just about right. According to the letter that accompanied the vouchers, Brad had been giving sums of cash to Felix Stockwell for over three years, a thousand or two at a time, in return for the option to buy—at a greatly reduced rate—stock shares in Platypus Equipment and Design at an unspecified future date. There were a lot of vouchers.

"How much of Platypus did Brad own?" I said.

"None of it," Felix said. "He unfortunately didn't live long enough to exercise his options. But if he had . . . about seventy percent. Seventy, seventy-five. I don't recall, off the top of my head."

"With Leonard's forty that didn't leave much for you, did it?"

"Not much at all, considering the effort I've put into this company over the years."

Leonard still hadn't said a word. He just stood in a pose of utter defeat, staring down at the ground. I wondered if he'd been drugged.

"You don't strike me as someone dumb enough to sell off a hundred and ten percent of his company," I said.

Felix shrugged. "In business all you need to be is less dumb than the guy you're dealing with. I was a lot less dumb than Brad Helfan. Besides, what was I supposed to do? Let the company collapse after ten years of hard work? No bank in the world would loan me a dime. Too high-risk, they said. They'll go ahead and give Brazil a hundred million, but nothing for me. I had to keep my business afloat. Whatever it took. And if you'd had time to read the fine print closer, Quinn, you'd have seen there was a time limit on the vouchers. If Brad didn't exercise his option within that time, I had the right to buy them back from him. It wasn't going to be a problem because Brad was flat-out broke. Up until U.S. Open week, that is. That's why I asked him to lose. All he needed to do was stay broke for another six months and everybody would've been fine. Brad would get a refund on his loan, I'd have my vouchers back. You can't say I didn't give him a chance. I warned him."

Felix tossed the shovel to me.

"You expect me to dig my own grave?" I said.

"No," Felix said. "I expect you to dig Leonard's grave. Now get started."

I looked at Leonard. He still wouldn't look up. Wouldn't return my gaze.

"You won't get away with this," I said.

"I've already gotten away with it," he said. "When fifteen million dollars is up for grabs, you think things out. The clues to nail Leonard's ass have all been laid out like colored eggs at an Easter egg hunt. *Brightly* colored eggs." Felix trained his gun on my ankle. "So start digging. That poor body of yours has been through a lot lately. Don't add a shot-up foot to the list."

I saw some pressure being applied to the trigger. Felix wasn't kidding. I bent down, picked up the shovel, and began to dig.

"How come Brad was so convinced the death threat was from Leonard?" I said, tossing aside the first shovelful of dirt.

"Because I told him so," Felix said.

"When?"

"The week before the tournament. When he first qualified I thought it was great. A respectable showing would be terrific for Platypus. But then it suddenly occurred to me that if Brad did *really* well in the Open he could stand to make a lot of money. Enough money to exercise his option to cash in his vouchers for Platypus stock. So I called up Brad and told him Leonard was getting aggressive about wanting to buy more stock in Platypus. That Leonard wasn't taking no for an answer. I told Brad that Leonard didn't believe me when I said Brad had the options on the remaining stock. I asked Brad to send me the original vouchers so I could show them to Leonard and shut him up, but Brad wouldn't do it."

Felix rubbed his eyes. His face was puffy. His chin was flecked with pinpoints of silver whiskers.

"I'm not a terrible person, Quinn," he said. "I liked Brad a lot. I really and truly did. I gave him every possible opportunity to get out of this with his life intact."

I kept shoveling, silent, thinking of what I could do. It was Leonard and me against Felix, two against one. If I tossed a sudden shovelful of sand in Felix's face, maybe Leonard could take the gun away. Except Leonard looked almost catatonic. If he didn't react, I'd be finished.

Felix held the cigar box in his hand, kept his gun trained on me with the other. He sifted through the vouchers, smiled a thin, weary smile. "When I was a kid, growing up in Los Angeles, I used to look around at my parents, friends, uncles and aunts. I was amazed at how easily they were able to settle for less. That was the one great mystery of my childhood. How people could settle for so little. For *nothing*. I made a vow to myself way back then that I'd never let that happen to me. I wanted it all. Now I'm on the brink of having it all."

"Don't you think it's going to be a little suspicious when the police find our bodies?" I said.

"Nope."

"Why not?"

"Because it went like this. You've been crazed with guilt about Brad's death ever since Pebble Beach. And then when you found Alison in that cabin in Winters you flipped. Deranged by the need for revenge, you bought a gun." Felix held up his pistol. "*This* gun, and went looking for Leonard. You lured him out here with some story about money, then shot him in cold blood. Only what you didn't realize was that I was with Leonard when you called him, going over some business matters in the wake of the Ameritime deal, and he asked me to come along because he didn't trust you. When you shot Leonard I jumped you from behind, we struggled, the gun went off . . . "

"Nobody'll believe you," I said.

"Why not? I have witnesses."

"What witnesses?"

"Nikki called me yesterday afternoon. She said you burst into her home and threatened her. You were wild. Like a madman. Waved a gun around." Felix held up the pistol again. "*This* very gun, coincidentally enough. You demanded to know where Leonard was because you were going to kill the sonofabitch. He'd done enough harm to enough people and now it was going to end. Nikki said one of her neighbors came over after you left to see if she was okay. This neighbor lives across the street. Said she saw you almost break down Nikki's front door. Nikki says this neighbor is a retired pediatrician. Well-respected member of the community. I think the authorities will give her corroborative testimony a lot of credence."

"So Nikki's in on it, too."

"Why not?" Felix said. Then, indicating Leonard. "This guy treated her like shit. A woman like that. Not the way I'll treat her."

"Congratulations," I said.

"Like I said." Felix smiled. "Why not have it all?"

For thirty seconds I dug in silence. Then Felix waved me away from the shallow grave with his gun.

"That's enough," he said. "You and I had our struggle before you finished."

Felix looked over at Leonard. "Sorry it had to end this way, partner," he said. "Sorry we couldn't enjoy all this together."

Then I saw it. I didn't know what it was at first. Down from the impossibly blue desert sky it came, fast and white, like a hard white bird, diving with mercurial speed. I barely had time to register it when a voice boomed from far off in the desert. *"Fore!"* the voice shouted. *"Fore!"*

The ball came whistling down like a mortar shell, cracked into the top branches of the nearest palm tree, and caromed straight down at our feet. Felix lurched to the side. The ball took one short bounce and the topspin kicked in and it skittered like a frightened animal off toward the Airstream.

Leonard came alive. He lunged for Felix, missed, fell, stood to lunge again. Felix pulled back and the gunshot boomed through the desert air. I felt it all the way to my molars.

Leonard backpedaled, a look on his face like he'd just bitten into a lemon, eyes blinking rapidly. Felix fired again, another tremendous percussive blast, and Leonard flew backwards through the air.

I didn't wait to see where Leonard landed. I rushed the still-disoriented Felix, clutching the shovel with both hands. He whirled on me. Fired. Another titanic explosion of sound and the hard metallic clank of the bullet hitting the broad face of the shovel, the force of the impact turning the wooden shovel handle a painful half-twist in my hands. Felix didn't have time to fire again. I swung the blade end of the shovel at his midsection in a kind of uppercut motion, as hard as I could.

The shovel hit and stuck, like the thunk of an axe in a chopping block. Felix's eyes went wide with surprise, hands up, mouth open, in a grotesque parody of a waiter dropping a plate of food. The gun fell from his hand. He staggered back, grasped the handle of the shovel, and pulled it out of his stomach. Let the shovel drop. Blood was gushing out of his midsection with the force of water breaking through a fissure in a levee. I'd never seen so much blood. It was terrifying to watch. The blood came and came and came and Felix just stood there, cupping both hands as if to catch it and put it back where it was supposed to be. Then he dropped to his knees, took one last look at the shovel in front of him, and toppled onto his side. Felix stirred once, and that was it. He didn't move again.

I tried to calm my breathing. Leonard was lying spread-eagled on his back, a dark red blotch on his chest, another on his shoulder. As utterly motionless as Felix.

On the horizon I could see Hank threading his way among the little papier-mâché hills, moving toward me, up to where he'd hit his shot. He was clutching his five-iron and doing little balletlike jumps to see if his ball was around. "Didn't mean to scare you!" he shouted. Then, when he got within fifty feet he stopped short. Looked at the two prone bodies. The club fell from his limp hands.

"Oh, my God!" he said. "Did I do this?"

"Yes," I said. "You did."

—31—

"Close your eyes and open wide," Kate said.

I did, leaning back on the park bench, mouth opened like a bird awaiting the worm.

"Not *that* wide," she said.

I adjusted my bite radius accordingly and Kate spooned the last of her crab cocktail down my throat.

"You can open your eyes now," she said.

"In a minute."

I took another ten seconds to feel the cool sun on my face. To let my senses concentrate fully on the last of the crab cocktail. I could feel and hear Kate's distinctive throaty laugh somewhere above me. The soft one. The one she uses when lascivious intent is around the bend. It was a nice sound. It kept me from rolling all the should'ves around in my brain. The "should've" immediately preceding the crab cocktail involved Felix's last phone call. It should've occurred to me to wonder how "Officer Orwood" knew which hotel Felix and Peggy had holed up in. But as I said, it was only the latest in a long line of should'ves, and could wait.

"True love," Kate said. "I almost never give my last bite of anything to anybody. Especially not crab cocktail. In fact, I'm already regretting it."

I opened my eyes. Kate was gazing down at me, smiling,

still holding the little plastic spoon near my lips. Above us sea gulls circled in the foggy afternoon, and behind us the usual hordes of summer tourists were exploring the shops of the Cannery.

"True love on this end, too," I said. "Usually it takes the threat of grievous bodily injury to make me come down to Fisherman's Wharf."

"You've just got a bad attitude," Kate said. "I like the Wharf. People on vacation are fun to be around. Beats those sour faces downtown."

"Says you."

"Says me. Besides, if I'm going to work right down the block I might as well enjoy my new surroundings."

Kate, for better or for worse, had gotten the advertising job she'd interviewed for while Hank, Carol, and I were on our Palm Springs junket. This Friday afternoon was going to be her last free weekday in a while, so we'd decided to celebrate with street vendor crab cocktails at the Wharf and Irish coffee at the reputed North American birthplace of Irish coffee, the Buena Vista Cafe. The coffee was coming up next, and I was getting in the mood. An especially cold fog was blowing in off the bay, the sun overhead a cool, gray disk in a cool, gray sky.

Two weeks had passed since Felix's childhood dream to "have it all" had come to a premature end in the scorched wastelands of the Mojave Desert. At first the culmination of the Brad Helfan murder got a lot of television airtime, but after only a few days the public's interest waned, and now the hubbub had virtually died out completely.

Initially there seemed to be some question as to whether the vouchers and accompanying letter were even valid documents. Some important legal buzz-phrases were missing from the agreement, and the vouchers, after all, were obtained with money earned from illegal hustling activities.

But public outcry is a powerful thing, and the consensus in the nation and on coast-to-coast talk shows was that Peggy and Alison should at least get a chunk of the Platypus payoff. Executives from Ameritime Sports, seeking to quickly shore up their weakening public image, came before the microphones to say that in their opinion the majority ownership in Platypus at the time of their corporate purchase belonged to Brad Helfan and his heirs. It was still being hammered out between lawyers, but things looked good for Peggy. Brad's "something big" turned out to be extremely big, indeed. The slow-talking country boy from West Texas had screwed up a lot along the road, but his instincts were good. The greatest treasures always get squirreled away in cigar boxes. Always. Any kid can tell you that.

Billy Useless had been on Felix's payroll all along—it was a bigger payroll—aiding and abetting any opportunity that came along to throw more guilt in Leonard's direction: the hiring of Mr. R.S., who had definite ties to Leonard in Palm Springs; the subsequent killing of Mr. R.S. in San Luis Obispo, with plenty of incriminating evidence pointing Leonard's way conveniently left at the scene.

It was Billy who told the dark man that it was Leonard, not Felix, who was behind the abduction of Alison. I remembered how Leonard had once warned me out on the fourth tee at Arroyo Seco that Billy was an independent agent, and that I should be careful. He couldn't have realized the deadly truth in his warning.

I felt comforted knowing that kidnapping had been thrown into the laundry-list of crimes Billy Useless was now being charged with. If convicted, he'd be looking at a nice long prison sentence, with years to go before being eligible for parole. I hadn't forgotten Lorenzini's warning that when the newly eunuched Billy was out and about again, he might make the demise of Quinn Parker his first order of business. One afternoon shortly after my return from Palm Springs I was having lunch with Kate at a restaurant in Pacific Heights when I had the vivid, out-of-nowhere sensation that one day Billy Useless and I would face each other again. It was a debilitating premonition, like the brief glimpsing of how one is destined to die. Kate put down her fork and asked if I was okay. I told her I was. She shook her head and went back to her food. "No you're not," she said. "You look like you've just seen a ghost." I hoped she wasn't right.

Nikki, on the other hand, was on the verge of getting off the hook completely. All her misconduct fell under the category of "conspiracy to": conspiracy to commit murder, conspiracy to aid and abet, conspiracy to commit fraud. She was waiting in the wings for Felix to tell her the Palm Springs end of it turned out as planned. Then she would back him up with tales of gun waving and death threats and a rabid Quinn Parker gone south to extract revenge from a husband who had vowed to "level" Brad if he played in the Open. As it was, she said she didn't know anything about anything.

Some aspects of the grand plan had gone to the grave with Felix Stockwell, and all I could do was speculate. What did they always tell you in those evaluation tests back in school? If there is no correct answer, choose the answer that fits best.

There was no obvious correct answer for the forged letters from the deceased Graham Kirby. I brooded on it for a day, and my best answer was that Felix had concocted them to put Brad in a difficult position. Kirby wanted a payoff or Brad's child was going to be in danger. Brad had no money to pay him off with. Felix might have approached Brad with a solution. Felix would give Brad a lump sum, enough to pay off Kirby, in exchange for the seemingly worthless vouchers.

I also didn't understand why Felix had to kill Leonard in the process. With Brad dead he still had sixty percent of Platypus. Nine million dollars. Surely he could swallow sharing the other six million with Leonard. But maybe not. Felix said he wanted it all, and you can't qualify "all." Nikki might've been worth the extra six million. Alas, I'd never gotten one of her frisks, but I'm sure if I came with a million-dollar bonus it would've been a frisk for the ages.

Leonard. Bagel-stuffing, Star-of-David-stamping Leonard. Mean, vulgar, and criminal to the core, yet in the days after his death I had to consciously remind myself to think horrible thoughts about him. Kitchen stores in Beverly Hills that will only stock high-priced imports irritate me, too. I thought of the story he had told me while we sat in the idling Cadillac in Palm Springs that first night. The kitten he'd seen being slowly devoured by the snake when he was a kid. The memory had been scalded into his consciousness for a reason. He thought it was a parable with which to warn others, but no. It was Leonard's own fate that he had crouched down and witnessed those many years ago. The kitten-devouring snake had come back to get him after all.

"It's getting cold," Kate said.

"Ready for the coffee?"

"Let's do it."

On a patch of lawn in front of us, thirty feet away, was the Human Jukebox. More accurately, the *new* Human Jukebox. The original Human Jukebox had worked the Wharf in San Francisco since the 1960s and had become something of an institution in the city. When the U.S. Postal Service decided to print a series of stamps with San Francisco as its theme, they actually considered giving the Human Jukebox his own stamp.

Whether they ever did it or not, I don't know. Whatever happened to the original Human Jukebox, I don't know. But the current bearer of the torch was still here—a chin-high cardboard "jukebox," with a couple dozen slots carved away, the name of a song written in Magic Marker above each of the slots. Put a dollar bill in a slot and the top of the jukebox flips open, a tall guy with long dark hair stands up out of his crouch, puts a trumpet to his lips, and plays the two-minute version of whatever song you picked. Tourists never could seem to get enough of the Human Jukebox. In the short time Kate spent nursing her crab cocktail three people had come up and inserted their dollar bills. One requested "California, Here I Come!" The other two ordered up "I Left my Heart in San Francisco."

But now several minutes had gone by and I couldn't stand to think of the guy sitting in there by himself, huddled in the growing cold, clutching his trumpet and waiting for the next person to ask for Tony Bennett favorites.

Kate had already taken a few steps in the direction of the Buena Vista and stopped when she realized I was still standing at the bench.

"Come on," she said. "Let's get warm."

"One second."

I went up to the Human Jukebox and slipped a dollar bill in the slot called Requests. The top of the jukebox flipped open and the man stood up. He was about forty-five years old and had an intelligent face. The kind of guy who might have been a bank president in an earlier life and then bagged it all to wear red tennis shoes and fly kites in Golden Gate Park. Kate strolled down to join me.

"What'll it be?" he said.

"Do you know any Dolly Parton?" I said.

"Dolly Parton?"

"Friend of mine used to like her a lot."

The Human Jukebox thought about it for a second. Nothing was coming.

"How about 'Queen of the Silver Dollar'?" I asked.

"Don't know it," he said.

"'Coat of Many Colors'?" Kate said.

He looked blank, then brightened. "Okay. Dolly Parton. How about 'Nine to Five'? From the movie."

Kate shook her head. "I start work on Monday," she said. "Too close to home."

"Then Dolly Parton's a blank," the Human Jukebox said. "Got another request? I'm good with towns. People like to hear songs about their hometowns."

Kate and I went down the checklist of Texas cities and decided on "The Streets of Laredo." A little south of Brad Helfan country, but close enough. Kate took my hand in hers and gripped it feelingly while the Human Jukebox settled into a surprisingly plaintive version of the sad cowboy song. All wrapped in white linen, and cold as the clay . . .

Then the song was over. As usual, the Human Jukebox sank back into his crouch and closed the top of the cardboard over his head without another word. I fished out another dollar and slipped it through the request slot. He popped right back out and looked at me like he'd never seen me before.

"No song this time," I said. "Just a question."

He shrugged. "Your dollar."

"Doesn't it get cold and lonely in there?"

The Human Jukebox stared down in the direction of his feet, shrugged again. "What can I tell you?" he said. "It's a living." Then he sank away and pulled the lid over his head.

For a moment I simply stood there, staring at the decorated cardboard box, thinking about the person huddled inside. Then Kate gently tugged my hand.

"Come on, Quinn," she said. "Let's go have our coffee. My treat."

So I turned and walked with her up the slope of the hill, toward the bar with the people sitting together on the other side of the window, where it was warm.